A RUTHLESS BLOODY BETRAYAL

ALSO BY LINDSAY CLEMENT

An Absolute Bloody Disaster

A
RUTHLESS
BLOODY
BETRAYAL

AN ABSOLUTE BLOODY DISASTER
BOOK 2

LINDSAY CLEMENT

To request permissions, contact the publisher at novelitica@gmail.com.

ISBN 978-1-7373593-3-3 (Hardcover)
ISBN 978-1-7373593-4-0 (Paperback)
ISBN 978-1-7373593-5-7 (Ebook)

First edition, April 2025.

Edited by Rachel Doyel

Cover design by Franzi Haase
www.coverdungeon.com | Instagram: @coverdungeonrabbit

Interior art by Dezaray Shuler
Instagram: @oblivionsdream

Interior Formatting and Map by Lindsay Clement
www.novelitica.com | Instagram: @novelitica

Printed by IngramSpark in the USA.

Novelitica
www.novelitica.com

For the ones who refuse to quit.

Dear readers,

Thank you so much for picking up A Ruthless Bloody Betrayal. This is a sequel and includes content warnings similar to the first book in the series, An Absolute Bloody Disaster. Please note that I consider this book to be rated PG-13 and it contains the following elements:

<u>On Page (and mentioned)</u>
Alcoholism
Blood/Gore
Character death
Emotional manipulation
Murder
Panic attacks
Sexual content - cracked door, mild to moderate
Swearing - mild to moderate
Suicidal ideations
Violence

<u>Mentioned Only</u>
Past sexual abuse (implied)
Past emotional/physical abuse
Past child loss

If you have any further questions about the content, I am happy to answer questions. Please reach out to me through Instagram @novelitica or email me at novelitica@gmail.com.

Best,
Lindsay

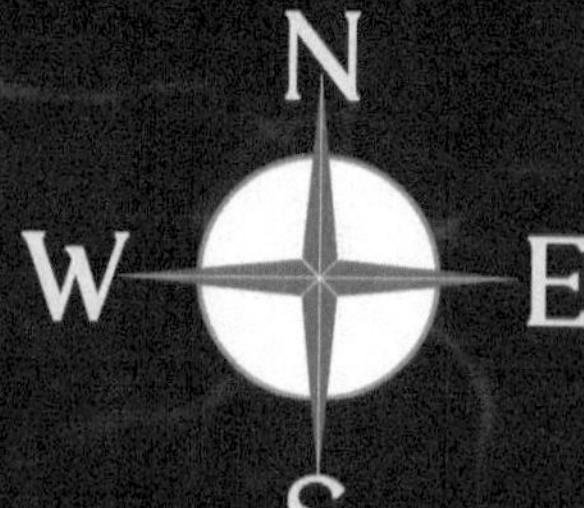

MARIN HEADLANDS
POINT MAREA
THE SAFE HOUSE
SAN FRANCISCO
CALIFORNIA
‹ PACIFIC OCEAN
THE CAGED BIRD
GOLDEN GATE PARK
N
W
E
S

SAN FRANCISCO BAY
FORT POINT
FISHERMAN'S WHARF
THE PRESIDIO
THE NOVIK MANSION
PACIFIC HEIGHTS
NIK'S HOUSE
THE GARAGE
RICHMOND DISTRICT
SUNSET DISTRICT

PROLOGUE

RAYNA KNEW IT WAS ONLY a matter of time.

She stares at the message on her phone screen, willing it to disappear, but it doesn't. The little bastard. It simply smiles up at her with its two words—two tiny words that she has dreaded for the last century.

He knows. Nothing else follows, but she infers Kaleb's meaning: *He knows where I am.*

Rayna drops her phone onto the bed and drags a hand over her face, swallowing a wave of nausea. She and Kaleb have been running from Konstantin for over two hundred years. It shouldn't surprise her to hear that he is finally catching up, but she can't stop the fear that crackles through her like a flame.

In the past, this wouldn't have concerned her. Kaleb would have simply whisked her away to a new location with a new house, a new life, a new name. She misses the days when she could step into the next room and see him sitting at his desk, tendrils of smoke swirling around his head as he read the morning newspaper. But those days are long past. The moment Kaleb became an Alpha, he started a ticking clock.

It seems his time has finally run out.

Rayna exhales sharply and paces across her luxurious bedroom, her feet wearing grooves in the plush ivory carpet. Damn Kaleb and his altruism, caring more about saving the vampires in a festering, salt-soaked city than he does about saving his own skin.

And what's worse, he involved their family. He involved *Nikolas*. Her brother should be far away from all of this, somewhere safe from Konstantin. Instead, he's in Kaleb's backyard. Directly in the monster's path.

Rayna sighs again and lets her head fall back, closing her eyes as panic claws its way into her throat. She inhales deeply, then exhales. Again. Again.

Memories flash through her head: a gold watch, a red dress, the glint of silver eyes in lamplight. Strong hands, cutting words. Kisses in the dark. Teeth buried in her neck, again, again, *again*. Nikolas begging for mercy. Konstantin refusing it. The sound of her brother's bones snapping as his body hit the pavement. She can still see Nikolas lying on the ground, blood pooling beneath him. It was the worst day of her life. *He cannot die,* she reminds herself. *He* didn't *die. We made sure of it.*

But Nikolas can't breathe.

Rayna can't breathe.

Dammit.

Her chest constricts. Fear flutters behind her ribs as silver eyes spark in her vision. She staggers backward, fighting for breath, and barely notices when her shoulders collide with the wall.

Breathe.

Konstantin knows where Kaleb is, but that doesn't mean he knows *everything.* It doesn't mean he knows Rayna is alive. It doesn't mean he will seek out her brother.

But Nikolas is broken on the pavement. He is still. *So* still.

After what feels like an eternity, he finally breathes.

Rayna breathes.

It's ragged. Jarring. Air tears through her chest like wildfire and her heart slows. Hot tears escape the corners of her eyes and in a sudden burst of clarity, she knows what she has to do.

Kaleb picks up on the first ring.

"Hello, darling."

"I'm coming home."

He scoffs. "Absolutely not."

"You just told me Konstantin knows where you are!" The anger in Rayna's own voice startles her and she forces a deep breath, cooling the heat that suddenly blazes inside her. "If he found *you*, that means he found Nikolas. I can't protect him if I'm a thousand miles away."

There's a beat. "Where are you?"

"New Mexico." She shrugs to herself. "I've been here for a few years, hiding out. Resting. Hoping. Honestly, I'm amazed Konstantin hasn't given up by now."

"Konstantin will never give up." It's a simple statement, but its chilly finality raises the hair on Rayna's arms. Kaleb exhales slowly and his voice softens. "If you grew tired of your own search—as I predicted you would, for the record—why didn't you contact me? We could have—" Another slow exhale. "I miss you, my heart. I would have helped you, had you asked."

Warmth spreads through her as she imagines the sincerity etched on Kaleb's face. It's almost enough to make her believe him. But even if he were telling the truth, this is something she had to do on her own.

If only she would have found Konstantin first.

"No, you wouldn't have," she says wryly. "We both know you never would have left your city."

Silence meets her words, followed by a familiar bright voice through the earpiece—someone calling to Kaleb.

"I'm sorry, darling," he says, distracted by some unknown problem. That seems to happen a lot these days. "I have something I need to attend to. In the meantime, don't—" He bites down on the words, and Rayna can practically see the tight set of his jaw, the way he fusses with the buttons on his blazer. "The situation here is already stressful enough, and your reappearance would only complicate things. I will keep you updated. Just . . . please. Stay where you are."

It takes a few seconds for her to reply with a simple, "Fine."

"Good. I love you, darling."

I love you, too, she almost says. She wants to say it. She *should* say it. But for whatever reason, her tongue is tied. She is silent for a beat too long and Kaleb sighs.

"I will talk to you soon. Stay safe."

"I—" she starts, but the call has already ended.

With a groan, Rayna tosses her phone back down and her eyes snag on the small bird figurine on the nightstand. She picks it up, appreciating the heft of the brass, and thumbs the familiar engraving on the bottom: *Všechno nejlepší k narozeninám, Magdaléna.*

Happy birthday, Magdaléna.

It has been too long since she celebrated the occasion with Nikolas.

The thought of Konstantin anywhere near him fills her with fear-fueled rage. If that bastard harms a single hair on her brother's head, there will be hell to pay.

Rayna has spent so many years running. For over half her life, she has been looking over her shoulder, watching for a flash of silver eyes. But now, for the first time, she may have the upper hand. If Konstantin isn't in San Francisco already, he will be soon. And Rayna will be ready.

It's time for her to come back from the dead.

Anticipation flutters in her chest like a caged bird, and her mouth twists into a grin. Konstantin will already have a plan in motion, that's for certain. But if he thinks he can beat her at his game, he's forgetting one very important thing.

"I am Rayna Magdaléna Vesely," she murmurs to the little brass bird, "and Konstantin taught me everything he knows."

CHAPTER 1

SAN FRANCISCO, CALIFORNIA

NOVEMBER 8, 2018

RAYNA VESELY IS DEAD.

She's been dead since 1897. One hundred and twenty-one years. Forty-four thousand, three hundred and twenty-four days.

But who's counting?

I am. Obviously. I've had a running tally in my head since the night she died. Since the night our world went up in flames.

Since the night Kaleb *killed her.*

But I didn't *see* her die, did I? There was never a body—only the burnt-out husk of what was once Kaleb's apartment building in New York. I can still feel the heat of the flames, smell the suffocating black smoke. And I see Kaleb—the way he watched, unflinching, as our world burned to the ground.

The way he worried at the buttons on his cuff.

Kaleb told us that Rayna was dead—that he killed the girl he risked everything for—and I believed him. I mourned my best friend. My *sister.* I watched as our family crumbled into chaos, and as her brother became a shell of his former self.

But Kaleb lied about all of it. Which begs the question: what else has he been hiding from us?

I stare at Nik where he stands in the doorway of the ruined ballroom, his arms wrapped tightly around the girl who may as well be a ghost. There's a stiffness to his shoulders, a desperation in the way he clutches the back of her jacket that screams, *This can't be real.*

The questions howling through my mind are enough to make my head spin. We just spent the evening living through literal hell while Konstantin watched. While Konstantin *laughed.* All because he wanted the truth about Rayna. But what truth? If he didn't already know she was alive, why would he be here in the first place? What else could he want from us? From *Kaleb?*

I glance around the room—at the blood-stained floor, the still-spinning disco ball, the toppled furniture—and wonder if this is all just a hallucination. If I'll wake up in a cold sweat from a vivid fever dream, only to realize that Konstantin was never here and that a small army of his fledglings never appeared from the shadows. That Victoria is safe. That Jason is alive, and that Rayna is dead.

That Ty is just Ty.

I pinch my arm. I pinch the other one. I press the heels of my hands into my eyes so hard that I see stars. But no matter what I do, the scene doesn't change. There is still blood on the floor.

Nik kisses the hair of the girl in his arms. She's curled against his chest, her eyes squeezed shut as she clutches at the front of his shirt. It's been so long since I've seen the Vesely twins together that their similarities are almost startling: broad shoulders, slim hips, square jawlines and strong brows.

And when the girl pulls away from Nik, smiling up at him with a century's worth of fondness, my last bit of disbelief evaporates.

It's really her. My Rayna. Standing there grinning like she didn't just come back from the dead.

She looks exactly the way I remember her, with her mischievous eyes and her confident air. But even the perfect memory of a vampire fades over time, and this Rayna is crisper. *Brighter.* I had forgotten how vivid her hair was: deep orange threaded with accents of gold and umber, falling straight to her shoulders and glowing in the dimmed ballroom lights.

Different, though, are her clothes: dark jeans, ankle boots, a black v-neck t-shirt, a jacket made of supple caramel leather. There's a large silver cross around her neck, inlaid with polished turquoise, and a matching ring adorns her right middle finger; the skin under each piece of jewelry is pulled tight in whitish scars. Everything is simple and perfectly tailored, the modernity a stark contrast to the elegant brocade and silks she once wore.

I rise shakily to my feet, ignoring the muffled grunt from Xander beside me. He hasn't moved since Konstantin disappeared with Victoria, but I don't blame him. He can barely walk as it is after his leg was snapped in half by one of Konstantin's fledglings.

My battle-tattered dress flutters around my ankles, and I can feel blood crusting in my hair, on my cheeks, on my hands. I'm a mess, the ballroom is a mess, but it doesn't matter. *Nothing* matters.

Because Rayna is alive.

Emotion surges through me like a riptide: disbelief, hope, relief. Confusion. Excitement. And underneath it all, the red-hot glow of anger, growing stronger with each beat of my frantic heart.

I cross to Rayna, stopping only when I'm close enough to touch her. I don't, though. Part of me wants to stay suspended in this moment forever. Because I know that as soon as I touch her—as soon as she becomes *real*—everything is going to change. Anticipation burns through me, and I get the distinct feeling that this moment is the start of something big. I just don't know if I'm ready to face it yet.

Unfortunately, Rayna doesn't seem to share the sentiment. She smiles softly at Nikolas, wipes a tear from his cheek, then turns to look directly at me, her mouth twisting into a wicked grin. I wait for the flash of mischief, the hint of bright humor that usually accompanied such a grin, but it never comes. There's something different about this smile—it's her eyes, I think. They're dark. Cold.

"Hi, Lottie," she says, and the embers in my chest ignite into flame.

With a snarl that makes the chandeliers shiver, I lunge forward and slap Rayna across the face.

CHAPTER 2

Rayna's head snaps sideways as a *crack* echoes through the ballroom. My hand tingles with the sheer force of the slap and I shake it out, satisfied by the pinpricks of heat dancing over my palm. Rayna stays turned away from me, fingers prodding her reddened cheek as Nik places a protective hand on her shoulder.

"*Charlotte,*" he chides, his tone incredulous. "What was that for?"

I don't know. I open and close my fist a few times, staring at the red-haired ghost in front of me. A hundred and twenty-one years, she's been dead. The number plays on a loop in my head, sticking there. One, two, one. Over half my life.

And now . . . now she's *here.*

"What the hell?" Rayna and I say at the same time, her eyes burning holes through me. Watching. Waiting.

I do nothing. I say nothing. There's nothing I *can* do, because everything I thought I knew was a lie. Every belief I held, every fear I had. *Lies.*

"You slapped me," Rayna says coolly, folding her arms.

I cock an eyebrow. "I had to make sure you were real."

"By *slapping me?*"

"Seemed as good an option as any."

The room settles into uncomfortable silence and I chew on the insides of my cheeks. I can feel Nik and Xander watching us intently, a shadow-wrapped Kaleb observing from his perch on the window sill. He hasn't moved—has barely *breathed* since Rayna walked into the room.

The silence stretches.

I've thought about this moment a million times—when Rayna would magically reappear and we would hug and laugh and celebrate with a tearful reunion—but I never thought it would actually happen. After all, how often do people actually come back from the dead?

And now that it *has* happened, I'm not sure how to feel.

Rayna gives me a once-over, her eyes dragging over me like a hungry cat: my stained burgundy velvet gown, the blood drying in my hair, the line of healing claw marks on my face. Her gaze lingers on the silver coin around my neck where it blisters the skin over my sternum.

Her coin.

I fight the urge to tear it off.

"Dear Lord, Lottie," she muses, wiping a drop of blood from my chin. I bat her hand away, frowning at her casual mention of deity. "You look like hell."

"Thanks for that," I snap, then sweep my arm sideways in a grand gesture. "As you can see, it's been one hell of a night."

And then I smile. It's forced and cold, and I can feel the bite in it. Something like confusion flickers in Rayna's eyes, so fast that I almost miss it.

I watch distantly as she steps back to survey her surroundings, as if noticing the room for the first time. She takes in the ballroom with its oak coffers and pale damask wallpaper, the white sheer curtains hanging limply in front of floor-length windows. Half the room is bathed in shadows, the other glittering with lights from the slow-spinning disco ball. It would be beautiful, except for the pools of blood drying on the floor and the handful of discarded, bloodied weapons strewn about the room.

"I can see that. What exactly—" Her eyes snag on Nik's haunted expression and she pales.

A droll voice behind me prevents Nik from speaking.

"And so," Xander drawls, "the Prodigal Daughter returns."

Rayna frowns at Nik but drags her attention away, her mouth splitting into an acidic smile.

"Alexander," she says through gritted teeth. "Charming as ever, I see."

My brother doesn't look amused. In fact, he looks like he's about a breath away from falling over. There's an oozing gash on his shoulder—a wound made from silver, no doubt; those bastards always take longer to heal—and he favors his injured leg, wincing with every other step as he limps toward us. Unfortunately for him, compound fractures don't heal quickly, either. He stops a few feet away, indignation in his emerald eyes.

"Xander," he says pointedly. "I go by Xander now."

Rayna inclines her head, crossing her arms as a beat of tense silence passes, then another. Finally, with a tiny nod, she bites out, "Noted."

"Rayna." Nik's voice rumbles beside her. "Be nice."

"Really, Nikolas?" She glances up at him, and there's a wealth of emotion in his expression: concern, uncertainty, and a flash of anger that mirrors my own.

The twins share a few sharp words, but I'm no longer listening. Green glints from the front of the room and I turn to see Kaleb still perched on the windowsill, the emerald glistening at his throat. His hands grip the ledge so hard that the wood has splintered, and his expression is unreadable as he watches the exchange with ice-chip eyes.

Rayna clears her throat loudly and my attention snaps back to her.

"Tell me what happened." The words aren't so much a request as a demand.

I open my mouth to retort but Nik makes a tiny noise in his throat. There's a hint of wariness in his expression, as if he's telling me to *wait*. To think about the words before they come out of my mouth.

In a surprising show of self-control, I do. How much should we tell Rayna about what happened here tonight? Will it even matter? Does she already have an idea?

Can we even trust her?

"What?" Rayna asks, her voice wavering, just a little. "What have I missed?"

Nik frowns. "It's been over a century, Rayna. What *haven't* you missed?"

There's movement by the window. Kaleb stands slowly and does his best to compose himself, re-buttoning his torn blazer and smoothing back his swath of chestnut hair. Despite his effort, his usual regal air is dulled, the sharp cut of his gaze now weathered and tired. His shoulders sag under invisible weight and his right eye is rimmed in deep purple, leaking blood into the white of his eye.

Our Alpha. My friend. His edges peeling, his foundation cracked. But still standing. Still *here*. And as long as Kaleb Sutton is still standing, so are we all.

There's a loud *bang as* Pippa and Rose burst through the ballroom doors, making me jump. Each of them is more haggard than when I last saw them: their chests are heaving, blood is smeared on their skin, and they're both holding their shoes in their hands.

The two of them look around wildly before they lock eyes with Xander, who perks up immediately.

"Anything?" he asks, a loose bit of hope coloring his voice. "Any sign of Victoria?"

Rose shakes her head sadly, tears slipping smoothly down her brown cheeks.

"I'm so sorry, Xander," she says, tearing the bow from her bright pink cocktail dress. "We lost her in the Presidio."

Xander sags and I reach for his hand, fumbling with it before our fingers interlock. For a few seconds, I worry that he'll pull away. But he stares down at me, his brow furrowed, and squeezes my fingers gently. Hesitant warmth fills me and I carefully hug my brother's arm, leaning my head on his shoulder. He releases a measured breath.

"They just . . . disappeared," Pippa adds, throwing her hands up in exasperation. She winces sharply and clutches at her heart, where a spiderweb of dark veins snakes over her pale chest, crawling upward from the neckline of her metallic purple dress—a permanent reminder of the hawthorn that almost claimed her life only yesterday. "We were hot on their trail, but they must have gotten in a car because—"

She chokes on her words as her gaze catches on a frowning Rayna, who regards her with thinly-veiled judgment. Pippa's eyes widen and she fixes me with a look that asks, *Are you seeing this?*

I just shrug. *I'm as confused as you are.*

Rayna cocks her head to the side. "Philippa Rees, what did you do to your hair?"

"I—um—I don't—" Pippa stammers, and it's one of the few times I've seen her speechless. She stares at Rayna with a frown of her own. "The hawthorn must have messed with my head, because the last time I checked, you were *dead.*"

"Last time *I* checked," Rayna counters, "I *wasn't.*"

Rose taps Rayna's arm gently, drawing her attention. There's a touch of hesitance in her expression, but her eyes are dark and focused. She raises one hand and lightly combs through Rayna's hair, toying with a few fiery strands that catch between her fingers.

"You're alive," she murmurs with the faintest trace of a smile. "I knew it."

I scoff. "You did *not.*"

Rose wets her lips then turns slowly to me, smiling sweetly. "You have no idea what I know."

"Oh, really?" I say, disentangling myself from Xander. There's a challenge in Rose's eyes—one that could be banter or something more serious. I'm never quite sure with her. "Try me."

"Yes, okay," Xander says brusquely, waving a derisive hand through the air. Though his arrogance is potent as ever, his face doesn't reflect it. His eyes are distant, his mouth turned down. "We're all very surprised that Rayna is alive. But can we please focus on what's actually important?"

I gape at him. "Are you serious, Alexander? Rayna is standing *right here*"—I grab her shoulder and give it a good shake to demonstrate the fact that she is, indeed, here—"and that's all you have to say?"

The black glare he fixes on Rayna could make a sunflower wilt. She meets his gaze steadily.

"I'm sorry," Xander says, "if you think Rayna's sudden reappearance is somehow more important than the fact that Victoria was just *kidnapped* by—"

He cuts off abruptly, snapping his mouth shut with a furtive glance at Kaleb.

Say it, I think. *Say his name.*

He doesn't. No one does. Instead, a chilly silence falls over the room, punctuated by the sharp *thud* of Rayna's racing heartbeat.

Good. Let her worry.

"I don't know who this Victoria is," Rayna says after a few slow breaths, "but I'm sorry that in the last century, you still haven't managed to remove the stick from your ass."

A growl rumbles through my brother's chest, but his reply is interrupted by a cool, British voice.

"Rayna, darling. Manners."

The commanding edge in Kaleb's tone sends a shiver down my spine. He steps forward, carrying with him the scent of eucalyptus and the lingering, acrid taste of cigarette smoke. Rayna's breath catches, and when their eyes meet—when they ignite with some long-cold fire—I suddenly feel like I'm intruding on a *very* intimate moment. Rayna's gaze slithers down Kaleb's body and she drags her lip between her teeth, causing Pippa to gag theatrically.

"Geez," I groan. "Get a room."

Rayna crosses to Kaleb in a few purposeful strides. She lifts a hand to touch the healing gashes at his neck but he snatches her wrist, eyes narrowing reproachfully.

"What are you doing here?" he hisses. I expect surprise—or maybe tenderness—but the growl in his words suggests he is anything but happy to see her. "I told you I have everything under control."

"Clearly." Rayna's jaw ticks. "If that's the case, am I to assume this ballroom demolished itself? That your wounds were self-inflicted?"

Kaleb stills, discomfort sharpening his pale eyes before he takes a step back, out of her reach. His posture is perfect and his head is inclined, even while one hand worries at a loose button on his blazer.

The Alpha's gaze flicks to mine and I glare back, my mind furiously working to make sense of this moment. I assume that Kaleb and Rayna have spoken recently and, if I had to guess, they speak often. Their exchange is too normal—too *comfortable* to be between two people reuniting after a long while. Somehow, that makes this all worse. Not only was Kaleb keeping her from us, but a few days ago, when I begged him to tell me what really happened to her, he only perpetuated the lie. Making me believe that it was all Rayna's idea.

Maybe it was.

Just when I think I can trust Kaleb again, I find a new secret. A new deception. I wish I could say that I'm surprised.

Something must change in my expression because remorse flashes in Kaleb's eyes, like he can see straight through me to the judgment underneath. The hurt. I don't bother hiding it.

"This was *him,* wasn't it?" Rayna's words slice into my thoughts, breaking my focus.

"Yes," Nik says, his voice low. Troubled. "Konstantin was here."

With a slow exhale, Rayna clutches both hands to her chest and squeezes her eyes shut, freezing in place like a marble carving of herself. It's no secret that Rayna and Konstantin once had an intimate relationship—one that ended *very* badly. Despite the fact that she spared me all the gory details of their time together, I know how much he terrified her. How desperate she was to get away from him.

I choose to ignore the sudden pounding of her heart and instead glance sideways at Kaleb, who is doing his best impression of an apathetic house cat. My eyes narrow. There's no way he can be so cavalier about being covered in Konstantin's blood with Rayna standing only a few feet away. He watches her carefully, his fingers obsessively worrying at that damn button. If he doesn't stop, he's going to rip it off.

Rayna's face softens suddenly. Her arms relax, her hands fall to her sides, and her mouth twists into a confident—albeit shaky—smirk.

"So, he beat me here after all," she says dryly, gracefully brushing a few strands of hair from her face. I see straight through her attempt at ambivalence, noting the sharpness in her words. "Figures."

Konstantin. Just the thought of him brings heat to gums and tightness to the hollows under my eyes. For a few minutes tonight, I had started to think I actually liked the boy I knew as Ty. He was brazen, beautiful, and just reckless enough to be alluring. And then I remember the look of horror on Kaleb's face when he recognized Ty for who he really was. I remember Ty's hands on Jason and the wicked glint in his eye when he snapped the human boy's neck. The anguish on Tristan's face as he watched his friend die.

"He's been here for the last week," I snarl, unable to hide my disgust, "and has been screwing with us the whole time. Until tonight, we didn't even know who he was."

Rayna eyes Kaleb disbelievingly. "A *week?* Don't tell me he managed to fool even you."

"I never saw him," Kaleb says carefully. "Neither did Nikolas. Not until tonight. It was clever of him, really."

"Yes, very clever," Xander bites out, glaring at Rayna. "And thanks to *you,* he has my fiancée."

Rayna blinks. "What do you mean, *fiancée?*"

"They've been engaged since 1956," I say, and Rayna bursts into laughter.

"Sixty years and you haven't tied the knot?" She makes a show of examining her nails. "It seems our little Alexander is still afraid of commitment. As I recall, you had a fiancée once before. Mira, was it?"

Xander lunges forward but I catch his arm, Nik assisting me with a firm hand on his shoulder. Mira was Xander's first love and though it's been centuries, I'm not sure if he ever truly got over her. She was beautiful as a porcelain doll and sweet as honey, and she had an uncanny ability to see straight into a person's soul. It's one of the many reasons we loved her so much. Xander may be wholly dedicated to Victoria now, but there's a little corner of his heart that he will always reserve for Mira.

"Don't you talk about her," Xander snarls. "*Never* talk about her."

"Temper, temper, *maly stín*." *Little shadow*. Rayna takes a taunting step forward. "There's so much anger in those pretty green eyes. You won't kill anymore, so you keep that hunger pent up inside you, tamping it down and pretending it doesn't exist. Is that it? How long before you snap? How long before you completely lose control again?" She taps a finger against her chin contemplatively. "We wouldn't want to tarnish that lovely little reputation of yours, would we?"

A snarl tears from Xander's throat as darkness blooms beneath his eyes. I'm not sure what's happening here, but my body is buzzing with nervous energy. Rayna is here. Rayna is *alive*. And she's doing everything in her power to piss everyone off. I'm not sure whether to laugh or cry, whether to let my brother throttle her or to hold him back.

"Konstantin is looking for you," Xander says to Rayna, his voice dripping with acid, "and as far as I'm concerned, he can have you."

A collective rush of adrenaline spikes in the room and the Veselys look at him with twin expressions of fury. I almost join them but can't summon enough energy for more than an unamused glare.

"Rayna is family," Pippa says firmly, but I notice the way she carefully avoids Rayna's eyes. "We're not going to sacrifice her."

"Why not?" Xander snaps. "She *abandoned us!*"

My brother's voice cracks, and I startle. His eyes are bright, his shoulders tense, and there's a touch of uncharacteristic wildness about him. I reach for his arm but he yanks it away.

Are those *tears* in his eyes?

"Rayna hasn't given a *damn* about us for over a hundred years," he says through gritted teeth. "Why should we give a damn about her?"

"Alexander, calm down," Rose says quietly. "We'll find Victoria, but you and I both know that she wouldn't want this."

Rayna steps forward, seething. "You don't know what you're talking about, *Xander*." She says his name with a condescending sneer. "If you had any idea the hell I've been through to protect all of you—"

"*Protect us*?" Xander shouts. "Abandoning your family is your idea of protection? Do we look *safe* to you?" He throws one hand out to the side, his mouth twisting into a snarl. "Konstantin was in my *home*. He murdered an innocent human in front of the poor boy's friends. He kidnapped my fiancée. He tormented Charlotte. *My little sister.*" Something in the way he says that makes my chest tighten. "If you really cared about protecting us, you would have killed that bastard centuries ago."

Almost imperceptibly, Kaleb winces.

Rayna's fangs shoot through her gums. "I'm not going to roll over just because your latest conquest was kidnapped," she says, drawing a tiny gasp from Rose. "I appreciate this newfound confidence of yours, but you're a fool if you think you have any authority over me."

Xander's cheeks flush a hot shade of red. "Get out."

Rayna rolls her eyes. "You're not serious."

"I said, *get out of my house*." His voice is laced with venom, and I'm silently grateful when Kaleb steps forward.

"I think we're all a bit exhausted after the events of the evening," he says calmly, though I can see the tension in his shoulders. "It would be best for us to rest and revisit this discussion tomorrow."

"Tomorrow?" Xander whirls on him, teeth bared. He looks absolutely feral, his pupils swallowing the emerald green of his irises. I almost shy away. "*Tomorrow?* Sure, that sounds like a great idea. Meanwhile, Konstantin could be torturing my Victoria while we all *rest*. Apparently, I'm the only one here who cares about finding her."

Kaleb exhales sharply, his expression bright with concern. "Alexander, that is not true—"

"*GET OUT!*" Xander's words echo loudly in the too-big room.

Pippa is the first to move. She offers me a sympathetic smile then gives Rayna a quick hug, patting her cheek a little too sharply. Rose casts a worried glance in Xander's direction and the two girls slip out of the room.

"Come," Kaleb murmurs to no one in particular, his troubled eyes locked on Xander. "We've overstayed our welcome."

Rayna cuts him a glare. There's a touch of annoyance there—probably at the idea of Kaleb bossing her around—but her common sense ultimately wins out. She follows him after flashing me her familiar devil's grin. My breath catches as memories of that smile whirl through my mind: racing through London's cobbled streets, breaking into the Kremlin, swimming the East River, climbing the Eiffel Tower.

"I'll talk to you soon, Lottie." She winks before disappearing through the ballroom doors.

I glance at Nik and mouth, *Are you going to be okay?*

He nods, then shakes his head, then shrugs. *I don't know,* he mouths back. And then he's gone, too.

I exhale slowly as an odd sort of numbness settles over me. I thought I had experienced the full spectrum of human emotion tonight, from my conversation with Tristan about my true vampire nature, to dancing with Ty at the party, to Jason's death and Konstantin's heart-stopping reveal. But then *Rayna* appeared after being dead for over a century. Standing here now, I wonder if I imagined it all. It seems too good to be true.

Maybe it is.

"Rayna's alive," I say as Nik's footsteps fade away. "How did I miss that?"

Xander's hand claps down on my shoulder and I flinch. The fury in his eyes is gone, replaced with . . . well, *nothing.* Just a yawning emptiness that makes my skin crawl. I press my palm to his damp cheek, brushing a tear away with my thumb.

Quietly, I ask, "*Tabie choladna?*"

Are you cold? It was a question we asked as children—a way to say, *I am here. Do you need me?*

The question barely registers in his eyes before they shutter completely. His hand drops from my shoulder as he stalks out of the room, vanishing into the shadowed hallway with the last traces of a limp.

"Xander?" I call, racing after him. "Alexander, talk to me!"

He doesn't stop—he doesn't even slow. I follow him through the foyer, past my bedroom, and watch as he disappears into his art studio, slamming the door behind him.

The house shudders, then stills, and then I'm alone.

CHAPTER 3

IF THERE IS ONE THING Konstantin has learned in his seven centuries of life, it is that everyone who has ever lived, and *will* ever live, has a weakness.

For him, it was his size. He was nothing but a runt among his peers. The larger, stronger boys counted him as useless. The adults, a nuisance. And if his size weren't enough to dissuade interest, his silver eyes were. *Copilul diavolului,* they called him. *The Devil's child.* Isolated and alone, he remained a small, weak boy. It wasn't until he was Turned—until that unholy disease claimed his humanity—that he became strong.

And now he can sense the weakness in others, as a trained dog may sniff out a cancer. Nikolas's weakness was his cowardice. Rayna's, her spineless brother.

And Kaleb's, his compulsive need to protect those closest to him, whatever the cost.

Konstantin took that need for granted. After all, it was once Kaleb's mission to protect *him*. But then they met Rayna, and all of that changed.

He'll be *damned* if he lets Kaleb's white king sweep him from the board again. He lost everything that night in Belarus: his empire, his power, his lover. And, most importantly, the man he once called brother.

But Konstantin is smarter now. Ruthless. A king with nothing else to lose.

The woman in the water cries out and he snaps to attention, tugging at the wire around her wrists and ignoring the lap of icy water at his chest. It has almost reached the woman's chin, soaking her raven hair and bringing tears to her slanted eyes. Wind howls outside the hiding place, bringing with it the crack of thunder and sporadic bursts of rain. It whips the sea into a frenzy, the waves surging in and out of the small cavern like the breaths of a mighty beast, crashing over the woman in angry swells.

"You're not going to win," she hisses, dark eyes blazing. Mascara runs in inky trails down her face, visible only by the small flashlight wedged into a crack on the cavern wall. "Alexander will come for me."

Konstantin offers a piteous smile, lowering his face to hers. "I'm counting on it."

"What can you possibly want with him?" she asks in a wavering voice, spitting out a mouthful of seawater. "He has nothing to do with any of this!"

He laughs, a low, sinister thing. "Oh, my dear, your Alexander is *far* from innocent."

"What is that supposed to mean?"

Konstantin considers her for a few long moments, watching with disinterest as the ocean's surface rises. The woman is oblivious. Pathetic. *Weak*.

"It doesn't matter," he says finally. "If Xander does come for you, he can join you in this hole. I've made the terms of your release very clear."

"You want the truth," the woman snaps, "and you can have it. Rayna is *dead*."

A wave crashes over her and she thrashes against her bonds, but there's no escape. Konstantin made sure of that. She sputters when the water retreats, choking on a sob. Konstantin smooths the hair back from her face, stroking it softly, and she shrinks back against the rock.

"Poor little bird," he says through a mocking smile. "So blind. So *foolish*."

The woman's eyes widen in horror and pain as Konstantin tugs once more on the wire at her wrists. Then, deeming it acceptable, he snatches the flashlight from the wall and clicks it off, plunging them into complete darkness. He drags a finger along her jaw and she shudders as he touches his mouth to her ear.

"I will have what I want." His voice is barely more than a whisper. "And in the meantime, you better pray that your precious Alpha moves quickly. The tide is coming in."

Konstantin hoists himself up the ladder, ignoring the slimy mildew coating each rung. Nothing can sour his mood tonight. After all, he is so close to victory that he can practically taste it. By the time he's done in this hellhole of a city, Kaleb will be begging for mercy. He will be groveling at Konstantin's feet—kissing the soles of his boots.

It is time the rightful king takes back his throne. And he'll do it by razing Kaleb's world to the ground.

A smile splits Konstantin's face as he emerges from the cavern, slamming the trap door behind him. He hums a discordant tune as he strolls into the night, the woman's screams swallowed by the relentless ocean's roar.

CHAPTER 4

NEW YORK CITY, NEW YORK
MAY 1926

"IF RAYNA WERE HERE, SHE *would never have let me drink so much."*

I stumble over a crack in the pavement, scuffing my patent leather shoes. Alexander catches me by the arm and rolls his eyes.

"You are right about that," he says, "because she would have stolen your drinks for herself, walked home alone, and not stumbled once."

"You are not as funny as you think you are."

Alexander only smirks in response, straightening his crisp tailcoat as I adjust the neckline of my sequined dress. My brother somehow manages to look regal in his finery, while I look like his kid sister playing at make-believe.

The ground sways beneath me as we make our way through a night-laden Times Square, and I swear the cobblestones are rising to trip me on purpose. Marquees flash above us, advertising Coca-Cola and Macy's and the Ziegfeld Follies, and the bright lights make my head spin. It's Pippa's fault, really. She convinced us all to attend yet another anti-Prohibition party at her favorite speakeasy, and Nikolas thought it would be a good idea to have a drinking contest.

He won, as usual. I am not sure why any of us try anymore.

Alexander, having stayed sober all evening, frowns as I stumble again, steadying me with a hand on my elbow.

"Really, Charlotte. You are making a fool of yourself tonight."

I laugh dryly. "And how is that different from any other night?"

Alexander opens his mouth to reply but is interrupted by a woman's nearby cry. His head snaps northward and he pauses, waiting. It is only a few seconds before we hear it again. My brother breaks into a run.

"Alexander!" I call, staggering after him. "Wait!"

He stops suddenly and I nearly crash into him, following his gaze as he peers into a shadowed alleyway. A woman is pinned against the grimy wall by a man twice her size. He's grinning at her with a predatory look in his eye, but the woman simply smiles up at him with smug contempt.

She is stunning. Layers of pale pink fringe fall to her knees, a long string of pearls hangs from her delicate neck, and her raven hair is pinned back in finger waves. A feathered band is wrapped around her head, dripping rosy jewels that sparkle against her ivory skin. Her eyes, upturned and dark, are lined with glittered makeup, and they shimmer as she glares at her attacker.

"Be a good girl," the man growls, "and hold still."

She laughs quietly, and her voice is calm when she speaks. Teasing, even. "Maybe if you ask nicely."

I glance up at Alexander, who is watching the exchange with wide, entranced eyes.

"Are you going to intervene or not?" I hiss with an elbow to his ribs. "Whatever you plan to do, do it quickly. I would love to get home and regain some semblance of sobriety."

Alexander blinks, coming back to himself, and yells, "You there!" just as the woman flashes a pair of fangs and buries her face in the man's neck. The man thrashes in her grip, his strength no match for hers. She shoves off from the wall and throws him to the ground with vampiric strength, pinning his wrists above him as she feeds. We watch, stunned, as the man's thrashing slows, then stops.

After a few long swallows, the woman sits up and throws her head back, the motion shaking a few strands of hair loose from their pins. She licks the blood from her lips with a sultry swipe of her tongue, then turns a bright gaze our way, smiling through red-tinged fangs.

Alexander doesn't breathe as she stands and saunters forward, stopping when she's barely a foot from him. She has to crane her neck to look at his face, but it's no matter; Alexander is pinned under her gaze, a fly caught in a widow's web.

"Hello," she says with singsong sweetness, walking her fingers up my brother's chest. She inhales deeply, tasting his scent, and I hear his heart stutter. "I haven't seen you before, fang. First time in New York?"

Alexander swallows stiffly. "No."

He doesn't elaborate. A beat passes, then another, and it might just be the excess of alcohol in my body, but I swear I see their shallow breaths synchronize. Alexander lifts one hand to thumb a smear of blood from the woman's mouth and she exhales slowly, her hungry eyes burning as he sucks his finger clean.

"Victoria." She smiles, glancing at his lips. "And you are?"

"Alexander."

The two stare at each other for a long moment, and I can almost see a connection form between them—reminiscent of a chemistry my brother has only shared with one other. But Mira is long-dead, and this woman's manicured fingers are toying with the open collar of Alexander's shirt.

"While I would love to stay and"—she traces one finger along Alexander's jaw—"get to know one another, I really must be going. Business, and all that." With a nod over her shoulder, she moves to leave, but my brother catches her hand. He draws it to his mouth, brushing a kiss against her pale knuckles.

Victoria's cheeks flush a demure shade of pink and the effect it has on my brother is audible. His heart leaps as she slowly pulls away, smiling coyly before she slips her hand free and disappears into the shadows.

"I have a feeling we'll meet again, fang," she calls through the darkness, and with the whisper of bare feet against pavement, she's gone.

Alexander stares at the place where she vanished for a few seconds too long, his hand lingering at his mouth and his heart splayed open on his sleeve.

IT TAKES ME all of seven seconds to break into Xander's studio. He added a lock to the room when we moved in, but it's all for show. I've been breaking into his rooms for two hundred years and we both know a little deadbolt won't stop me.

I did give him some time to himself, however, since I'm not *completely* heartless. After the shock of Rayna's appearance wore off, I finally managed to track down a bucket, a bottle of ammonia, and a mean-looking scrub brush. Where blood once stained the ballroom floors, there are now only a few worn areas where the harsh cleaner ate away some of the varnish. Victoria would kill me if she knew.

But she doesn't know. Because she isn't here.

Her absence is a hollow ache that mingles with the guilt and fear already writhing in my chest. It's my fault she's gone.

It's *my fault.*

Konstantin's warning rings in my ears: *You have one week to tell me the truth about Rayna, or the girl dies.* The thought of his crooked grin when he snatched her away is enough to raise the hair on my arms. Despite taking a shower so hot it would make the Devil uncomfortable, I can still feel Konstantin's cold presence all over me—touching my bare back, breathing in my ear, kissing my neck.

I should have known who he was. *What* he was.

With a shudder, I force the thought away. I'll have plenty of time to wallow later. Right now, I need to focus on my brother. If the crashing sounds coming from his studio earlier were any indication, he is not doing well. I quietly turn the door's handle and peer inside.

"Xander?"

The room is quiet and dark despite its wall of windows, the air ripe with the overpowering scent of wet paint. Through the dimness I can make out the carnage: broken pencils littering the floor, sketches ripped in half, the tall easel upended with one leg snapped. A huge splatter of turquoise paint covers the windows, obscuring my view of the San Francisco Bay and dripping into a puddle on the floor. The gallery wall has suffered a similar fate, and I stifle a gasp. Splotches of black paint cover Xander's favorite works: the New York skyline, our cottage home in Belarus, and his impressionistic piece of Victoria. Dark streaks drip down her watercolor face like tears.

Xander is lying on his back in the middle of the room, his arms and legs limp, his eyes closed. He is still in his party clothes—black everything, as usual—but it now looks less menacing and more like he's in mourning. Blood is caked into his hair, his tie is missing, and his collar has been torn open to reveal the remnants of a shallow gash on his throat.

I've only seen Xander like this three times in his life. First, when Mama died. Second, when he was Turned and realized he would never—*could* never—see his Mira again. And third, the Chicago afternoon with Nik, which he has never fully explained. Though, based on the fact that Xander dragged a half-dead Nik inside on the first sunny day of the year, I think I have an idea.

It was the first time we almost lost Nik to his own devices, and it certainly wouldn't be the last.

My stomach clenches as I crouch next to Xander, smoothing sticky hair from his forehead. When I press my palm to his cheek, his eyes snap open.

"Victoria?" he murmurs, his voice thin.

Something cracks in my chest. "No, Alexander. It's Charlotte."

He blinks a few times, as though waking from a stupor.

"Oh," he says quietly, doing nothing to hide the disappointment in his voice.

"Nice to see you too," I mutter, but he doesn't seem to hear me.

"I thought that maybe—that she had found her way back." He swallows and squeezes his eyes shut. "*Mnie choladna, siastra.*"

I'm cold.

I need you.

When I asked the question earlier, it was more of a formality than anything. I never expected him to actually take me up on it. Xander *never* asks for help. To be honest, I'm not sure how to respond when he does. Trying to comfort Xander is like trying to calm an injured rattlesnake.

"Get up," I say, grabbing one arm and coaxing him to his feet. He is unsteady, his gaze unfocused, but at least his leg seems to be healing nicely. "You need some rest. And a shower."

"No shower," he groans. "I just want to sleep."

"You're not going to sleep smelling like that. And you'll kill me if I let you get blood on your sheets." I pause, then add, "At least let me wash your hair."

It takes a good few minutes to get Xander upstairs, but I manage to tow him into the bathroom he and Victoria share. He leans over the tub while I scrub the blood from his scalp, silently obeying when I tell him to, "Turn your head," or, "Stop trying to help, you're making it worse." After about two minutes he slaps my hands away, grumbling something about being able to take care of himself. I almost snap back, but stomp away before I say something I'll regret. Instead, I dig through his closet for sweatpants and a t-shirt.

When I return, he's using a towel to carefully squeeze water from his hair, twisting his curls into careful ringlets. Leave it to Xander to maintain his hair routine in the middle of a crisis. I shove the black clothes into his arms and he takes them methodically, but there's a patronizing gleam in his eye.

"Don't baby me, Lottie. You're not Mama."

I balk and Xander blinks quickly, as though startled by his own words. In truth, Xander is more like our mother than I am, with his olive skin, dark curls, and affinity for plants. Alena Novik was charismatic and loving, but could be fiercely protective when she needed to be. She taught me how to bake rhubarb pastries and taught Xander how to tend a vegetable garden. Whenever I would ask about our father, she would say he was a gentle soul. That I reminded her of him, despite the fact that I never knew him.

We may each take after a different parent, but the one thing Xander and I do share is our green eyes, inherited from Mama—a similarity I once took pride in. Now, I wish we didn't share the feature at all.

"Thanks for the reminder," I say coolly, ignoring a pang of grief as I back into Victoria's adjoined bedroom. "I bet you wish she were here instead of me."

Xander's face falls. "Charlotte—"

"Get dressed. I'll be in here when you're done."

I close the bathroom door and then I'm alone. Again.

Taking a deep breath, I glance around the room. The oversized bed is made, covered with textured pillows in shades of pink and white, but the comforter is mussed where a self-help book lies open, likely abandoned when Victoria readied herself for the party. A sprig of lavender rests in the crease alongside a pink sticky note with the words, "Share with Charlotte?" written in a delicate hand.

The sight of my name surprises me and I crawl onto the bed, snatching up the book. A few tiny leaves break off the lavender as it falls into my lap. I peel off the sticky note to see a highlighted passage.

There are those who believe they are destined for greatness. Others, that they are destined for failure. They believe that no matter their choices, their lives have already been determined—that there is no way to change what has already been written.

To those people, I pose this question: What is the purpose of life if not to choose our own destinies? Are we truly born into this world only to follow a fixed path that the universe has laid out for us, like a train on its tracks? Or are we here to find the tools that allow us to carve our own path?

When you realize you are the one with control over

your own life—your own mind—*a new world of possibil-
ities will open up to you. The universe will have no choice
but to give you what you want. In the words of the author
Paulo Coelho, "When you want something, all the universe
conspires in helping you to achieve it."*

I scoff, snapping the book shut. The cover boasts the title,
*Conquering the Universe: Seven Simple Steps to Choosing Your Own
Destiny*, and the author's name: Dr. Sonya Romero, M.D., Psy.D. I'll
never understand why Victoria reads this stuff.

Tossing the book back onto the bed, I turn my attention to the
bookshelves where I see a plethora of romance novels, more self-help
books, and dozens of sparkling crystals. There's a glass-top desk on
another wall with containers of perfectly organized pens, and a street
light shining through the sheer curtains on the window gives the room
a dream-like feel.

Anxious longing claws its way into my throat. If we don't get
Victoria back—if Konstantin does anything to hurt her—I'm afraid
her loss will change me in a very real way. One I haven't felt since I
lost Rayna. But unlike Rayna, Konstantin will make sure that Victoria
never comes back. And Xander will never recover.

The door opens behind me and I turn to see my brother shuffle out
of the bathroom, his gaze lowered. He looks a little better, at least—I
think he might have even shaved—but his eyes are haunted and rimmed
in red.

A sisterly instinct awakens in me and I lurch forward, wrapping my
arms around his chest. He freezes for a mortifying moment, and I'm
sure that he'll shove me away. But slowly—*so* slowly—he returns the
embrace, resting his face against my hair.

We stand in silence for a few minutes, unsure of what to say. Since
the two of us became vampires, the emotional side of our relationship
has been strenuous, at best. Not because we stopped caring for one
another, but because we, as individuals, changed irrevocably that day.

We have spent so much time trying to take care of ourselves that we've forgotten what it means to take care of each other.

Not for the first time, I wish I could open my eyes and wake up in Belarus, with Mama baking in the kitchen and Xander harvesting vegetables for the town market.

"Xander?" I say, but his expression is vacant. I grab his chin and jerk his face upward, forcing his eyes to meet mine. "Hey. I need you to be present, okay? Can you do that?"

He blinks slowly, like a bored house cat, and I frown. Before tonight, I thought the worst thing Xander could be was drunk, but I was wrong. This distance—this hopelessness—is much worse.

"I don't—" he murmurs, his gaze wandering again. It snags on Victoria's bed and a muscle in his jaw feathers. "I don't know where she is."

"None of us do, Alexander. But we'll find her. It's not your fault."

"I should have helped her." His voice rises in pitch and his expression sharpens. "She was right in front of me. Why didn't I help her?"

"Hey." I lead him to the edge of Victoria's bed and practically force him to sit next to me. I know I'm being brash, but it's the best I can do right now. I'm barely holding myself together as it is. "Do you remember what Konstantin said? If you tried to save her, she would have been dead before you had even taken a step. You did the right thing in letting her go. Now we have an entire week, which is more than enough time to find her." I purse my lips, hearing the insecurity in my own voice. "Besides, if anyone is to blame for her kidnapping, it's me."

Xander actually scoffs. "And why the hell would you think that?"

"Because I was the closest to Konstantin. I'm the one who invited him to the party. If it wasn't for me, Victoria would still be here."

"Don't be so dramatic," Xander says, but even his annoyance lacks its usual vivacity. "Konstantin would have found a way to hurt us regardless of whether or not he was invited to some stupid party."

I shrug. "I suppose we'll never know."

"Stop that."

"Stop what?"

"Torturing yourself. You know it could have happened to anyone—"

"Just let me wallow, will you?"

Xander swallows thickly. After a few seconds, he says, "It's just—I can't lose her, Lottie. I've already lost one love. I can't lose another. I—I don't think I would survive it."

My heart sinks even further. Xander rarely mentions Mira anymore. After we were Turned, I always assumed she moved on and lived a normal life—I wouldn't be surprised if she married the stablehand on the other side of the village. Though it doesn't matter, really. She's long gone. I miss her sometimes, with her chestnut curls and round, doll-like face. She was sweet, steady, and soft—qualities I always envied.

But she had nothing on Victoria.

"Victoria is strong as hell," I say. "You remember who she was when we first met her." The corner of Xander's mouth twitches, and I know I'm on the right track. "If she could work in a business like Mei's for a decade, I think she can handle one week with Konstantin."

Xander inhales deeply then nods once, though the panic doesn't leave his eyes.

"You're right," he says, leaning his head on my shoulder. "She'll be okay. She *has* to be."

We sit together in silence, my hand resting awkwardly on Xander's back, and I try not to notice his tears as they fall into my lap.

CHAPTER 5

When Rayna left the Noviks' house, she had two options: either spend the night with Kaleb, or spend the night with Nikolas. She almost suggested that the three of them speak together—Hell knows they have a lot to discuss—but she couldn't deny the frigid air between her brother and her . . . well, she isn't sure what Kaleb is to her right now. But she'll figure that out later.

Because she chose to go home with her brother, and things are not going well.

Nikolas curses loudly, brushing damp strands of freshly-washed hair from his forehead. "What did you think was going to happen, Rayna? That you would come back from the dead and everything would still be the way it was?"

Rayna sits on the edge of Nikolas's sofa while he paces in front of her, pausing every few steps to hurl another accusation, another insult, another wild question at her. Each one is a barb that lodges itself in her chest; if Nikolas keeps going like this, she's eventually going to bleed out. Her brother was once calm and soft-spoken. Now he holds nothing back.

"Why did you leave in the first place?" he asks, expression bright with anger, disbelief, confusion, and a slew of other emotions Rayna can't place. "I could have come with you! Why did you have to hide from *me, straka?*" *Magpie.* An old nickname—one she hasn't been called in a long time. "You should have involved me! But you didn't trust me to keep your secret. Your own *brother.* What kind of—" Nikolas sighs loudly, dragging a hand over his face. "Is this really what you wanted? To ruin my life?"

He plants his feet and turns to face Rayna, cognac eyes ablaze. She fights the urge to shrink away from his scrutiny, forcing herself to meet his gaze. In hindsight, she probably should have expected this. But she was convinced that her brother would be happy. That he would *understand.*

"Are you finished?" Rayna drums her fingers on the leather sofa, projecting an air of calm control despite her racing thoughts.

Nikolas laughs humorlessly and stalks to the bar cart, muttering under his breath.

Rayna inhales shakily. "Nikolas—"

"Nik."

"Really?" Rayna folds her arms to hide her trembling hands. "You're my brother. I'll call you whatever I like."

"You'll call me Nik." He pours himself a glass of whiskey and immediately downs it before pouring another.

"Fine."

There's a long stretch of silence, and Rayna can feel ice burning its way up her throat. She squeezes her eyes shut and balls her fists, swallowing her growing panic. *Not here,* she thinks. *Not now.*

What she wouldn't give to have Harper with her right now. She had considered asking her friend to come but ultimately decided this reunion would be best done alone. A stupid decision, if she has ever made one. Harper would have made a great buffer between her and whatever version of her brother is leaning casually against the wall and getting drunk on top-shelf liquor.

Rayna's hand twitches to the phone in her pocket, desperately wanting to send a text message to Harper. She could use some of her unfiltered Southern wisdom right about now. But she hesitates a moment too long and Nik speaks again, yanking her from her thoughts.

"You didn't answer my question," he says, now on his third glass of whiskey. The decanter is nearly empty.

"Oh?" Rayna keeps her tone level. Neutral. "Which one? You've thrown quite a few at me in the last twenty minutes."

Nik narrows his eyes and his voice drops to a near-whisper when he asks, "Why did you leave?"

Rayna opens her mouth, then closes it again. Despite the fact that Nik has enough alcohol in his system to knock out a small town, she knows he can hear everything. *See* everything. As twins, they have always had a unique connection: Nik can see through Rayna's bullshit the way Rayna can see his heart.

Right now, it's bleeding.

"I left—" she starts, then amends her words. "*We* left because we were trying to protect you."

"Oh, you're going to drag Kaleb into this now?" Nik moves to an armchair and sits heavily, swirling his glass of whiskey. With each drink, his demeanor softens a fraction; now, instead of anger, there's a fluidity to his movements, a languorous glint in his eyes. He looks up at her, scrutinizing. "It's just like you to try to pass the blame. Tell me, how exactly did you convince Kaleb to agree to such an idiotic plan?"

Fire crackles through Rayna now, chasing away the ice, but it only fuels her racing heart. *You knew this would be a possibility,* she reminds herself. *If he faked his death and showed up alive a hundred years later, you would be angry, too.* Still, his blatant disdain is enough to make her blood boil.

"Listen here, *Nik*—"

"*No.*" He holds up a hand, and Rayna bites her tongue. "You are in no place to chastise me. Either explain yourself or go away. I'm sure you would rather be staying with Kaleb anyway. Hell knows he could use a good lay."

She gasps, heat rising to her cheeks. "*Nikolas.*"

"Oh, don't tell me you haven't thought about it. We all saw the two of you lusting over each other in the ballroom."

He isn't wrong. She *has* thought about it. In fact, she hasn't been able to *stop* thinking about it. The last time she and Kaleb were in the same room was in 2001, barely a week after he became San Francisco's Alpha. Rayna had left without saying goodbye. She still doesn't know if Kaleb has forgiven her for that.

"I couldn't let Konstantin get near you again," Rayna says, forcefully changing the subject. "Kaleb and I made a deal a long time ago, that if Kostya ever found us, we would do whatever it took to protect you and the rest of our family. He had no quarrel with you; if we were gone, you were safe. It was as simple as that."

Nik regards her for a few long moments, his pointed glare softening, just a little. Something shifts in his expression and, with a sigh of long-suffering, he sets his now-empty glass on the coffee table.

"I'm going to bed," he says, standing, "and will be sleeping for the rest of the year. There's a guest bedroom on the second floor you can use. Goodnight."

And just like that, Rayna's anger cools to embers. Nik moves to stride past her but hesitates, making her breath hitch. He's facing away from her, but she can see the muscles straining in his neck, the strong tick of his jaw.

"I understand why you thought you had to leave," he murmurs, turning to look at her. The anger is gone from his eyes, replaced with a deep sadness. "But you were wrong. Losing the two of you . . . it destroyed me, Rayna."

The pain is his voice is enough to bring her to her knees, but she wills herself to stay upright, to keep her shoulders square and her chin high. She presses a palm to her brother's cheek and he sighs quietly, relaxing into her touch.

"It was for the best, Nikolas," Rayna says quietly, and she feels the tension return to his jaw. "I had to keep him away from you—"

He jerks away, teeth bared. "Dammit, Rayna! Will you listen to yourself? You're not the only one who had to watch that bastard torture your twin."

Fire reignites in Rayna's belly, and a low growl rumbles through her. "You were his *subjugate,* Nikolas—"

"So were you!"

"—for seven years."

"He *owned* you."

"He auctioned you off to the highest bidder!"

Nik's fangs are out now. Veins snake beneath his eyes. Rayna can feel the same change in her own face, her cheeks blazing with heat and her lips curled back in a snarl. She didn't want to talk about this tonight. She simply wanted to share a drink with her brother for the first time in a hundred and twenty-one years. Clearly, he had no intention of letting her off easy.

Just thinking about Konstantin's hold on him makes Rayna's stomach roil. Nik has always been one to draw attention, with his movie star good looks and charming demeanor. Kostya used that to his advantage. And Rayna let it happen.

She won't let it happen again.

"You have no idea what it was like," she almost snarls, "watching those vampires tear into you every night—"

"Of course I did! Hell, are you even listening to me? I had to stand by and watch while that *monster* took advantage of you for *decades.*" Nik's lips press into a tight line and when he speaks again, his voice is low. Deadly. "I would sell *myself* a thousand more times if it meant I could keep you away from Konstantin. You say you left to protect me?" He scoffs and takes a step back, raking a hand through his damp hair. "Did you ever stop to think that maybe I wanted to protect you, too?"

Rayna's retort dies on her tongue. She stares at her brother—at the man she would willingly die for—and takes a slow, steadying breath.

"I don't need your protection, Nikolas."

"You're my sister, Rayna. Whether you think you need it or not is irrelevant."

With a long exhale and an indecipherable frown, Nik strides into the hallway, taking the stairs two at a time. Rayna stares after him, no longer fighting the tremor. The ice. The ghostly memory of fangs on her neck. A shudder rocks her body and she lets the feeling overtake her, refusing to acknowledge the real reason—the *weakness* that sent her running all those years ago.

Konstantin had finally found her, and she was afraid.

And now she's walking right into his trap. Maybe she should run again. This is all about her, after all. If he follows her away from San Francisco, then her family will be safe, like before.

But how long with that last, Rayna? She wants to believe that she can still understand Konstantin's intentions, but something feels different this time. He used to be predictable; spontaneous, yes, but she always knew how he would react in a given situation. He was confident, violent, and most of all, cunning. There was never a doubt that his plans would work because they always had. They always *did*.

There is a plan at work here in San Francisco. If Konstantin has been here for the last week—though Rayna suspects it has been *much* longer—what exactly has he been doing? And why reveal himself in such a way? Why *now?*

Rayna's mind spins in dizzying circles as she tries to piece together everything she has learned tonight. It isn't nearly enough. If she's going to beat Konstantin, she needs to know *everything:* who is working with him, where he is staying, how long he has been here, what exactly he's looking for.

And, more than anything, she needs to learn *why*. What is his endgame? To win her back? To torment Nik? To kill Kaleb? The ideas send a trickle of ice through her veins.

There's a *bang* from upstairs as Nik slams a door shut. Dragging her mind out of its downward spiral, Rayna stands and walks into the dim kitchen, rifling through the wooden cabinets until she finds a stemless wine glass and a bottle of nameless chardonnay. Training her ear upward, she hears the faint sound of her brother crying.

Rayna squeezes her eyes shut and leans heavily against the counter. If she knew coming back would cause Nikolas so much pain, she never would have returned. The last thing she wanted to do was hurt him.

Though it seems leaving in the first place may have already done enough damage.

She needs to change that. She *has* to. And, luckily for her, the timing of her return couldn't be more perfect. Because tomorrow is their birthday, and she knows just the thing to cheer Nik up.

RAYNA VESELY

CHAPTER 6

SAN FRANCISCO VAMPIRE TAKES
FIRST BREAK IN FIVE DAYS

I grimace at the news story on my phone and let my head fall back, resting it against a nondescript wall where I paused to metaphorically catch my breath. I don't know how long I've been running, but I've been sprinting up every street, tracing a map of San Francisco with my footsteps. The first signs of morning have appeared, cars passing more frequently as humans leave for early-morning work shifts, and the air carries that almost-dawn feeling, the day's anticipation bleeding into the last dark moments before the sunrise.

I went on a run to think—about Konstantin, about Rayna, about Victoria and Tristan—but in reality, I haven't been thinking about anything. Just the pounding of my feet on the pavement and the wind yanking at my hair. Thankfully, last night's storm has passed, but moisture still hangs over the city, manifesting as chilly fog that clings to the uppermost floors of nearby buildings and carries the scent of cool earth and green things.

Glancing down, I continue swiping at my phone screen, the motion propelling me through an endless torrent of perplexed news stories. They're doing nothing to calm my nerves.

Of course, I should be grateful that Ty—*Konstantin;* I'm still not used to that—didn't make yet another conspicuous kill. The media's obsession with the so-called San Francisco Vampire was getting worrisome and, frankly, tiring. It's bad enough that we, as vampires, have to exist in a world ruled by humans. The last thing we need is for those humans to start sticking their noses where they don't belong.

Konstantin's most recent murder may not have caught the public eye, but it's a moment I'm sure I'll never forget: the cold look of terror on Kaleb's face, the shift in Ty's once-cool demeanor, the dark grin he flashed as he snapped Jason's neck.

The glint of his fangs as he laughed in Kaleb's face. The soft *I love you* on Victoria's lips only seconds before Konstantin took her away. Xander's howl of anguish when his fiancée disappeared.

Xander. My poor brother.

Sighing, I close the Internet app and open my meager list of contacts. I sneer down at the name *Ty* and furiously replace it with *Konstantin.* His contact jumps up to the space right below Kaleb. I consider deleting him from my phone altogether, but decide against it. I'm not sure who has this particular number, and having a direct line of contact with him could potentially prove useful.

I shove my phone in my pocket and start running again. Buildings rush by in a blur and soon the city disappears, replaced by scrubby trees and rolling green hills. I put on a burst of speed. Then another. I will my legs to carry me as fast as they will go—away from the fear, the anger, the confusion of it all.

Rayna is *alive.*

Memories come rushing back at hyper-speed—every good moment I've relived millions of times, and other, less savory moments. Moments that were long-forgotten, but are returning with a vengeance: Rayna playing cruel tricks on Xander, Rayna getting us into trouble and pinning the blame on me. The way she put herself first. Every. Single. Time.

It's true what they say: absence makes the heart grow fonder. And now that Rayna is back, I'm not sure if I was ever fond of her at all.

Light kisses the eastern horizon and I skid to a stop. I'm in the middle of open field and I don't want to be stuck here when the sun rises. I move back toward the city, but not before checking my phone again.

I have one message from an unknown number.

I'm going to need you and your morose brother at Nik's tonight.

Narrowing my eyes, I type out a quick response.

Rayna?

Who else would it be?

My lips pucker. Never in my modern life did I expect to receive a text message from Rayna Vesely. I'm still half-convinced that I made it up—that she's not really alive and that I have finally gone completely insane.

This is so weird. It's like I'm texting a hallucination. Maybe they should fit me for a straight jacket.

You better get used to it, my girl. I'm sticking with you from now on. Starting at Nik's house at sunset.

Why? What are you planning?

You really have no idea? I take offense to that.

What are you talking about?

When Rayna doesn't answer immediately, I pocket my phone, grumbling under my breath. Who does she think she is, anyway? Not the Rayna I used to know, that's for sure. That girl would *never* have lied to her brother. She and Nik once shared everything—every secret, every promise, every moment—and it almost seemed like they even shared a mind. But if she managed to hide herself from him—from *us*—for so long, I'm starting to think she has more secrets than even Nik knew. As thrilled as I should be to have her back, I can't help but be wary.

I know I've changed in the last hundred and twenty-one years. Why not Rayna?

I consider calling Kaleb, just to hear him attempt to explain himself, but I'm not exactly in the mood to talk right now. In fact, I think I would rather scream.

Instead, I stare at the approaching dawn as anger takes root in my chest and I hold it there, letting it bloom.

◊   ◊   ◊

When I get home, I find Xander asleep in Victoria's bed. He has her pillow clutched to his chest and his brow is furrowed, even in sleep. There's something so soft about him—so *vulnerable*—that I feel the urge to curl up next to him. To tell him that I'm here and that everything is going to be okay.

But I know my brother, and that would do nothing but make him angry. I settle for a gentle press of my fingers to his cheek before I slip out of the room.

Sighing, I trudge down the stairs, passing through the entry before descending to the basement. I step into the cellar and yank open the door of the walk-in refrigerator where we keep our blood bags. My appetite has all but vanished after the events of last night, but I find myself drawn here anyway. There's something strangely comforting about the damp air and the low buzz of the fluorescent lights. I close my eyes and inhale deeply, relishing in the scent of cold metal and refrigerant.

And just as quickly, the familiar scent turns sour. My mind conjures the memory of standing here with Ty—with *Konstantin*. I feel the brush of his fingers against my cheek, the press of his hips as they pinned me against the wall. His lips commanding mine. At the time, our kiss seemed harmless. Stupid, even. But now, the thought makes my stomach turn.

Almost like I can feel him watching me.

Fear shivers through me and my eyes snap open, but I'm alone with the wire racks and rows of organized blood bags. I snatch a few and practically run from the room, slamming the refrigerator door behind me.

Goosebumps dance over my skin. I fight to steady my breathing as I lock the wine cellar door and walk into the game room. *He isn't here,* I think to myself.

But what if he is?

My phone buzzes but I ignore the message, choosing instead to focus on the navy-painted ceiling with its pinpricks of twinkling light. Another memory surfaces—this one *much* brighter—of Tristan's awe during his first tour of the house. His excitement was admittedly adorable.

It's becoming increasingly obvious that I fell for him immediately. Serves me right, falling for someone I can never have.

Stupid, stupid Charlotte.

Tristan Carr, with his golden hair, toned shoulders, and fading summer tan. I can still picture his wide grin when he first saw me on the Embarcadero and the way he held me close at Pier 39. I can feel the warmth of his body against mine in the backseat of Xander's Maserati.

Heat simmers in my abdomen and I release a frustrated breath, tossing my blood bags onto the side table. I shouldn't want to be with Tristan. He's *human.* Just being near me puts him in danger. Because of me, both his sister and one of his best friends are dead. He's a ray of human sunshine; he deserves more than this life of blood and darkness. Besides, it's not like I can keep him. He'll age and die like every normal human, but me? I'll be here, stuck forever at nineteen.

Still, I can't help but feel a deep ache in my chest when I think about how we parted last night. He didn't even give me a chance to explain. Maybe he's just another boy who will break my heart—one who will paint me as the villain, the tragedy, the girl who ruins everything.

So why do I feel the urge to call him?

When I check my phone, I see a new text message and silently hope it's from Tristan.

It isn't.

> Hey, hot stuff. Last night was an absolute delight. How is that brother of yours? I assume he misses his girl.

Konstantin.

All confusion over Tristan leaves me, replaced quickly by white-hot anger. Before I can stop myself, I tap the call button.

Ring. Ring. Ring. A beep, and the call ends.

"Coward," I grumble, opening our conversation.

> If you text me again, I will murder you in your sleep.

> Is that any way to speak to an old friend?

> I could do more speaking if you would answer your phone. In fact, I have a few choice words I would LOVE to share.

But where's the fun in that?

A sharp stab of fury rockets through me. I want to murder him. I want to tear his heart from his body and wash my hands with his blood. I want to show him what happens when he makes Charlotte Novik angry.

But I can't do that. Not yet. Until Victoria is home safe, we need him alive. A fact that brings a sneer to my lips.

We'll talk again when you muster up the courage to actually answer my phone calls, you coward.

Now, now, Charlotte. There's no need to get testy. I'm only having a bit of fun.

I can practically see his smug smile. That son of a bitch.

Instead of responding, I scroll through my contacts and make another call, my nerves prickling.

"Hi, Tristan," I say when it goes straight to voicemail. My voice trembles with leftover rage and I do my best to smooth it, focusing instead on the memory of Tristan's golden eyes. "It's Charlotte. Look, I know I'm probably the last person you want to talk to right now, but I just wanted to make sure you were okay after, you know, everything. Things got a lot more complicated after you left, and I'm—*we're* all a little lost."

I pause, not sure what else to say. I hate how bad I want to talk to him—I want to see the warmth in his smile and hear the honey in his laugh. My cheeks flush at the thought.

"Anyway," I continue, clearing my throat. "I'm, uh . . . I'm sorry about Jason. I know you two were close. And Ty . . . he has Victoria, and right now, I can't do anything about it. Xander is practically catatonic, Nik is broken, Kaleb is . . ." I hesitate, unsure if I want to talk about Kaleb or even mention Rayna at all. "I don't know. I don't know what to do about any of this. I just . . . I need a distraction, Tristan. If you—I'm not—look, just call me sometime. Please."

I need you, I should add. But I don't.

Ending the call, I collapse onto the sectional with a huff. I wish I knew where Tristan lived. If I did, I would show up on his doorstep the way he did on mine nearly every night for the past week. I would bring him coffee and ask for a tour of his house and convince him to play the guitar for me.

He told me once that he's an amazing singer. Maybe I'd ask him to sing.

CHAPTER 7

NEW YORK CITY, NEW YORK

NOVEMBER 9, 1897

MY HEART POUNDS AS *I ascend the staircase to the Veselys' Upper East Side apartment.*

Though I suppose it only belongs to Nikolas now.

The stairs are carpeted in rich blue velvet, the railing a masterpiece of gilded wood carvings. Nikolas lives in the only all-vampire apartment building in the city, owned by a severe vampire woman named Mei. I've never met her, but from what I've heard, she adores Nikolas—enough that she put aside her dislike of Rayna to allow them to live here. I glance up at the chandelier with its thousands of shimmering crystals and sigh softly. Alexander echoes it behind me.

It has been just over four months since Rayna's death. At times, I still refuse to believe it. I have known Kaleb for most of my life, and I never would have suspected him to do something so deplorable. The flat expression on his face that night still haunts me, hovering behind my eyelids as I hear his cold, British voice echo in my ears:

Rayna is dead. And I am the one to blame.

Alexander bumps into me and curses under his breath. "Charlotte."

I blink away the memory to find that I've stopped halfway up the stairs, my knuckles white where I grip the railing. Frowning, I let go, offering my brother a forced smile.

"Sorry," *I mumble, continuing my climb.* "I was thinking about

Kaleb again."

My brother is silent for a few seconds. When he responds, his voice is tight. Tired. "Me too."

We reach the upper floor, our steps muted by the plush carpet. Gold sconces light our way to the apartment at the end of the hall, banishing shadows from the corners and bathing the building's interior in warm, flickering light. I clutch a small box in my hand, turning it over and over in my palm.

I hope it will make Nikolas smile, is all I can think. I hope he is alright.

We reach the apartment door, the gold number "19" standing out beautifully against the deep oak. Alexander and I share a wary glance before I knock softly. Once, twice, three times.

We wait. And wait. But there is no answer. Not that we expected one. Alexander's brow creases and he presses an ear to the door, his green eyes narrowed in focus.

"You may as well come in." Nikolas's deep voice sounds from inside, and Alexander startles. "I would rather you not hover about my door like a pair of solicitors. Mei does not take kindly to loitering."

Alexander looks at me sideways before turning the knob. The door opens slowly, revealing a sight that makes my heart sink.

Nikolas lounges in the middle of his crimson brocade sofa, the fireplace cold, the sconces bare and dark. Candles on the coffee table and sideboard have long-since guttered, leaving lumpy wax formations on the once-shiny surfaces. Wan moonlight spills in through a single uncovered window and glints off scattered piles of liquor bottles—some empty, others half-full and dribbling onto the carpet. The room reeks of alcohol. The vapors burn my nose and I swallow the urge to cough.

The room may be a mess, but Nikolas himself is in shambles. I thought I knew the extent of his struggle these past few months, but it seems I barely knew the half of it. It looks like he hasn't bathed in days, his clothing is disheveled, and his hair is a wild mess of tangled auburn.

The beginning of a dark beard lines his jaw. It makes him look older, somehow. Harder. His eyes are fixed on a chair near the fireplace where an intricate gold dress is draped, its beauty radiant in the broken room.

Rayna's dress. A gift from Kaleb the first time he asked her to marry him.

When we enter, Nikolas waves an ornate bottle of absinthe in our direction. "Welcome, friends, to my humble abode." He glances around with a frown, then shrugs. "I am sure there is a comfortable seat somewhere."

My grip tightens around the tiny box in my hand as I cross the room, my other hand lifting my skirts in an attempt to avoid dragging them through spilled alcohol. I perch on the arm of the sofa, my chest in knots. I'm tempted to snatch the bottle from Nikolas's hand and take a drink of my own, but I can't afford to lose my wits right now. I have to stay strong for him, the way he has always been strong for me.

Alexander lingers by the door, a mere shadow in all black with his arms crossed over his chest. To anyone else the gesture might seem a bit rude, but I can tell by my brother's flitting eyes that he's doing it to mask his concern.

"Nikolas," I say quietly, resting a hand on his shoulder. Are you alright? I almost ask, then think better of it. Of course he is not alright. One day, maybe, but not today. Instead, I offer him a small smile. "Happy birthday."

Nikolas hurls the absinthe into the fireplace. I shriek as the bottle shatters, liquid exploding into the room and splattering Alexander. He grimaces and jumps back, shooting a glare at Nikolas as he takes off his coat and shakes it brusquely.

"Ah, yes," Nikolas says. His expression has sharpened, his mouth twisted into a grimace. "And what a wonderful birthday it has been. Alone in his hell-forsaken apartment, surrounded by the belongings of my murdered twin sister. She always loved our birthday." He laughs grimly. "Now that she's dead, what am I supposed to do? Celebrate?"

"You were both born on the same day," Alexander says, his voice

surprisingly gentle, "but that does not mean you can't enjoy today without her. It is your birthday, Nikolas. You are allowed to be happy, even with Rayna gone."

I flash Alexander a grateful look but Nikolas isn't listening. He leans forward, rummaging through the bottles piled at his feet, and sits up when he finds a wine bottle with a few swallows left. He downs it in one gulp and it quickly meets the same fate as the empty bottle of absinthe.

"I—here. For your birthday." My heart thuds as I present the box—an offering. He stares intently as I open it, then his shoulders go slack. Inside is a small Bohemian coin on a leather cord, a twin to the one around Nikolas's own neck.

"Is that . . . Rayna's coin?" he asks, and I nod. His fingers tremble as he lifts it, watching it spin in a lazy circle. "How—where did you find this?"

"It was in my pocket that night." I swallow hard, the words thick in my mouth. "She must have taken it off when we went for a swim, and I picked it up by mistake."

Nikolas's eyes shimmer. He sets the coin back in the box and closes my fingers around it. "Keep it."

I blink. "What?"

"I have one, remember?" he says, touching the coin at his throat. "Maybe this can be Rayna's gift to you, after everything. Besides,"—he motions vaguely around—"I have plenty of Rayna's belongings. I don't need . . . I don't want more."

Tears well in my eyes but I nod, carefully pocketing the box. I smooth my skirts and give Alexander a look that asks, What now? He only shrugs.

"Alright, then," I say, standing quickly. I don't know when things changed—when my interactions with Nikolas went from easy as breathing to . . . this. I lift his chin with my fingers and he looks up at me woefully, the expression on his face now one of pure agony. My chest tightens and I fight to keep myself composed. Strong. "I love you,

darahi. Now and always. Please . . ." My lip trembles. *"Please take care of yourself. I—we miss you."*

Nikolas slouches back onto the sofa, hiding his face in his hands. I frown down at him but Alexander opens the door, beckoning. With one last glance at Nikolas, I stand and follow my brother out. We close the door to the sound of quiet sobs.

As we descend the staircase and return to the bustling world, a thought grips me—one that terrifies me but that I know, deep down, is true.

My darling Nikolas—the strong, beautiful, amazing man I have loved since the moment I met him—is gone.

"ARE YOU READY?" I stare up at Nik's house, the white Victorian facade looming like a specter in the dark.

"No, Charlotte. I'm not." Xander's lips press into a thin line while his hands fidget at his sides. "Victoria is gone and it's all I can think about. Konstantin said he would give us a week, but what if he was lying? What if he's torturing her?" He tugs at the hem of his sweater, that wild touch of panic returning to his eyes. "What are we doing here? We should be *looking for her*—"

"Hey." I grab Xander's wrists and turn him to face me. Worry creases his brow. Mine too. "Victoria will be okay."

Xander takes a deep breath, coming back into himself. "How do you know?"

"Because she's a badass. We both know she's not going down without a fight."

My brother's mouth twitches, but concern is still etched on every plane of his face. I squeeze his hands gently, bracing myself to say something that might just kill me.

"Look. I know I've been a bit insufferable lately, but this thing with Konstantin—" I chew on my bottom lip, not sure how to go about this. I've never been good at the touchy-feely stuff. By the way Xander is staring at me, I'd guess he's just as uncomfortable with it as I am. "I'm not going to magically stop being a pain in your ass"—Xander snorts—"but you're my brother and for better or for worse, I've got your back. We're going to figure this out together. Even if that means bullying Rayna into helping us."

I mean it as a joke, but I can't keep the sincerity from my expression. The look is mirrored on Xander's face, the corner of his mouth curving into a wry smirk.

"Nothing would make me happier." He exhales slowly, his jaw working, and hesitates for a moment before pressing a gentle kiss to my hair. "Thank you, Ksusha."

My old name. My *real* name. I usually hate when Xander says it, but it feels different tonight—like a peace offering. I smooth a wrinkle from his black turtleneck then back away, hastily wiping a tear from my eye.

"You're welcome, jackass."

We say nothing else as we head up the marble stairs to Nik's house, our steps perfectly in sync. Like we haven't been at each other's throats for the past few decades. I feel a tentative camaraderie forming between us—a few threads in a fragile tapestry that's just beginning to knit back together. A bright pinprick of hope roots itself in my chest. Maybe if we survive this whole ordeal with Konstantin, my brother and I can learn how to be friends again.

I knock on the door and hear Rayna's voice. "Come in!"

We're greeted by the comforting warmth of Nik's living room. The walls are painted a rich shade of forest green, and three Tiffany lamps fill the elegant space with an inviting glow. There's a huge fireplace on the longest wall, a leather Chesterfield sofa stretched in front of the hearth. The wall next to the fireplace is plastered with gilded mirrors in all shapes and sizes, reflecting pieces of the grand piano nestled against the bay window.

But tonight, all that elegance is hidden behind what Rayna must think is a good idea.

She stands in the middle of the living room in a fitted green blazer—the color radiant against the vivid orange of her hair—and her arms are thrown wide, as if to showcase how completely clueless she is. There are no fewer than thirty bottles of expensive alcohol adorning the surfaces—the coffee table, the grand piano, the mantle—and black and gold balloons float aimlessly from where they're tied to handles and lamps and hooks. Just as prevalent are decanters of blood, filling the room with a sharp, metallic scent that has my mouth watering. A giant *HAPPY BIRTHDAY* banner adorns the wall above the lit fireplace, the flames huge and menacing.

My jaw goes slack. "What the *hell* do you think you're doing? Are you out of your mind?"

Rayna looks affronted. "It's our *birthday*, Lottie. I'm offended that you didn't remember."

"Of course I remembered," I snap, biting back a twinge of guilt. The truth is, I absolutely did *not* remember. Nik hasn't celebrated his birthday since Rayna died, and his refusal to acknowledge it has all but erased it from our minds. "It's just—" I frown, dragging my gaze around the empty room. "Where's Nik?"

Rayna drops her hands with a scowl, crossing to the coffee table to snatch up a blood-filled glass. "Oh, I don't know." She takes a prolonged sip. "He's been gone all day. It gave me plenty of time to decorate."

"So he doesn't know about this?"

"No. I wanted to surprise him."

Xander scoffs and I laugh, loud and humorless. "You have no *idea* what—"

"Rayna!" The lively British voice cuts me off, and I whirl to see Henry Albright stride into the house, a grimacing Kaleb in tow. The Alpha's deep rose blazer is pristine and he looks considerably better than he did last night, but the irritated expression on his face says he would rather be anywhere else.

"Darling," he says to Rayna, "please tell me you didn't summon us here for a *birthday party.*"

Ignoring Kaleb completely, Henry throws himself at Rayna, lifting her into a bone-crushing hug. "My dear, I knew you wouldn't be away for long."

"It's been a century, Albright," Rayna chides, but there's a smile in her voice.

Henry rolls his eyes good-naturedly. "Yes, yes. So everyone keeps telling me."

I stare at the two of them in turn, taking in Henry's usual uniform of crisp charcoal slacks with a matching vest and white dress shirt, and idly wonder what would happen if I tore that stupid pocket watch from his chest. These two are a little too familiar for my liking. Which means . . .

"Are you kidding me?" I snarl at Henry, and his head whips in my direction. "You knew Rayna was alive, too?"

Henry has the decency to look sheepish. "I may have had some idea."

"Charlotte," Kaleb sighs, "please, don't start—"

"Quiet, you," I say, and he balks slightly. "Apparently Rayna wasn't as much of a secret as I thought, and I'm not in the mood to reason with liars."

Xander stiffens behind me just as a pair of female voices chatters through the doorway. Pippa and Rose appear, arms filled with whiskey, wine, and a huge bottle of vodka. Pippa grins at me and waves a sleeve of red Solo cups with a leather-clad arm.

"Lottie! Glad you guys could make it. You up for a good old game of beer pong?"

"No!" I shout, bringing the bustle in the room to a halt. Even the fire seems to still. "We are not playing *beer pong,* Pippa! Why am I the only one who's upset about this? You all know what happens to Nik on his birthday."

Rayna sighs heavily. "It's a *party,* Lottie. Everyone loves a good party."

"Nik doesn't. He doesn't love *anything* anymore. And after what happened at last night's little soirée . . ." I drag a hand down my face. "What's to stop Konstantin from crashing this one, too?"

Silence follows my words and doubt prickles through me as Pippa and Rose exchange a look. *Am I the crazy one here?*

Pippa purses her lips, her eyes gentle. "It's been so long since Nik has celebrated his birthday. He deserves a night of fun."

Rose nods, her blue sweater shimmering, and Rayna grins in response.

"See?" she says. "Nik needs this."

Xander *hmphs* and glares at her. "Clearly you know nothing about what your brother actually needs."

Kaleb snarls. "Please, all of you. I haven't the time nor the patience for this level of bickering."

"And *you*." I jab a finger into Kaleb's shoulder. "I can't believe you're even here. Victoria was *kidnapped,* for Hell's sake! Why are we having a party when we should be looking for her?"

Rayna's lips pucker. "Lottie—"

"You've been dead for the last century," I bite out, seething. I'm not exactly sure where all this anger is coming from, but I don't tamp it down. I stoke it. "Nik hasn't celebrated his birthday since then, and we all assumed he never would again. You got back *yesterday,* Rayna, which is hardly enough time for him to process everything. You have to get rid of all this"—I jerk my head toward the birthday banner—"right now."

Rayna opens her mouth to reply just as a soft footfall sounds in the entry. Nik stands in the open doorway, keys in one hand, a half-empty bottle of scotch in the other. There's an off-kilter air to him, present in his ruffled hair and the missed button in his dark blue shirt. His gaze sweeps the room, snagging on the banner, the balloons, the obscene amount of alcohol, and his eyes land on Rayna like an executioner's axe.

His lip curls, he blinks once, then he turns heel and disappears into the night.

CHAPTER 8

"Now look what you've done," I say to Rayna, not waiting for a response before I dart after Nik.

The night air is fresh and damp, cooling the fire under my skin. It's been less than twenty-four hours since Rayna returned and she's already acting like she's the boss. If she had any idea the hell Nik went through after she died, there is no way she would be throwing a birthday party, of all things. But she doesn't know, because she didn't bother to ask. She just waltzed right back into our lives and expected everything to be exactly how it was the night she left.

But that's not how this works. If Rayna expects our forgiveness—*my* forgiveness—I'm not just going to hand it to her. I expect her to *beg*.

I catch up to Nik at the edge of the porch and freeze when I see Noah, Tristan's friend, standing with him. I know he and Nik have been spending time together—made obvious by the compromising position I found them in last night, with Nik pinning Noah up against a bookcase while he fed on him—but I thought it was just a fling. A physical attraction. But the way the human boy leans close to Nik and the way Nik gazes back at him has me wondering if their relationship is more than just a passing fancy.

I clear my throat and Noah springs back, a flush rising to his cheeks.

"Oh. Hi, Charlotte." His expression is wary but not unfriendly, and he awkwardly adjusts his grip on the bag of Chinese takeout he's carrying.

"Don't take this the wrong way, Noah," I say, ignoring Nik's warning frown, "but this probably isn't the best time for you to be here."

Noah's response is cut off by the sound of a car door slamming; a black Mazda sits at the curb, moonlight glinting off its hood. Another boy steps into view, a guitar slung over one shoulder. He clicks a button on the key fob in his hand and there's a bright chirping sound as the car locks. I gape at the tousled golden hair, the broad shoulders, the freckles dusting his cheekbones, made visible by the warm light from a street lamp.

The boy who ran. The boy I worried I would never see again.

Tristan adjusts the guitar at his back. "Nik, do you have any—"

He chokes on the words when he sees me, freezing with one foot on the bottom porch step. Standing here, looking down at him, it's all I can do to stop myself from falling to my knees.

He's here. He came *back*.

Clearing his throat, Tristan asks, "What are you doing here, Charlotte?"

The question takes me off guard and I blink a few times, studying his expression—a mask of careful indifference as he stares up at me, his golden eyes unreadable.

"What do you mean?" I ask, attempting nonchalance to hide my hesitant excitement. *He's here.* "I think the better question would be, what are *you* doing here?"

"Nik was at our place," Noah cuts in a little too loudly, "and he filled us in on what happened after we left last night. We ran out of booze, so"—he gestures to the front door—"he invited us over."

"What Noah said." Tristan takes a slow breath and continues up the steps, his movements unsteady. Frowning, I examine him as he draws closer: red-rimmed eyes, mussed hair, a rumpled white t-shirt. He takes a moment to right himself when he clears the last step and I reach out to steady him.

"Tristan." My fingertips brush his bare forearm, his short sleeves exposing far too much skin to the chilly November air. "Are you drunk?"

Hurt flashes in his eyes, accompanied by a small pout that tells me those are the worst words that could have come out of my mouth. *I'm sorry,* is what I should have said. *It's my fault that Jason is dead. It's my fault you lost your sister.* He meets my gaze unflinchingly and I wonder if he can see into me—*through* me. If he can see Alison's blood on my hands. We stare at each other for a few long seconds, something dark radiating from Tristan before he forces a tight smile.

"I'm fine, Char."

Before I can reply, Nik grabs my wrist—thank goodness—and drags me to a darkened corner of the wraparound porch. He glances at the human boys before looking down at me, his gaze filled with rare fire.

"Tristan isn't doing well, to put it lightly," he murmurs. "Last night really shook him."

A huge understatement, if the poorly-controlled tremor in Tristan's shoulders is any indication. The last time I saw him, he was running from me—from everything I am, from everything that had happened since that damn Halloween party. It was only yesterday that he learned we were all vampires, and I told him that we weren't going to hurt him. That nothing was going to happen to him. That he could trust me.

And then Konstantin had to go and ruin everything.

I can still hear the vicious *crack* of Jason's snapping neck and the solid *thud* when his body hit the floor.

"What about Noah?" I whisper. "How's he doing?"

Nik just shrugs. I nod, unsure of what else to say. In reality, I should be asking Nik how *he's* doing. He saw Konstantin last night. He saw Rayna, his long-dead twin who has been the cause of so much pain for the last century. Based on his reaction tonight, it seems he isn't exactly thrilled about seeing her again.

I wrap my arms around him, trying to force back the memory of Nik's first birthday after Rayna left: the dozens of empty bottles, the acrid stench of alcohol, the misery in his expression. He returns the embrace and rests his forehead on mine, a deep sigh rushing out of him.

"Are you okay, *darahi?*" I ask quietly.

With a furtive glance at Noah and Tristan, he says, "Honestly, this all feels like a bad dream. I've wanted Rayna back for so long, but seeing her again . . . I don't know, Lottie. It's surreal."

"I know what you mean. So far she's done nothing but piss me off."

That startles a laugh out of him, but he quickly sobers again. "I don't know if I can walk in there and pretend like everything is okay. I'm sure Rayna had good intentions, but . . ." He pauses, then scoffs sharply. "No, I take it back. Rayna never has good intentions. She only cares about herself."

"Any idea what they're talking about?" Noah whispers loudly to Tristan, drawing my attention.

There's an edge to Tristan's voice when he says, "No idea."

"They're awfully close," Noah murmurs, frowning.

"Yeah. And they can probably hear us."

I snort and glance at them, catching Tristan's eye.

"Strike that," he says, smacking Noah's arm. "They can *definitely* hear us."

"I just—"

"*Shut up.*" Tristan mutters something about ditching his guitar then slips back down the porch steps.

"I'm not happy about this either," I murmur to Nik. "Believe me, I don't want to be at this terrible family reunion anymore than you do. But it *is* your birthday, and your family wants to celebrate it with you. Give it a couple of hours. If it turns into a disaster, I'll take you to Kaleb's club and we'll drink all his top shelf liquor. Deal?"

Nik smooths a thumb over my cheekbone. His eyes are dark and cold, devoid of the warmth I once knew so well. I miss the old Nik, sometimes.

"Besides," I add, fastening his missed shirt button, "if you leave now, Rayna will never let you live it down. You'll be hearing about ditching this party for the rest of eternity."

Nik sighs and draws a hand over his mouth. "Fine," he says at a normal volume, making Noah jump. "If it's a party she wants, then it's a party she'll get."

He yanks a flask from his back pocket and takes a swig before striding back into the house. I follow hesitantly, the human boys bringing up the rear.

Conversations halt when we return to the living room, but Nik doesn't seem to care about the attention. In fact, he revels in it. He snatches a bottle of scotch from the bar cart and lifts it into the air.

"To my sister on our birthday," he says, his grin bright and wicked. He pins Rayna with a flesh-melting glare. "May she live to die another day."

A shadow passes over Rayna's face, bruising the hollows beneath her eyes. Nik's grin sharpens. The tension thickens, creeping over my skin like hot needles. I can practically hear the air crackle.

"Nik." Noah steps up behind him and takes his hand, smiling warmly. Whether the gesture is genuine or if it's meant as a distraction, it's hard to tell. "Be nice."

Pippa snorts. And just like that the tension is gone, dissipating like water on hot pavement. Everyone breaks into soft chatter, Kaleb pulling Xander aside while Pippa drags Henry to the back of the room, loudly chastising him for something. Rose busies herself by filling a few glasses with bourbon.

I consider approaching Tristan, but I can't seem to look away from the Vesely drama unfolding in front of me.

Rayna looks at Noah, who is pressed close to Nik, and says, "I see you brought dinner."

Nik ignores her and looks at Noah instead, his smile turning wry. He motions to his sister with all the grace of a wilting flower. "This is Rayna."

Noah lifts a scrupulous eyebrow. "Your dead sister." It isn't a question, and he doesn't seem surprised by the fact. It seems Nik did tell him about last night—he told him *everything.*

"Yes, Noah. That one." Nik's smile is deadly. "It's a miracle she came back from the dead, isn't it? Our very own messiah."

"Nikolas, *please,*" Rayna says. She fixes a vulpine stare on her brother, but her shoulders are relaxed now, the dark cloud gone from her features. "If you're going to introduce me, do it properly." She steps forward and extends a hand to Noah, grinning through her fangs. "I'm Rayna Magdaléna Vesely, Nik's *older* sister."

"By eight minutes," Nik mutters. "And I think you're forgetting that you're stuck forever at nineteen. If we're going to get technical, I was Turned at twenty-three, which means I'm four years older than you."

She rolls her eyes as Noah takes her hand, flashing her a winning smile.

"Noah Tomas Santiago Romero," he says. "Nice necklace."

Rayna touches the turquoise cross at her neck, then motions to the little diamond cross around Noah's.

"I like yours, too." She drops his hand. "I'm not sure what Nik has told you about me, but contrary to popular belief, I'm not dead. I did, however, let everyone believe I was until last night."

"Why would you do that?" Tristan's question slices into the conversation, sharp enough that even Rayna startles. His expression is bordering on vicious, his brow is creased, and my chest constricts now that I see him in the light. He looks *awful*—there are dark circles under his eyes, his jaw is dusted with gold stubble, and he's still wearing his burgundy slacks from last night.

"Have you slept since the party?" I murmur into his ear, but he pushes me away, his touch like ice.

Only a few nights ago, Tristan took me to the Land's End Labyrinth, a makeshift stone maze on a cliffside overlooking the ocean. Everything about him was warm and welcoming, and I felt wanted—*hopeful*—for the first time in a long time. He lit up when he spoke about his sister, Alison, despite the pain he was hiding behind that sunshine smile—a deep ache etched into his words, adding sharp edges to his bright demeanor.

Because Alison is dead. And I'm the one who killed her.

I fight the urge to reach for him again, choosing instead to shove my hands into my back pockets.

"What could you possibly gain from faking your own death?" Tristan continues. "Didn't you know what that would do to your brother?" He throws a hand in the air, ignoring a warning nudge from Noah. "What kind of sister are you?"

Nik exhales a laugh and I expect him to jump to Rayna's defense, but he doesn't. He gives Tristan an appraising look, then turns a withering glare on his twin.

"Yeah, Rayna," he says acerbically. "What kind of sister *are* you?"

Rayna doesn't even look at Nik. She just blinks slowly at Tristan, tilting her chin upward. "I'm sorry, but have we met?"

"Leave him alone," I snap at her, but he answers anyway.

"Tristan," he says bluntly, narrowing his eyes. "And you didn't answer my question."

A pause, and then Rayna slowly raises an eyebrow, lips twisting into a knowing smirk.

"Hello, Tristan," she purrs. "Nice to meet a human *friend* of Charlotte's." Her eyes flick to me, then back. "Frankly, it's none of your business why I did what I did. You don't know me from Adam, and I don't owe you an explanation."

"Oh yeah?" Tristan says, the confusion in his eyes morphing into anger. "Well, you sure as hell owe Nik one."

Rayna bristles and I snatch Tristan's arm, yanking him into the hallway. He doesn't struggle, just follows me with clomping feet as I drag him into the dark.

CHAPTER 9

"WHAT ARE YOU DOING?" I hiss, whirling on Tristan. We're in Nik's kitchen, where cool moonlight filters through the windows and spills onto the dark wood floor. The San Francisco Bay twinkles in the distance, framed by a thick canopy of night-dark trees.

"Making new friends. What does it look like?" Tristan's pulse flutters at his throat, just below the skin. My gums prickle and I take a small step back, distancing myself from the blood singing in his veins.

"You can't just pick a fight with Rayna like that," I say. "Do you have a death wish?"

"Of course not. But what she did . . ." Tristan scoffs. "I don't blame Nik for reacting like this. If Alison suddenly showed up a hundred years after faking her death, I would be *furious*."

Music starts up in the living room, filling the house with the upbeat pulse of a pop song. I'm transported back to the night on Pier 39 before everything fell apart, when Tristan asked me to dance and my problems disappeared for a while. When we were in our own little world.

That is, until "Ty" showed up and everything went to Hell in a handbasket.

Tristan and I aren't close enough to touch, but I can still feel his heat, sense the strain in his shoulders. He scrubs the back of his neck with one hand, and the motion lifts the hem of his t-shirt, a strip of tan skin peeking out from underneath it. The pressure in my gums sharpens.

"Sorry," Tristan murmurs, rubbing at his eyes. When he opens them again, they're slightly clearer. "I didn't mean to show up and antagonize Rayna, I just—I didn't get much sleep last night."

"Join the club," I say, daring to rest a hand on his upper arm. His muscles flex slightly under my touch, his skin just too warm.

Tristan raises a brow. "But you never sleep at night. I hardly think it's a fair comparison."

My head tilts to the side, considering him. "Touché."

We stand in silence for a few uncomfortable seconds before Tristan hesitantly wraps his arms around me, pulling me into a tight hug. It takes far too long for my surprise to wear off, but I let myself sink into him, burying my face in his chest. Breathing him in. There's still a slight tremor in his shoulders so I hold him closer, urging his body to relax.

"How is Noah?" I ask lamely, not sure what to say. Not sure what Tristan expects of me. "Olivia and Bree?" Tristan's girl friends disappeared after the party, and I'm not sure what they've been doing since.

"Noah is . . . fine." Tristan sags slightly. "He wasn't as close to Jason as I was. He'll be alright. Bree and Olivia are okay, too. From what I can tell, they think Jason died in a car accident that Nik apparently staged. I assume we can thank Rose for Compelling them to forget what actually happened." He trails off at the end like a question, and I nod. "So, yeah. The funeral is scheduled for next Saturday. I think we're all going to fly home for it."

Again, I'm at a loss for words. What am I supposed to say to a human boy who just had his world turned upside down? I settle for nothing, instead rubbing my hands slowly up and down his back in what I hope is a comforting gesture. He sighs softly and rests his chin against my hair.

"About last night," Tristan says. "I'm sorry for calling you a—for saying those things about you." His words come back in a rush, and they pack a surprising sting: *I should have called this off the moment*

I learned about . . . about you. You're a monster. All of you are. Why couldn't I see that? "It was just . . . a lot. But it wasn't fair of me to respond like that. It's not like you killed Jason yourself."

Guilt sits like a stone in my chest. I may not have snapped Jason's neck, but I'm the one who invited Konstantin to the party. I'm the one who messed up Tristan's Compulsion on Halloween, making him unwittingly obsessed with me. I'm the one who brought him and all his friends into my life—one filled with blood and death.

And I'm the one who killed Alison.

It was a cruel twist of fate when Tristan and I met that night at Kaleb's party. A grieving boy and the girl who started it all. A vampire. A murderer.

"Tristan," I say, surprised by the tremor in my voice. "I'm so sorry."

"Don't be sorry, Char. It's not your fault."

"But it *is*."

"No." The word is firm. Final. Tristan pulls away, holding me by the shoulders while his eyes bore into mine. "It's not."

My gaze drops, snagging on the hem of his t-shirt. *You're wrong!* I want to shout. *I did it! I killed her, I killed her, I killed her!*

"I just want to make sure you're okay," I say. "Last night—"

"I'm fine," Tristan bites out, but he sounds more tired than angry. "Or at least, I will be. But I'd rather not talk about me right now."

I consider him for a few seconds. There's a dull gleam in his eyes tonight, like all the warmth has been sucked from him—so unlike the Tristan I met on the Embarcadero. Now he's colder. Brittle. A sunflower touched by the first frost of winter.

"Okay," I say warily. "Then what do you want to talk about?"

Tristan leans back and perches on the edge of the granite countertop, his shoulders heavy. "I want to talk about Ty."

I shake my head vigorously. "No. I don't want you getting involved."

"Too late," he says flatly. Something tells me he isn't as drunk as I thought he was, because his eyes are crisp and cutting, like chiseled topaz. "I was involved the minute he murdered my friend. So tell me who he is and what the hell is going on."

There's a slight command in his tone that makes my stomach flip. I suppose he deserves the truth—or at least part of it.

"Ty's real name is Konstantin," I say reluctantly, "and he's an old vampire. And I mean, *really* old. I'm pretty sure he was born in the Middle Ages. Kaleb, Rayna, and Nik were part of his circle for a long time—I'm sure you can guess that he wasn't a good guy back then, either. Eventually, the three of them left him behind, and they've been running from him ever since."

I expect Tristan to be surprised by the fact that Konstantin is close to 700 years old, or that he knew Nik, but he doesn't bat an eye.

"When we met Ty, I—*we* had no idea who he really was," I say, twisting a lock of hair between my fingers. "It was that night at Pier 39. When I ran away from our dance, it was because I smelled blood. A lot of it."

Tristan's eyes widen but he stays quiet, allowing me to tell the full story, uninterrupted. I quickly explain what happened with Ty—about finding him standing over a body, chasing him down, then tackling him to the ground and grinding his face into the pavement. Tristan smirks a little at that. I explain how Ty lied about being a fledgling vampire, and how he tricked us into letting him into our lives. Into our *home*.

Humiliation burns through me as I recount my time with Ty— training him at Hyde Street Pier, feeding him in our dining room, kissing him in the basement. Konstantin was right in front of me and I didn't see him. Looking back, it should have been obvious: he was too confident, too *controlled* to be a brand new fledgling.

The cocky smirk alone should have been a dead giveaway.

I tell Tristan how careful he was—how he avoided Kaleb and Nik so they wouldn't recognize him. I tell him about his relationship with Rayna, and how she faked her death to get away.

I tell him every detail—except one.

Though I have no proof, I'm almost positive it was Konstantin who sent the texts to Tristan connecting Alison's murder to the San

Francisco Vampire. If I shared my theory with Tristan, it would only be a matter of time before he put two and two together. Until he puzzled out the truth. And it will be a cold day in Hell before I let that happen.

When I finish speaking, Tristan is quiet for a few minutes, contemplating. I can see him turning the information over in his head, reconciling it with what he already knew.

"I'm so sorry, Tristan," I say again, emotion burning at the corners of my eyes. "I should never have invited him to the party. He was supposed to be harmless. He was just some *kid*—"

Tristan takes me by the wrist and yanks me forward, catching me just before our bodies collide. I inhale in surprise. This closeness is nothing like our hug only a few minutes ago—this is sharper. Warmer. Heat rushes to my cheeks as I hear Tristan's heart begin to pound.

"What are you doing?"

"Distracting you," he whispers roughly. He traces gentle fingers along my jaw, trailing down my throat. A little flame of desire dances in my chest as his hand dips lower, brushing the sensitive skin near the scar over my heart, his touch leaving a tingling trail of heat in its wake. He takes a deep, steadying breath as his gaze falls to my lips.

I frown up at him. "What?"

"In your message, you said you needed a distraction." He leans his forehead against mine, his breath hot between us, and his mouth curves into an alluring smile. Callused fingers trail over my collar bone, waking a flock of butterflies in my stomach. I force my hands to stay still, even as I have the overwhelming urge to snake them under his shirt. To trace the ridges of his spine. "Maybe I need one too."

Tristan has known about vampires for one day. Last night, he wanted nothing to do with me, all but blaming me for Jason's death before he disappeared. I should be worried about that. I should be asking him if he's *sure* he wants to be here. To be with me.

Instead, I blurt out, "You listened to my message?"

"I'll never ignore something from you, Char. I can't."

Despite the sincerity in his words, I wilt, just a little. "You were

Compelled—"

"I *was* Compelled, but not anymore." He leans close, his mouth a whisper against mine. There's no pressure to the touch—it's barely a touch at all, just a slight brush of air against my lips—but it fills me with light, a honeyed glow that threads its way through my veins. "Now, I can't seem to keep you out of my head, and Compulsion has nothing to do with it."

Tristan's mouth finds its way to the corner of my jaw and he traces kisses down my neck. He's gentle at first, but he grows more confident with each press of his lips against my skin. My breath catches, even though I know this is a terrible idea. Too much has happened between us in the past week, and I know we both need some time to process. Victoria is *missing*, for Hell's sake.

But there's a plea in Tristan's touch: *Help me.*

I slide one hand into his hair and tug sharply, drawing a small gasp from him. Under his usual scent of vanilla and linen is the bittersweet scent of beer, clinging to him like a second skin. It reminds me so much of Nik that I almost pull away, but I don't. Instead, I draw him closer. He shudders, breathing my name against my throat.

I can feel my family's presence on the other side of the house, hear their voices pitched over the excited pulse of the music. In that room, all my problems are waiting for me: Victoria's kidnapping, Rayna's reappearance, Xander's emptiness.

But here, in Nik's moonlit kitchen, Tristan and I are utterly and completely alone. We can do anything we want. We can *be* anything. We can build walls that no one can penetrate: not Rayna, not Alison, not Jason or Konstantin.

We can just *be*. The two of us, here, in the dark.

"After everything," I breathe, "are you sure about this?"

"Absolutely," Tristan says gruffly, hooking his fingers under my waistband. He yanks me close and heat blooms in my abdomen. "Stop second-guessing everything and just *kiss me*, will you?"

Hope, bright as a sunrise, fills me almost to bursting. He still wants to be here. He still wants *me*. I ignore the little voice in my head that warns me away—that reminds me of all the things we have going against us—and press my lips to his.

Tristan sighs quietly, the tension in his shoulders draining with his breath. The kiss is soft and slow, and it feels like a promise. *I'm here*, it says. *And I'm not going to let you go.*

I break away and find Tristan smiling at me, his eyes crinkling at the corners. But there's an iciness in that smile, a touch of darkness hovering behind the gold of his irises.

"Tristan," I murmur. "I'm so sorry."

He twirls a lock of my hair around his fingers, flashing a wry grin. "So you've said. Three times now."

I kiss him again, more fiercely this time, and my teeth scrape at his bottom lip. *I'm sorry for hurting you*, the kiss says to him. *For being the monster that killed your sister. For dragging you into this mess. For being selfish now.* Tristan inhales in surprise, then melts into me. One hand slides under my shirt, his calluses rough against the bare skin of my back. But his hand is warm. *So* warm. I let him pull me against him, a little helpless sound escaping me as our bodies press together.

Warm. Safe. *Here.*

My hands tug at the hem of his shirt, pushing it up enough to reveal a few inches of skin above his waistband, hot to the touch and smooth as silk. Tristan breathes deeply as I tease the ridges of his hip bones, his skin pebbling under my fingertips. He wraps his arms around me, holding me too tightly, clinging to me like a lifeline.

Desire simmers deep in my abdomen and I hitch one leg up, making Tristan groan as my hips pin him against the edge of the counter. His heart is pounding and I'm *melting* and I can almost taste the blood under his skin, just waiting to be taken—

My fangs pop, and Tristan yelps.

Hunger scorches its way through me and I kiss him harder, sweeping my tongue over his lips, sighing at the bright, coppery taste of him. My hands fist in his hair. My hips grind into his. Holding him in place.

Trapping him.

I want him. I want *more*.

"Char," Tristan gasps, one hand pressing hard against my ribs. He tries to push me away but I barely feel it. I'm too focused on the strength of his pulse hammering under my fingertips as I rake my nails down the side of his throat.

More. *More.*

"*Char,*" he says again, more forcefully this time. His voice is sharp and commanding, and reality shivers into focus.

I shove away from Tristan as horror roils in my stomach, and he winces as one of my fangs slices a shallow gash along his lower lip. He stares at me, wide-eyed, as fresh blood leaks onto his chin.

"Tristan," I gasp. The fire that burned inside me mere seconds ago is gone, doused by the touch of fear in his eyes. He sidesteps me slowly and touches two fingers to his mouth, paling when they come away red. "I'm so sorry. I didn't—I wasn't—"

"It's fine," he says quietly, but he's retreated into himself, just a little. He jabs his thumb in the direction of the hallway. "I'm just going to go take a look at this in the bathroom."

He watches me warily for a few seconds, smooths his hair back with one hand, and disappears into the hall. After a few strained breaths, I lick a drop of blood from my lip and a new type of warmth shivers through me, sweet like honey and tinged with darkness.

Delicious.

CHAPTER 10

FOR A FEW MINUTES AFTER Tristan closes himself in the nearest bathroom, I consider lying on the floor right here in the middle of the kitchen and wallowing for the rest of night. It's been too long since I've had a good wallow. The only thing that prevents me from collapsing onto the polished wood is the sound of Rayna's voice drifting from the living room.

"Konstantin has endless patience. He made the last move, so he'll be waiting for you to make the next one. Stop worrying and enjoy yourselves."

I stomp back down the hall, making a beeline for the party. A quick scan shows Pippa and Henry on the sofa, Rose chatting with Noah near the bookshelves, and no sign of Tristan. I swallow a pang of nausea and stalk through the doorway. It's probably for the best that he isn't here. I'm not sure how in control I am at this point.

Not with Rayna grinning like that.

She is perched on the back of the sofa, a glass of cognac in her hand and forced humor etched on her face. Nik, Kaleb, and Xander stand around her, listening. Though she is the only one sitting, it's clear by her body language that she's in control of the conversation.

I snatch a glass of blood from Pippa's hand where she's draped over Henry's lap. She barely protests, distracted quickly by Henry teasingly kissing his way down her neck. With a roll of my eyes, I empty the glass in one gulp. It isn't *nearly* enough. After that taste of Tristan, I'm positively ravenous. Rayna catches my eye and grins, motioning for me to join her circle.

"Welcome back to the party, Lottie," she says as I push between Kaleb and Xander, prompting a grunt of annoyance from my brother. "Did you have a good time with your little human friend? He sure smelled good."

Nik's nostrils flare. *"Rayna."*

"What? It's not like it's a *secret*." She winks at me, glancing at my shirt where it's hiked up to my ribs. "We could all hear you."

I hastily tug my shirt down, expecting a judgmental frown from Xander, but he just looks at me—*past* me, like I'm not even here. His eyes are rimmed with red, and based on his fluid movements and the flush on his cheeks, it's safe to assume that he's had a few too many drinks. *Just how long were Tristan and I in the kitchen?*

"Please, darling," Kaleb says to Rayna with an air of long-suffering. "Behave."

Rayna looks up at him and I expect her to snap back, but instead, I hear her heart skip a beat. When we first met them, Rayna and Kaleb were closer than any couple I had ever seen: constantly touching, deferring to one another, sharing everything from their clothing to their meals. It was the type of love that seemed too good to be true and I found myself envying them more often than not.

Now, looking at the cool distance in Kaleb's eyes, the way Rayna lets their legs brush only to have Kaleb move away, has me wondering what's really going on here. I catch Rayna's eye, ignoring my frustration to give her a questioning look. She stares at me with an unreadable expression then makes a show of shifting in her seat, putting herself farther from Kaleb.

"Only having a bit of fun, *darling,*" she says to him. There's a barb in the endearment, but if Kaleb notices, he doesn't show it.

"Can we get back to the matter at hand?" he asks coolly.

"Yes, of course." Rayna blinks prettily at him—trying to soften him up, I'm sure—but he only purses his lips in response. Shrugging, she turns her attention to me. "These lovely men were just catching me up on the events of the past week. It sounds like Konstantin really gave you a run for your money."

I raise a brow. "That's putting it lightly."

"What did he say *exactly*? When he offered you this little deal to get Victoria back."

It's Nik who speaks, clearing his throat quietly. "He said, 'You have one week to tell me the truth about Rayna, or the girl dies.'"

"Not very specific, was he?" Rayna hums as she takes a sip of her drink, her wheels turning. "Do you suppose, *láska*"—she looks pointedly at Kaleb—"that he knows I'm alive?"

Láska. Love. Kaleb has gone carefully still, his face a mask of indifference. "I had assumed as much, with his arrival in San Francisco and his insistence that I 'tell him the truth.' But . . ." He trails off, frowning. "No, he has not said anything to suggest he knows, without a doubt, that you are alive." He glances to me and Xander for confirmation, and we both shake our heads.

"Nothing," we say in unison.

"So he likely *suspects* I'm alive, but doesn't know for sure." Rayna taps her chin pensively. "Interesting. Though, since he didn't specify *which* truth would get Victoria back, there are many secrets that could fit the bill. I always love a good loophole."

Xander grimaces. "I am not gambling Victoria's safety on the possibility of a *loophole*. You may not care about her, seeing as you abandoned us for a hundred years, but I am going to do everything in my power to make sure Konstantin gets exactly what he wants."

The threat hovers in the air, my brother's eyes fixed on Rayna. She stares back at him with her head inclined, as though daring him to take her on.

"You want to hand me over to him?" she asks in a familiar condescending tone. It's the one she always reserved for Xander, and *only*

Xander. "I'd like to see you try, boy."

Xander lunges forward but is stopped by Kaleb's firm hand on his chest.

"Alexander," the Alpha warns, glaring pointedly at Xander. "A word."

Something unspoken passes between them, and I watch curiously as they stride to the piano on the other side of the room. They strike up a hushed conversation, pitching their voices low enough that even I can't hear. From the looks of it, neither one is happy.

"On that note," Rayna says, raising her glass, "I need another drink."

She saunters to bar cart, leaving Nik and I alone.

"Are you okay?" we ask at the same time, then both chuckle.

"You first," Nik says, and I sigh.

"I suppose you're referring to what happened in the kitchen just now?" When Nik nods, I wince. "I didn't bite him on purpose, you know."

Nik only smirks. "I wouldn't judge you if you had."

Embarrassment heats my cheeks just as Tristan's small voice sounds from behind me.

"Char, can I talk to you?"

I swallow hard but Nik just smiles, motioning over my shoulder to where Tristan must be standing. Bracing myself, I turn around—just in time to see Xander punch Kaleb in the face.

CHAPTER 11

CHICAGO, ILLINOIS
DECEMBER 2001

"Xander, we're going to press *play without you!*"

My brother has been on the phone in his room for over an hour, speaking so softly that neither Victoria nor I can hear. We've had American Psycho *queued up for at least forty-five minutes, and the repetitive music from the DVD menu is about two cycles away from making me throw the remote through the TV screen. Victoria nudges me with her foot and looks up from her book.*

"Don't rush him," she says, grinning slyly as she waves the paperback in the air. The cover boasts a blonde girl with her arms wrapped around a man's shiny, muscled chest, their hair blowing in some directionless wind. "I'm just getting to the good part."

I roll my eyes at her. "So they're kissing."

"Yeah, kissing," she says with emphasis. "Let's go with that."

There's a distant beep, signaling the end of Xander's call. He emerges from his room a few minutes later, returning the phone to its receiver on the side table.

"Well," I say, looking at him expectantly. "What was that all about?"

Xander is standing very still, his arms crossed and his gaze fixed on the wall of windows overlooking Lake Michigan. Ice glistens near the shore where the water has frozen in the frigid Chicago winter, the city's lights making it sparkle. Despite the beautiful scene, Xander chews on his bottom lip—a habit left over from childhood that always signals anxiety or frustration.

"What is it?" Victoria asks, marking her page with a manicured finger. "Is something wrong?"

"That was . . ." Xander pauses, his jaw working. "We're moving to California, come January."

I bolt upright, and Victoria's book falls to the floor.

"What?"

Xander's eyes are distant. Calculating. "We've been in Chicago long enough. It's time for a change of scenery."

"Hell, no." I stand and stalk over to my brother, noting the way he avoids my eyes. The way he balls the hem of his shirt in his fists. "You can't just make a decision like this on your own."

Xander exhales sharply. "Charlotte—"

"Don't we get a say in this?" I ask, waving an arm in Victoria's direction. "We happen to like Chicago."

"Actually," Victoria says with an apologetic shrug, "a new city might be nice."

"Oh, you're no help," I snap, then turn back to Xander. "Where in California, exactly? Los Angeles? San Diego? In case you've forgotten, the sun doesn't exactly agree with us—"

"San Francisco."

I choke on my next words. "Excuse me?" Xander opens his mouth, but I don't let him speak. "You mean to tell me that you're going to drag me to the hellhole of a city where Kaleb Sutton lives? The city he rules? No. Absolutely not. I refuse to live anywhere near that homicidal piece of shit."

Xander glares down at me, his eyes hardening to flint.

"Well, in this instance, you don't have a choice." He turns and stalks back into his bedroom, bare feet slapping on the wood floor. "We're leaving in a month. I hope you like seafood."

"Wait!" I follow him, swinging around the doorframe so hard

that I swear I feel the wood splinter. "Who were you talking to? Who convinced you to drag us to California?"

"The homicidal piece of shit," Xander says simply. "Who else?"

Then he strides back to the door and slams it in my face.

"YOU SELFISH *BASTARD*," Xander snarls.

Kaleb stumbles sideways, catching himself against the wall. The gilded mirrors shudder on their hooks. When he turns back to my brother, his jaw is red and his expression is livid.

It's a look I've never seen on Kaleb's face. Something like fear wraps around my spine.

The music is still playing, but every conversation has come to a grinding halt. Xander looks at Kaleb furiously, and the Alpha's lip curls into a snarl. My instincts ring a warning bell and I move to intervene, but Kaleb beats me to the punch. Literally.

Xander's nose cracks under Kaleb's fist and he staggers backward, blood pouring over his mouth and down his neck. There's a tense pause, a sharp intake of breath, and then Xander launches himself at Kaleb. They careen into the wall, knocking a mirror to the ground. It shatters loudly, littering the floor with angry shards of glass.

Nik cries out in dismay. *"What the hell?"*

I want to stop them, or at least *try*, but I'm frozen in place with the rest of the room. Doing nothing, just . . . watching.

Kaleb hits Xander again, this time with a sharp jab to the throat, and Xander releases a strangled gasp. He wastes no time grabbing Kaleb by the lapel in an attempt to throw him to the ground, but Kaleb twists out of his grip and slams the heel of his hand into Xander's sternum.

My brother chokes, clutching at his chest as the wind is knocked out of him. Seeing him breathless and raging snaps me out of my stupor and I stalk forward.

"Stop!" I yell, shoving Kaleb hard in the shoulder. "What do you think you're doing?"

He barely flinches. His pupils are wide and he's focused on Xander, regarding him with outrage and disgust. It's so rare for Kaleb to lose his cool like this, fangs out and feral, that I sometimes forget just how powerful he is. He stands tall and regal, ever the Alpha, and stares down his nose at Xander.

"Your brother struck first," he growls. It resonates deep in his chest, making the hair on my neck stand on end. "It seems he has forgotten who he works for."

Before I can ask what he means, Xander's breath returns to him in one huge inhale, and he *roars*. He lunges for Kaleb again and I stumble out of the way, surprised to find Tristan behind me. He catches at my arm and steadies me, his eyes wide in confusion and horror. *What is going on?* they seem to ask. I shrug in silent answer.

Xander roars again and my attention snaps back to the battle unfolding in front of me. *Swing, block, swing, block.* Every time Xander attacks, Kaleb brushes him aside like a harmless fly. His pale eyes glint with triumph, knowing that Xander won't win this fight. He *can't*. The alcohol is making him reckless and sloppy. The fight was over before it began.

I am vaguely aware of someone moving toward the pair, but I still can't seem to tear my eyes away. It isn't until Rayna steps in, catching Xander's thrown fist in her hand, that I come back to myself, blinking quickly.

"Enough," Rayna hisses, wrenching Xander's wrist sideways. He winces and she shoves him backward into Nik, who catches him with a look of surprise.

Xander tries to free himself but Nik tightens his arms around his chest, holding him back. My brother does *not* like it. He struggles in Nik's grasp, his fangs flashing, fury coming off of him in waves.

"*Bastard!*" he says again, glaring daggers at Kaleb. "Selfish, cowardly *bastard.*"

Kaleb straightens, mirror shards crunching under his pristine black

Oxfords. A bruise is blooming on his jaw and my brother's blood speckles his face, but otherwise, he's unruffled.

Meanwhile, Xander looks like he just did ten rounds in a boxing ring.

"How dare you, Alexander," Kaleb snarls dangerously. "I am not the one at fault here. You are in no position to make such demands."

"What demands?" I ask, looking at each of them in turn. "What the hell is going on here?"

A derisive grin splits Xander's face, his eyes still fixed on the Alpha. "Kaleb refuses to do what it takes to get Victoria back. We all really know what Konstantin wants, and it isn't some magical answer to his question. It's simple, really. He wants *her.*" He spits the word at Rayna. "But Kaleb . . ." He chuckles quietly, cold and dark. "Kaleb only cares about himself."

"You are out of your bloody mind," Kaleb grinds out between clenched teeth, "if you think I will trade Rayna for Victoria. We aren't even sure that she is what Konstantin is after. There are other options— some that I would actually be willing to consider."

I glare at Xander. "I thought we talked about this."

"What options?" he asks Kaleb, ignoring me completely. He sags in Nik's arms, his voice turning desperate. "There's nothing to consider!"

"We will get Victoria back," Kaleb says softly—an attempt to diffuse the tension, no doubt. "But until then, I expect you to fall in line."

Something strikes me, suddenly. A distant warning, the fleeting feeling of imminent danger. I glance around the room—at Pippa and Henry, now standing; at Nik's dark expression; at Rose, at Noah and Tristan—and can see the same uncertainty reflected in their eyes. Something important is happening here. I just have no idea what it is.

"Oh, you want me to *fall in line?*" Xander's voice is wild, rising in pitch and hysteria. It tears at my chest, sinking deep into my heart—pain echoes there, followed by fear. "The love of my life was just kidnapped. I have no idea where she is or what Konstantin is doing to her. What he may have already done. She is my *world*, Kaleb." His voice cracks. "I can't lose her. I won't."

"Xander," I say, stepping closer to him with a nod at Nik, who reluctantly relinquishes his hold. Panic makes Xander's eyes bright, and blood oozes from his broken nose and a split on his brow. I grab his chin and force him to look at me. "Hey. I know you're worried about Victoria—I am too—but infighting isn't going to help. We're going to find her."

"How, Ksusha?" he asks quietly, his tone cooling. "Kaleb won't let us."

Kaleb looses a breath. "That is not what I said."

"You know what?" Xander snaps. He steps back—*away*. Leaving me alone. Confused. More worried about my brother than I have ever been. His next words are feral. Dangerous. "I'm done with you. I knew moving to San Francisco was a bad idea, but I *trusted you*, didn't I? We're only here because you practically demanded it, and it's been nothing but trouble for all of us." He throws his hands outward, his green eyes ablaze. "I wish you had kept all your stupid secrets to yourself. If I had known how little you really cared, I never would have agreed to come here and be your *fucking Beta*."

The word echoes in my ears. My brain is still processing everything that just came out of Xander's mouth, but that one word rang out loud and clear. Beta.

Beta?

"I'm sorry," I ask, disbelieving. "What did you just say?"

Xander freezes, staring at me in dismay. In those familiar eyes I see fear, I see surprise, and something else that it takes me a moment to identify.

Uncertainty.

"Charlotte," he says, holding a hand out like he's trying to keep an animal at bay. "Let me explain."

Everyone watches and I sense their scrutiny as they, too, realize the implications of what Xander just said. My brother must feel it as well, because his shoulders curl forward in what could be mistaken for a gesture of submission.

Nearly twenty years of memories flash before my eyes: Xander's late-night phone calls, his "moonlighting" to help with fledglings, his unexplained knowledge of everything happening in this damn city. I think back to our meeting with Kaleb the other night, when Xander led us straight to The Caged Bird—Kaleb's club—with no hesitation. I think of the strange familiarity between the two of them and the way Xander has spent the past week submitting to Kaleb at every turn.

And I feel like an absolute bloody *fool* for not seeing it earlier.

"Dammit, Alexander," I groan, pressing the heels of my hands to my eyes. "Is that why Kaleb brought us here? So you could be his *Beta*? Does that mean you've been lying to me for *seventeen years?*"

Xander hesitates, but resolve hardens his expression. "Yes."

He glances at Kaleb, who offers a subtle nod. The gesture is comfortable. Practiced. Now that I'm looking for it, I can see the easy camaraderie between them, the slight acquiescence in Xander's expression that should have been clear to me from the moment we set foot in this city.

"What about Henry?" Pippa asks. "Isn't he Beta?"

Henry's gaze drops, guilt written on every plane of that pale, boyish face. "Not exactly."

I mumble a curse and pinch the bridge of my nose. "I guess I'm the idiot for not seeing it sooner. Everything suddenly makes *so much sense.*"

Xander frowns warily. Blood still trickles from his nose while bruises form under his eyes and at the base of his throat. There's a frantic energy about him—prey caught in the gaze of a predator. Poised to run.

I'm distantly aware that a few in the room *do* leave—Noah, followed closely by Tristan. He whispers a quick, "I'll call you," then slips away. The space behind me feels cold and empty, and I'm surprised how quickly I yearn for his warmth. But this is a family matter, and

Tristan doesn't need to see or hear anything that might happen in the next few minutes.

Xander exhales slowly, all signs of hostility gone. Now he just looks tired, his shoulders sagging, his fingers worrying at the hem of his sweater.

"I wanted to tell you, Lottie."

A laugh escapes me, dulled by exhaustion. "You could have fooled me. If I recall correctly, you moved us here without explanation, even though I asked for it *dozens* of times. You left me to assume the worst: that you brought us to San Francisco because you were just following daddy's orders."

A snarl tears from Kaleb's throat. "Do not make judgments on matters you know nothing about, Charlotte."

"Stay out of this," I snap. Kaleb bristles and Rayna's eyes widen, but I'm too annoyed to care. "Unsurprisingly, you keep giving me more reasons to hate you."

"Leave Kaleb alone," Xander says, his tone defensive. "He asked the question, but I'm the one who agreed to come here."

"Kind of a dick move," Pippa grumbles.

Xander huffs in exasperation. "Lottie, I'm sorry—"

"Don't," I say with a wry chuckle. "Don't try to act all high and mighty. If anything, I should be apologizing to you, the Beta vampire of San Francisco." I throw my arms wide and offer a sweeping bow. "Do forgive my insolence, *Your Highness.*"

My brother flinches.

"Xander." Nik has been surprisingly quiet during this whole exchange, and his deep voice rumbles through the room like the first shudder of an earthquake. "What did you mean when you said you wished Kaleb had kept all his secrets to himself? What exactly did he tell you?"

Rayna's heart stutters. And I feel it again, that sense of dread. The shadow of impending doom.

Xander blanches. "I—Nothing. I don't know why I said that."

Nik's eyes narrow and he steps forward, rising to his full height. Broad-shouldered and imposing, he stares at my brother with all the heat of boiling magma.

"You're hiding something," Nik growls, "and I think I know what it is. It will be better if you offer it freely, rather than waiting for me to beat it out of you." He lowers his voice, and with a curl of his lip, he asks, "What did Kaleb tell you?"

Xander stares back defiantly for only a moment, but Nik's fury seems to break something in him. He unravels; slowly at first, but then Xander—my confident, strong, asshole of a brother—starts to cry. His eyes shine, a single tear escaping down his cheek as he and Kaleb share a tense look. I turn to the Alpha, who is watching Xander with bated breath, his icy gaze calculating. So quickly that I almost miss it, his eyes flick to Rayna and back, and a few things shiver into sharp focus.

"Everything," Xander whispers, the word a gunshot in the silence. "He told me everything."

Clarity strikes me, pure and unrelenting. It presses on me like a knife: a gentle prick, a tiny sting, and then metallic fire as it slices into my chest, buried to the hilt.

When Rayna died, something changed in Xander. He became distant. Detached. Every time I so much as mentioned her, he would close himself off, refusing to engage. It was like a switch would flip in his mind, cutting off his emotions—no sadness, no joy, just a total and complete ambivalence that never sat right with me. It didn't matter that they spent most of their time at one another's throats. Xander, despite all his denial, really did love Rayna in his own way. Like a sister.

What could have happened, I asked myself, *to make him feel absolutely nothing?*

Everything inside me stills. My heart. My breath. Even my mind slows its racing, every thought replaced by a faint ringing. Louder and louder it grows, blocking out the gasps of the others around me, the music still blaring, the sound of someone whispering my name.

My consciousness splits in two: one frozen forever in the *before,* and the other moving forward into the here and now. The *after*.

Because hearing those words is the nail in the coffin—the one I have been building around myself for as long as I can remember, the one I use to protect myself from my brother and his judgment, his demands, his condescension. Tonight, for just a moment, a small prickle of hope made me think that maybe—*maybe*—I could finally start to pry it apart. To destroy the box that I have so carefully crafted to keep him out. To let my Alexander back in.

But now that hope is gone—shriveled and scorched and formless, like the remnants of my brother's heart.

After this moment I know, without a doubt, that nothing will ever return to the way it was. And nothing will ever be the same again.

Because Xander *knew.*

Nik slams his fist into Xander's temple so hard that he crumples to the ground. He catches himself with both hands, wincing as mirror shards slice into his palms. My instincts are screaming to go to him, to help him, but I don't. I just watch, numb, as he struggles to his hands and knees, spitting blood onto the floor.

You're my brother and for better or for worse, I've got your back. Words I said only a few hours ago. Words that, now, stir nothing in me but a sense of bitter emptiness.

Pippa says something behind me, met by a retort from Rose, but I don't hear it. I hear nothing but the wild pounding of my heart and the furious crackling of fire in my veins. Xander's head lifts slightly, and he hesitantly meets my eyes.

"Lottie?"

It sounds like a plea. An apology. The last hope of a desperate man. Maybe if I were a different person, I would have taken pity on him. If he hadn't spent the last few decades making my life a living hell. If he hadn't dismissed me as his incompetent little sister—as the girl who ruined everything.

If I were the old Charlotte, none of that would matter.

Unfortunately, that girl died the night Rayna did.

"I—I don't know you," I say at last, my voice breaking. At least, I *think* I say it. My world and everything I knew is shattering to pieces, creating a strange disconnect between my mind and body. My disembodied voice continues. "How could you do that to me?"

Xander chokes back a sob and scrambles to his feet, grabbing my wrists with bloody fingers. "Please. You have to understand—"

"*How could you?*" I practically scream, the force of his betrayal slicing through me like a scythe. Hot tears pool in my eyes, streaking down my cheeks as I yank my hands away. Red bleeds into my vision. "You knew she was alive! You knew and you said *nothing!*"

Xander exhales dejectedly. "It isn't that simple—"

"It is!"

"Charlotte—"

"How long have you known? Twenty years? Fifty?"

He drops his head in shame, and my anger flares anew.

"You've known the *whole time?*"

"*Please,* Ksusha—"

"*Don't call me that!*"

Xander looks at me with an expression of pure agony. He opens his mouth to protest, to plea, but I don't let him.

"You *knew,*" I snap, but it sounds more like a sob. "Rayna's death *ruined me,* and you just let it happen! All you had to do was tell me the truth. And Nik—" I choke on the words, swallowing hard to quell the emotion bleeding into my voice. It doesn't help. "He tried to kill himself, Alexander. And you did nothing to stop it."

Rayna gasps and Xander wilts. Nik seizes him by the collar.

"Get out of my sight," he growls, and Xander stares at him with wide, fearful eyes.

Rayna hurries forward, putting a hand on her brother's arm. "Let's not be hasty—"

Nik cuts her off with a Czech insult that has her staggering back a step.

"Nik," Xander practically whimpers, grasping the hand at his throat. He's panicking now, his words coming fast and breathless. "I'm sorry. I'm *so* sorry. I didn't want to hide it from you, but I had to! Please, *please* understand. If you will just let me *explain*—"

"*LEAVE.*" Nik's voice shakes the house like a crash of thunder. The mirrors shiver.

Xander's frantic gaze sweeps around the room, silently pleading for someone to come to his defense. To tell him to stay. No one does. Rose only shakes her head sadly while Pippa stares right at him, her expression dark and unflinching. Kaleb and Rayna are conspicuously quiet, and Henry's eyes are on the floor.

In a last desperate attempt at sympathy, Xander looks to me. "Lottie, please. I'm your *brother.*"

The words should make me feel something. *Anything.* Instead, there is a cool numbness spreading through me, turning the man in front of me into a complete stranger. If he wants pity, he's not going to get it from me.

"No," I say softly, and the light drains from Xander's eyes. "I don't have a brother anymore."

With a sound that might have been a sob, Xander yanks himself from Nik's grasp. His eyes shimmer with unshed tears before he turns and vanishes through the front door, trailing a soft breeze in his wake that makes the balloons sway.

Silence. Dead and hollow and black.

"*Darahi.*" Rayna moves to stand beside me, resting a hand on my shoulder. "Calm down and let us explain—"

I jerk away. "There's nothing to explain." For a moment, I wonder if I'm the one who actually spoke. I've never heard my voice sound so cold before. "Besides, you have no authority here. You've been back less than a day and you're already more trouble than you're worth. I'm glad I found out so quickly that this new Rayna is nothing but a lying, conniving *bitch.*"

"Charlotte," Kaleb warns. "Watch your tongue."

"Shut up, Kaleb." I turn to the Alpha, barely registering the shock on his face. "You're hardly innocent here. But hey, at least you let me hate you for the last century. Kudos for that."

The tension in the room shifts suddenly, only moments before Kaleb's expression sharpens. With a dangerous tilt of his head, he methodically buttons his blazer and uses a handkerchief to wipe Xander's blood from his face, all the while keeping his wintery eyes locked on me. The Alpha persona slides over his face like a mask, fierce and furious. Instinctively, I shy away.

"If your Alpha were anyone else," he growls, low and lethal, "you would have just lost your head."

I stare back at him coldly before dropping my gaze, cowed by the ice in his tone. Still, betrayal simmers in my chest, a writhing mass of anger, sadness, and disappointment. My jaw clenches.

Fighting back a sudden burst of emotion, I take a quick inventory of the others. Pippa and Rose are both crying, Henry has disappeared, and Nik is fuming, leveling Rayna with a scorching glare that tells me he's only moments away from a full explosion.

I don't want to hear what he has to say. I don't want anything. But I want answers. I want to be alone, but not *alone*. I want, I want, I want.

I *need*.

I bolt from the room, throwing myself through the kitchen and out the back door. The wooden deck is wide and dim, overlooking an empty street and the vast darkness of the Presidio. Catching myself against the railing, my stomach empties itself over the edge. I retch again and again, my muscles aching, my throat burning as huge, agonized tears stream down my face.

My own brother betrayed me. The man who has been to Hell and back with me, who has held my hand during my darkest times. Who has been my one constant—my distant, burning star. He knew Rayna was alive and he said nothing. He did *nothing*. He let me spiral into oblivion while Nik drank himself to near-death.

He should have told me. Instead, he kept a secret that ruined my life. It ruined *all* our lives. Just because he couldn't trust me not to screw things up.

Xander will never share his secrets with me, just like he will never grant me compassion or sympathy. He will never include me or listen to me when it matters.

I was starting to think that everything between us might just be okay. But I was wrong.

My knees buckle and I collapse onto the deck, sobs tearing through me as the same words cut through my thoughts over and over again.

Never enough. I will never be enough.

CHAPTER 12

I DON'T KNOW HOW LONG I sit on the deck, my hair buffeted by a howling wind that ushers in yet another storm. Minutes? Hours? Not that it matters. I doubt anyone misses me.

Tear trails stain my cheeks, making my skin feel tight. I roughly scrub them away. It does nothing to soothe the ache, the yawning chasm that has opened inside me, but the pressure of my palms is calming, somehow.

Voices carry over the wind, an emotional storm a hundred and twenty-one years in the making.

"You're a real piece of work, you know that?" I hear Nik snarl from inside. "Confiding in *Xander,* of all people."

"I didn't confide in him." That's Rayna. Strange, how her voice can be so familiar and yet so foreign. "We told him out of necessity, and it was not a choice made lightly."

"Oh yeah? And what *need* were you filling? The need to do whatever you want? The need to betray your own brother? The need to be a lying piece of shit?"

Rayna scoffs. "Since when have I been obligated to tell you everything?"

"Rayna." There's a warning in Kaleb's voice. He seems to be doing a lot of that lately. Warning us. Chastising us. "Employ a bit of tact, will you?"

Silence follows. Wind gusts over the deck, bringing with it the first drops of chilly rain. A shiver rattles through me. Not from cold, but from a familiar eerie feeling—like someone's attention is fixed on me.

I leap to my feet, my eyes darting through the darkness as I examine Nik's deck, the balconies on the neighboring houses, the street below. Nothing. At least, nothing I can see. But the cool dread remains, reminding me that even when I can't see him, Konstantin is always watching.

Fighting another shiver, I hurry into the house, locking the door behind me. Not that a lock will keep Konstantin out, but the action brings a modicum of comfort.

I make my way back into the living room where Nik, Rayna, and Kaleb are still arguing. The numbness of a few minutes ago slowly dissipates, replaced with white-hot rage that quickly bubbles to the surface. They all turn to look at me when I enter—just the three of them; Pippa and Rose have vanished—and consider me with varying levels of concern. I can only imagine what I look like right now: mascara smeared down my cheeks, a windblown nest of tangled hair, a sneer on my lips.

"You."

I stalk toward Rayna, put both hands on her chest, and shove. She gasps and flies backward, slamming into the piano with enough force to make the strings hum. Her expression turns vicious.

"*God,* Lottie!" she snarls, and I flinch again at her casual mention of deity—one of those vampire immunities I've never had the patience to master. Rayna's fangs flash. "A little warning would have been nice."

A snarl grates in my throat. I'm distantly aware that I've lost all semblance of control—that I might do something I regret. But I don't care.

"Why?" My voice is low. "Why should I do anything you say?"

Why? Why did you leave? Why did you tell Xander and not me? Why did it take you so long to come back? Why, why, why? Too many questions. Not enough damned time to ask them all.

"Come on, Charlotte—"

Before I know what I'm doing, I launch myself at Rayna. But she's prepared this time, and she catches me around the middle. She hooks one foot behind mine in an attempt to throw me off balance but I twist out of her grasp and swing a fist, catching the corner of her jaw. My knuckles spark with pain. Rayna snarls and grabs a fistful of my hair, dragging me sideways. Fire screams over my scalp as I trip over my own feet and momentum sends me sprawling face-first onto the wood floor. My chin takes the brunt of it and my fangs slice through my lower lip. Bitter, stale blood fills my mouth. I spit it out as I push up to my hands and knees.

"You were supposed to be my friend," I say through gritted teeth. "How could you do that to me? To *Nik?*"

"I *am* your friend!" Rayna snaps, and I glare up at her ruefully. Her jaw is an angry shade of red, already turning purple at the edges. "But are you mine? I'm pretty sure friends don't attack one another unprovoked."

Unbelievable.

"Oh, okay," I say with a derisive laugh, hoisting myself to my feet. I swipe blood from my chin with the back of my hand. "If you think that was unprovoked, then you're more delusional than I thought."

Kaleb's hand closes around my wrist and he yanks me sideways, spinning me to face him. His eyes are bright with frustration and incredulity.

"You are far too old to be acting like a petulant child," he scolds through clenched teeth, fingers digging into my skin. "Get a hold of yourself."

I sneer at him. "Maybe if Rayna would stop being such a—"

He grabs my chin, cutting me off. "Choose your next words carefully."

The chill in his voice has the desired effect, cooling the fire in my veins. Replacing it with shame. Rayna approaches with a smug look on her face and Kaleb releases me with a final warning glare. When he turns to Rayna, he matches her expression, but with an added bite of annoyance.

"You are also at fault here," he says to her, a bit of calm superiority transforming his demeanor. "I told you not to come to San Francisco, and now you see *why.*"

Rayna glowers. "You're all a bunch of jackasses," she says, then points at a frowning Nik. "And *you* had no right to hit Xander like that."

Nik's scowl turns murderous. "You're defending *Xander* now?"

"None of this was his fault. If you would have given him the chance to—"

"That's *it.*" I lunge at Rayna again, but Kaleb steps into my path. "Get out of my way, Kaleb."

"Charlotte," he bites out, "that is quite enough. I think you've made your point."

"And since when have I ever cared what you think?" His eyes flash, and I recoil. "Just . . . will you *please move?*"

Kaleb's eyes narrow ruefully and he makes a show of planting his feet, tucking his hands into his pockets.

Pompous ass.

"Outside," I bark at Rayna, skirting around Kaleb to storm out the front door.

Icy raindrops pelt my face and I inhale deeply, relishing in the way the air chills my lungs. The shadow of Xander's Maserati sits at the curb, dark and lifeless, rain sluicing over its slick matte surface. If I hadn't just disowned him, I might be worried that he left without taking his car. Under normal circumstances, I know he would rather die than leave it behind.

Then again, I'm not sure I know him at all anymore.

Rayna appears beside me, her blazer gone and her hair pulled back. I can't help but smirk at the bluish bruise on her jaw.

Her voice is soft and serious when she says, "I didn't do anything to Nik."

"What?"

"You asked how I could do that to him. But I didn't do *anything*."

I look at her incredulously. "You can't be serious."

"I know what you must think," she says, and the words are slow, almost practiced. "But I was protecting him. If you knew what Konstantin put him through"—her voice wavers—"you would have done the same. I wasn't about to let that monster get his hands on my brother ever again, and that meant getting as far from him as possible. I only did what was best for him. For all of us."

I scoff loudly, scrubbing rainwater from my eyes. "You may have protected him from Konstantin, but no one can hurt Nik more than he hurts himself. Frankly, he would have been better off dead."

"Excuse me? I think I would rather have my brother living without me than not living at all."

"Rayna, you weren't there!" Heat rushes into my face and my fangs pop, surprising her. She leans back slightly, her expression wary. "Nik died the day you did. He started drinking—*really* drinking. He barely left his apartment for the first few years. He would disappear for days at a time—*weeks* even—only for us to find him wasting his life away in pubs and gambling dens. It was like watching a bonfire burn out. Everything bright and beautiful about him was just . . . gone."

The memories pack an unexpected punch, my vision blurring with unshed tears. Nik was once such a strong presence. His emotions were so real—so *raw*—and he showed me what it truly meant to feel and to not be ashamed. He taught me how to love myself even when others didn't.

If only I could do the same for him.

"I—I didn't know," Rayna says, and her surprise seems genuine. She touches her fingertips to her lips. "Kaleb never said anything to me."

I raise a sardonic brow. "Before tonight, I might have believed he didn't know about it either. But now that I know Xander is his Beta,

I'm sure he knows far more about our lives than we realize. When's the last time the two of you actually talked?"

Rayna leans back against the porch's railing. "We talk all the time. But we haven't actually seen each other in . . . God, it's been seventeen years. Since he became Alpha." There's a touch of wistfulness in her voice, colored by frustration. "It seems he's been keeping secrets from me, as well." Anger simmers in her eyes and she slams a fist into the railing, splintering it into fragments.

I wince. "Destroying Nik's porch isn't going to get you back in his good graces."

"That is not what Kaleb promised," she snarls, her gaze distant. "He was supposed to tell me everything. *Everything.*"

Part of me wants to feel a touch of triumph, but I don't. I feel only a deep, resounding sadness. Drawing a hand down my face, I ask, "What are you really doing here, Rayna?"

I expect a quick response but she lets her head fall back, closing her eyes against the rain. I study her profile: she's just as beautiful as I remember, her sharp cheekbones slanting down to full lips and a jawline that has always made me jealous. With everything that has happened since she got back, I haven't let myself think about her motives. But now, it's *all* I can think about. What exactly is she planning to do? What is she really doing in San Francisco? Is she going to disappear again or will she stay with us—try to assimilate into a family that is nothing like the one she remembers?

Rayna takes a steadying breath and turns to face me, her eyes piercing. Sincere. Mischievous.

"I'm here," she says, enunciating every word, "because I'm your only hope of beating Konstantin."

◊   ◊   ◊

I tell Rayna everything.

Well, everything that doesn't involve my relationship with Tristan.

She and I may have once been like sisters, but I don't think I'm ready to talk to her about my boy problems just yet.

When I finish, she huffs out a breath.

"Kostya really got you good, didn't he?"

I grimace. "Don't give him a nickname. It makes him sound like an actual person."

"Sorry, old habit." Rayna shrugs, letting her hair down now that the rain has stopped. She shakes it out, spraying me with water droplets. "Interesting how he singled you out, don't you think?"

"Yes," I say, only half listening, "very interesting. Completely misplaced, if we're being honest."

The squeak of tires on wet asphalt catches my attention, and I turn to see a police car make its way slowly up the street. It's strange to have a patrol passing through here. Officers usually stick to downtown and the tourist areas, not side streets in the wealthier districts. I wonder if it has anything to do with the San Francisco Vampire case; it wouldn't surprise me if they were doing extra patrols in an effort to thwart any future murder attempts.

Though I doubt Konstantin would be fazed by a few human officers and a taser.

"No, I don't think so," Rayna muses. She watches the police car as it disappears around the corner, a glint in her eye. "Konstantin was watching you when you killed that girl by the coffee shop. I suppose he could have assigned someone else to keep an eye on you . . ." She pauses, tracing her lips contemplatively. "No. He was there. I'm sure of it."

I think back to the empty sidewalk, the piece of spotty shade outside a coffee shop, the girl with bouncy brown curls . . . and there, across the street, a group of raucous boys chattering about some nonsense, one of them recording something on his phone. I had thought they were tourists at the time, but now that I think about it, the phone wasn't angled at the boys. It was facing *me,* as if on purpose. Capturing the video that would eventually be leaked to the press. And the boy holding it . . .

He had silver eyes.

Groaning, I lean on the porch railing and let my head fall into my hands. Of course. Of *course* he was there.

"Why is he so obsessed with me?"

Rayna's mouth twists into a smirk. "If Konstantin has been watching you since March—or longer—he has a good reason. He knows your habits, your interests, and the status of every one of your relationships. In addition, he knows the same things about Nik, Xander, Pippa, and Rose. Victoria. Even Kaleb."

And Tristan, I add silently, dread pooling in my stomach. But that's another detail I left out of my little story. As far as Rayna knows, the girl in the Shakespeare Garden was a nobody. I won't have her pity me for crushing on the girl's brother.

"Clever, really," Rayna says, "that he would take Victoria over anyone else."

"What do you mean?"

"Konstantin views the world like a game of chess." Rayna drags her fingers along the railing, tracing an invisible grid. "There are pawns and rooks, knights and bishops. The queen. The *king*. It is his ultimate goal to lock Kaleb in a checkmate. Victoria," she says through a revelatory smile, "is just a pawn. Meaningless. Disposable. He could have taken anyone, really, but it had to be her. He knew that Xander would do anything to get her back, no matter the cost."

I nod, unsure where she's going with this. "Meaning?"

"Who better to convince Kaleb to cooperate than his Beta?"

Xander. Kaleb's *Beta*. Traitor. Bastard. Brother.

Not anymore, I remind myself. *My brother is dead.*

I suddenly feel the urge to retreat. To get as far from Rayna and Konstantin and Xander's sleeping Maserati as possible.

"I've had enough of this conversation tonight," I say, striding purposefully away.

Rayna catches at my arm but I yank it free. "Where are you going?"

"I don't know. I just—" I sigh loudly, avoiding Rayna's searching gaze. "I need a minute."

I hurtle down the stairs, letting my legs take me wherever they want to go.

Konstantin came here to destroy us—to tear us apart. I can't help but wonder if Rayna returned to help us defeat him, or if he somehow manipulated her into coming back. Either way, Rayna is part of his game. I'm just not sure whose team she's playing for.

CHAPTER 13

Konstantin whistles tunelessly as he strolls up Jackson Street. For the first time in multiple lifetimes, he feels a spark of nervous anticipation. He has been planning his revenge on Kaleb for so long, he was beginning to think it would never actually happen. But tonight, the stars finally aligned when he saw the red-haired demon setting up birthday decorations in Nikolas's house.

How mundane.

Rayna herself wasn't a surprise; Konstantin has known she was alive since Kaleb became San Francisco's Alpha. What he didn't expect was for Rayna to arrive in the city so quickly. He thought he would have to play with Kaleb for a few weeks—*months,* even—before her weakness finally won over. Perhaps he was wrong about her. Any protégé of his should never have given in so easily.

Though he must admit that it's quite poetic, Rayna returning the very night Konstantin revealed himself. A king and his queen moving together for the first time in centuries.

Seeing Rayna again brought a rush of old feelings to the surface: relief, anger, and a mouth-watering desire so intense that it took every ounce of Konstantin's willpower not to rush into Nikolas's house and steal her away.

But then he wouldn't have seen Xander punch Kaleb in the face.

He wouldn't have seen Nikolas knock Xander to the floor. And he wouldn't have seen Charlotte escape from the house, her umber hair catching the wind as her life disintegrated.

He wouldn't have felt that protective instinct flare to life inside of him—one he has just started to feel again. One that he needs to extinguish immediately.

Now that Rayna is here, everything is going to happen very fast. If Konstantin knows anything about her, it's that Rayna is dangerously competitive. He has no doubt that she is already concocting a plan of her own, learning everything she can about the city's weaknesses in an attempt to bring him down.

Unfortunately for Rayna, she has only been here for a day. Konstantin has been here for eleven years.

He would have been able to act sooner if Kaleb hadn't been so hell-bent on shunning his dysfunctional family. If he hadn't insisted on playing the villain. So Konstantin watched and waited, biding his time until the moment Kaleb showed his hand.

The first move, made by the white king.

Everything changed the morning Kaleb showed up on Charlotte's doorstep, and Konstantin finally, *finally* put his plan into motion.

And it is going far better than he expected.

Playing the role of Ty may have been infuriating—he would rather die than let Xander order him around again—but it was also surprisingly enjoyable. He appreciated having an excuse to be close to Charlotte after watching her for so long, wanting to play with her but choosing to lie low. As he suspected, she was pliable and easily manipulated, and it was almost too easy to coax that kiss from her. The taste of her lips still lingers in his memory, tinged with fresh blood and a colorful bouquet of wine.

The rain intensifies as Konstantin turns onto Sutter Street, so much that he almost doesn't hear the tiny noise behind him—the scuffle of sneakers on wet pavement. He pauses mid-stride, training an ear backward. Under the constant patter of the rain and the distant roar of late-night traffic, he can just hear a hissing, ragged laugh, followed by two haunting words.

"New blood."

Alarm heats Konstantin's skin. He whirls around to see three white-haired figures emerge from a narrow alley, twisted smiles on their cracked lips. There is something dangerously beautiful about them as they creep forward as one, their movements synchronized and more fluid than they have any right to be. For another vampire, encountering these creatures might mean a slow and agonizing death. Fortunately for Konstantin, he has had more than his fair share of experience with demons like these.

One of them—a young woman with gray-brown skin—lunges forward, elongated fangs snapping shut mere inches from Konstantin's throat. He stifles a gag at her decaying stench as he spins out of her reach, grimacing at the familiar sharp pain in his shoulder, then dodges a second attack from a chalk-skinned boy with a manic grin. With practiced ease, he punches a hole through the boy's sternum and yanks out his shriveled heart, his hand dripping with blackish blood.

The third creature snarls and leaps, his fathomless black eyes filled with malice. Konstantin curses and staggers sideways into the woman's arms, who wraps him in a skeletal embrace. He roars as her fangs pierce his neck.

"Get off me!"

Konstantin throws his head back and hears a *crunch* as he connects with the woman's nose. She screams in rage and falls away, her teeth tearing at his skin. He takes the opportunity to sprint away from her, ignoring the duo's otherworldly howls as they watch their prey escape. After a few seconds, Konstantin is far enough away that he can barely hear the sound. After a few minutes, he catches himself against a weathered railing looking out over the Bay, heart pounding and shoulder seizing. He crosses his arm over his chest in an attempt to release the tension from his muscles, but his left hand remains stiff as a dull ache radiates from the middle of his back.

This constant pain . . . this is where it all started. This is why he's here.

There were only three, he reassures himself, letting his arm hang limp at his side. With his right hand, he presses two fingers to the bite at his throat. It twinges under his touch. *Well, two now. They won't be a problem.* But even as he thinks it, he knows it's a lie. He has kept a very close eye on Lorenzo's little horde since he arrived in San Francisco, and these three creatures are none he has seen before.

Sighing, Konstantin leans forward to rest his good arm on the railing, already reassessing his plan to account for a volatile, blood-thirsty new enemy. Because if he isn't careful, the pale-faced demons will put an end to everything before he has even begun.

CHAPTER 14

NEW YORK CITY, NEW YORK

FEBRUARY 1899

*C*ANAL *S*TREET IS PITCH BLACK *and empty tonight, the below-freezing temperatures forcing everyone inside. The winter has been abnormally cold, but the brisk wind carries the strange warmth of an oncoming snowstorm. Even as I walk, ice falls from the sky and bites into the chapped skin of my cheeks. I hardly feel the cold anymore, but somehow the recent weather has driven a chill into my bones, untouched by warm coats or a roaring fireplace or the energetic rush that comes from drinking human blood.*

I have trekked through Chinatown countless times in the last few weeks looking for Nikolas, checking all his frequented haunts—restaurants, tiny shops, bars filled with hopeless drunkards—but, as usual, he is nowhere to be found.

That hasn't stopped me from searching.

I shiver as the wind whips my hair into my face, tiny crystals forming on my eyelashes as I squint down a familiar dark alley; Nik's favorite bar is tucked between the back doors of two brightly-painted restaurants, remaining secret to all but those who already know where it is. I visit it every night, hoping he hasn't frozen to death. Hoping I won't find him here.

The red door is glaring in the darkness, a dragon knocker with ruby eyes watching me as I knock once, then twice, then once again. After a few long seconds, the door swings inward, the arctic air rushing in ahead of me with a flurry of shimmering snowflakes. A petite vampire woman with heavy eyeliner and red lips looks at me disapprovingly. Her jet black hair is pulled back into a painfully-tight bun, the skin on her forehead stretching upward and adding severity to the already sharp angle of her eyes. Her mouth curves into what, for her, might be a smile.

"Nǐ hǎo, Mei," I say, giving her a little bow. "Have you seen him?"

She narrows her eyes in pointed judgment—Mei has never liked me, for reasons she has never confirmed—then motions behind her with a flick of her head.

I gaze past her into the bar. Despite its unsavory location, Mei's bar is the picture of luxury. Red velvet furniture fills the room in intimate groupings around the four fireplaces, humans and vampires alike lounging languidly together as they drink and smoke and feed from necks. A solid jade bar stretches the length of one wall, decorated in gilded carvings and crystal glasses in all shapes and sizes. The dark-haired bartender expertly mixes a drink with a gold shaker, red nails glinting, and the walls behind her are hand-carved and gilded in gold, the long, fluid body of a dragon winding its way around the room until its head emerges, snarling, from above an archway that leads into the back room.

The room Mei just motioned toward. I groan.

"Again?" I grumble to no one—least of all, Mei—and brush past her into the club. Mei closes the door behind me and I'm bathed in sudden warmth. I yank the wool gloves from my hands—an old gift from Nikolas—and shrug off my coat, handing them to the woman at the coat check.

I step through the beaded curtain under the archway and am met by complete darkness. Not even a hazy gold glow from the fireplaces finds its way in. This is one of my personal ideas of Hell—a small dark space, trapped with no end in sight—but I've been down this narrow hallway many times. Always with Nik, and almost always begrudgingly.

I emerge into the dark gambling den and my nose fills with the overpowering and nauseating scent of blood mixed with alcohol and a suffocating cloud of cigar smoke. Five poker tables are packed into the small room, six or eight or ten vampires crowded around each one. Green light glows sickeningly from a collection of large pendants with emerald glass, and gold lamps flicker near the dealer at each table, offering a tiny amount of light for the players to read by. A few humans wander zombie-like around the tables, their eyes glassy, holding out their wrists to any vampire who will take them.

It takes me a few seconds to locate Nikolas but I finally spot him at a table in the far corner, a bright grin lighting up his face as he stacks a neat pile of chips in front of him. A cigar is clamped tightly between his teeth, a habit I never thought he would adopt. But Nikolas has adopted many uncharacteristic habits as of late. I can't say I'm surprised by the addition of one more.

Someone at the table displays his hand and Nikolas laughs sharply, removing the cigar from his mouth with a flourish. The laugh is cold and dark and languorous, and his smile doesn't reach his eyes. Nothing reaches his eyes anymore. They flicker around, numb and unfeeling, as he flashes his own cards before gathering a pile of chips from the middle of the table.

I move toward him, watching, hoping he won't disappoint me as a human wrist is extended in front of him. Unfortunately, Nikolas has been nothing if not disappointing for the last few years.

"Nikolas."

He freezes, teeth buried in a pale wrist, and his eyes snap up, searching for the source of his name. The confusion in his expression evaporates quickly when he spots me, morphing into distant horror as he releases the girl's arm, wiping his mouth with the back of his wrist. He stands, extinguishes his cigar, and, mumbling a low excuse to the dealer, weaves through the tables until he reaches me. No one pays him any notice.

"Charlotte," he says, his eyes not quite meeting mine. He takes one of my hands and pulls me a few feet into the dark hallway. "What are

you doing here?"

The eerie glow etches his silhouette in green, a color I have always loved when paired with the deep auburn of his hair.

"I have been looking for you, Nikolas!" I say, and am surprised by the intensity of my tone. Nikolas recoils slightly. I want to feel relieved that he is here, that he is alive, but I only feel a cold fury igniting in my chest. "You have been gone for over three weeks! Did you think I would not come looking for you?"

With each word my voice grows louder and Nikolas looks over his shoulder nervously. "Maybe we should continue this conversation outside."

I glance past Nikolas and am met by a collection of sharp glares from the poker dealers. Mei's bar is known for its all-female staff, each one a near-perfect clone of the others: dark hair swept into tight buns with jeweled chopsticks, gold jewelry, high-necked shirts of red silk, blood-red lips. They glare at me acidly through the haze and I force myself to look away.

"That would probably be a good idea."

Nik leads me back through the hallway, his hand firm and strong as always, but with the unwelcome addition of a cool clamminess. Whether it indicates anxiety or a vampiric version of alcohol poisoning, I cannot tell.

We pass quickly through the main bar and I keep my eyes on the ground. Nikolas may be a standard fixture here—he has known Mei since our first night in New York—but the staff and patrons seem to think I'm the enemy. It may have something to do with my first visit, when I accidentally knocked over an entire shelf of ancient baijou liquor, which is now kept in a locked cabinet bolted to the wall. It may also have to do with the fact that I'm dating Nikolas and Mei doesn't think I am good enough for him. Either way, I feel the venomous stares of a few dozen pairs of eyes—Mei's included—as we slip outside into a raging blizzard.

Mei frowns and murmurs something to Nikolas in Mandarin before she slams the door shut behind us.

The wind has picked up considerably in the last few minutes, whistling angrily through the alleyway and lifting my skirts around my knees. I cry out in surprise and Nikolas wraps a tight arm around me, leading us around the corner into a sheltered alcove. A small doorway stretches into blackness behind us and I smell the faint aroma of onions and roast duck before it is carried away by the wind.

"Charlotte," Nikolas says, taking my shoulders. "I'll ask again: what are you doing here? You shouldn't be alone in this part of town."

"I can take care of myself, Nikolas," I spit. "And I told you. I have been looking for you. We all have. Alexander said this morning that you were probably dead and I almost believed him."

Nikolas frowns, rubbing the back of his neck with a shaky hand. Now that we're away from the golden light and smoke-soaked air of the bar, I see how haggard he looks. He is still wearing the suit he was in when I last saw him, sans coat, and there are tears and dark stains lining the edge of his waistcoat. His shoes are scuffed and unpolished. Dark circles hang under his eyes, which are dull and unfocused. His shirt, once white, is now dingy with soot and grime, and the top few buttons are undone to reveal the familiar silver coin winking at his throat. The same coin that Rayna wears—wore—to remind them of their vulnerability. If only Nikolas could stay sober for long enough to remember.

"Nikolas," I say, touching his face softly. "Where have you been?"

He leans into my touch and closes his eyes, his jaw trembling.

"I'm sorry, darahi," he whispers, though the words are nearly indecipherable over the howling of the wind. "I was—I didn't know you were looking for me."

If only I could tell him everything—that I have hardly slept since he left, that I have spent every waking moment crippled by anxiety and scouring the city for any breath, any trace of him—but I can't. I shouldn't. I'm afraid of what might happen if I break an already broken heart.

But at the same time, I wonder what might happen to my own heart if I allow Nikolas to break it any further.

"Nikolas, I—" A knot forms in my throat but I swallow it, forcing myself to speak the words I've been thinking for months. "I don't know if I can do this any longer."

His eyes snap open. "Do what?"

"This. Us. I don't—I can't live like this."

His frown deepens and he takes my face in both hands. Somehow his skin is simultaneously warm and cold, sending an odd chill through me. I stare at his cognac eyes—the eyes that have the capacity to both raise and ruin—and see none of his old fire there. They are nothing but dark pits of despair, staring back at me intensely as he struggles to stay focused. I wonder how much he has had to drink. And how many days it has been since he last slept.

"I won't run away again," he says, his vowels a little too drawn-out, his consonants soft. "You have my word. I'll only drink once a week. Twice." He scowls at my shoulder. "Maybe three times. Three times is okay, right?"

"Nik. It isn't just about your drinking." I have heard Alexander, Pippa, and Rose give Nikolas the same speech many times in the last two years, but it never seems to get through to him. I have done my best to hold my tongue—to give Nikolas the sense that at least one person remains on his side—but as soon as the words start coming, I can't seem to stop them. "You have changed since Rayna died. You have lost your sense. Your kindness. Your fire. I do not see the Nikolas I have known and loved for the past seventy years. He is gone, replaced by some ghost of his former self. The man I see in front of me is a stranger, and I cannot love a man I have only just met."

Something cracks in Nikolas's expression. "Lottie, I—"

"You cannot explain this away. I am done hearing your reasons and excuses. Nothing you say will convince me I am wrong." The gravity of what I am doing finally hits me and a weight lands heavily in my stomach. I clench my teeth.

"Charlotte. Darahi." His voice wavers as he realizes my intentions, too late. "You promised me—" He blinks a few times, refocusing. "You promised once that you would never leave me. Don't leave me. Not now. Please."

"I have never left you, Nikolas. I have never stopped loving and supporting you as you spiraled into this abyss. But enough is enough. I will be by your side, one way or another, until death claims us. But I cannot be with you as we are." My voice wavers. "Not as your partner. My heart cannot take it anymore."

His hands fall from my face, hanging limply at his sides. I watch with stinging eyes as he forces on a mask of indifference, a terrifying numbness filling his gaze as it fixes on a point just over my shoulder.

"I—I understand," he says, the softness in his voice jarring against the stiffness of his shoulders. "'So farewell hope, and with hope farewell fear. Farewell remorse: all good to me is lost. Evil, be thou my good.'"

My heart stutters anxiously at his sudden clarity. "Nikolas? What—"

Taking me gruffly by the arm, he yanks me toward him, his sudden kiss stunting my words. His lips are hard and urgent, crushing mine for a few agonizing seconds before he pulls back. Then he turns and strides away into the ever-growing blizzard without so much as a backward glance, the thick flurries of snowflakes swallowing him in a matter of moments.

"Nikolas!" I cry, but it is no use. My words are lost to the wind, my feet frozen to the ground as I watch my heart vanish into the storm.

A chill settles over me. I'm alone in the dark alcove, the air still touched by the scents of simmering oil and vegetables. I stare down at my hands—at my dry skin and bony fingers—and frown.

I forgot my gloves.

I'M GONE FOR maybe twenty minutes—just enough time to clear my head—and I find Rayna right where I left her.

"What," I say, "too embarrassed to go back inside?"

"Pippa's in there," she mutters, her expression distant. "I'm not sure I want to."

Good hell. If Pippa came back to see Nik after a night like tonight, there's only one thing she plans on doing. I bolt inside, Rayna following with a begrudging groan, and sigh in exasperation when I see the disastrous scene playing out in the living room.

Nik is lounging on the sofa with a bottle of very expensive scotch in one hand, his hair rumpled, his shirt open, and Pippa draped over his lap. She lets out a nauseating giggle as he wraps himself around her, dragging kisses down her neck. The room reeks of alcohol, which is quickly explained when Pippa clumsily reaches for a glass of bourbon and knocks it to the floor.

"You're wasting all my good liquor, Philippa," Nik murmurs against her throat, fangs flashing through a grin. "You're going to have to make it up to me somehow."

"Oh?" Pippa says, visibly swooning. "What did you have in mind?"

"I'm sure you'll come up with something worth my while."

Oh, Nik.

"Nikolas, *co děláš?*" Rayna hisses, and his head snaps up, his grin turning sour.

"Ah, *moje sestra!*" he slurs, untangling himself from Pippa and falling back onto the sofa. The scotch bottle stays glued to his hand. "Here to ruin our good time?"

"Where is Kaleb?"

Nik makes a show of looking around, then shrugs theatrically. "The hell if I care."

"Dammit, Nik," I say, snatching the bottle from his hand. He glowers at me. "How much have you had to drink?"

"Not enough!" Pippa sings, taking the scotch from me and downing it in a few over-eager gulps.

I grimace. "You know Nik's mouth was all over that."

Pippa's grins languidly and she pulls Nik closer. "His mouth was all over *me* a second ago."

Rayna audibly gags.

"Absolutely not," I say, yanking Pippa off of Nik's lap. He doesn't protest but his eyes narrow minutely. "The last time this happened, both of you came crying to me the next morning filled with regret. I do not have time to deal with the fallout from your ill-fated sexual shenanigans right now."

"Philippa Rees regrets *nothing,*" she says, though she frowns, just a little. She stumbles sideways and I catch her arm as a small hiccup escapes her. "I've never regretted anything in my entire life."

"Sure, you haven't," I mutter, recoiling from the alcohol fumes on her breath. "What are you two doing, anyway?"

Pippa looks at me with glossy eyes. "Hmm? Oh, I just wanted to give Nik a *real* party, is all. He was sad and now he's not. Mission accomplished." Nik smirks as Pippa shoots finger guns at me.

"Come here." I drag her into the hall, patting her cheek sharply in an attempt to snap her out of it. "You are *not* going to sleep with Nik, do you hear me? I have enough to worry about without helping the two of you navigate your 'one-night stand' for the umpteenth time."

"But *Lottie*—"

"No buts. Go get a blood bag from the fridge and sober up."

Pippa looks like she might actually apologize but glass shatters in the living room, strangling whatever she was about to say. We turn to see Nik and Rayna nose to nose, broken glass at their feet. Remnants of the wasted scotch are splattered on the cuffs of their jeans and the twins are bristling, energy blazing between them like wildfire.

"You have always acted like you were the smarter twin," Nik snarls, digging a finger into Rayna's shoulder. She doesn't budge, just stares up at him with fury in her eyes. "Perfect Rayna and her perfect brain. Always thinking your way out of problems. But what happens when that isn't enough, huh? What happens when your crazy schemes can't save you?"

Rayna sneers. "Those *crazy schemes* of mine have kept us safe for almost three hundred years. Where do you think you'd be without me?"

"Dead, most likely!"

"Exactly!"

"Yes, Rayna. *Exactly*." Nik storms away from her, retrieving a decanter of whiskey from the bar cart. He doesn't bother with a glass. "I'd be dead. And hell, do you know how many times in the last hundred years I wanted to be?"

Rayna stills. "You don't mean that."

"Oh," Nik says with a wry smile, "I assure you, I absolutely do."

"I left to *protect you,* Nikolas. I didn't do anything wrong."

Nik laughs. "You keep saying that, but let's not pretend it was anything more than what it actually was."

"And what, pray tell, was that?"

"A ruthless, bloody *betrayal*."

"Hey," I snarl, leaving Pippa in the hall. "Cut it out. I'm going upstairs to get some much-needed sleep, because there's no way I'm going home right now." Just the thought of confronting Xander has my stomach clenching. "If you keep me awake, I will come down here and slit both your throats."

Nik's brow knits in confusion. "But Pippa—"

"Was just leaving. Right, Pippa?"

I turn to look at her, but she's already gone.

"I'm leaving too." Rayna snatches her green blazer from the back of a chair, takes one sweeping look around the ruined living room, and jabs a finger into Nik's chest. "Next time you think about dying, *don't*."

Nik and I stare after her as she stalks out of the house and slams the door behind her.

"When Kaleb told us he killed Rayna," Nik says coldly, almost to himself, "I wished he had been lying. Now I wish he had been telling the truth."

His words should surprise me, but they don't. Not when I almost agree.

Nik tosses his decanter aside—I wince as it shatters near the bookshelves—and trades it for a bottle of blood from a nearby credenza. The scent of it is overpowering and I feel the heat rushing to my cheeks, the veins pulsing below my eyes. Tristan's blood stoked my hunger, but I haven't had a chance to sate it.

Without a word, I grab the bottle from Nik's hand and take a few deep swigs, closing my eyes as relief sweeps through me. *Not enough.* I slam the bottle down and reach for another, but Nik stops me with a firm hand on my wrist.

I look up at him—at his wild eyes and flushed cheeks—and realize he is standing close to me. *Too* close.

"Nik?"

"Darahi," he murmurs, and I freeze as he smooths a lock of hair behind my ear. "You're so beautiful."

Wariness fills me, my hunger forgotten. "What are you—"

"Shh."

Nik presses a finger to my mouth, silencing my question. Traitorous warmth trickles through my veins and I lose myself momentarily in his eyes, dark and bottomless and blazing.

Dammit.

It's damn near impossible to resist Nik when he gets like this: emotional, existential, and with more alcohol in his veins than blood. The combination lowers all his inhibitions, and the effect it has on him is dazzling. His mouth quirks into a heart-breaking smile—the one he uses to lure humans to bed—and I silently wonder if he was actually Adonis in another life.

"Aren't you sick of all the lies?" Nik asks, voice dripping with honey. "Don't you ever just want to run away?"

Stop this, Charlotte. Don't let him drag you down with him.

I chew on the insides of my cheeks before quietly saying, "Yes."

"Then why don't we?"

I exhale slowly, wetting my lips. Nik's gaze drops, tracing the movement with hungry eyes. My heart responds with an erratic leap.

You just told Pippa off. Don't be a hypocrite.

"You want to run away together?" I ask, all nonchalance despite the familiar ache of anticipation in my chest. *Don't do it, Charlotte.* "How nauseatingly romantic."

"I'm serious, Lottie. We could escape it all, just you and me. We don't owe these bastards anything."

Stop this, stop him, stop, stop, stop—

When Nik lowers his face to mine, all thoughts leave my head. My entire body goes soft, my knees threatening to buckle under the sudden heat. The anguish. The overwhelming disappointment. Nik's touch is warm and gentle, and he folds me into his arms like something precious. Like a prized possession. Like something he can't bear to lose.

I melt into him, allowing myself a moment to picture a life on the run with Nik. We could be *together:* Charlotte and Nikolas, the wild ones. The ones who put themselves above everyone else. The ones who bring out the worst in one another. The ones who enable and excuse and destroy.

But we have always been too much alike—too volatile to be anything but a cautionary tale.

I put a palm to Nik's chest and gently push him away, easing myself out of his embrace. He frowns at me, dejected.

"Nikolas," I whisper. "I—*we* can't do this."

"Charlotte—"

"No."

Nik's jaw feathers and he shoves his hands in his pockets, frowning in frustration. "Why not?"

"You know why."

We have lives here. We have *family* here. And as much as it pains me to even consider it, we have to do what's best for them. I refuse to leave them at Konstantin's mercy because I'm too afraid to face him.

I'm not Rayna.

When Nik's expression remains uncertain, I ask, "What about Noah?"

"Noah," he murmurs, like he doesn't quite grasp what I'm saying.

Then, after a few seconds, the fog clears from his expression and his eyes widen in alarm. "Oh my hell, *Noah.*" He takes a few stumbling steps toward the sofa and collapses onto it, staring into the fireplace with dull horror, all traces of Adonis gone. "What have I done?"

"Nothing," I say firmly, crouching in front of him. "You did nothing."

"I almost kissed you, Charlotte! And Pippa . . ." Nik buries his face in his hands. "What am I supposed to tell him?"

"But you *didn't* kiss me," I say, playing at humor. "I've gotten more action from a tube of lipstick." I smile hesitantly, but he doesn't return it.

Nik groans through a string of Czech curses. "And worse, I got you and Pippa involved."

"We both know Pippa brought this one on herself." I climb onto the sofa and pull him into a hug. "It's been a rough twenty-four hours. Let's just chalk this up to an aftershock, yeah?"

Nik is quiet for a few seconds, considering, then offers a tiny nod.

Heavy silence fills the room and I curl into Nik's chest, letting his steady presence ground me. After all this time, he is one of the few people I can always lean on—he never judges, never chastises, never tries to turn me into something I'm not. Nik has always encouraged my bad behavior—celebrated it, even—and I did the same for him. Maybe that's why our relationship was doomed from the start.

"Do you think we would still be together," I ask quietly, watching the flames writhe and crackle in the fireplace, "if Rayna had never left?"

Nik's chest fills, then he exhales a long, slow breath. "You mean if I never turned into a raging alcoholic and destroyed any chance I had at happiness?"

I scoff. "You're such a drama queen."

"Sue me."

"If you'll remember," I muse, "it was Rayna who encouraged us to hook up in the first place. I think she wanted us to be together more than we did."

Nik chews on the idea, combing gentle fingers through my knotted hair as the fire spits a few sparks onto the hearth. "You're probably right. And if Rayna had left earlier, maybe we never would have gotten together in the first place." His voice drops, taking on a sharp edge. "That sure would have saved us a lot of heartache."

"Yeah," I say idly, ignoring the twinge of guilt in my chest. "Maybe."

Silence falls again, but neither of us breaks it. We stay curled together on the sofa until the fire burns down to embers, until Nik's breathing settles into the steady rhythm of sleep, until the outside world shifts from inky black to watery gray.

Until I almost forget why I don't want to go home.

NIK VESELY

CHAPTER 15

ALL RAYNA WANTED WAS TO talk to Kaleb alone. She didn't expect, well, *this*.

"Kaleb is running a *subjugate club*?" she snarls at Henry, who led her into The Caged Bird only minutes ago. "After everything Kostya did to me? To *Nik*?"

She would have been impressed with the lavish club if it weren't for the well-dressed vampires lounging on the furniture, drinking sensually from a collection of dreamy-eyed humans. *Subjugates*. Humans Compelled to submit to vampires. As pets. As playthings. Just thinking about it is enough to bring back the phantom bite of teeth at her neck, but actually seeing it has ice slinking down her spine.

Henry cowers against the damask wall in a back hallway and offers a sheepish grin. "If it makes you feel any better, he doesn't *want* to run a subjugate club. But it's the easiest way to keep the elites satisfied."

Rayna scoffs, tugging on her cross necklace as she fights back the panic, the fear, the untamed anger. When Kaleb became San Francisco's Alpha, she knew everything was going to change. It went against the one thing they had always promised each other—that they would do whatever it took to stay hidden. To stay *safe*. But then Kaleb broke his own rule: *Nullum corpus*. Leave no bodies. He told her that killing the previous Alpha was an accident—that he hadn't recognized the vampire cornering that poor girl in an alley—but Rayna knew better. And honestly, she couldn't blame him. The bastard deserved it.

Everything had happened quickly then. Kaleb had always been a natural leader, but something changed the night he became Alpha. He grew fiercer. Sharper. More determined—and maybe more reckless, too. Because staying in San Francisco was the single most idiotic decision Kaleb had ever made.

He did everything he could to convince Rayna to stay, even going as far as asking her to marry him. Again. But when he told her of his plans to invite their family to join them, Rayna knew she couldn't stay. With Kaleb forcing himself into the public eye, it would only be a matter of time before Konstantin found him, and therefore Rayna. And if he found Rayna, he would find Nik, too.

It wasn't even a question. When given the option to protect either Kaleb or Nikolas, her brother has always come first. So she ran. She left Kaleb behind, only to find out that he continues to make idiotic decisions—like ignoring their family for nearly two decades. Like choosing Xander as his Beta. Like running a damn *subjugate club.*

"What the hell does he think he's doing?" Rayna snaps at Henry.

A droll British voice speaks behind her. "Maybe you'd like to ask me yourself."

The cool edge in Kaleb's tone prickles along Rayna's skin, stoking the embers already burning in her gut. She doesn't look at him, instead attempting to reign in the fury grating against her ribs, screaming for a release. Now is not the time to lose control. Not in Kaleb's club. Not with so much at stake.

"I'm sorry," Henry says brightly, but his voice shakes, just a little. "I—she wasn't supposed to enter the main club. We were heading for your office and she went rogue . . ."

The boy trails off, and Rayna finally allows herself to look at Kaleb. His glare is fixed on Henry, his pale eyes alight with fury.

"You have work to do," he bites out. "I suggest you get to it."

With a tight nod, Henry mumbles a quiet, "Yes, sir," before

disappearing back into the club.

Kaleb watches him go, and there's something in his expression—an odd mixture of displeasure and unease—that piques Rayna's interest. It softens his countenance just enough that she forgets her anger for a moment. The man standing in front of her is so similar to the man she once knew, but somehow *very* different. Like being an Alpha has forced him to put up a wall around himself—like he no longer knows who he can trust.

"Come," Kaleb commands, striding away without a second glance.

Rayna follows, of course. She would follow Kaleb anywhere.

He shoves through a pair of carved walnut doors into what Rayna assumes is his office. The room is completely lined with books, and it boasts an impressive mahogany desk covered in piles of meticulously-organized papers. The doors close behind them with an ominous thud, and then Kaleb and Rayna are alone—truly *alone*—for the first time in seventeen years.

A barrage of questions and accusations whirl in her head, but she forces herself to stay quiet, her jaw clenching with the effort. She watches as Kaleb shrugs out of his blazer—this one a deep purple—and drapes it over a rose-colored lounge chair. His white dress shirt is unbuttoned to his sternum, a few white scars visible on his pale chest, and the emerald glints from behind his collar.

The emerald that Konstantin stole from him. The one Kaleb stole back.

"You shouldn't be here." Kaleb perches on his desk and folds his arms over his chest, fixing Rayna with an accusatory stare.

Her breath hisses through her teeth. *"That's* what you're going to lead with? Not, 'Hello, Rayna, good to see you, allow me to explain myself'?" When Kaleb doesn't so much as blink, she narrows her eyes. "I wanted to see where the mighty Alpha lives. Is that so hard to believe?"

Kaleb scoffs. "Yes. But I wasn't talking about the club. I want to know why you're in San Francisco when I expressly forbade you from coming."

"If we're asking stupid questions," Rayna shoots back, blood boiling, "I have one: why are you running a subjugate club?"

Kaleb's jaw ticks. "Do not change the subject, darling."

"Why not?" The anger she's been repressing bubbles to the surface, and she jabs a finger in Kaleb's direction. "You know what Konstantin did to us. You know *exactly* what happens to subjugates." Her voice breaks and she closes her eyes tightly, feeling the weakness, the fear, the hopelessness as though it was only yesterday. It was torture, being aware of everything happening to her while she was Compelled to let him touch her. *Feed* on her. "And now you're letting it happen to all these innocent people?"

Kaleb exhales through his nose, visibly fighting to keep his composure. "I am not hurting them, Rayna. Not like Konstantin. *Never* like him."

"Are you sure about that?" She starts pacing, gathering fistfuls of her jacket in her hands. "You're holding humans here as prisoners—"

"They are not prisoners."

"—for *years*—"

"Most are here for barely a week."

"—and take away their free will so you can, what, keep a few of the high-brows happy?"

Rayna can feel herself losing control. Her logical brain is fighting against her emotions, but they're stronger than they usually are. She has grown complacent. She has forgotten how angry Kaleb can make her.

She's forgotten the way he makes her feel.

Cool disinterest smooths the wrinkles on Kaleb's forehead, softening his shoulders. He uncrosses his arms and leans back against his desk, watching Rayna pace, his eyes tracking every movement. It's *maddening*.

Rayna stops in front of him, shooting daggers with her words. "And then there's the matter of what you've been hiding from me."

That brings wariness to Kaleb's face. "To what are you referring?"

"You brought our family here with a promise to tell me everything you learned about Nikolas. But if I knew you were just going to keep things from me, I wouldn't have let you contact them at all."

"Oh?" Kaleb straightens, his lip twitching. "You wouldn't have *let* me?"

"No." Rayna's tone is sharp. Unflinching. "I would have dragged you from this city, kicking and screaming. I should never have let you stay here in the first place."

Kaleb rises from his desk and takes a step forward, pale eyes flashing.

"You do not control my actions," he says darkly, and Rayna shivers as his fangs slide from his gums. "And I do not owe you an explanation."

"Of course you do!" Rayna says, wincing at her shrill tone, but Kaleb doesn't flinch. Doesn't move, doesn't breathe. His gaze flickers to her feet and back up again, like he's sizing her up. His eyes, which used to display his emotions readily, are cold and distant, revealing nothing but mild contempt.

"Why can't I see what you're thinking?" Rayna asks before she can stop herself. "Why are you hiding from me?"

Kaleb scowls and takes another step forward. Another. They're breathing the same air now, and heat flares in Rayna's chest.

"Is that what you think I'm doing?" he growls, brushing his knuckles along her jaw.

She takes a few deep breaths to slow her heartbeat, which is now racing. "I don't think anything, Kaleb. I *know*. I thought you might be excited to see me when I got back. Angry, even. But you've given *Xander* more attention than you have me." Her voice is rising with her temperature, her veins simmering with rage. "What is wrong with you? You're abandoning our family, keeping humans as pets . . . this isn't like you, Kaleb. What happened to the man I—"

Rayna's words are cut off as Kaleb takes her face in both hands and crushes his mouth to hers. Fire licks through her, hot and urgent, stealing her breath and stalling her thoughts. Her chest ignites with surprise, with relief, with desire that has been too-long buried. And just when she expects the kiss to deepen, Kaleb pulls away, barely enough to draw breath.

"Rayna, darling," he rasps, leaning his forehead against hers. "Shut. *Up.*"

Oh.

Awareness shivers through Rayna like fracturing ice. Exhaling slowly, she slides her hands into Kaleb's hair and he hums softly, his eyes drifting closed. She presses her body against his, *feeling* him, losing herself in his familiar scent of eucalyptus and cigarette smoke that mingles with her rose petal perfume. There is so much unsaid between them—so many questions she has yet to ask—but her mind has gone blank. The only things that matter are Kaleb's waiting lips, his closeness, his cool hands where they cup her jaw. Tension coils in her abdomen.

It has been far too long.

"I have not been ignoring you, *mé srdce,*" Kaleb murmurs into her ear. The chill in his breath raises the hair at her nape. "On the contrary. I have been keeping my distance because I knew if I got too close, I wouldn't be able to keep my hands off of you."

To illustrate his point, Kaleb hands slip under her hemline, thumbing circles on her hip bones. It's a gentle touch, the *slightest* pressure, but they've spent thousands of nights together. Kaleb knows exactly what he's doing.

By the same token, Rayna ducks her head to trace a line of kisses down Kaleb's throat, through his open collar to the point of his sternum. He exhales shakily as her lips brush the scar there—a perfect white circle—and she smiles against his skin before lifting her face to his.

This time, *she* kisses *him.* He inhales deeply, fingers digging into her sides as his mouth opens readily, and he tastes like smoke and ice, of old promises and the darkness of desire. His lips are hard and unyielding, and he wraps his arms around her torso, holding her. *Commanding* her.

She grins, letting her fangs pop.

The kiss grows wild. Desperate. Colored by seventeen years of yearning, of uncertainty, of loneliness. Based on the low moan that rumbles through Kaleb when Rayna's fingers dip beneath his waistband, she guesses he has missed her as much as she missed him.

She tugs the hem of his shirt free and slides her hands up his abdomen, raking her fingernails across his skin, over the familiar pattern of scars that criss-cross his ribs. Kaleb grabs the front of her jacket and practically tears it off, letting it fall to the floor with a soft *thud*. Tension roils between them—questions and fears and so many *layers*. Rayna reaches for Kaleb's shirt buttons, but her hands are shaking. It takes entirely too long for her to release the first button, and she huffs in frustration.

Kaleb's hands close over hers. "Let me, love," he murmurs, deftly finishing her task. He shrugs out of his shirt then rests it atop his blazer before drawing Rayna's shirt over her head in one smooth motion. His eyes spark.

"Rayna," he growls and she goes slack in his arms, groaning when his fangs graze her throat. When he drags his tongue over her pulse point. Her hands trace every ridge and scar that graces his skin. Exploring. *Remembering.*

Kaleb's hands find the clasp of her bra and she sucks in a breath, ready to be laid bare, but he pauses, a line forming between his brows.

"Are you sure—"

"Why did you stop?" Rayna demands, grabbing a fistful of his hair. *"Never stop."*

Kaleb's throat bobs. "Darling, there is so much—"

"Just *kiss me, láska.*" She tugs his face toward her, dragging her lip between her teeth. Kaleb's gaze drops to her mouth and desire flares in his winter-blue eyes, and with a quick flick of his fingers, the clasp comes loose. Fire, wild and urgent, flares inside Rayna and she gasps. "Kiss me senseless."

She doesn't have to ask again.

CHAPTER 16

CHICAGO, ILLINOIS

JULY 4, 1997

COLORS EXPLODE IN THE SKY *over Lake Michigan. I brace myself for the delayed chorus of booms and cringe as the penthouse shudders around me. In the park below, throngs of people are gathered on the waterfront to watch the fireworks, oohing and ahhing with each new explosion. Reflections sparkle on the lake's surface. The crowd cheers.*

I want to murder every single one of them.

Time moves differently as an immortal. When I was human, each second felt important—like I needed to savor every moment because I had so few. Now I find myself drifting through days at a time with nothing to show for it. Grief can do that to a person.

One hundred years have passed since the night my world fell apart. Somehow I've lived an entire century since then, though I'm still younger than Rayna was when she died. When she was murdered. *She had so much more to give: more excitement, more mischief, more love. If only Kaleb weren't such a coward, maybe the two of them would still be here. Maybe the last century would have meant something.*

As it stands, living for another hundred years has meant nothing at all.

Boom. The chandelier shivers, casting tiny rainbows on the walls and ceiling, and I clamp my hands over my ears. Ironic that Rayna would die on one of the most celebrated days in the United States.

Maybe we should have moved back to Europe so it felt less like the whole country was celebrating her death.

"Charlotte?" Xander steps through the front door, followed closely by a young man and woman. He closes the door softly behind him and strides into the living room, setting a large paper bag on the coffee table. "I brought—"

"Dinner?"

The two Compelled humans are looking around in awe—at the crystal chandelier, the carved marble fireplace, the glossy grand piano on its pedestal—and I bite back a smile. It's been a while since Xander brought humans home and I often forget how jaw-dropping our multi-million-dollar penthouse can be.

My brother rolls his eyes. "I was going to say 'drinks'"—he motions to the bag on the table—"but yes. Dinner as well."

After another chorus of window-rattling booms, I snatch up the bag and remove a variety of different alcohols. Xander rolls his eyes as I pop open the bottle of vodka.

"I should have known you'd start with that."

The drink burns its way down my throat. "Yes, you should have. And don't expect me to share." I point to the humans, who are still gaping at our extravagant decor. "Which one do you want?"

Xander frowns, eyeing me critically before turning to the humans. "Go wait in the kitchen," he says in his smooth, Compelling tone, "just down the hall. We'll be there in a minute."

The boy obeys immediately, but the girl offers a little pout before disappearing.

Boom. I glare at Xander as he sighs and sits down next to me, resting his elbows on his knees.

"You okay?"

I scoff and take another swig. "What do you think?"

He sighs again. "Are you enjoying the fireworks at least?"

Boom.

"I'm thinking about carving out my eardrums for the night." I

glance sideways at him. "Do you think they'll grow back?"

"Lottie—"

"Stop." The bottle clangs against the coffee table when I set it down. "I don't want your pity. Just let me suffer in peace, alright?"

Xander says nothing, but his gaze falls to his hands where they're hanging between his knees. In another lifetime—one where Rayna was alive—we might have joined the crowd of people on the waterfront. We might have played drinking games with Nik and Pippa then raced through the park with Rayna and Rose while Kaleb looked on. But everything changed a hundred years ago, and things have never quite been the same between me and my brother.

"I'll race you to the waterfront," he says suddenly, eyes glinting.

I raise an eyebrow. "Come again?"

But Xander is already halfway across the apartment. I tear after him, calling his name, but he doesn't respond as he slips through an open window and rappels down the building's face.

Cursing, I squeeze through the window and force back a wave of vertigo as I orient myself, peering down at the sidewalk thirty floors below. As a vampire, I would survive the fall, but I would rather not break every bone in my body tonight. Instead, I take a deep breath and ease my way downward, bare feet skimming the wind-worn brick. It's been so long since I've done something like this—something Rayna would do. I smile at the rush of adrenaline, at the thrilling idea of getting caught, and for a moment—one beautiful, shining moment—I can almost imagine that my best friend is scaling the wall below me.

Boom.

Boom.

Boom.

The firework finale explodes with so much force that it nearly knocks me loose. My toes slip from their ledges, my fingers straining as they suddenly take the entirety of my weight. Panic seizes me as one hand loses its grip, and I wonder what will happen if I splatter on the sidewalk in front of hundreds of human onlookers.

A strong hand seizes my arm, and I look to see Xander on the windowsill next to me, brow creased in concentration.

"I've got you, repa," he says, voice tight with concern. "Try not to fall in front of all these people, okay?"

I can't help an ugly snort. "Yeah, best to avoid that."

We carefully make our way down the building, and the moment my feet touch the ground I sprint toward the waterfront. Xander shouts after me, but I don't slow. It's a race he wanted, and it's a race he'll get.

Boom. Boom. Boom.

A chorus of too-loud bangs fills the sky, accompanied by blinding flashes that illuminate Millennium Park in a colorful strobe. I skid to a halt in a small clearing, not wanting to miss the big finale, and Xander slams into me with a muffled curse. We careen sideways onto the grass, tumbling for a few bruising seconds before landing in a heap in a manicured flower bed.

Groaning, I rise to my knees and see Xander trying to disentangle himself from an overzealous bush. I can't help but laugh.

"Shut up," Xander grumbles, yanking his arm free. A branch catches on his shirt and rips a tiny hole in the fabric. "This is your fault."

"How do you figure?"

"Because you stopped in the middle of a race."

I gesture wildly to the sky as if to say, Fireworks!

My brother only rolls his eyes before flopping onto his back, yanking me down with him. Explosions of gold, red, and blue fill the night, glittering like stars in the smoggy Chicago sky. I rest my head on Xander's arm and he idly plays with my hair, our breaths syncing, my sadness ebbing. Rayna may not be here, but I still have Nik, Pippa, Victoria, and Rose. I still have Xander, despite the fact that I want to murder him most days. And lying here, staring up at the crackling sky, I almost forget that we're vampires. We're just Aleksandr and Ksusha, two siblings with a bond that runs deeper than the blood in our veins. My brother. My home.

We lie in silence as the finale finishes, as the crowd disperses, as the night turns to early morning and then to dawn.

"I have a question," I say, rousing Xander from a light sleep.

"Hmm?"

"Those humans you brought home. Do you suppose they're still waiting for us in the kitchen?"

Xander bolts upright, looks at me with wild eyes, then bursts into laughter, the sound warm and wonderful as it skips through the dewy morning air.

FIRE SIZZLES AGAINST my face. Pain forces my eyes open and I'm blinded by sun blazing through Nik's bay window. Hissing, I throw myself from the sofa, seeking shelter in the shadows by the fireplace. The darkness is cool against my skin and the fire retreats, leaving a faint sting in its wake.

A white slip of paper on the coffee table catches my attention and I pick it up, reading the note left in Nik's elegant hand:

> *Thank you for being my rock, darahi.*
> *I'll be at Noah's. I love you.*

I crumple the note in my fist, trying not to think about last night—about Nik's heat or Rayna's scorn.

Or Xander. Damn him.

The Maserati is still sitting at the curb when I slip out the front door, a dark stain on the street's canvas. I hurry down the steps and slip into the driver's seat, fishing the keys from the center console. I guess it's *my* Maserati now.

It's early afternoon when I pull the car into our basement garage next to my rarely-used silver BMW, cutting the engine with a flourish. The immediate silence is deafening, broken only by the sound of the garage door closing with a terminal clatter.

Somewhere in this house, Xander is waiting. Brother, leader, bastard. Beta. Betrayer. My grip tightens on the steering wheel, the metal bending under the force. There have always been secrets between my brother and I, but not like this. *Never* like this.

Before last night, I thought I deserved all the vitriol Xander spewed at me. He was always the perfect sibling. The picture of control. The example I could never seem to emulate. But if he was lying about Rayna, what other life-altering secrets has he been hiding? Is his perfect facade just that: a facade? A mask? A *lie?* Do I really even know him at all, or have I only ever seen what he wanted me to see?

Groaning, I drag myself out of the car and trudge into the house. The downstairs hall is cool and dark, still in a way that suggests it hasn't been occupied in some time. In fact, the feeling lingers as I make my way through the game room and to the bottom of the stairs.

Stale, undisturbed air. A house that is *just* too quiet.

Unease slithers over my skin and I shiver, pausing halfway up the stairs to listen. The refrigerator hums softly in the kitchen, the clock ticks away in the living room, the crystals in the entry chandelier ring. But there's nothing else: not the scratch of pencils on paper, nor the soft thud of another heartbeat.

"Xander?" I whisper. "Are you here, you bastard?"

Silence. A pulse of nerves. If his absence means anything, it's that he feels too much shame to face me again so soon. It's probably for the best. If he *were* here, he would have another black eye the moment I walked through the door.

Without thinking, I pull my phone from my pocket and dial. The call goes straight to voicemail, Xander's bored greeting tinny through the earpiece.

"If it's not an emergency, I don't want to hear it."

I end the call without leaving a message, absently drumming my fingers on the railing. His phone is off, which means he doesn't want to be found. Unless . . .

Unless he isn't the one who turned it off. Unless someone already found him.

My phone clatters to the ground, making me jump. I'm not even sure how I dropped it. All I know is that I'm alone in this giant house, and there are far too many places for those silver eyes to hide.

I snatch my phone and scramble up the stairs, noticing two unread text messages. Frowning, I open the first one from Pippa.

I guess I should thank you for stopping me from doing something hot and stupid last night.

It's a good thing I did. You're a sloppy drunk, you know that?

Don't make me rescind my thanks.

I step into the foyer and am met with a blaze of afternoon light. It burns my eyes and I cringe, hurrying from the room and its clerestory windows. Only when I'm in the kitchen do I open the second text, this one from Tristan.

I have a confession to make. After Noah and I left last night, we may have lingered for a while. Did Xander really know Rayna was alive?

Even though they're nothing but words on a screen, I can practically hear the bite in Tristan's voice. In the short time I've known him, he hasn't seemed like the cynical type. But when he confronted Rayna last night, demanding answers to questions he had no business asking, I saw a spark of anger there. Of hurt. Of betrayal.

Because he knows what it's like to lose a sister. And if Alison betrayed him in the same way Rayna betrayed Nik, it would destroy him.

I ignore his question and ask one of my own.

> Are you okay?

> I asked you first.

> You didn't, actually. You asked if Xander knew about Rayna, but I am no longer acknowledging his existence, so I'm avoiding the question altogether.

> Ah. That bad, huh?

> Worse.

> I can come over later, if you'd like.

Something flutters in my chest, bringing with it a mixture of disbelief and anticipation. Somehow, after everything—even after my unhinged moment in the kitchen last night—Tristan still wants to see me. And I don't deserve it.

Before I can respond, I get another message from Rose.

> I'm assuming you have no idea where Xander is.

My hand freezes on the fridge's handle.

> No, I don't. How did you know he was missing?

I've been trying to call him all night but he hasn't answered.

I repress a shudder and yank open the fridge, grabbing a blood bag. The stopper comes out with a satisfying *pop*.

"Dammit," I mutter, taking a swig. If anyone had heard from Xander, it would be Rose. Or maybe Kaleb. Come to think of it, Kaleb is more likely to know where he is than anyone.

My screen lights up with another message from Rose.

Don't be angry with him. He was just doing what he thought was best.

I almost spit out a mouthful of B-negative. Of course Rose would side with Xander. I start typing out a reply but it's too cumbersome. Instead, I call her.

"Don't be *angry?*" I snarl as soon as she answers. "Xander—I'm sorry, Kaleb's *Beta* knew Rayna was alive the entire time. How can I *not* be mad at him? Aren't you?"

Rose is quiet for so long that I wonder if she's even there. But I can hear her shallow breathing, indicating that she's thinking very carefully about her answer. My eyes narrow, a tendril of suspicion winding through my mind.

"Don't hate me," Rose says slowly, as though trying to soften whatever blow she's about to deliver.

"Out with it, Rose."

"Fine. It's just . . . I—I knew."

A distant ringing echoes in my ears and I let out a deep, unhurried breath. Of course. Of *course.*

Rose's special little relationship with Xander has always overshadowed me. He tells her practically everything, so why not this? And then I remember something she said the other night, after Rayna returned:

You have no idea what I know.

"You weren't lying," I scoff after another swallow from my blood bag. "You *did* know Rayna was alive."

"What? *No,*" she says quickly, and a bit of the tension releases from my chest. "Not about Rayna. I swear, Xander never told me anything about that. It was just a sneaking suspicion I've had for a long time. But I did know he was Kaleb's Beta." There's a pause, and I find myself sneering. "Victoria knew too, but she was always very hands-off, as you know. She wanted nothing to do with Xander's job, so when he needed help, he called me. It wasn't often, but it was enough."

Right. It shouldn't surprise me that Victoria knew, too. Everywhere I look, I find someone else keeping secrets from me, and I'm *tired*. Tired of always being on the outside. Tired of not being trusted.

"He did always like you more than he ever liked me."

"Lottie—"

"Whatever, Rose." The blood bag is almost empty now, so I chug the dregs. It makes my throat burn. "I'm not mad at you, it's just . . . it's a lot. At least you didn't know about Rayna, right? I can take comfort in that."

"Xander doesn't hate you, Lottie. I know you're mad at him, but I believe he had his reasons for keeping all this from you."

"Oh, I'm sure he did." I can think of about a thousand excuses that Xander would offer, but they would all boil down to the fact that he doesn't trust me. That I'm too much of a mess. "But, unlike you, I'm not willing to forgive him so easily."

The words hang between us as I wait for Rose's response. She doesn't give one.

"Well, let me know if you hear from him," I say finally, retrieving a wine glass from the cabinet. "And if you don't . . . I'm going after him. We're going to need his help to find Victoria, and I'm not about to let him wallow while we work."

"Charlotte, don't—"

I hang up before she can finish.

The too-quiet house folds itself around me, every hum and tick and buzz like a scream in the silence.

As if sensing my unease, my phone vibrates in my hand. Too many texts, too many people. I may not love being by myself, but I would sure like to be left alone right now. I glance down, hoping for a message that won't make me want to throw my phone out the window, but anger grips me the moment I see the name on my screen.

> Just under six days, pet. I hope you haven't forgotten about me.

I glower at Konstantin's words and my skin prickles. *Pet.* Like he's my master.

> How could I? You are currently— actively—ruining my life.

> There's no need to be dramatic. It's your move, if you'll remember. Kaleb knows what he needs to do.

> Does he though? From where I'm standing, he's just as confused as the rest of us. Maybe you should have been a little more specific about what TRUTH you are looking for. Maybe you'd like to know that Rayna is a Scorpio? Or maybe that she has a thing for brunettes. Oh, I know! How about I tell you exactly how she felt about you? Would that TRUTH suffice?

Konstantin doesn't respond immediately and I worry that I've gone too far. The last thing I want is to get friendly with him, but I don't want to lose this line of communication, either. It may be the only method we have of speaking to him directly and I'll be damned if I screw it up.

Don't take me for a fool.

I exhale in relief, then chastise myself for being relieved to hear from Konstantin.

Whatever do you mean, darling?

You are not as incompetent as everyone seems to think you are, Charlotte.

I almost call him. Almost.

Gee, thanks. Would you like to get to the point?

Be warned, my girl: I will not amend the deal. I will not tolerate any of your little games. Kaleb will tell me the truth or your precious Victoria dies.

Fear shivers through me, ice cold and suffocating.

First, I am not your girl. Don't take ME for a fool. Second, you still haven't answered my question. What truth?

And then I hear it: a deep laugh, like a rolling ocean wave. Quiet—distant—but unmistakable.

A chill lifts the hair on my arms but I ignore it, tossing the empty blood bag into the trash. If Konstantin is watching me, then let him watch. All he's going to see is a wild-haired girl drinking her weight in alcohol and blood before passing out on the sofa like an over-zealous college student. Not much of a show, as far as he's concerned.

Besides, I'm not the one he's after. He doesn't want to hurt me. At least, I don't *think* he does, so I message him again.

Stalker.

That's quite the accusation.

If the shoe fits.

I stare at my phone for a few long minutes, pouring a glass of wine while I wait for Konstantin's reply. Out of curiosity, I open the location app on my phone to see if I can track him but, as expected, he isn't sharing his location. It was worth a try, at least.

Fifteen minutes pass. Thirty. Forty-five. Konstantin doesn't text back. I empty two wine bottles in the meantime, lost in swirling thoughts of Rayna and Tristan and Nik and Victoria. Kaleb. *Xander.*

Fury has me grinding my teeth and I chuck a bottle into the sink where it lands with an echoing *clang.* I would rather have Konstantin walk through the front door right now than have to deal with my traitor brother.

Fuming, I storm out of the kitchen, squinting at the light coming through the windows. I head for my bedroom but something catches my eye in the dining room: a small black card propped on the table, tied with a thin piece of black satin ribbon.

That was not there an hour ago.

For a moment, I don't move, uneasiness rooting me to the spot. But curiosity eventually wins out and I hurry to the table, tearing the ribbon from the crisp paper. Words are scrawled inside in shimmering silver ink.

Tell Kaleb I want the truth. Tell him I want to know the real reason why Rayna left.

And tell that insufferable brother of yours that you deserve more than the half-assed apology I witnessed last night. A betrayal of that magnitude should have him groveling at your feet.

K.

So he *was* there. I knew I felt someone watching me on Nik's balcony. Which means he saw everything and everyone at Nik's house tonight—he saw *Rayna*.

And he did absolutely nothing. What the hell is he playing at?

He was also just inside my house, slipping a note into the dining room while I drank in the kitchen, just on the other side of the wall.

Holy *shit*.

I whip my phone out again, typing another message with shaking fingers.

> Stay out of my house.

> Are you sure? You must be lonely in there, all alone. Wouldn't you like the pleasure of my company?

The words finally send my heart into overdrive and I sprint into my bedroom, locking the door behind me. Locking the window. Checking in my closet, behind the shower curtain, under my bed. When I'm sure I'm alone, I drag my comforter into the closet and shut myself in, burying myself under the weight of the blanket.

He doesn't want to hurt me, I tell myself in a desperate attempt to calm my nerves. *He won't.*

But I'm alone in this house. The two people who have always been here for me are gone—one kidnapped, the other disowned—and I don't know who else to call. Nik is unstable, Pippa is distracted, Rose is on Xander's side. Rayna is volatile. And Tristan is . . . complicated.

That only leaves one person. Surprising myself, I send a quick message before losing myself in the darkness.

I need you.

CHAPTER 17

I HEAR THE LOW RUMBLE of his Mercedes first. The engine cuts off in front of the house, and I track one set of footsteps as it makes its way up the front walk.

Three, two, one.

There's a syncopated knock on the door.

I untangle myself from my comforter, groaning in pain as I move for the first time in what feels like days. I hoped I would be able to sleep, but that was just wishful thinking. And while vampires don't technically need sleep, it sure helps. The house's silence is deafening and my mind is far too loud—I'm not even sure where one train of thought ends and another begins.

Konstantin is here.

Victoria is gone.

Rayna is alive.

Xander knew, he knew, he *knew.*

The knock sounds again. "Charlotte, darling, open the door."

"Patience is a virtue, Kaleb," I grumble, and am met with a quiet *hmph.* I scrub my hands over my face a few times to clear the grogginess from my head then slip out of my room.

Clouds have moved over the sun, turning the once-bright foyer into a hall of shadows. I shuffle in just in time to see the front door open.

Kaleb enters, letting pale gray light leak into the house before he closes the door behind him.

"Did you seriously just pick the lock?" I ask a tad too forcefully. I'd rather die than let him hear relief in my voice. Relief that he's here. That I'm not alone.

The Alpha's eyebrow quirks as if to say, *You were taking too long.* His velvet blazer is such a deep purple that it's almost black; it isn't buttoned, and a few strong creases mar what would normally be a pristine lapel. There are wrinkles in his white dress shirt as well, and his hair is a bit too stiff, like he styled it in a hurry.

"I grew impatient," he says. "A single lock is a very poor security system, as I'm sure you know."

I note the slight upward tilt of his mouth. There's something different about him—looser—and I think I smell a hint of rose petals mingling with his ever-present eucalyptus scent. His gaze is bright, his lips red, and a fading round bruise sits at the base of his throat, peeking out from behind his collar . . .

"Oh, okay," I say smugly, folding my arms. "I see why it looks like you're wearing yesterday's clothes."

Kaleb frowns, glancing down at himself. "What do you mean?"

"Tell me: was the sex as good as you remember?"

There's a brief moment of silence before mortification creeps into Kaleb's expression. He hides it quickly then smooths both hands down his shirt, re-tucking it into his waistband. I fully expect him to snap a retort, but he just chews on the insides of his nearly-flushed cheeks.

"That obvious, is it?"

"Please. I can smell her on you."

Kaleb exhales sharply then strides through the foyer without so much as a passing glance. I hurry after him, not bothering to hide my amusement. There isn't much I can say to make Kaleb squirm, but talking about his sex life has always done the trick.

"I suppose that's what I get for forgoing a shower," he grumbles.

With a grin, I say, "I haven't seen you this relaxed in a century."

"You haven't seen me at all in a century."

Kaleb stops in the living room and removes his blazer, folding it carefully before draping it over the back of a lounge chair. The curtains are drawn but muted light leaks around the edges, soaking the room in pale shadows. He sinks onto the sofa and kicks one foot onto the opposite knee, his expression cool as he retrieves a gold cigarette case from his pocket.

"What do you think you're doing?" I ask, all feelings of amusement gone. "Why are you acting like you've been invited to stay the evening?"

"Because," he says, lighting a cigarette and taking a slow drag, "I *will* be staying the evening."

I plant my hands firmly on my hips. "I'm flattered, Kaleb. Truly. But—"

"You asked me to come here." Annoyance flickers in his eyes, accompanied by the ever-present pity that brings heat to my cheeks. "Besides, I'm afraid I must insist, darling. I won't allow you to stay here alone while Alexander is absent. Not with Konstantin on the prowl."

But Konstantin was already here, I almost say. Though I doubt that would do anything but add to Kaleb's anxiety.

"And how did you know Xander was *absent*?" I say instead, grimacing through his name.

Kaleb cocks one eyebrow. "He is my Beta, Charlotte. I make it my business to know."

I get the sudden and barely-repressible urge to punch Kaleb in the throat.

He sighs, exhaling a slow stream of smoke, and I examine the tight set of his shoulders, the distance in his eyes. Looking at him now, disheveled and concerned, brings back an echo of the fondness I once felt for him. He always was the first one to leap to my rescue. There was a time when I told him everything—when there was no one else in the world I trusted more. After all, he listened to me when no one else would. I never knew my own father, but Kaleb was more of a father to me than that man ever was.

Kaleb's eyes narrow slightly, as though sensing my shift in thought. He motions to the cushion next to him and I begrudgingly oblige, stomping across the room and plopping down with a huff.

"Are you alright, darling?"

I fix my gaze on the empty fireplace. "A lot has happened recently. You're going to have to be more specific."

"Learning everything about Alexander last night . . . that can't have been easy for you." There's a touch of genuine concern in his voice and I avoid his eyes, feeling suddenly vulnerable.

"How very observant of you," I say, too emotionally numb to do anything but shrug. "I don't even know what to think right now. I know I should be just as angry with you, or *Rayna,* but Xander—" I sigh. "With Xander, it's different."

"He is your brother, and you feel that he betrayed you. Your anger is completely understandable. And, dare I say, justified."

"Damn right. And don't think I'm not mad at you, too." My mouth trips over the words as they tumble out of my mouth. "Or rather, I'm mad at you all over again. Why didn't you just tell us the truth? Why tell Xander? And why make him your *Beta?* Why did you even ask us to come here in the first place? Did you know where Rayna was? Why—"

"Slow down, Charlotte." Kaleb rests a staying hand on my shoulder. "One question at a time."

"Fine. Let's just start with last night. What happened?"

Kaleb exhales and props his cigarette in an ashtray, its tip glowing orange. "Alexander and I were discussing our options moving forward, regarding Victoria. He insisted we do whatever Konstantin wants, even going as far as to hand Rayna over to him. I, of course, disagreed. The conversation grew heated and"—he rubs at what remains of the bruise on his jaw—"the rest is history."

I can't help but smirk. "How is your face, by the way? It looks like Xander got you good."

"Yes, well," Kaleb says with a faint trace of good humor, "I had my guard down. On any other day, he wouldn't have been able to touch me."

It occurs to me that until last night, I had never seen Kaleb and Xander fight. *Really* fight. I may not know firsthand who would win, but seeing the confident look on Kaleb's face now, I believe him.

"I don't doubt it."

Kaleb regards me for a few seconds then twists in his seat, resting his arm on the back of the sofa. "Are you familiar with the process of becoming an Alpha?"

"You have to kill the previous Alpha, right?"

Kaleb nods, moonlight flashing off the emerald at his throat. "You must either kill him or usurp his power via coup or war. Most find murder to be the more savory option."

"*Nullum corpus,*" I say with a condescending I shake of my head. "Did you really break your own rule? I always knew you were a hypocrite."

"You have no idea." Kaleb almost smiles, and I *almost* think he's joking. "Though, if you'll recall, the rule only applies to vampires killing humans, not other vampires."

I consider asking him exactly how *he* became an Alpha, but there's a hint of discomfort in his expression—almost regret—so I bite my tongue.

"The vampire community here is . . . well, *volatile* is putting it lightly." A muscle feathers in Kaleb's jaw and he fusses with his shirt cuff. "When I took the seat of power, my position was challenged almost immediately. Fortunately, I have both the experience and fortitude to withstand such efforts, though it still took a few years to garner a fraction of the respect given to the previous Alpha. Henry was my Beta for a while, but it was never going to last. Some began to view him as a weakness, others, a liability. Neither of which I could afford."

I exhale, nodding slowly as the picture comes together. "That's when you called Xander."

"Yes," Kaleb says. "I needed a Beta who would exude strength, not exuberance. Since taking the position at my side, Alexander has proved himself invaluable. He has saved my life countless times. He commands respect when I cannot. Without his generosity, I would have failed a hundred times over."

A flash of anger starts low in my gut and licks its way into my chest. For decades, I've lived in my brother's shadow. He is the commander. The persecutor. The last beat of poignant silence before the asp strikes. He has beaten me down, destroyed my confidence, and convinced me that I wasn't worthy of his trust. I truly believed that he had lost any ounce of humanity he once had, but apparently, he was saving it all for Kaleb.

"That is such *bullshit.*"

Kaleb doesn't flinch at the snarl in my voice. "I beg your pardon?"

"Oh, just the fact that Xander knew how to be a decent person to everyone but his own sister." My hands knead at my sweater. One fingernail snags on the fabric and I yank it back, pulling a thread loose in the process. "He hid all of this from me for seventeen years! Not to mention the *century* he kept Rayna's secret."

Kaleb's eyes narrow reproachfully. "Based on your reaction last night, I think his decision was entirely warranted."

"He—*you* should have trusted us from the beginning!" I snap, the fire tearing from my throat in a guttural snarl. "What was the worst that could have happened? I would have been pissed for a few days, but it would have been fine. *It would have been fine.*"

"Charlotte—"

"I guess it was easy, though. Xander has kept secrets from me our entire lives. What's one more?"

Kaleb stills with blazing eyes on me, the muscles in his neck straining. The ferocity in his gaze is enough to douse the fire in me, and I shrink away by pure instinct. I'm not looking at Kaleb anymore. I'm looking at the Alpha.

"Allow me to set the record straight," he says with alarming calm, his head inclined, his lip curled back over his fangs. I fight the urge to drop my gaze. "Alexander is a brilliant Beta. He is intelligent. Even-tempered. A true force to be reckoned with. It may sound like 'bullshit' to you, Charlotte, but he has been protecting the lot of you since the moment he learned the truth." Kaleb's icy mask slips for only a moment, but it's long enough for me to see the flicker of pain in his eyes. "When I first told Alexander about Rayna, he demanded I tell you, too. Believe me, that would have been much easier. I will never forget the way you looked at me when I told you that Rayna was dead. That I—" He briefly looks away, hiding his discomfort with a small cough. "It will haunt me until the day I die.

"But that is why I had to tell Alexander. Someone needed to know, if only to prevent you—or anyone else—from unearthing the truth."

I shake my head, trying to process the string of garbage coming out of his mouth. "I don't understand, Kaleb. Why was it so important to keep me in the dark? Or *Nik?*"

"Because," he says with a long-suffering sigh, "if you knew Rayna was alive but that she had simply run away, you would have burned the world down to find her. But Konstantin is *everywhere*. He is a man possessed, following Rayna for centuries—across continents, across oceans. The only way for her to fully escape him was to die. To leave everything behind and start a new life, far away from anyone who Konstantin might use to find her.

"I guarantee that he has been watching you for longer than you know. Years, even. *Decades.* And if you had given any indication that you knew Rayna was alive, he would have used you. Broken you. Done everything in his power to get Rayna back. And then he would have ripped the heart from your chest, just because he could. Your brother understood that."

Cold seeps down the back of my neck, spreading through me in icy tendrils. *Konstantin is everywhere.*

"Well," I say numbly, balling my hands into fists, "it looks like all you did was delay the inevitable."

Kaleb's expression darkens, his mouth twisting into a snarl. "Alexander did what he had to in order to protect you for as long as he could. I apologize if he hurt your feelings, but he is a good man and a better brother than you give him credit for."

"Xander is *not* a good brother." I cross my arms in defiance, feeling less like a confident centuries-old vampire and more like an obstinate toddler. "He is controlling and manipulative and only ever sees the worst in me. When we moved here from Chicago, he didn't even ask how I felt about it. Did you know that? I just—" My voice wavers, and I blink back a wave of angry tears. "I didn't want to move. Especially knowing that *you* were here. But he didn't listen. He never does. He just treats me like a child who needs constant supervision."

"What choice does he have, Charlotte?" Kaleb says, his voice rising in pitch and volume. I startle; it isn't like him to raise his voice about *anything*. "You behave as though nothing matters. Before Rayna left, you were doing so well. Only one kill in over six years. Alexander was so *proud* of you. But now . . ." Kaleb scoffs and rakes an exasperated hand through his hair, making it stick up wildly. It gives him the air of a disgruntled cockatoo. "You let yourself believe that your actions have no consequences. You kill without a thought. You do whatever the hell you want then throw a tantrum when someone dares call you out for it."

I blink at him. I blink again. If I had known Kaleb was going to lay into me like this, I would have come prepared with an arsenal of ready-made retorts and insults. As it stands, I'm too stunned to respond at all. *Kaleb: one. Charlotte: zero.*

"If I've learned anything in the years I've known you," Kaleb continues, letting his head fall back, "it's that you hate being wrong. It is always someone else at fault: Alexander, Rayna, *me*. When are you going to start taking responsibility for yourself? You have no self-control, no confidence, and somehow you've found a way to blame Alexander for that, too."

His words pack a surprising sting and I shrink back into the sofa.

I've come to expect these types of dressing-downs from Xander—from *Nik,* even—but Kaleb is usually more tactful.

Something dark and heavy tugs me down, making my gaze drop and my shoulders sag.

"I don't blame Xander for that," I mumble, but the lie feels weak on my own lips.

"Yes, you do," Kaleb replies tersely. "You blame him because you are too proud to admit your own failings." I glance back up in time to see him rise from the sofa, snatching up his blazer. "Alexander adores you, Lottie, more than you know. All he wants is for you to be safe."

"Well, he should have considered that before he stabbed me in the back."

"He did no such thing."

"Hilarious that you truly believe that," I say, sneering up at him. "You should have told me about Rayna just so Konstantin would find me. If he killed me back then, it would have made everyone's lives easier."

Kaleb's arm slices through the air. "*Enough!*"

The word reverberates through the room, vibrating in my chest, and I can practically feel the air heat with his temper. If I sink any further into the sofa, it's going to swallow me whole.

"I have grown tired of your relentless self-pity," Kaleb snarls, his eyes veinous and dark with agitation. "Clearly, you have no idea just how incredible you are."

How the hell am I supposed to respond to that?

"I'm—I don't—" My mind searches for the words, but it comes up blank.

Kaleb strides to the fireplace and back again. "You are the only thing holding this goddamn family together. Do you really think Alexander and Nikolas would have tolerated one another for so long if it weren't for you?"

Even if I wanted to speak, I'm not sure if I could through the knot in my throat. All I can do is watch Kaleb pace through my living room while he loses his damn mind.

"Philippa is one of the most independent women I have ever known." He shakes his head, chuckling almost to himself. "And Ambrosia? I guarantee that Rose does not *need* any of us. And yet, here they remain. Why do you think that is?

"Better yet," Kaleb continues, pausing in front of me, "why do you think Rayna decided to return to us right now? She could have done so at any point in the last century. Why *now?*"

I've never seen this version of Kaleb. Sure, I've seen him angry too many times to count. But this is . . . I don't know what this is. He's crossed the threshold from frustration to desperation; every word is both a plea and a demand: *listen to me, Charlotte.*

Why *did* Rayna come back when she did? Surely, it wasn't because of some text message Kaleb sent her. But if what Kaleb is inferring is true, then she came back . . . for *me.* Because Konstantin is here. Because his presence puts me in danger.

But that's *ludicrous.* If anything, she came back here for Nik. Believing she would risk so much for me specifically is a huge leap in logic. Not to mention, extremely pretentious.

My mouth flutters open and closed a few times, but still, no words come out. Kaleb's eyes bore into me—*through* me. Uncovering answers to questions he has yet to ask.

How does he do that?

When I don't respond, Kaleb closes his eyes, exhaling his anger in one long breath.

"I'm going to get situated downstairs," he says coolly, tugging once on each shirt cuff as he fights to regain composure. "I know these past few days have been difficult for you, and I acknowledge my role in that. I don't expect you to forgive me"—his voice wavers slightly—"but I do expect you to reconsider what you think about your brother."

I scrub a tear from my cheek as he stalks away, numbness settling over me like a thick fog. *Difficult,* he says. If only it were that simple. In the past few days, I've been lied to, yelled at, beaten down. Kissed.

Stabbed. Manipulated.

Betrayed.

Difficult is putting it lightly.

"You have the power over your own life, darling." Kaleb pauses at the room's threshold, his fingers tapping a syncopated rhythm on the door frame. "No one else: not me, not Rayna, and certainly not Alexander. If you are ever going to regain that sense of power, it has to come from you. Do not forget that there is more to you than simply being a vampire." His voice is filled with conviction. "You may be cursed with immortality like the rest of us, but you are the one who decides if you will simply endure it, or if you will revel in it."

Cold fire blazes in his eyes, piercing through the anger, the shame, the guilt. Reaching into the hidden parts of me that have long-since been snuffed out. There's a spark of recognition there—reminding me that somewhere, even after all this time, the little girl from Belarus is still there. The girl who played jokes on her older brother and laughed when he returned the favor. The girl who ran wild through the grassy fields and relished in the feel of dirt under her fingernails. The girl who wore her confidence proudly, never wavering, and who knew from an early age that she was destined for something more.

The girl who knew what it meant to be human. The one who would be ashamed of the monster she had become.

Kaleb studies me for a few long moments before finally striding away, crossing the entry to disappear down the stairs. I watch him go, dumbfounded, and internally kick myself for inviting him over in the first place.

CHAPTER 18

Darkness. Inky and suffocating.

Trees surround me on all sides, towering over me like sleeping giants. Their branches shudder and creak despite the lack of wind, and a chilly layer of fog seeps between their massive trunks. It clings to me like a second skin. Misty tendrils twine around my ankles, hiding my bare feet where they leave imprints in the tepid earth.

"Hello?" The fog dampens my voice to a whisper. "Is anyone there?"

I take a step forward, then another. The darkness parts for me—a living thing. Awareness dances over my skin and I whirl around, sure there is someone behind me, but I see only an endless grove of blackened trees. My heart pounds as a familiar feeling creeps up my neck: the dread that accompanies impending disaster.

I inhale deeply and continue walking, my feet sinking into the soil; I smell sea spray and pine and freshly-turned earth. The bitter scent of berries. The metallic tang of blood.

The scene in front of me morphs into something else entirely: a brick path lined with trees, a stone sundial, and a red-haired girl with arms full of painting supplies. She lifts a phone to her ear. I don't see who calls. I'm on her in an instant, my fangs buried deep in her neck. I drain the life from her. And I enjoy it.

Alison? Alison, are you there?

"*Alison!*"

My blood runs cold. I look up from my meal to see Tristan, gold-haired and white-clad, staring down at me in horror.

"Tristan," I breathe, "I—I can explain—"

But I don't get the chance. The vision is gone, dissipating into mist as another scene takes its place.

A dark street. A lone house surrounded by trees. In the distance, lights from the Eiffel Tower glow through the pouring rain.

"You promised."

I whirl around. "Nik?"

He looks down at me with dark, unfocused eyes, and his clothes are ragged and dirty, his hair dripping. "You promised you wouldn't leave me."

Pain and guilt rocket through me, the memory of our separation like a wound reopened. I inhale to reply, but someone else speaks instead.

"Nikolas, please." It's Rayna's voice. I turn to see her staring at Nik, fire in her eyes. She's wearing the same dress she wore the day she died—the day she left: *warm brown linen cinched tight around her waist. "I didn't leave you. I was trying to protect you."*

It's like they don't know I'm here—a ghost, watching their conversation, undetected.

"You left me!" Nik cries, and launches himself at Rayna. At me.

I yelp and close my eyes, bracing for the impact, but it doesn't come.

When I open my eyes again, the twins are gone.

Then I hear a voice call my name. My real name. The voice is familiar. Heartbroken.

"Xander?" I sprint in the direction of his voice, a new scene materializing as I run. Trees again, but these are familiar. Through their towering trunks, I can see lights from the Golden Gate Bridge shining eerily through the thick fog.

I hurtle toward the rocky cliffside. The wind screams in my ears as I search the shadows, churning the ocean below me into white-capped waves.

"Ksusha," Xander says again. His voice echoes around me, filling the air, whispered on the wind. "Ksusha, I found her."

A figure swims into focus a few yards away, crouched on the ground with a girl held tightly against his chest. I dash toward him, concern mingling with relief.

He found her. He found Victoria. She's safe.

"She's okay," I breathe, touching my brother's shoulder.

"No." Xander's voice is dark. Wavering. "She's not."

Panic lances through me as Xander begins to shake, his body wracked with sobs. No, she can't be—

Victoria is draped across his lap, but the sight of her makes my stomach turn. Though her eyes are closed in what could be mistaken for peaceful sleep, there is a gaping, gruesome hole where her heart should be. Blood soaks the front of her satin party dress, seeping into the ground and staining the earth red.

Xander's sobs grow louder. More hysterical. And then I realize he isn't sobbing anymore—he's laughing.

"Oh, Charlotte," he says in a deep, accented voice. "You didn't think it would be so easy, did you?"

The figure lifts his head and grins up at me with a bloodied, fanged grin. Silver eyes flash in the darkness.

"Say nothing, little bird," Konstantin orders, touching a red finger to his lips.

And I obey.

I BOLT UPRIGHT in a cold sweat, my heart hammering against my ribs. Visions of darkness swim in my eyes and I press my palms into them, fighting a growing sense of panic. I have no idea where I am. It's dark—*too* dark—and there are plants here, *trees,* looming over me like—like—

There's a flash of something. Light? A reflection?

A shock of adrenaline throws me forward and I fall—falling, falling, falling. A tree looms ahead of me. I crash into it and it topples, landing next to me in a chorus of shattering ceramic and crunching foliage. Soil flies, covering me and the rug I'm lying on with a pungent layer of powdery dirt.

The *rug*. And suddenly, it all comes crashing back.

I'm in Xander's bedroom, where I finally fell asleep. Because Xander is missing, and Victoria is dead.

Wait . . . no she's not. *Why did I think that?* She's fine . . . isn't she?

"We have five more days," I say to myself. To the omnipresent silver eyes that I can feel watching me. "You promised. You *promised!*"

And without fully knowing why, I start to cry. A dam bursts somewhere deep inside me, letting everything out: the fear of being watched, the guilt that came from killing Alison. My brother's betrayal and, with that, a growing rage.

My eyes trace the dim lines of Xander's room: off-kilter furniture, piles of haphazard sketchbooks, and dozens of neglected house plants. His discarded clothes from the night of the party, still in a rumpled pile near the bathroom door. A half-empty bottle of scotch on his nightstand. I've never seen his bedroom this messy. By Xander's standards, it's practically in shambles. It makes me wonder just how hard all this Konstantin business has been on him.

He was so devastated when Victoria was taken, broken in a way I have never seen. I practically had to drag him upstairs. I even washed his damn hair in an attempt to comfort him. And this is how he thanks me? Disappearing right when I need him the most?

No. I don't need Xander. I *need* to drink blood. I *need* to booby-trap every entrance to our house. I *need* to figure out a way to get Victoria back without waiting for Xander's help.

My mouth twists into a snarl and I dig my fingernails into the dirty rug. I *need* him to grovel at my feet. To beg for my forgiveness. Even then, I don't know if I'll give it. If he would have just . . . told me everything . . . from the beginning . . .

My thoughts slow, then come to a grinding halt. An odd feeling of disconnect shudders through me and I hear Kaleb's words in my head: *When I first told Alexander about Rayna, he demanded I tell you, too.* He wanted Kaleb to tell me. He *demanded* it. But he also understood me well enough to know what would happen if he did. Because Kaleb was right: if I had known Rayna was alive, I would have hunted her down like the coward that she is, if only to put an end to her myself. I never would have let her abandon me like that. Abandon *Nik* like that.

Fresh tears fill my eyes. Am I really so predictable? So volatile? I want to deny it—to convince myself that I wouldn't have been so reckless—but I can't. As it turns out, I *can* be trusted to be exactly as disastrous as everyone expects.

If I weren't so unstable, maybe Kaleb would have listened to Xander that night in New York. Maybe he would have let me in on the secret, if only because Xander asked.

Somewhere, deep in a sealed-off corner of my heart, something cracks. It's the wall I built to keep Xander out—the one I thought I might finally be able to tear down. The fissure is small, barely noticeable, but it's there, straining to let him back in.

I don't know if I'll be able to forgive my brother. I don't know how I'm ever supposed to trust him again. After last night, I feel like an irreparable wedge has been driven into our relationship, forcing us apart.

But there's no one else I would rather go through this immortal Hell with. There's no one else who shares the same inside jokes or who understands my obscure movie references. No one else has been there for me at every turn, celebrating my victories and grieving my losses. Under that shadowed exterior is nothing but a lost Belarusian boy who has always done whatever it takes to protect his little sister.

Dammit.

"Charlotte, are you alright?"

My head snaps up and I see Kaleb standing in the now-open doorway, light haloing him from the hallway beyond. The top few buttons of his shirt are undone, his shoes are off, and his hair is a tousled mess, as if he ran upstairs without checking a mirror. Fear is alight in his eyes, but it's quickly replaced with concern when he sees the state of me, sprawled on the floor in a pile of dirt and the tattered remains of Xander's fiddle leaf fig.

My lip trembles. *"Kaleb."*

His shoulders soften and he crosses the room, lowering himself to the floor beside me. I resist the urge to shy away when he reaches for me, instead letting him pull me to his chest. The familiar scent of cigarette smoke, scotch, and eucalyptus washes over me. It's over-powering—not good, exactly, but not bad either.

Just like Kaleb himself. Desperately trying to maintain a sliver of humanity, but always doing what is necessary, even if it hurts everyone around him. Even if it means being ostracized and hated for a literal century. Even if it means breaking his own cardinal rule.

And yet, I find myself curling into his embrace, clutching at his shirt, finding comfort in his presence. Somehow, inexplicably, I crave this closeness. For so long, I believed I would never speak to Kaleb again, but now I feel like I'm well on my way to forgiving him.

And if I can forgive Kaleb for everything he has—and hasn't—done, there may be hope for Xander yet.

"A nightmare, was it?" Kaleb murmurs against my hair, rocking me gently as though trying to soothe a frightened child. I welcome it. I *cherish* it. Because I no longer care about what Kaleb did in the past. Sitting with him in the dark, my tears soaking into his rumpled clothes, I am safe. I am *home*.

"There, there." The sound of his voice anchors me, a guiding light in a relentless storm. It takes on a sharp edge as he adds, "Konstantin cannot hurt you as long as I'm here."

I sniff, glancing up at him. "How did you know he was in my dream?"

"Because, darling," Kaleb says, his arms tightening around me, "he has haunted mine for three hundred years."

CHAPTER 19

"So," I say to Kaleb, breaking what must have been an hour's silence, "you and Rayna seem to have picked up where you left off."

Kaleb stiffens and gently pushes me away, though I get the sense that he would rather shove me back into the pile of dirt.

"After all that, you want to talk about my love life?" A twitch of his nose. The ghost of a smile on his lips.

"Can you blame me for being curious? After decades of hearing how good you were in bed, I'm surprised Rayna didn't jump you the moment she got back." I immediately clap a hand over my mouth, offering him a sheepish smile. "She's going to kill me for saying that."

Kaleb stares at me with a carefully neutral expression for an uncomfortable amount of time. But then he says, "All in a night's work, darling," and smiles.

I gasp in mock astonishment, clutching my metaphorical pearls. "My goodness, a *smile?* I better call the Devil to see if Hell has finally frozen over."

We both break into hesitant laughter, made all the more ridiculous by the fact that Kaleb Sutton is actually *laughing.*

My phone vibrates loudly on the wood nightstand, making us jump. I glance over at the screen to see Tristan's name and groan loudly, pressing a button to silence the incessant buzz.

Kaleb raises a brow. "Is there a reason for your reaction, or am I just to assume you don't like the boy as much as you lead on?"

"Haven't you heard? The girl from Golden Gate Park—you remember?" Kaleb nods contemplatively. "That was Tristan's sister."

"Hmm." He exhales, long and even. "I did know, actually. From Alexander. Have you spoken to Tristan about it?"

The laugh that explodes from me can only be described as indecent. "Are you *kidding*? That's never going to happen."

"You do know that if you continue to spend time with him, he will find out sooner or later."

My phone buzzes again and I snatch it from its place on the nightstand.

"I'm sorry, I can't hear you. I'm on the phone."

I accept the call and press a shushing finger to Kaleb's open mouth. He snaps it closed with a good-natured glare then stands stiffly, brushing the dirt from his pants. I wait until he's well into the hallway before I say anything.

"Hello?"

There's a beat of silence before Tristan asks, "Are you okay?"

I clear my throat hoarsely, hammering my chest to clear a few hours' worth of tears. "You keep asking that. Do I really sound that bad?"

"A little." Another pause. "Are you home?"

I close my eyes and release a controlled breath. "Please don't tell me you're outside with coffee again. I really don't think you want to see me right now."

"I'm not outside with *coffee* . . ." Tristan trails off, a smile in his voice, and I brace myself. "But I am outside with all of your friends."

At that, I hear the front door burst open and Pippa's loud voice as she yells, "It's a slumber party, bitches!"

"Yeah, bitches!" Henry's laugh echoes through the foyer.

Nik groans. "I told the two of you not to say that."

"Why? It was funny." Rayna's tone is dismissive. "And I've always said that humor is the best coping mechanism."

I end the phone call and reluctantly stand, staring down at my dirt-caked clothes. I contemplate raiding Xander's closet for something clean to wear, but I'm still furious with him. The last thing I want to do is to walk around in his funeral-attire wardrobe.

Maybe I should burn all his clothes, just for the hell of it. It wouldn't accomplish anything, but it would be worth it to see the look on his face.

"I hope you're all here to actually make a plan," I say as I stride out of my disowned brother's room. "Otherwise, get out of my house."

I look down from the loft to see everyone—Nik, Rayna, Pippa, Rose, and Henry—milling about in the foyer. Tristan and Noah hover among them, and I get the sense that they're going to be fixtures in our group for the foreseeable future. At least, I hope they will. The seven of them look up at me with matching expressions of confusion.

Pippa frowns judgmentally. "What the hell happened to you?"

"Long story," I say, descending the stairs just as Kaleb ascends from the basement.

Rayna grins at him and walks straight into his embrace. He catches her with a small sigh and she wraps her arms around his neck, pressing a hard kiss to his lips.

Pippa shoves an upward-facing palm toward Rose. "Pay up."

Rose huffs in annoyance. "This proves nothing."

"It proves everything!" Pippa's attention snaps to Kaleb and Rayna. "You've totally hooked up already, haven't you?"

Kaleb regards the two of them with a look of pure exasperation. "Why must you all be so interested in my love life?" he asks, at the same time Rayna says, "Of course we have."

"Ha!" Pippa punches the air triumphantly, making a *gimme* gesture at Rose. "I win. Fifty bucks, just like you promised."

"That wasn't the only stipulation!" Rose argues. "Timing is key here, remember?"

A heated discussion ensues—something about timing and "how many times" and "where"—but my attention strays to the golden boy making his way toward me. He brightens when I meet his gaze, and his smile lights up the entire room.

I hurry down the stairs and Tristan traps me in a hug. He's so *warm*. I didn't expect this level of closeness—of *trust*—after what happened between us last night. His heart beats a steady rhythm in his chest, the scent of him bringing heat to my cheeks, my gums. It's like I can still taste his blood on my lips . . .

"Hey, Char," Tristan murmurs against my hair. "How are you doing?"

You have the power over your own life, darling.

After a slow breath to cool the fire building in me, I lean back to look up at Tristan's honey-gold eyes. Once, I would have interpreted his expression as pity. Now, I see only care.

"Do you want the easy answer or the truth?"

Tristan chuckles quietly. "The truth, please. How do you expect me to come to your rescue if you won't tell me what's really going on?"

"I wasn't aware I needed rescuing."

"You don't. But that won't stop me from trying."

I bite back a smile. "Okay, then. If you want the truth . . ." I toy with the neckline of his sweater, my fingers brushing the skin over his pulse point. He swallows, and I watch his Adam's apple bob up, then back down. My fangs prick at my gums. "Not great. After everything with Xander, I'm just—I'm really confused. And with him gone it's been—"

"What do you mean, gone?"

"He ran off last night and I haven't seen him since."

Tristan's eyes widen in alarm. "God, Char. Has anyone else heard from him? Is he okay?"

I shrug, feigning disinterest. "No idea."

"What's this about Xander?" Pippa interrupts, shouldering her way through the group. "He isn't here?"

Everyone turns their attention back to me—everyone, that is, except for Rayna. She's looking down at her phone, her brow furrowed.

"Yeah." I pull away from Tristan, but his hand lingers on the small of my back, making my stomach flutter. "After he left the party, he just . . . never came home. I've tried calling him, but his phone is off." I chuckle wryly. "I wouldn't want to talk to me, either. He's probably afraid I'm going to bite his head off." When Pippa's brow quirks, I add, "He's right, of course."

"Alexander," Kaleb cuts in, "is one reason I invited you all here this evening. There are a number of things we need to discuss."

Of course Kaleb called them. I make a mental note to chastise him for it later.

"I'll say," Nik grumbles, looking from Kaleb to Rayna. "Starting with why you involved Xander in your little betrayal mission in the first place."

Rayna rolls her eyes. "Nikolas—"

"Downstairs," Kaleb says, eyeing Noah and Tristan. Noah mumbles a hurried goodbye to Nik and moves to leave, but Kaleb adds, "All of you."

Noah and Tristan exchange a dubious glance, then Nik takes Noah's hand and whispers something in his ear. They both grin and the pure joy on Nik's face is enough to melt my heart. It's so good to see him smiling again—even when I can see the flask still tucked into his back pocket.

The group files through the foyer and down the stairs, a chorus of chattering voices filling the once-empty house. And to think, last night I thought it was too quiet in here. Now I crave the silence.

Rayna doesn't follow immediately, instead watching Tristan and me for a few seconds. There's something in her expression that seems strange—so different from the vision of her I've held onto for all these years. With every minute Rayna is back, that rose-colored memory of her cracks a bit, reminding me that while I loved her, she was far from perfect.

Reminding me that I'm still not sure if I can trust her, even though I want to.

She stalks away, her ginger hair flashing. I take a step to follow but

Tristan catches me softly by the hand.

"Char," he murmurs, "can I talk to you for a minute?"

"Sure," I say distractedly, my gaze lingering on the spot where Rayna disappeared.

Tristan ushers me through the front door then closes it gently behind us. Dusk is in full force, the sky glowing in muted shades of gold, red, and purple; the light halos Tristan and casts his face in shadow, giving him the appearance of an avenging angel. We stand in silence for a moment, letting the cool breeze wash over us like a wave, and I admire the way Tristan's green sweater hugs his chest, his shoulders, his fore-arms. It's a shame the weather has been so chilly lately. I'd much rather see those muscular arms bare.

"So," Tristan muses, rocking onto his heels, "I wanted to talk to you about—"

"Can I say something first?" I interrupt, forcing myself to stop ogling. Tristan nods, a smile playing at his lips. "About last night . . . I'm so sorry. Sometimes my fangs just get a little too excited and—"

"Hey." Tristan presses a finger to my lips. "It's okay. Really. It was—" He drops his hand with his gaze. Is that a touch of pink on his cheeks? "It was fine. I'm fine."

The air between us jumps up a few degrees. Tristan must feel it too, because he clears his throat and attempts a non-flirtatious smile. It doesn't work.

My gums prickle and I press against them with my tongue, forcing my fangs back. "So . . . what did you want to talk to me about?"

Tristan contemplates his answer for a few seconds, then his smile turns wry. "Do you want the easy answer or the truth?"

"Oh, stop," I say, swatting his arm. "You've got me on pins and needles here."

"Okay fine." Tristan drops his voice, wringing his hands. The sudden change in his demeanor sets my nerves on edge. "It might sound crazy—and hell, maybe it is—but I'm going to find Alison's killer. And I need your help."

My heart plummets into my stomach and settles there like a hunk of lead.

"The other night in Xander's car," Tristan continues, his enthusiasm growing, even as I gnaw on my bottom lip, "I said that I thought she was killed by the San Francisco Vampire. But that was before I knew that you guys were actually *real*. And if there are a lot of you out there, she could have been killed by an actual vampire. Right?"

I'm nodding along with his words, making a show of listening, but I'm lost in my own thoughts. He can't know it was me, can he? How am I supposed to help him look for Alison's killer without implicating myself? *Why is this happening right now?*

Tristan is still talking, gesturing animatedly with his hands. "I was thinking that maybe you would know something. Or that one of your friends would. Maybe Kaleb? He seems important."

I snort. "He likes to think so." When Tristan looks at me quizzically, I say, "He's the city's Alpha—a seat of power, like a mayor or something. But also not like that at all, because mayors don't usually kill people who piss them off."

Tristan's eyes widen, accompanied by a considering nod. "Hmm. I guess I shouldn't piss him off, then."

"Probably a good idea."

"As mayor of the vampires"—he smirks—"I'm sure he has connections. Maybe he would be willing to help."

It sounds like a question—a quiet, hopeful question. I sigh, hugging my elbows. If it were any other time, *maybe* I would try to "help" him. But with Konstantin on the prowl, Rayna back, and Xander and Victoria missing, I don't have the brainpower to be deceitful.

"Tristan—"

"*Please,* Char." He takes both my hands, his thumbs tracing slow circles on my wrists. "Alison was everything to me. What would you do if someone killed Xander?"

Xander. His name brings a fresh wave of anger, but underneath, a deep, gaping wound has started to fester with the first inklings of panic. I mentally remind myself that this is an instinctual feeling. It doesn't mean I actually care about him. It sure as hell doesn't mean I *forgive* him. He's been gone for barely a day and I know without a doubt that Xander can take care of himself. I'm sure he's fine.

Still, the wound festers.

"Sorry," Tristan says, frowning. "I know you're not exactly on good terms with him right now—"

"If someone hurt Xander," I say resolutely, answering his question with more force than I intend, "I would find the bastard who did it and make him regret he'd ever been born."

A slow smile splits Tristan's face, and he cups my face with a calloused hand. Warmth fills my veins when he says, "You're terrifying, you know that? Yet somehow, I can't seem to stay away from you."

I inch closer and smile when Tristan's eyes drop to my mouth.

"Maybe you should stop trying so hard and just"—I lift my face to his—"give in."

"Hey!" Pippa's voice echoes from inside. "Get in here, lovebirds!"

I cough and take a hurried step back from Tristan.

He frowns. "What?"

"Oh, just Pippa ordering us around." I motion to the door. "Come on. I guess you're part of the dysfunctional family now. Even Kaleb said you can stay, and that's a lot coming from him."

Tristan's face lights up. "Does that mean you'll do it? Since, you know, I'm 'part of the family?'"

Even though it's bound to be a disaster, I know I have to agree, if only to keep him as far from the truth as possible. Because nothing—*nothing*—will ever get me to tell him what really happened that night in the Shakespeare Garden. It's a secret I'll take to my distant, immortal grave.

"Okay, golden boy," I say. "I'll help."

"I knew I could count on you, Char."

I return the smile he flashes me, but I feel it again: the sense of impending doom. We head back inside and I try to brush away the feeling that I'm making a huge mistake.

Stupid, stupid Charlotte. What exactly are you getting yourself into?

CHAPTER 20

We've been sitting in the game room for *hours* going over everything that has happened in the past week and a half, starting with Kaleb's Halloween party and ending with the moment Rayna walked through the ballroom door. Despite Xander's absence, we've managed to fill in most of the little details, even going so far as to note exactly where he was and when.

It hasn't been an easy conversation, to say the least. Not only have I forced myself to relive every humiliating moment of my time with Konstantin, but I can feel the discomfort coming from everyone else when they recount their own experiences. Even Tristan and Noah contribute, noting the few times they met Konstantin while he claimed to be friends with Jason. Based on the huge number of holes in their memories—notably the lack of any experiences with him before last week—we come to the conclusion that they were most likely Compelled to believe Jason's friendship with "Ty."

After all this talking, I've been able to glean three things. First, that Konstantin has been here for at least six months. Based on the fact that he knows I killed Alison—made clear by his text to Tristan about the San Francisco Vampire video—I would guess eight months, maybe longer.

Second, he has endless patience. He could have put his plan into motion at any time, but he waited for the perfect moment. As Rayna once said, he is the black king. In chess, it's the white pieces who always move first, which means he was waiting for Kaleb to make the first move—though we're still not exactly sure what the move was.

And third, he is invisible. The fact that Kaleb—the Alpha, with all his spies and connections—didn't know he was here is testament to that fact. Even at my stealthiest, other vampires have always noticed me. Known what I was.

Whatever his game is, Konstantin knows what he's doing. I once thought he wanted Kaleb dead, but now I'm not so sure. Even at the party the other night, Konstantin barely lifted a finger when Kaleb attacked him. In fact, he laughed in his face.

Konstantin is king. Konstantin will not stop until he recovers what was taken, and only Kaleb can return it. The unsettling mantra the fledglings have been reciting all week plays on a loop in my head, and I've been wracking my brain trying to figure out what it means. My first instinct is that he's talking about Rayna. Who—or what—else would warrant this much psychological torture? But Kaleb didn't *take* Rayna . . . maybe Konstantin just *thinks* he did. And if that's the case, I don't know if he'll ever get the answer he's looking for.

Which would be terrible news for Victoria.

"Until we have determined exactly what truth Konstantin is demanding," Kaleb says thoughtfully, perched on the sofa's arm, "there isn't much we can do. I am not about to risk losing an eye by confronting him without a proper plan."

"That's all well and good," Nik says, "but how are we supposed to figure that out?" His flask is nearly empty now, having spent the night taking a swig every time something particularly upsetting came up. Which means he hasn't put it down once. Noah sits next to him and idly plays with his hair, the pair striking in their shared beauty. "It's not like we can just call him and ask for clarification."

I fiddle with the satin ribbon tied to Konstantin's note, which I've had hidden inside my jacket pocket for the entirety of our conversation.

I know I should have said something before now, but Konstantin's comment about Xander has me holding onto it out of pure embarrassment. The last thing I need is for everyone to think Konstantin actually cares about my feelings.

And that he saw everything that happened at the twins' birthday party.

"Why not?" Rose asks from the corner of the sectional. "Kaleb, why don't you just set up a meeting with him? You'll have to talk to him eventually anyway."

Kaleb considers her for a moment, eyes glinting, but it's Henry who speaks.

"Who's to say the smarmy git won't just kill him?" His proper London accent is particularly pronounced tonight, garnishing a grin from Pippa, who is curled into his side with her head on his shoulder. "If he has wanted Kaleb dead for this long, a one-on-one meeting would be the perfect time to do it."

"If Konstantin wanted Kaleb dead," Rayna says coldly, "he would be headless at the bottom of the ocean by now."

Henry frowns and turns his head pointedly away from Rayna.

"I—" The word catches and I clear my throat. "I have something."

Bracing myself, I slip the note from my pocket and offer it to Kaleb, but not before Rayna tries to snatch it from me. Kaleb glares at her and snatches it instead, reading the silver scrawl in a few torturous seconds. A tiny quirk of his eyebrow is all the reaction he gives, and he catches my eye in question. I shake my head subtly. *Please don't say anything.*

The room holds its breath as everyone waits for Kaleb to speak, but they're all staring at me, confusion plain on their faces. Even Tristan frowns, shifting in a way that makes our thighs brush together. There's something odd in his expression—anxiety? Or maybe just discomfort. He rests a comforting hand on my knee, squeezing it gently.

"Konstantin," Kaleb says, "wants to know the real reason Rayna left."

Nik laughs sharply. "Which one? I could list about fifty without even breaking a sweat."

"It must be something specific," Rose says. "Maybe something you've lied to him about before?" She eyes Rayna, who only shrugs.

"Like Nik said, there are endless reasons and endless lies. How am I supposed to know which one he's referencing?" With a frown of suspicion, Rayna turns to me. "I'd like to know how you got such a fancy little note, Lottie. Have the two of you been talking?"

"What? No!" The protest comes too quickly and Rayna narrows her eyes. I backtrack, focusing on the bits of truth I'm not ashamed to share. "I mean, we talked before the party, obviously. But today I—" I glance at Kaleb, who is listening intently. "I found this note on the doorstep when I got home from Nik's." There's no use telling them that Konstantin texted me. No use saying that he was *in* my house.

"You're saying he gave this to you completely unprompted?" Rayna reaches for the card again but Kaleb yanks it out of her reach, tucking it into one of his blazer's inner pockets. "It seems pretty convenient, if you ask me."

"I have something too." Tristan's interjection signals a prick of warning in the back of my mind, and I fight to keep my expression neutral.

"And the plot thickens," Pippa murmurs.

Tristan opens up his messaging app, the screen displaying a collection of increasingly angry texts sent to Konstantin, all unanswered. The most recent message, however, is one Tristan received.

"'If you think she is yours, don't be fooled,'" Tristan says, imitating the haughty cadence of Konstantin's voice. "'I have already claimed her, as Kaleb claimed Rayna. I would run away now, little human, before—'" He cuts off, voice catching. "'Before you meet the same tragic fate as your sister.'"

I gape at him, my body going rigid. Too close. Konstantin is getting *far too close* to telling Tristan the truth about Alison. About *me*. And I'm positive he's doing it on purpose—I just don't know *why*.

Noah sits up, eyes widening. "He really said that?"

"More importantly," Rayna says, "you have Konstantin's phone number?"

"Before you go asking me to text him," Tristan says through pursed lips, "I've already tried. Incessantly. He never responds."

"No offense, golden boy," Pippa says, "but why did he text *you?*"

Tristan shrugs in annoyance. "Do I look like someone who knows the answer to that question? Until a few days ago, I thought vampires were just a spooky story that people once used to explain away the Black Plague."

Henry chuckles. "He does have a point."

"What exactly is Konstantin after?" Rose asks, keeping us on topic, true to form. She looks at Rayna, Kaleb, and Nik in turn. "You three know him better than anyone, and you're clearly not telling us the whole story."

Nik and Rayna exchange a wary glance, the first sign of solidarity I've seen between them since Rayna returned. Something buzzes in the air—a nervous energy that immediately permeates the room and makes everyone squirm a bit in their seats. Even Tristan, a human with no extraordinary senses, wraps his arm around mine in an attempt to ground himself. I take a measured breath to stop myself from melting into him.

I expect Rayna to say something but she is uncharacteristically quiet. Kaleb looks at her for a few seconds before turning to Nik, who nods stiffly. With a defeated sigh, Kaleb folds his arms as if to say, *Fine, but you asked for it.*

"When it comes to Konstantin," he starts, "I will never be able to tell you everything. Having known him for nearly five hundred years"—Tristan balks at the number, but Kaleb doesn't seem to notice—"I have seen him from every angle. I have seen the good sides of him—the protector, the charmer, the lover." Rayna tenses, but makes a show of looking bored. "But I have also seen the worst of him. The man who murdered those who refused him. The man who would tear the world apart just to prove he could.

"To make a long story slightly shorter," Kaleb continues, "I had been Konstantin's right hand—a Beta figure, if you will—for most of my life. He once brought me back from a very dark place, and I felt I owed him my life. You all know how infuriatingly charismatic he can be. I followed him without a second thought. I never had reason to do otherwise.

"But then we met Rayna and Nikolas, sixteen years old and half-starving. I saw them as two children we could save. Konstantin saw them as an opportunity."

I glance at Nik and Rayna, both of whom are staring at the floor. Rayna's hand finds Nik's and she squeezes it hard, their anger forgotten, if only for a moment.

"For three years, I watched him manipulate them." Kaleb says. "Control them. Then when Rayna was Turned"—Rayna looks up at him with an indecipherable expression—"he was furious. He had planned on doing it himself, you see."

"Wait, wait, wait," I say to Rayna, scooting to the edge of my seat. Tristan reluctantly releases my arm. "Konstantin didn't Turn you?" When Rayna shakes her head, I ask, "Then who did?"

"That is not relevant," Kaleb says firmly, cutting off Rayna's reply. For once, she looks grateful for the interruption. "All that matters is that she was Turned, and it was another four years before I finally Turned Nikolas."

I glance at Nik, who now has his face buried in his hands. Noah rubs his back in slow circles as he tries—and fails—to mask his own horror. Meanwhile, I'm trying to wrap my head around the fact that *Kaleb Turned Nik*. How have I known them for two hundred years and they've never said a word about it?

Unwittingly, I wonder if they *have* spoken about it. Just not to me.

Kaleb presses his lips into a tight line. "Something changed in me during those seven years. I was finally able to see Konstantin for what he truly was: a soulless, self-centered monster. It became clear that I needed to escape, and that I must take Rayna and Nikolas with me. But in order to do that, I would first need to dismantle

Konstantin's empire."

Pippa grins. "Now we're talkin'."

Kaleb pointedly ignores her. "For seventy years, we traveled the world with a power-hungry Konstantin, slowly corrupting his followers. I showed them the truth: that despite Konstantin's promises of wealth and control, he would just as soon see them in a grave than allow them to share in his glory. Rayna eventually joined me in my efforts and by the time we left Konstantin in 1804, he had no foundation to stand on. All it took was a single blow and his entire world crumbled to the ground."

A long beat of silence follows. Rayna has moved to the floor, lying flat on her back with her fox's eyes fixed on the star-flecked ceiling.

"It was so satisfying," she muses, absentmindedly tugging on her turquoise cross, "to see the look of betrayal on that bastard's face."

"Would have been nice," Nik drawls, lowering his hands to glare at her. "Unfortunately, the two of you didn't think to involve me in your little game. I'm pretty sure you surprised me as much as you did him."

With a huff, Rayna props herself onto her elbows. "We both know you wouldn't have been able to go through with it. You're too soft. It was better to keep you in the dark than have you ruin everything."

"Too soft?" Nik growls, leaning forward. "I'll show you *soft*."

Noah squeezes his arm and Nik instantly relaxes, but he still glares murderously at his sister. So much for the twins' tentative camaraderie.

"*God,* you two," Tristan scoffs, his words laced with annoyance. "Can you stop trying to bite each other's heads off for two seconds? There are more important things going on here than"—he waves a hand in their direction—"whatever this is." They stare at him with expressions of incredulity. Tristan doesn't flinch, which only makes Rayna's stare more piercing. "You may think you know everything about *everything*, but you're all too high on your own drama to see things clearly. If you ask me, I think Konstantin blames Kaleb for Rayna leaving. Why else would he be tormenting Kaleb so much? With Rayna here, why wouldn't he just take her now and be done with it?"

Kaleb's lips purse as he considers Tristan's claim, fingers tapping against his velvet-clad bicep. I note the slight tilt of his head, the sharp glint in his eye. He glances at me, a question in his gaze: *What do you think?* I point to myself in a, *Who me?* gesture, and he nods.

"Ooh!" Pippa blurts before I can respond. "What if he thinks you literally *stole* Rayna from him? That you said something to her to convince her to go with you, even though she wanted to stay?"

"Maybe he thinks you have her hidden away," Rose says, "and that's why he has never been able to find her."

Nik scoffs. "For two hundred years? That would be a hell of a long time to keep someone prisoner."

It *would* be a stretch. Kaleb can be stealthy, yes, but even he wouldn't be able to keep something like that secret for so long, especially while moving from place to place. And I'm sure that if Rayna wanted to stay with Konstantin, Kaleb wouldn't have questioned it. He would have been supportive of whatever she chose, so long as it made her happy. Regardless of the consequences.

Everyone is still chattering, speculating about Konstantin's beliefs, but Kaleb's attention is fixed on me. I can't remember the last time he— or anyone, for that matter—asked for my opinion first. Maybe in this instance, with Xander gone, he is defaulting to the only other Novik in the room. Regardless, it's a few minutes before I find the words.

"Okay, hear me out." The chatter stops abruptly, and I instantly become the center of attention. Rayna seems particularly interested, swinging her legs around to a sitting position. "From what I know about him, Konstantin is extremely arrogant. He believes that he can do no wrong, and that he is entitled to the things he wants. It would make sense, as illogical as it seems, for him to believe that Kaleb took Rayna from him. Because in his mind, there is no way she would ever willingly *choose* to leave him."

Even as I say it, I get the sense that I'm missing something. That there's more to Konstantin's suspicions. Sure, Kaleb could have taken Rayna—either by convincing her verbally or taking her by force—but what was to stop her from running right back to Konstantin the moment she could? Rayna isn't an idiot and Konstantin knows that. So what exactly is he fishing for?

A faint smile plays on Kaleb's lips. "Exactly. And while I would *love*"—he puts a little too much emphasis on the word—"to confront Konstantin straightaway, I will not risk my life on a whim. If our goal is to have Victoria returned safely, I will need to think on the matter, and we still have five days until Konstantin's deadline."

"In the meantime," Rayna interjects, "the rest of us can work on gathering more information: where Konstantin might be hiding, who is working for him, etcetera, etcetera. Starting tonight."

Kaleb arches a brow in silent question and she smirks.

"I heard a bit of chatter on the police radio," she says nonchalantly, examining her nails. "Something about an elevated level of 'suspicious activity.' I think we should check it out."

Nik's eyes narrow. "And where exactly is this 'suspicious activity?'"

"Chinatown," Rayna says, her grin a little too bright, her eyes too sharp.

I know that look. She's *lying*.

Kaleb regards her for a few seconds, then says, "Very well. If you truly think it might be a lead, then by all means, investigate it."

"Perfect. You're coming with me, right, moon girl?" Rayna looks at me and I nod hesitantly, unable to refuse while trapped in the fox's gaze.

"I'm in," Pippa says, much to Kaleb's chagrin.

"Me too!" chimes Rose.

"Be careful," Kaleb adds, eying Rayna and Pippa as they share a conspiratorial glance. "If you find yourselves in any danger at all, you leave. Understood?"

We nod solemnly, but with Rayna in charge, I suspect we'll be running straight *toward* danger, not away from it.

"Nikolas?" Kaleb asks. Nik just stares at him. "May I speak with you?"

Nik blinks, clearly taken aback by a request from the man who was, until a few days ago, his mortal enemy.

"I—I guess so."

"Good. Let's get to it, then." Kaleb stands and buttons his blazer. "After the girls leave," he says to Tristan and Noah, "the two of you are welcome to stay. It may be safest for you here."

Without another word, he strides out of the room, touching my shoulder gently as he passes. Nik exhales slowly before rising to his feet. He follows Kaleb with visible trepidation, leaving the rest of us in an exhausted, sudden silence. It's Tristan who speaks first.

"I guess the meeting's over," he says with a decisive clap of his hands. "I think I'll take Kaleb up on that offer and make myself at home. Who needs a drink?"

I smile at him as six hands shoot into the air.

CHAPTER 21

While Tristan runs off to the wine cellar, Rayna slips upstairs. The sound of soft footsteps floats down from the loft and she hurries to the second floor just in time to see Kaleb and Nik disappear behind a swinging bookcase. It closes with a decisive *click*.

Careful to make her own footsteps silent, she creeps to the bookcase and closes her eyes, focusing on the hushed sound of voices in the mystery room beyond.

"How are you doing?" Kaleb's voice is low.

"I'm sorry?"

"We haven't had a chance to speak alone since—" He clears his throat. "Since the fiasco the other night. I wanted to make sure that you were alright."

Nik laughs once, loudly and without humor. "How sweet of you. Not that you deserve an answer, but it *has* been a hellish few days, dredging up all sorts of past trauma. Did you know that you can still have panic attacks about something that happened over two hundred years ago? I didn't, but I sure do now."

Rayna's chest tightens at the dull anger in his voice. The hopelessness. She would have given anything to prevent Nik from facing Konstantin again. In fact, she gave up *everything*: her family, her home, her life. Unfortunately, that all amounted to nothing. A hundred and twenty-one years of hiding and now she's right back where she started.

"Has he spoken to you at all?" Kaleb asks carefully. "Any calls? Notes?"

"From Kostya?" Nik replies, voice strained. "No. Nothing."

"Me neither."

Rayna hears glass clinking, followed by the sound of liquid being poured. She'd like to add that Konstantin hasn't reached out to her either, but that isn't surprising. If he hasn't been able to track her down thus far, she doubts he would suddenly have her phone number.

Nik exhales, long and slow. There's a quiet sip and a loud swallow. "But he's leaving notes for Charlotte and texting Tristan, of all people."

Someone—Kaleb, most likely—drums his fingers on his glass.

"Strange, isn't it?"

Nik takes another drink. "What do either of them have to do with this? Why would he even be talking to them in the first place?"

Yes, why? It seems odd that Konstantin, who hadn't officially met Charlotte until a week and a half ago, would focus so much attention on her. As for Tristan, Rayna doesn't even know what the hell he's doing here.

"Honestly?" Kaleb clicks open a lighter. "I can't be sure. There must be something we're not seeing—something significant that connects Charlotte to Konstantin."

"Did she do something to offend him?" Nik does nothing to hide the worry in his voice. "Whatever it is, I don't want her mixed up in all of this. She's too important. I'm afraid Konstantin wants to hurt her."

"On the contrary, Nikolas," Kaleb muses, and there's an audible spark when his lighter ignites. His voice drops when he says, "I think he is quite taken with her."

Rayna considers that for a moment. Maybe there's no real connection between Kostya and Lottie at all. Maybe he just wants to lure her into his bed.

The thought makes Rayna squirm. That is just like him, lusting after one of her friends while he continues to claim her as his "one true love." And it wouldn't be the first time. He was always such a—

"Cheating bastard," Rayna grumbles, and the men's conversation halts.

There's a sigh followed by a few sharp footsteps, then a glowering Kaleb swings the bookcase open, a freshly-lit cigarette between his fingers. Even while wearing an expression of pure annoyance, he manages to radiate power; she can see it in the perfect set of his shoulders and the sharp cut of his jaw. Even in the way he wears the ever-present emerald at his throat—always on display, always a warning. Rayna forces back the fluttering in her stomach and smiles coyly before planting a kiss on Kaleb's parted lips. He inhales sharply—in surprise or excitement, it's hard to tell—and she uses the momentary distraction to slide her hand over his chest, quickly slipping it into his blazer. Her fingers brush a sharp corner of paper and she draws it out, twirling away before Kaleb realizes what she's doing. With another sweet smile, she surreptitiously tucks the card into her own pocket, warming at the taste of smoke on her lips.

"Please, darling," Kaleb grumbles as the door closes, drawing a hand over his mouth. "Do come in."

Rayna finds herself in a dim and airy office, though it seems rarely used. The walls are lined with walnut bookshelves but they're half-empty, and the marble fireplace is conspicuously free of soot. At least the furniture looks comfortable.

Nik swirls the drink in his glass, rolling his eyes away from Rayna. "Of course you were eavesdropping."

"What did you expect?" Rayna plops into a lounge chair in front of the cold fireplace, throwing her legs over the arm. She shoots a glare at her brother. Her *brother.* God, it feels good to be in the same room again. "Besides, it's not like you were going to invite me to this super secret meeting. If I didn't eavesdrop, how else would I be able to find out what's going on?"

"Here's a crazy idea: you could *ask.*"

"I doubt you would have told me about your panic attacks."

Nik's nostrils flare. "That was not for you to hear."

"Oh yeah?" Rayna's words sharpen and she can feel her old belligerence surfacing. She knows she shouldn't argue with him but she can't help it. Nik has always known how to drive her absolutely *crazy*. "Did you ever stop to think that maybe I *wanted* to hear about it? I've been having them too, you know—"

"*Enough,*" Kaleb snaps, though his confidence is wavering, worry dancing in his eyes. He sinks into a chair next to Rayna's and Nik follows suit more slowly, watching them with mild trepidation. "The two of you need to get over yourselves. Konstantin's return is what we have been dreading for two hundred years. We cannot afford to be divided. Even when"—Kaleb narrows his eyes at Rayna—"we blatantly ignore one another's instructions."

Rayna responds with an irritated huff. Of *course* she ignored Kaleb when he said to stay away. Nik was in danger—she wasn't about to leave him to his own devices. Though, in hindsight, maybe she shouldn't have come. It's not like her brother is happy to see her. She turns a sour expression his way.

"Or when we don't thank our sister for throwing us a birthday party."

Nik doesn't flinch. "Or when we lie about *dying.*"

Chilly silence falls over the room, the three of them sharing looks of accusation and uncertainty. There's something comforting about it, though. Familiar.

Rayna can't help but grin. "This is going to be difficult, isn't it?"

Kaleb's eyes spark with a touch of old mischief, but Nik's expression remains flat.

"Since you're here, you might as well make yourself useful," he says, and Rayna swallows a retort. "What does Konstantin want from you? He has to know the reason you left. It must be more than that." Frowning, he stares down into his drink. "Maybe it has something to do with Belarus. Did something happen that night that could have given him the wrong idea?"

Belarus. Rayna can still see the firelight reflected in Konstantin's eyes, the glint of the emerald at his throat, the twist of his cutting smile. She almost felt bad for him after what they did. Almost.

"I don't think so," Rayna says, and Kaleb shakes his head.

"Then," Nik continues, turning to Kaleb, "what could he possibly think you did to 'take' Rayna from him? He should know better. Rayna never does anything she doesn't want to do."

"Damn right," Rayna says, raising her glass.

Silence falls again as they all consider Nik's question—one Rayna has already been turning over in her mind. A few centuries ago, understanding Konstantin's intentions would have been as easy as opening a book, but now she's out of practice. Konstantin is different. *Rayna* is different. What she wouldn't give to see him in person—to look into those dead eyes and unravel his twisted mind.

To see what kind of monster they created that autumn night in Belarus.

Rayna watches Kaleb's eyes spark with intelligence as he examines whatever details he has spinning around in his head. It's refreshing to see him shed the Alpha persona, if only for a few minutes, and relax into their old comfortable routine: Nik asking questions, Rayna testing theories, and Kaleb keeping the two of them from throwing punches. There was once a time when they had fun together—when they smiled and laughed and celebrated little victories—but time and distance have stolen that kinship away.

"Listen." Kaleb leans forward, resting his elbows on his knees. He casts a furtive glance over his shoulder, as though someone might be listening; Rayna can hear the others in the basement discussing something juvenile, unlikely to be paying much attention to the hushed voices upstairs. Kaleb continues, his tone taking on a sense of urgency. "We are not the only ones looking for answers. The others—the Noviks, especially—will all be asking questions, picking our brains for information in an attempt to learn more about our history with Konstantin. But they cannot know the truth about what we did in Belarus. We are the only ones who know exactly what happened that night and we are going to keep it that way. Agreed?"

Rayna swivels in her chair, planting her feet firmly on the floor. "I've kept the secret for two hundred and fourteen years. I don't plan on spilling it now."

Nik looks from Rayna to Kaleb, his eyes wary but resolute. Rayna wonders how he feels about that night; he wasn't directly involved, but he saw the aftermath. He knows what she and Kaleb did. At the time, he seemed happy—vindicated, even. But as the years went by, she could see a small kernel of guilt wedge its way into his heart, despite the fact that Konstantin deserved every horrible thing that happened to him.

Rayna hasn't seen Kostya since that night. She hasn't seen the long-term effects of the injury, physical or mental. She doesn't know what he'll do when he sees her again.

A breath of fear shivers over her skin.

Nik inhales deeply, then releases the breath as he sets his empty glass on a side table. Jaw set, he holds both hands out in front of him.

"To the grave?"

Kaleb and Rayna share a glance before they each take one of Nik's hands, then Kaleb's free hand finds hers. It's cool to the touch but soft. Pliant. She squeezes it in solidarity, nodding as they answer in unison.

"To the grave."

They speak for only a few more minutes before Rayna excuses herself, mumbling something about needing to speak with Charlotte. In reality, she creeps out of the office and passes silently through the loft, shutting herself into a large fragrant bedroom. She grimaces at the piles of fluffy pink pillows on the bed, choosing to sit in a velvet desk chair instead. The desk is tidy, with only a few gold stationery items and a framed photo of Xander with his arms around a beautiful Chinese woman who Rayna can only assume is Victoria. The woman blushes as Xander presses a kiss to her cheek, and she flashes a bright, delighted grin.

A touch of sadness prickles under Rayna's skin, then she shudders when she realizes the feeling is directed at Xander. She refuses to feel sorry for him.

Ignoring the emotion, she pulls the small black notecard from her pocket, smoothing her fingers over the delicate satin ribbon. It's simple but elegant, and when she opens it, the sight of Konstantin's familiar cursive sets her heart racing. He was never one to mince words, and this note is no exception.

It seems Konstantin isn't as clueless as she originally thought.

Rayna reads the note three times, committing it to memory. She leans back in her chair, re-tying the thin ribbon, and smirks as a few more puzzle pieces slide into place.

CHAPTER 22

AFTER A FEW ROUNDS OF drinks, tongues start to loosen and I'm getting so *tired* of hearing Rayna's voice. She has spent the better part of twenty minutes describing Santa Fe—where she has been living for the past few years—in vivid detail, from the dusty desert roads to the fiery sunsets. She has also mentioned someone named Harper more than once, but hasn't provided any information about her. I assume it's a friend of hers. The thought sends an unexpected pang of jealousy through me. I frown, chastising myself. I can't expect her to have lived the last hundred years without making *friends*.

"Harper is always telling me I'm too cautious." Rayna scowls and throws back yet another glass of bourbon. "'Live a little,' she says." Rayna's impression of Harper carries a heavy Southern accent and I choke back a laugh. She is *terrible* at it. "But she doesn't *get it*, does she? It's not like that ancient psychopath is after *her.*"

"Sociopath," Noah says, then recoils a bit when Rayna shoots him a withering look. He quickly recovers, shaking out his shoulders. "Sorry, it's just . . . based on what I've heard about him, Konstantin is impulsive, charming, manipulative, controlling . . . textbook sociopathic traits."

When Rayna's glare doesn't soften, Tristan jumps in. "Noah is studying psychology," he offers by way of explanation. He stopped drinking after a few glasses of whiskey, but there's still a faint flush to his cheeks and when he speaks, his consonants are soft. "Finals are in a few weeks."

Noah's eyes widen at that and he checks his phone before leaping to his feet. He mumbles a curse under his breath and darts out of the room.

"What was that all about?" Pippa asks, waving after him with a bottle of vodka.

Tristan chuckles. "Homework."

Despite the smile on his face, there's an edge to his words. The first time I met Noah, we were with Tristan and their other friends at Olivia's house. Tristan mentioned that he wouldn't be going back to school in the spring, and Noah's face fell when he asked, "What about psychology?" They must have been studying it together.

"You've got to be kidding," Rayna says with an exaggerated amount of judgment. "He's been unwittingly dragged into the world's oldest revenge plot and he's stuck in a house full of vampires. You're telling me he's worried about *school?*"

Rose levels her with a challenging gaze. "Why shouldn't he be? I've got finals too, and I sure as hell don't intend to miss them."

Pippa gawks at her. "You're in school *again?* What is this, your twelfth degree?"

"Fourteenth," Rose says coolly, but there's a smug glint in her eyes. "I'm majoring in forensics this time."

While Rayna and Pippa grill Rose about her fourteen degrees, I stand and take Tristan's hand, pulling him to his feet. He follows silently as I lead him up to the foyer, up the curving staircase, and finally close us in Xander's room. It's pitch black as always, and I flip a lamp on for Tristan's benefit. He doesn't say a word the whole time, but grins slyly when he sees the huge bed with its plush white comforter.

"If you wanted to take me to your bedroom, you could have just asked."

I smack his arm, but I can't help the flush that rises to my cheeks.

"Shut up," I say, and Tristan laughs, too. He's a bit tipsy, his smiles coming easily, and it somehow makes him even more endearing. "Besides, this isn't my bedroom. It's Xander's."

He sobers instantly, examining the messy plant-lined room with a frown. There's still a pile of dirt on the rug from the fiddle-leaf fig, which is now in a mangled heap next to the bed.

"That sure kills the mood."

While I would love to indulge his teasing, there are more important things to talk about. I chose Xander's room for this conversation because it's furthest from anyone else in the house, minimizing the likelihood that we'll be overheard. Still, I drop my voice to a low whisper, motioning for Tristan to do the same.

"Why did you jump in back there?" I ask, practically mouthing the words. "When they were asking me about the note? You didn't have to say anything."

Tristan's expression turns conspiratorial, and he leans in to whisper, "Because I could tell you were freaking out a little bit."

I scoff. "I was not—"

He touches a finger to my lips. "Yes you were. And I could tell where Rayna was going with her interrogation." Lips pursing, he says, "I stepped in because I knew how it would look if everyone found out you were still talking to him."

There's no question in his words, but I can hear it in the suggestive tone of his voice: *Are you?*

I nod. "We've been texting a little."

Shame has me dropping my gaze, suddenly worried about how this will look to Tristan. Not three days ago I danced with Konstantin while Tristan looked on, unable to hide his jealousy. There was a moment on the dance floor when I felt drawn to Konstantin; I thought that maybe—just maybe—I might grow to like him. *Really* like him. It isn't hard to imagine how easily Rayna was swayed by his charm and good looks; I was enthralled from the moment I first saw his face.

Tristan nods, his expression unreadable. "Good."

I frown, wondering if I heard him right. *"Good?"*

"Yes," he says simply. "Because Konstantin knows who killed Alison, and I need you to ask him who it was."

I fight to keep my jaw off the floor. Of all the reasons Tristan could have given, this never even crossed my mind. Anxiety jump-starts my heart, my nerves prickling, but I school my features into mild annoyance.

"You want me to casually text Konstantin and ask him who killed Alison?" Just the idea summons a pulse of adrenaline. "And you think he'll actually tell me?"

"I mean . . ." Tristan scrubs at the back of his neck. "It couldn't hurt, right? The worst he could say is no."

I open my mouth. Close it. There is no way I'm going to call Konstantin and ask him to reveal my deepest, darkest secret.

"I'm not sure that's a good idea," I say, fighting the tremor in my voice. "Even if he did answer, how would we know he was telling the truth? He could just be messing with you."

Tristan considers that for a few seconds, then shakes his head. "Why would he do that? I'm nothing to him. Unless you're referring to his obsession with *you*, in which case, I'm enemy number one."

"He's not obsessed with me," I say a little too defensively. "He's just . . ." *What is he, Charlotte?* "He's incorrigible. I think he sees me as an easy target."

Tristan scoffs. "Char, since the moment I met you, you have been playing the world's most competitive game of hard-to-get. Nothing about you is easy."

We both chuckle at that, but it quickly falls flat.

"We already know that he has been here since before Alison died," Tristan says, back on track. "And if he's as observant as he seems, he has probably been paying attention to every vampire in the city, trying to find a way to exploit Kaleb's weaknesses. Right?"

After a beat, I offer a hesitant nod. "You're pretty astute for a human."

"Which means," he continues a little too loudly. I shush him and he nods, pressing closer. Our breath mingles. My skin pebbles. "Which means he probably knows about everyone who was killed by a vampire." Tristan pauses, brow furrowed in concentration. "I know he's the one who texted me about Alison and the San Francisco Vampire the night I—when I saw you as a vampire for the first time." He cringes a little, and so do I. "There has to be a reason. Why would he do that unless he eventually planned on telling me?"

If only he knew. As far as I'm concerned, Konstantin texting Tristan is a threat. I'm not stupid enough to believe otherwise.

"I don't know, Tristan. He does have a long history of torturing people. Maybe playing with human emotions really gets him off."

I work to keep my voice light, but my unease is growing by the second. My mind is screaming, my heart thudding at a rapid uneven rhythm. I have to stop this before it goes too far.

Tristan. Cannot. Know.

"Hey, I saved you back there," he says, and a bit of clarity returns to his eyes. "The least you could do is send a text."

He smiles, eyes crinkling at the corners, and I know he does it to soften his words. To make them less of a demand. But I can hear the sincerity in his voice. The desperation that mirrors my own.

How am I supposed to say no to this? After all, it's a simple request. If I had nothing to hide, I would have texted Konstantin already. But he's unpredictable. Cruel. I have no way of knowing if he'll play along with any attempts to steer him away from the truth or if he'll tell Tristan just for the hell of it.

An unwelcome idea creeps into my head and I immediately hate myself for thinking it: if Konstantin *did* tell the truth, I could just Compel Tristan to forget. He would never know the difference. For that matter, I could Compel him now. Convince him that Konstantin doesn't know anything and we shouldn't text him.

But even as I consider it, I know that if Tristan ever finds out what happened to Alison, I'll never Compel him. I once asked him to trust me, and he did. I can't break that trust now. He deserves better than that. He deserves the truth.

Just not right now. I'm not ready to lose him yet.

"Please, Char."

I squeeze my eyes shut, grimacing as I whisper a quiet, "Okay. But don't be mad if he doesn't reply."

Tristan nods excitedly, then peers over my shoulder as I pull out my phone and send Konstantin a text—one that might end everything, right here, right now. I choose my words carefully, hoping to prompt a response that is anything but the truth.

> Tristan wants to know who killed his sister.

I tap send. My breath stills as my whole body tenses, my lungs turning to concrete in my chest. Tristan's pulse is racing but I can barely hear it over the dull pounding in my own ears. We stare at the screen for a minute. Then another. Three dots appear and I nearly throw my phone across the room in wild panic, but then they vanish. They appear and disappear two more times before they stop altogether.

"We don't have to sit here staring at my phone," I say with a breathy smile, sure even Tristan can hear my heart slamming against my ribs. "He's probably just going to—"

My phone vibrates and I nearly leap out of my skin. Konstantin is *calling* me. I stare at his name as the phone vibrates again, then again.

"Answer it," Tristan hisses.

I don't.

"Answer it," he says again, more urgently this time, and grabs at my phone. "Or I will."

I snatch it away and slide my thumb across the screen, the motion like the swipe of an assassin's blade. Tristan angles his head close as I lift the phone to my ear and say a quiet, "Hello?"

"Hello, love."

My breath leaves me in a rush and my once-racing heart turns to solid ice. The last time I heard Konstantin's voice, he was using Victoria as a shield, holding her there with a dagger pressed to her chest. While she cried in fear, he did nothing but laugh. Like it was all just a joke to him. A game.

And just like that, the ice in my chest melts. Fire takes its place, hot and ruthless and all-consuming. I inhale to snap at him, but Tristan beats me to it.

"You son a bitch," he hisses, and his jaw tenses as he attempts to stay quiet. I glance up at him, surprised by the vitriol in his expression. There's no sign of tipsiness now, only a quiet fury as his eyes meet mine. "What are you doing, tormenting Charlotte like this?"

"Temper, temper, little human." There's a smile in Konstantin's voice. "Is that any way to talk to your elder?"

"Don't patronize me," Tristan snaps, and I shush him when his pitch rises. "Just tell me what I want to know."

"What makes you think you can simply demand information from me? Who am I, your idiot friend? Oh, wait. I killed him, didn't I?"

Panic seizes me and I clap a hand over Tristan's mouth before he can shout a response, the force of it jolting him backward. He bumps into the wall and I hold him there, his breath hot on my palm, and light from the table lamp glints in his eyes, turning them electric.

Let me do the talking, I mouth, and Tristan offers a tight nod. His chest heaves with unspoken rage.

"The boy was quite forthcoming," Konstantin continues, "when it came to sharing details about you and your darling sister."

"Shut up," I snarl, clamping down on another surge of anger from Tristan. "You called *us,* remember? Now tell us"—I take a beat, searching for the perfect words—"do you know who killed Alison?"

Konstantin is silent for a few agonizing seconds. Tristan's heart is beating sporadically, but he doesn't move from where I have him trapped. His hands are balled into fists at his sides, his knuckles white.

Finally, Konstantin says a simple, "Yes."

And I can hear it, then: the slight stretch of the vowel, the downward cadence in his tone. All the implications of that one word.

Yes, Charlotte. I know it was you.

Tristan mumbles something against my hand and I remove it, poised to shut him up again.

"How?" he asks, his voice both furious and eager. "You sent me those texts, didn't you? How do you know?"

Konstantin chuckles, a low, ominous sound. "Because I was there, of course."

Oh, hell. This conversation is getting worse by the second. Not only does he know I killed Alison, but he actually saw me do it. My stomach heaves but I swallow it down, jaw trembling. Lungs aching. A spark of memory—a glimpse of red, I thought. Or silver. A flash of watching eyes in the dark.

While I'm having a miniature crisis, Tristan's eyes turn murderous.

"It was *you*," he almost snarls. "You—"

"No," Konstantin says, his tone leaving no room for argument. "I may be a killer, boy, but I'm not careless. I would never leave such a mess."

I can't find it in me to be offended.

"Then who was it?" Tristan asks, sounding desperate now. Pleading. Begging. "Tell me who it was!"

Silence. The soft rush of Konstantin's breath. Tristan's erratic heart. My own thoughts, going quiet as the reality of the situation sets in.

This is it. Konstantin is going to tell him. I've barely had ten days with Tristan and now it's all over. How will he react? Will he tell Noah? The police? Will Kaleb have to work his connections to erase yet another disastrous Charlotte story from the media?

I let my eyes trace the shape of Tristan's face: the straight line of his nose, the welcome curves of his golden eyes, the angle of his jaw, the white scar on his cheek that creates a permanent dimple. And his freckles, smattering his cheeks and nose like sun-kissed constellations.

Emotion wells in my eyes, my lip trembling.

I don't want to lose him.

"No, I don't think I will," Konstantin muses, and it takes me a moment to understand. *No. He said no.* He's not going to tell him. Before I have a chance to be relieved, he adds, "Not yet, anyway."

I can practically see the wicked quirk of his mouth when the line goes dead.

"No!" Tristan cries, and I don't bother covering his mouth this time. "Is he serious?"

With a few sharp curses, he grabs my phone and calls Konstantin back. It goes straight to voicemail one, two, three times.

"*Shit,*" Tristan groans, sinking onto the edge of Xander's bed.

I can only stare at him, numb, knowing he shouldn't worry; something tells me he'll find out sooner rather than later. I don't know what Konstantin's game is, but I now know one thing with absolute surety: it isn't a matter of *if* Konstantin tells Tristan the truth about Alison's death, but *when*.

CHAPTER 23

Things are not going according to plan.

In fact, one might argue that they are going much, *much* better.

Konstantin watches from a shadowed crag as the tall, dark figure makes his way over the sea-slicked rocks. After receiving a very cryptic text message from the man with the promise of information about Rayna, Konstantin immediately set a meeting. In reality, he knows his question will not be answered tonight, but he couldn't help himself. He will always jump at the chance to make someone suffer.

The man draws closer and Konstantin grimaces. He wishes it were Kaleb approaching, but the little Alpha is probably hiding away like the back-stabbing coward he is. It shouldn't surprise Konstantin that one of Kaleb's mongrel family has come to negotiate on his behalf. They have proven time and time again that they fancy themselves above the rules. If only they would listen, maybe they wouldn't have found themselves in such a predicament in the first place.

Then again, Konstantin isn't complaining. He does love watching them squirm.

The ocean slams against the rocky cliffside, spraying water and salty foam into the air. Konstantin slithers up from his perch, pulling himself onto the walkway surrounding the weather-worn lighthouse. Wind whips off the open ocean and buffets his hair relentlessly, but no matter. He has no one to impress tonight.

The shadow is still inching toward him, using the deafening roar of the waves to mask his movements. Clever man. Konstantin watches as he creeps up to the lighthouse, pressing an ear to the door.

Konstantin chuckles, slow and deep. "Hello, Xander."

Kaleb's Beta staggers backward, his back colliding with a metal railing. The poor thing looks terrible, with dark circles under his eyes and the remnants of injuries on his lip and brow. It brings a smile to Konstantin's face.

Xander regards him warily, banishing his surprise in an instant. "You came."

"Of course I did," Konstantin says, folding his arms. "I am, at my core, a man of my word."

There's something wild about Xander tonight: his usual smug air is gone, replaced with a touch of panic. Of *fear*. After spending a week under his thumb, letting the man order him around while he pretended to be the fledgling, Ty, Konstantin had begun to think that Xander was incapable of such feelings. But the Beta's anxiety is palpable as he tugs hard at the hem of his rain-soaked sweater, balling it into his fists.

"I have information," he says, a slight tremor in his voice, "about Rayna." He pauses, as if waiting for a response, but Konstantin waves him on. "She's—Rayna is alive. And she's here. In San Francisco."

Konstantin swallows a laugh, schooling his expression into calm interest. "Oh?"

"She showed up the other night after"—he pauses, jaw clenching—"after the party."

"Interesting," Konstantin muses, walking a slow circle around Xander. A wolf circling its prey. "She's in the city, you say? Where exactly?"

"Right now?" Xander frowns, searching for the answer. "She's been staying with Nik, I think. Or Kaleb. I don't know."

"Very interesting." Konstantin considers the information for a few moments, continuing his slow walk. Tightening the circle. He's barely an arm's length from Xander now, and he can feel the Beta's green eyes tracking him. "Though I am surprised at your lack of familial loyalty."

Xander snarls. "Rayna is *not* my family. She can rot in Hell."

That stops Konstantin in his tracks. He takes a deep breath as he fights the twitch in his shoulder, the stiffness that creeps down his arm, the pain that shoots up his neck.

"I suggest," he says with lethal calm, "you refrain from saying such things in the future."

"Or what? You'll kidnap my fiancée?"

The two men stare at each other while lightning flashes overhead, and Konstantin is struck with—dare he say it—a touch of *respect*.

"You have quite the mouth on you. If you weren't actively working against me, then I might find you entertaining. Valuable, even."

"I'm *not* working against you," Xander says, narrowing his eyes. "You wanted the truth about Rayna, and now you have it. Now it's your turn. Where is Victoria?"

Konstantin had expected this.

"While I do appreciate your effort," he says, "I've known Rayna was alive for quite some time. Would you believe it if I said I saw her with my own eyes just last night?"

Xander rears back slightly, bewildered. "What do you mean? What—when did you see her?"

"Ridiculous, wasn't it? That she decided to throw a birthday party, of all things. Charlotte told her it was a bad idea and it lived up to that warning rather magnificently."

Horror sparks in Xander's eyes. "You were there?"

"Just observing." Konstantin eases closer to Xander, grabbing his chin. He has to look up at the Beta, but the expression on Xander's face is one of complete submission. He doesn't fight when Konstantin rotates his face one way, then the next, eyeing the bruise at his temple.

"If you ask me," Konstantin says, tightening his grip, "you owe Charlotte an apology. I can only imagine how it must feel to be betrayed so completely by your own brother."

Even though he says it casually—*mockingly*—Konstantin can't help the surge of anger in his chest. He knows *exactly* what such a betrayal feels like. Though he and Kaleb weren't related by blood, they were brothers in every way that mattered—that is, until Kaleb stabbed him in the back.

His shoulder ticks.

"If you already knew Rayna was alive," Xander says, muscles tensing, "then why are you here? What else could you possibly want to know?"

Konstantin releases him with a condescending scoff. "Only Kaleb can answer that."

The fight visibly drains from Xander and he sags, his expression a mixture of exasperation and desperation.

"Please," he says, eyes shining. "Let her go. I'll give you anything you want."

"Hmm." Konstantin taps his chin in mock consideration. "Tempting, but"—he shrugs—"no. You know the terms of our arrangement. Kaleb tells me the truth about what he did to Rayna, and your Victoria goes free."

"*Our* arrangement?" Xander snaps, pitch rising in hysteria. "I did not agree to this!"

"Unfortunately for you, that doesn't matter."

Xander growls deep in his chest, an animalistic sound that cuts through the ocean's din. "Give her to me."

A wave crashes over the rocks, splattering Konstantin with icy water. He doesn't flinch.

"No."

Xander lunges at him, but Konstantin dodges the attack with an artful sidestep. He whirls around and lands a blow to the other man's head, hard enough to knock him down. His knees crack against the pavement and he releases a cry of pain.

Konstantin clamps a hand around Xander's throat, forcing his head back. Panic blazes in the man's eyes as he claws at the hand holding him, but Konstantin only smiles. He leans down to whisper in Xander's ear, his voice low and full of menace.

"How does it feel to fail so spectacularly?"

Xander snarls and surges upward, but Konstantin is faster. Stronger. He slams him back to his knees and twists out of the way, stomping on Xander's foot. *Hard.* There is a chorus of loud cracks, accompanied by a howl of agony.

"While I did promise I would not harm Victoria until your week is up," Konstantin grinds out, "I made no such promise to you. Who knows?" He squeezes the Beta's throat harder, his nails cutting into skin. Blood beads at his fingertips. "Maybe a second hostage will make my demands a little more *enticing.*"

Raw terror floods Xander's expression and Konstantin grins, snapping the man's neck with a sharp flick of his wrist.

CHAPTER 24

SOMEWHERE IN BELARUS

WINTER 1826

I DON'T OFTEN GO OUT *alone, but tonight I am feeling adventurous.*

After Alexander leaves for the evening—most likely to join Kaleb and Nikolas at a nearby tavern—I slip from our room at the inn to do some exploring on my own. If they knew I was doing this, I would most likely receive a lecture about my lack of self-control—about how dangerous it is for me to be wandering the town unsupervised. After all, vampirism hasn't exactly come easy to me. But it has been almost a month since my last kill, so I call that progress.

The town where we've camped for the night is charming: simple stone buildings, tidy dirt roads, and kind people who have been nothing but hospitable since we arrived. I wander the streets for a while, taking time to enjoy my newfound abilities. I have been a vampire for two years, but I still find myself surprised by my superior speed and strength. An exhilarating sprint takes me miles from the outskirts of the village, walking through snow-covered fields in the brittle, moonlit night.

It isn't long before I see a cluster of small homes in the distance. It isn't much longer before a shadow slithers through the space between buildings.

At first, I think it is an animal—there is something primal in its movements as it glides through the night with preternatural grace.

But no animal that I have ever seen resembles a human so perfectly.

As I creep toward the silent village, careful to step lightly on the icy ground, I see another shadow. This one stands tall and proud, haloed in what looks like a mockery of human hair. There is no fluidity to it, no shine. Just a tangled, pale cloud strewn about the creature's head.

A warning voice in my head says, Stop! Turn around! I am not one to give heed to such a cowardly order, but once I start walking down a cobbled street, my heels clicking loudly in the icy stillness, I realize my mistake.

Here, the shadows seethe.

"Hello, miss," a voice croons from my right. "Come for a taste?"

Fear rockets through me, freezing me in place as I turn to face the disembodied sound. A young man leans against a stone doorway. But no, not a man. A vampire. The first one I have met since Kaleb, Nikolas, and Rayna. I am not sure how I can tell—he looks human, after all— but I just know. *An instinct, maybe. Another of those vampiric abilities.*

The man straightens and walks slowly toward me, moonlight shining in his bone-white hair and deepening the shadows beneath his eyes. There's something strange about him, but I cannot put my finger on it; whatever it is, it's enough to make my blood run cold.

"Of—of what?" I stammer, just as a white-haired woman appears in front of me.

"Pretty thing," she rasps, her voice crackling like footsteps on gravel. Small drops of dark blood ooze from her chapped lips and she stares at me with hungry black eyes. "So young. So fresh."

The pair inches closer. A rancid smell fills my nose—the scent of stale blood and decay, stronger and more putrid than the vampire smell I'm used to—and I swallow a gag. Ice glints on their sallow cheeks. I take a step back, then another, but the two of them only smile. They follow, just as another pair of pale-haired vampires emerges from behind a crumbling stone cottage.

"New blood," one of them murmurs, and the words are caught up on the breeze, echoing from every alcove, every hollow between houses.

Whispers in the dark.

New blood.

New blood.

New blood.

My heart slams against my ribs. I turn to run but a girl blocks my path. She looks so young—barely ten—but there's a darkness in her eyes that betrays her years. A blood-crusted silk ribbon is tied in her white hair.

"Mama," she says to the first woman, her tiny fangs glinting. "She smells so good. Can I be first, Mama?"

The woman grins. "Of course, darling. Take all you need."

"What?" I whirl around, aware of the circle of phantom vampires closing in around me. "I don't—I am not human! I am a vampire, like you!"

"No," the little girl says, her laugh like chimes in the wind, "you are nothing like us."

She lunges and I throw my arms in front of me, bracing myself for the inevitable blow just as a familiar snarl tears through the night. I open my eyes to see Rayna cutting down the pale demons, her fangs and daggers drawn. A man is thrown in my direction and I stagger sideways, barely avoiding a collision. He slams against a stone wall with a loud crunch.

Rayna calls through the din. "Charlotte, run!"

"But Rayna—"

"Go!"

I obey. My legs carry me back down the street and I hike my skirts up around my knees, heels pounding on stone, then hard dirt, then the snowy field beyond. I don't slow until I am sure no one has followed me, and I pause in a patch of scraggly bushes. A scream slices through the air and I turn to see Rayna standing in front of the little girl, whose mouth is open in a monstrous snarl.

Rayna raises a dagger and I flinch, squeezing my eyes shut as the girl's scream cuts off, plunging the night into suffocating silence.

My breath clouds around me as I count aloud, barely a whisper. "One, two, three . . ."

I have reached nearly five hundred when I see Rayna exit the village on the same path, running so quickly that she is nearly a blur. She skids to a halt in front of me, blood-stained and wind-swept.

"Charlotte," Rayna says, "are you alright?"

"Yes, I think so." I nod shakily, lip trembling. "I was only exploring. I thought the town was empty. I didn't think—"

"Never do that again," she growls, jabbing a finger into my chest.

"Do what?"

"Run away without telling me! Alexander tasked me with keeping you safe. If I hadn't realized you were gone, the immortui *would have eaten you alive. Not only that, your brother would have had my head."*

Guilt sweeps over me, but I don't apologize. Instead, I ask, "What are im—immu—"

"Immortui." Rayna tucks a few strands of hair back into her chignon and swipes a drop of blood from her brow. "Flesh eaters. When a vampire is desperate—when she cannot find a reliable blood source—she may feed on another of our kind. If she drinks enough, it causes a mutation in the vampire gene. She becomes less human. More monstrous."

I swallow, glancing over her shoulder at the eerie, abandoned town. "Is that what happened here?"

Rayna nods, sneering. "The mutation—it's like a different breed of vampire. Some would argue it makes them stronger. Others, that it causes madness. Either way, I would advise you to avoid small villages at night. Especially if they look abandoned. If the immortui *catch you, they'll drain you dry then tear you apart for good measure."*

Her words shiver through me with an added spike of horror. I had only wanted to be adventurous. But Rayna was right—if she hadn't appeared to fight the creatures, I would most likely be dead.

Not only that, I would be in pieces.

Rayna softens when she sees my expression, her mouth curving

*into a smile. "Good thing I always have your back, Lottie. I don't
know what you would do without me."*

*She wraps an arm around my shoulders and leads me back toward
the bustling town. When I turn to look at the cobblestone road one
more time, I swear I see a flash of white slip into the shadows.*

RAIN SLUICES DOWN the Maserati's windshield, catching the glow of
nearby street lights as we glide through the stormy night. Pippa and
Rose are in the back while Rayna sits in the passenger's seat, her feet
propped up on the dashboard and her eyes glued to her phone. We're
on our way to Chinatown, black-clad and armed to the teeth; I have no
idea what we're going to find there, but I sure as hell won't be caught
unprepared.

The fact that the girls are on a mission without the boys isn't lost
on me—Rayna inconspicuously roped us into a Girls' Night, just like
she used to.

The thought of Girls' Night makes my chest burn. The last time we
had one, we snuck into Alcatraz, playing tricks and skirting security
and mourning Rayna. And now Rayna is alive, and Victoria is gone.

"Turn left here," Rayna says, and I slam on the brakes mid-right
turn.

"I'm sorry, have you been to Chinatown before?" I say, glowering.
"Pretty sure I know where I'm going."

"I'm sure you do." Rayna's eyes spark with mischief. "But we're
not going to Chinatown."

Pippa scoffs. "Then where *are* we going?"

"You'll find out."

I crank the wheel to the left, heading north toward the Bay, and
Rose sighs loudly. "So we're lying to Kaleb."

Rayna shrugs, still staring at her phone. "I didn't tell him because I
didn't want him to intrude on our party. You know how he worries, and
I would rather not have him hovering around us like an overprotective

little honey bee."

She says it so flippantly that I'm almost convinced she's telling me the truth. But the tension in her jaw suggests there's more to it than she cares to admit. Just as I'm about to pry, Pippa laughs.

"That is a surprisingly apt description. And did you feel all that *testosterone* today?" She shudders. "I'm just glad to get away, no matter where we end up."

Rose nods, her eyes widening pointedly. "Agreed. I'll be surprised if Kaleb and Nik survive the night together with how much posturing they're doing."

"Even your little golden boy held his own tonight," Rayna muses, twirling a lock of ginger hair around her finger. "I'm actually kind of impressed. And you know," she adds, leaning toward me, "he sure seems to like you."

Too bad I killed his sister and he wants me to help him investigate her murder, I almost say, but Pippa saves me from incriminating myself.

"That's because Lottie is a hot piece of ass and Tristan wants a slice."

I glare at her in the rear-view mirror and forcefully divert the attention back at her. "I would *love* more information on whatever you and Henry have going on."

"Well," Pippa says, tossing her platinum braid over her shoulder, "I'm sure you've noticed that we make an absolutely *ravishing* couple. We simply decided that we, being the generous beings that we are, simply couldn't live with ourselves if we denied the world our beauty any longer."

Rose rolls her eyes while Rayna makes a sound of annoyance.

"He's a *child,*" she says, fingers tapping at her phone screen.

"The man is a hundred and seventy-six years old," Pippa protests. "Only thirteen years younger than me. In immortal terms, it might as well be thirteen days."

"Yeah," I say, "but he was Turned at sixteen. *Sixteen,* Pippa."

Pippa waves a dismissive hand in the air. "Turned age doesn't matter.

All that matters is if he knows his way around a female body. And I can assure you, Henry is an expert." The three of us make dramatic shows of disgust, which only brighten Pippa's grin. "You know, Lottie," she adds, tapping her chin, "I think it's *you* we should be worried about. How old is Tristan again? Eighteen?"

"Twenty," I grumble. "*Technically* legal." *Still physically older than I'll ever be,* I mentally add, cringing at the thought.

"Hmm." Rayna finally pockets her phone, motioning for me to make another turn. "So, you're almost two hundred years older? I think that makes you a—what do they call them now? A cougar?"

The others burst into laughter as we make our way through the night-laden city, and I can't help but smile, just a little.

◊   ◊   ◊

I have never wanted to *not* be somewhere so badly.

Ahead of us is a huge brick structure nestled against the rocky coast at the base of the Golden Gate Bridge. Wind whips off the water as we creep through the dark, filling the air with a perpetual mist of sea spray. We skirt around a rock face and I drag my hand along it, the surface slick with moisture, moss clinging to every surface. The combination makes it feel slimy and I recoil, wiping my palm on my jeans. Rayna shoves her hands in her jacket pockets, grumbling something about the "damn sea," but I'm too nervous to give her any grief.

Rayna dragged us to *Fort Point,* of all places—a military fort that once protected the San Francisco Bay from enemy warships. Now it stands empty and unused except to entertain tourists and look intimidating. And, if the locals are to be believed, it's still haunted by the ghosts of the soldiers who died there. Based on the eerie feeling spider-crawling over my skin, I wouldn't be surprised.

Just because Rayna heard something on a police radio doesn't mean we're going to see Konstantin tonight. Hell, the chances of that are slim to none. The "suspicious activity" could have been something as innocent as a bunch of teenagers trying to sneak in.

I'm sure it's nothing.

We slink along the cliffside, keeping to the shadows in case of prying eyes. The bridge's massive silhouette looms above us like a sleeping giant, its pinprick lights shining through the mist in a hazy orange glow. When we reach the huge iron doors, Rayna makes quick work of the chain and padlock—meaning she tears them from the door's handles, dropping them on the asphalt with a *clang*.

I give her a, *What the hell?* look, but she just shrugs and pushes on the doors. They open with a low, resounding creak.

We walk into a concrete courtyard open to the sky, surrounded on all sides by brick archways that are duplicated on three levels. There's a dull roar that rumbles through the walls, no doubt a combination of the relentless ocean waves and the constant traffic on the bridge overhead. I take a deep breath of salty air and cough at the reek of damp wood and mildew.

"Well, this is *lovely*," I whisper, and Pippa slaps my arm, shushing me as we creep through the fort.

At first glance, the place seems completely empty. Abandoned. But for some unknown reason, goosebumps shiver down my arms, making my skin prickle inside my hoodie. Rayna motions us toward a small opening that reveals a narrow staircase ascending into blackness.

Realistically, I know I shouldn't be afraid of the dark. A few weeks ago, I wouldn't have given it a second thought. But now, with the threat of Konstantin around every corner, I can't help but be wary.

Rayna ascends the staircase and with a strong mental shove, I follow.

The second level is similar to the first. On one side of the walkway, the arches are open to the courtyard below. On the other side is a series of large alcoves—each one must be at least twenty feet deep—and they're engulfed in darkness. I can just make out tiny windows cut into the walls, where I assume cannons were once positioned to shoot out into the Bay. The smell is stronger here—*wetter*—like an underground cave that never dries out, and a touch of rot permeates the air.

For all our skill in stealth, it still feels like every breath, every scuff of my Converse shoes on the concrete is as loud as cannon fire. We're practically begging to be ambushed.

Something rustles in one of the alcoves and we all freeze, straining to hear anything over the howling wind and the deep roar of the ocean. There's a scratch. A thud. The scrape of something being dragged over a rough floor. The spine-tingling feeling that from deep in the shadows, someone is watching us. I squint into the darkness—so complete that I can barely see, even with my heightened sight—and slowly draw one of my throwing knives from the leather sheath around my thigh.

And then I recognize the rotting scent. It cuts through the wood and mildew and brine, tugging at a memory of fetid blood and the unmistakable reek of decay.

Fear shoots through me, all-encompassing, and I grab Rayna's hand.

"We've got to get out of here—" I say, just as she clicks on a flashlight.

Dozens of chalky faces snap in our direction, their eyes bruised and their lips curled. Rose gasps quietly. White hair shines. Black eyes glint.

Rayna curses under her breath and a damp chill creeps over my skin as one of them smiles, blackish blood oozing from the corner of her mouth.

I stifle a scream.

Immortui.

CHAPTER 25

If I was expecting anything tonight, finding a venerable horde of cannibal vampires in San Francisco was not it. The white-haired creatures are staring at us curiously, some showing their fangs, others sniffing at the air. Some are in modern clothes—t-shirts, sundresses, blue jeans—while others look like they were plucked from the pages of a Victorian novel, donning corsets and overskirts and tailored breeches. All are covered in grime and crusted with dried blood, and they taste the air, chuckling quietly to themselves. Dozens of solid black eyes shimmer in the cold light.

"New blood," one of them whispers, his voice like the rasp of a crow. It's enough to send adrenaline down every nerve, every vein, burning through my chest like an electric current. The other creatures join in—only a few at first, but the whispers quickly turn into a growling predatory chant. Voices echo from above and below, surrounding us. *Trapping* us.

We have *got* to get out of here.

Rayna's hand tightens around mine and Rose presses close on my other side, Pippa's breath cool and rapid at my shoulder. All of our hearts are racing, the rhythms rising in panic and fear. In contrast, I hear nothing from the *immortui*: no heartbeats, no breathing. Just their words—*new blood*—echoing in their hollow chests.

We take a step back, moving as a group. Slowly. *So* slowly. Afraid that any wrong move may startle the *immortui* into a frenzy. Pippa stumbles slightly and winces, clutching at the snaking veins over her heart. Hissing in warning, Rayna throws her a scorching, fear-fueled glare.

A few more steps and we might be able make a run for it. *Left. Right. Left. Right.* But the *immortui* are catching on. They may look like a horde of zombies, but that's where the resemblance stops. The creatures are just as lucid, intelligent, and calculating as the rest of us, but they have lost any sense of the humanity they once possessed, making them lethal. Destructive. Impulsive.

Unfortunately, it also makes them extremely territorial, which means they view our presence here as a threat. As if they can hear my thoughts, a few of the *immortui* growl quietly.

With each step we take, one of the creatures moves closer, tracking us with its black eyes and tasting our scent on the tepid, rank air. *Almost there. We're going to get out of this. We just need to—*

The creature closest to us locks eyes with me, and his cracking lips stretch into a wide grin. Snarling, he leaps forward and I stagger back, nearly knocking Pippa over. She curses loudly and shoves Rose toward the exit, the pair barely maintaining their footing as the *immortui* surge.

"Come on!" I bark at Rayna, dragging her behind me, but three *immortui* materialize in our path like a trio of ghostly wraiths. We skid to a halt in time to see Pippa and Rose disappear into the stairwell. I call after them but can barely hear myself over the wild snarling that echoes through the cavernous fort.

I dart for the nearest archway, meaning to throw myself through the gap into the courtyard below, but an icy hand catches at my wrist, wrenching my shoulder. I fly backward and land with a *crack* as my head slams into the concrete. Pain reverberates through my skull, reducing every sound to a high-pitched ringing.

"Let's go!" Rayna yells, dragging me to my feet. Nausea grips me and I nearly double over, but she doesn't let me. Black creeps into the edges of my vision as we shove our way past a handful of *immortui*, my feet singing with each slap of my Converse against the hard ground.

Rayna has us careening around a corner, too fast. I slam into a wall—a dead end—and there's a loud, jarring *snap* where my collar bone meets my shoulder. I cry out in pain as Rayna crashes into me and we tumble to the floor, a mess of limbs and hair and panicked breaths, the beam of her flashlight flying wildly around us.

Rayna manages to stand and looks down at me with wide eyes. Tension crackles in the air and she clicks off her light, plunging us into darkness.

"What are you doing?" I hiss.

"Hiding."

"Are you *crazy?*" I almost shriek. I attempt to stand but pain screams through my shoulder again. I sink backward and Rayna catches me, clapping a silencing hand over my mouth. I blink away the tears of pain, the stars swimming through the dark.

So this is how I die: trapped in a grimy tourist trap with a broken collar bone, sucked dry by a bunch of vampire cannibals. Not exactly the glorious death I always hoped for, but there isn't much I can do about it now.

It's so dark now that Rayna's light is gone. I can just make out a few barrels against the wall to my left and a stack of old cannonballs ahead to my right. Maybe if I could grab a few of those, we might have a chance—

But I don't get to test my theory. A figure cuts through the mist of darkness, then another, then another. In less than three seconds, the entire hallway is blocked by a mass of petticoats and bone-white hair, the smell rancid enough that I actually gag. The man at the front of the horde grins—the same one who lunged at me—and blood leaks from a cut on his lip.

"*New blood.*"

I curl into Rayna's chest and she clutches me tightly, muttering the Lord's Prayer under her breath. As if her god can save us now.

I'm sorry, Xander. Please forgive me.

"Diego, *fermare!*" a deep voice orders, and my head snaps up. *Stop.* "*Famme vedere.*"

The *immortui* man freezes and immediately backs away, joining the throng as a path opens down its middle.

Click, click, click.

Footsteps, heading in our direction. My heart is pounding so hard that I'm worried it might literally break through my ribs. Rayna hasn't moved, but I can feel her muscles coil with tension, ready to fight. Ready to *run.* But there's nowhere to go. Even if we could break into that opening, we wouldn't make it through—at least not in one piece.

A yellow glow appears around the corner, growing brighter as the footsteps draw nearer. I see the source first: a gold lighter, held between the pointer and middle finger of a broad hand. It's followed by a wrist, then an arm, then the hand's owner comes into view, stepping into the dead-end hallway while the *immortui* part around him like Moses and the Red Sea.

This man—this *vampire*—is not *immortui* at all. In fact, he's extremely handsome, with a square jaw and a head of dark, wavy hair that falls elegantly over his forehead. His skin holds a deep tan and his hair is tousled, but clean—a stark contrast to the collection of ghouls gathered around him. For a moment, all I can do is stare at his face—at the bright azure of his eyes.

Then there's a glint of metal somewhere on his person, and I notice his bold choice of clothing. His legs are long, fitted in a pair of pale breeches and tall leather boots. He wears a gold-trimmed blue coat that falls to his knees and it hangs open over a linen shirt that is held closed by a single button, a bullet casing hanging from a gold chain around his neck. To top it all off, there's a literal sword in a scabbard at his hip.

Good hell. I'm about to be murdered by a pirate.

Rayna releases me and leaps to her feet, a viper poised to strike, but the man doesn't flinch.

"*Ciao, bellezze.* My apologies." His voice is warm and deep, and it carries a slight Italian accent. He motions to the group of *immortui*, flashing a disarming half smile. "We don't often have visitors at night, and unannounced guests have a tendency to work my Bonded into a frenzy, as I'm sure you've noticed."

Bonded? All I can do is nod, wincing as the motion rattles my collar bone. Rayna stands completely still but I don't dare look up at her, afraid to tear my eyes away from undead Johnny Depp. Leaning slightly to one side, I slowly—painfully—get my legs under me and take up a place next to Rayna.

"That being said," the man continues, "I do appreciate the company of beautiful women. Though I can't recall having afforded either of you an invitation." He takes a step forward with a tap of his chin, looking at Rayna for a tense second before turning to me. "So, I must ask, what exactly are you doing here?"

I stare at his hand, then the other, frowning at the hint of strangeness that catches my attention. Almost like there's something missing—

"How do you hold a sword without thumbs?" I blurt out, and Rayna smacks me across the chest. I bite back a cry of pain but my attention fixes on the man's hand that holds the lighter, where it looks like his thumb was severed cleanly. No evidence of that fifth finger remains at all.

The pirate's easy demeanor sharpens. "I beg your pardon?"

"I, um . . . I didn't mean anything by it," I stammer. "I just—I'm curious."

He reaches for his sword, a challenge in his gaze. "Would you like me to show you?"

"No!" I say a little too quickly, and a low chuckle ripples through the *immortui.* "No, that's fine. If you wouldn't mind, we"—I motion between Rayna and I—"would actually just like to get out of here. So if you could call off the hounds, I'd really appreciate it, Mister . . . ?"

The pirate considers me for a few long seconds. Shadows flicker under the lighter's tiny flame, the only movement in a sea of mannequin-like bodies.

"Who I am depends entirely on who *you* are." His posture is relaxed, but his voice carries a slight edge.

"Could you be a little more vague?" I snap with a too-grand hand gesture that makes my shoulder scream. I swallow a curse and curl my left arm tightly against my chest. *Damn,* it's been a long time since I've broken a bone like this. I think I would rather have my thumbs cut off.

The man catches Rayna's eye before his gaze drifts down her body, sizing her up as he offers a rakish grin. She stares back, unbothered— *too* unbothered, if I'm being honest.

"My name is Lorenzo de Luca," the pirate says, bowing with a flourish. "But my friends call me Enzo. And you are?"

"Charlotte Novik," I say, realizing belatedly that I could have— *should* have given him a fake name. "And this is—"

"Lena," Rayna says quickly. "Lena Sirakova."

"You?" Enzo drawls in my direction, as though Rayna hadn't spoken. "*You* are Charlotte Novik?"

"Uh . . . yes." Unease prickles through me. "Is that a problem?"

"*Porca miseria,*" Enzo grumbles, glancing upward with an exasperated expression. He scrubs at the scruff along his jaw, rings glinting on three fingers. "I thought dealing with one Novik was bad enough. If Xander thinks he can get more information out of me by sending his kid sister, he doesn't know me as well as I thought."

I try not to be insulted. "You know Xander?"

Enzo arches a brow. "Of course. What self-respecting vampire doesn't know his own Beta?"

Me, apparently.

"Okay, then." I shrug, immediately regretting it as my shoulder screams again. "What did you mean, more information? Is Xander looking for something?" My pulse spikes. "Was he here?"

"Obviously," Enzo says wryly. Movement flickers at his waist, his fingers tapping the hilt of his sword. The *immortui* to his left mirrors the motion, a pale echo tapping at empty air. "Xander visited last night asking for information about Konstantin, but I had nothing to tell."

I gape at the pirate as the name ripples through the *immortui*.

Konstantin.

Konstantin.

Konstantin.

Repressing a shudder, I ask, "What exactly did he want to know?"

"Do I look like a mind reader?" Enzo asks sharply. "I assumed you would know, being his sister and all. The man sure does *love* to talk about you. From what he has told me, I thought you would be . . ." He studies me, lips pursed. "Taller."

"If the only things you've learned about me are from Xander, then you probably think I'm a certifiable lunatic with a penchant for breaking the rules."

Enzo blinks a few times in puzzlement. "On the contrary, *bellezza.*"

He doesn't elaborate, and I don't pry. I would prefer not to hear the unhinged tales Xander tells about me.

"You must know *something* about Konstantin," Rayna interjects, her tone all bite. "Where he has been, what he's doing here . . . you *must* have seen him at some point."

The name carries again, louder this time, hissing through the *immortui*'s cracked lips. A few of them twitch, their black eyes locked on me. One flashes his fangs while another has moved into a slight crouch, her full skirt bunching on the ground. They're getting restless.

A long pause follows as Enzo considers her question. "And why would you think that?"

The two lock eyes, but after a few seconds, Rayna's expression turns wary.

Enzo exhales sharply, an amused sound that I hear again, and again, and again. Endless, phantom echoes. The *immortui* nearest the wall chuckles, taking a small step toward me. I'm starting to wonder if any of these ghouls are going to let me out of here alive. There are far too many for us to fight off, and panic is starting to simmer behind my ribs.

"As the unofficial leader of San Francisco's underground,"

Enzo says slowly, as though weighing each word, "I am sometimes privy to certain pieces of . . . *unsavory* information. Unfortunately, Konstantin"—he spits on the ground with a sneer—"has always been a tricky bastard. If he is here, I haven't seen him." His words are firm, but I catch a flicker of apprehension in his eyes. "I do not know where he is, but even if I did, I wouldn't be idiotic enough to share it with one of the most important men in San Francisco."

"You're afraid of him," Rayna says, impatience creeping into her voice. Impatience and fear and a touch of recklessness. "You have all these nightmarish creatures at your disposal and you're afraid of one man?"

Enzo's eyes narrow in accusation. "Aren't you?"

Rayna winces minutely and I twine my arm with hers, something like kinship flaring in my chest. An ember being fanned. There's a connection here, between her and I. Shared fear, shared fight—a desperate need to survive.

"She has a point, you know," I say, trying to sound more confident than I feel. "These *immortui* sure seem to like you. I bet Konstantin would only be able to kill one or two before the horde ripped him to pieces."

Enzo's poise falters, his expression shuttering in an instant. Gone is the self-assuredness, replaced by cool hostility. The shift in his demeanor must affect the *immortui* as well, because their control all but vanishes. Dozens of hungry eyes fix on us, their pallid faces flickering in and out of shadow.

"I will have nothing to do with this childish feud between Kaleb and Konstantin." Enzo takes a threatening step toward us and we stagger back, shoulder blades kissing the frigid wall. He leans in, blue eyes pinning us in place. Rayna swallows hard. "You should stay away from that man if you know what's good for you. Not a person who has pursued him has lived to tell about it." My hand slides down my thigh, fingers curling around the handle of a knife. Slowly, I draw the weapon from my sheath, gripping it firmly in my fist. "I suggest you run far away, little mice, before the king makes a meal out of you."

Using every ounce of strength I have, I drive the knife upward—straight into Enzo's ribs. His lighter clatters to the ground, the flame snuffing out as he stumbles sideways with a furious roar. He curses in snarling Italian as I grab Rayna's hand and drag her behind me, running straight for the wall of *immortui*.

My first mistake is believing we'll be able to slip easily through the throng. Unfortunately, I'm as wrong as I am dead. Bodies close in on all sides, the *immortui's* animal snarls rising in a tumultuous wave. Rayna cries out as her hand is ripped from mine but I press forward, shoving my way through the clawing horde as they slice and swipe and grab. Cuts open on my arms, my cheeks. One of my shoes is yanked off. The pain in my shoulder is near-blinding, and I can feel the break worsening with each movement, each pull, each shove.

"Rayna!" I shriek. "Rayna, *help!*"

But Rayna has disappeared, swallowed by the mass of petticoats and pallid skin.

One of the *immortui* wraps her arms around me and clutches me against her chest. Before I have a chance to react, to fight, to *scream*, she plunges her fangs into my neck.

White explodes in my vision, terror and pain fighting for dominance in my exhausted, broken body. I thrash in the woman's grip but she is unyielding, her teeth like daggers, her arms like an iron cage. The harder I struggle, the tighter she holds. No matter how hard I try, there is no escape, no hope—only the sway of the floor and the deep pull of blood from my neck.

A distant part of my mind wonders if this is how Alison felt.

Another *immortui* joins my captor, his fangs clamping down on my forearm. Then another on my shoulder. Another. Another.

Someone barks a command, but I barely hear it over my own broken cries. The darkness seethes and a pale face appears above me, fangs gleaming behind a twisted smile. A memory snags in the back of my mind: the smell of burned pastries, the reek of stale blood, the glint of a kitchen knife protruding from a broad, bloodied chest . . .

And the pain—oh, the *pain* as he tears into my throat, a fire that scorches through my veins as the shadow drains my life away.

I'm dying, I'm dying, I'm dying.

It wouldn't be the first time.

"Abbastanza!" Enzo's voice thunders through the air, and I swear I can feel the ground shake. "Leave her!"

The pressure in my neck, my forearm, my shoulder is gone in an instant, leaving behind a deep throbbing ache. The *immortui* release me and I crumple to the ground; my body hits the concrete hard, sending a bolt of nausea through me.

"Bellezza," Enzo says, lifting me gruffly to my feet—despite the ringing in my head, I can just make out the hard angles of his face, the way his brows are knit together in an emotion I can't decipher. "Get out of here. I won't have a Novik die under my watch." When I don't move, he adds, *"Now."*

He gives my good shoulder a gentle shove and I stagger backward, barely keeping my footing when my shoe catches on a jagged crack in the concrete. Enzo snaps a few orders at the *immortui* as I stumble away, but the words fade into background noise. My ears fill with a dull roar, growing louder with each wavering step, threatening to pull me under, but I don't let it. I force my legs to move faster, *faster,* and they carry me back down the stairwell, through the courtyard, and into the misty world beyond.

LORENZO DE LUCA

CHAPTER 26

"Rayna, *help!*"

But Rayna has her own problems at the moment. She fights her way through the knot of *immortui*, their claws scratching and their teeth bared. Fear fuels her, urges her forward, even as nails tear her skin. As fangs snap mere inches from her neck.

And then she is free. She doesn't look back, knowing Charlotte will follow. *Assuming* she will. Rayna sprints through the fort in a panicked frenzy, practically falling down the stairs, and throws herself through the door. It isn't until she is halfway up the cliffside that she allows herself to slow, forcing her racing heart to settle.

As she picks her way up the rocky path, she realizes two things. One, she can no longer hear the *immortui* snarling. And two, Charlotte is not behind her.

Rayna stops and turns around, staring down at the dark, imposing building. She listens for a set of footsteps or the sound of Lottie's panicked breathing, but there is nothing but the crashing of the wind-tossed sea. Dread pools in her stomach as she considers the implications of that sudden silence.

"Rayna?" Pippa calls, peering over the cliff's edge. She huffs a sigh of relief. "Thank *hell*. Are you alright?"

Rayna takes a moment. Another. She forces her mind to rationalize.

She and Charlotte were trying to escape together, but the *immortui* separated them—it's not like Rayna left her behind on purpose. They were fighting for their lives, surrounded on all sides by bloodthirsty creatures intent on killing them. It was only natural for Rayna to run. To get out as fast as she could. It isn't her fault Charlotte wasn't strong enough to get away.

Besides, Rayna didn't run from Konstantin for two hundred years only to die at the hands of cannibals.

Something like guilt pricks at her chest, followed by a pang of worry. If the situation were reversed, Charlotte never would have left without her, even if that meant they died together.

But Charlotte isn't *dead*. If she were, Rayna would know. She has to make herself believe that.

Suddenly she's running back down the path. Pippa calls after her, followed closely by a concerned Rose, but their voices are carried away by the wind. *What was she thinking?* How could she leave Charlotte behind?

The most important lesson that Rayna has ever learned is that fear is a powerful motivator. A person will do anything if it means banishing the terror, the unhinged anxiety that sinks its claws deep. It's why Konstantin was able to manipulate her for so long; he preyed on her worst fear—losing her brother—and it worked almost too well.

The same fear that had her running away from the fort now has Rayna running back, her mind imagining all the ways the *immortui* might have torn Charlotte apart. Panic seizes her in a vise-like grip, squeezing her lungs and shooting ice into her throat.

If Lottie is dead, Nik will never forgive her.

"Charlotte!" she calls into the darkness. "Charlotte, *where are you?*"

Barreling through the doorway, she nearly runs into a scowling Enzo.

"Rayna," he growls, catching her by the shoulders. "Do be quiet, *bellezza*. Are you trying to wake the dead?"

Rayna blinks a few times, taken aback by her true name on Enzo's lips. "I'm not—"

"Don't be an idiot," he growls. "Do you really think I didn't recognize you? I know it has been a few centuries, but"—he taps a finger to his temple—"this old mind is sharp as ever."

Grimacing, Rayna yanks herself from Enzo's grip. In reality, she knew her old frenemy had recognized her; it was obvious by the way he took her in, the way his mouth quirked as though enjoying his own silent joke.

"What do you want, Lorenzo?"

"As I said, I want you to *be quiet.*" His frown sharpens into a sneer. "And it would have been nice to know you were alive before Kaleb broke the news a few days ago. I thought we were friends, love."

"We were never friends."

Enzo smiles, though it doesn't reach his eyes. He traces a finger down her jaw. "Weren't we?"

Rayna shudders and backs away. "Kaleb told you about me? That I was alive?"

"He thought it would be best that we know you're here, so we would be prepared if Konstantin"—he spits on the ground—"came knocking."

"Who is *we?*"

"The Lesser Alphas, of course."

When he doesn't elaborate, Rayna frowns. She wants to press him further, to ask what a Lesser Alpha is, but now is not the time.

"What do you know about Konstantin?" she asks instead.

Enzo scowls, his fingers tapping the hilt of his sword. "Rayna, I don't know anything—"

"Maybe you didn't hear me," Rayna says, grabbing him by the chin. His eyes widen a fraction. "While I appreciate the fact that you lied to Charlotte, I won't be so easily cowed. Now tell me: *what do you know?*"

Squeezing his eyes shut, Enzo pulls away and spins in a slow circle before glaring acerbically at Rayna. "Fine. But as far as Kaleb knows, this conversation never happened."

Rayna folds her arms, biting her cheeks to keep from smirking. "Deal."

"When you have one foot in the vampire underground," Enzo begins, "it's common to hear rumors circulating through unsavory circles. A few years ago, I started hearing whispers of a powerful vampire in the city, though his whereabouts were unknown. At first, it was simple: a rogue kill here, a new fledgling there. But it didn't take long for them to get unsettlingly specific."

Rayna's arms tighten around herself and her hands start to fidget, releasing little bursts of the anxious energy buzzing through her veins.

"People started mentioning a man with silver eyes," Enzo continues, fiddling with the bullet casing hanging from his neck, "who was working his way through the vampire underground, gathering followers in his wake. Rumor had it that he was turning them against Kaleb, sowing discord in whatever way he could. It was then that I started to suspect Konstantin."

Rayna punches him hard in the shoulder and he responds with a sharp, "*Ow.*"

"Why didn't you say anything," she snarls, "if you suspected this for *years?*"

"I didn't want Kaleb worked up over nothing," he snarls back, rubbing at his shoulder. "Especially when I had no proof. You would have done the same thing."

Rayna's lips press into a tight line. He's right, of course. She *would* have hidden her suspicions from Kaleb if it meant she could save him the agonizing stress it would inevitably cause him. If only he didn't feel the need to carry the weight of the world on his shoulders.

"Fine." Rayna frowns as two *immortui* slip from the shadows behind Enzo. They don't approach or attack, they just hover. Listening. "Where is she?"

Enzo raises a scarred brow, not questioning the abrupt change of subject. "Who?"

"Charlotte, obviously."

He shrugs. "The hell if I know."

"What do you mean?"

"I *mean,* I called off my *immortui* and she ran. The poor girl looked terrible, but she was very much alive when she left. However, I can't guarantee she has remained so since she disappeared. Once she left my territory, she became someone else's problem."

Rayna snarls and grabs Enzo's lapel, yanking him close, and he smiles languidly when their noses touch.

"My, my," he says, gaze dropping to her lips. "I'll admit this is a bit forward, but I'm open to it if you are."

Goosebumps rise on Rayna's arms, not entirely unwelcome. After all, Enzo has always been incredibly attractive. It isn't the first time she's been tempted by those seaglass eyes.

She shakes the thought away and shoves the pirate backward, drawing a soft laugh from him.

"Which way did she go?" Rayna demands.

"As I said," he muses, "that's not my problem."

"You are no help," she grumbles and turns to leave, but Enzo catches her by the arm, pulling her into a rough hug. For a moment, she lets herself sink into him, oddly comforted by his familiar cologne-laden embrace. Then, not wanting him to think she actually *missed* him, she shoves away, flashing him her middle finger.

"I missed you too, *straka,*" he says with a crooked grin, striding backward into the shadows. He vanishes with a thumbless wave and a flash of gold at his hip, the *immortui* swallowed by the darkness in his wake.

Anger and panic and guilt roar through Rayna's chest. Overwhelming her. Consuming her.

Charlotte is gone, gone, gone.

And I left her to die.

Rayna crumples to the ground, wrapping her arms around herself.

Trying to force back the ice trickling through her veins. But she's too late. It numbs her, freezes her, pulls her under.

Alone in the darkness, her mask fractures.

CHAPTER 27

BLACK CIRCLES MY VISION AS I sprint away from Fort Point, rocks jabbing into my single bare foot with every other step. Fire burns at my throat. Blood and rainwater drip into my eyes. The ocean is an endless roar in my head, adding to the pressure. Blinding me with sound. I have no idea where I'm going, I just know that I have to *run*.

Run away.

Run from.

Run to . . . what? *Who?* How will I explain this mess?

Streets pass in a blur. I run, even as my strength ebbs, as the jackhammer in my head threatens to split my skull in two. I'm almost grateful when my foot clips a curb and I fly through the air, crashing into a neatly-trimmed hedge. I've stopped running, at least. I tumble to the ground, landing face-down in a puddle, and my pain amplifies a thousand-fold before everything goes suddenly cold.

"Don't you dare," I mutter to myself, pushing to my hands and knees. "You are a *vampire*. Vampires are too badass to go into shock."

A shudder rocks through me and I grit my teeth as I force myself into a sitting position. Red soaks into the wet pavement around me, leaking from a wound on my forearm that can only be described as horror movie-esque. Three sets of parallel slashes overlap one another, the furrows deep and jagged, the skin peeling away from muscle and bone. My breath catches and I choke back a gag, then a sob.

I've lost too much blood. If I lose much more without replenishing it, it will take far longer for my body to heal than usual. The process is going to be excruciating as it is, with the broken collarbone, the blood loss, and the multiple bites and scratches that tore ragged holes in my flesh. Not to mention the obvious concussion and the fact that I am *definitely* going into shock. Even a vampire's body can only do so much at one time. As if in warning, a wave of dizziness pulls me sideways and I barely catch myself, my hand slapping against the wet pavement.

Fighting past the pounding in my head, I gingerly remove my ruined jacket and yank the drawstring from my hood. It takes a few tries—my shoulder is unstable and the water makes the fabric heavy and cumbersome—but I manage to tie the string tightly around my upper arm. A tourniquet may prevent blood from healing the wounds, but at least the blood will stay *inside* my body until I make it home.

But how am I supposed to do that?

Rayna's face flashes in my mind and I grimace, chucking my jacket into the hedges. We should never have gone to Fort Point. We should never have lied to Kaleb—knowing him, he probably sent scouts to Chinatown to keep an eye on us if something went awry. But Rayna just couldn't stand the idea of him knowing her plans. Watching out for her. *Protecting* her. I fail to see how that would have been a problem tonight. In fact, if we had told him we were going to Fort Point, he could have told us about the *immortui* and saved us all the trouble.

He's going to lose his mind when he finds out what really happened.

Headlights cut through the darkness and I turn to see a car making its way down the street, its engine a low rumble. I scramble backward, ignoring my body's protests as I dive for cover, too slow. It's only seconds before the car passes me—no, it stops *right* in front of me. I don't dare look up, fixing my eyes on its wet black wheels and glistening wine-red paint.

Don't look at me, I think. *Just leave.*

There's an electronic hum as the tinted window rolls down, and a chill shivers up my back.

"Get up," says a dark voice from inside, "and get in."

There's a tiny tug beneath my ribs, urging me to my feet. Something is calling me forward—curiosity, maybe—and I slowly make my way to the car, gripping the handle with bloody, trembling fingers. The warm air bleeding from the open window brings with it the scents of coffee and leather, tinged with something heady and sweet, like roses falling to rot.

"Come on," the voice says, a smile leaking into it. "I don't have all night."

My mind immediately rebels but my hand acts on its own, pulling the door open before I slide into the passenger's seat with a grunt of pain. Warmth engulfs me, and the lack of torrential rain is a welcome reprieve. But then I see a hand resting on the gear shift, a ring glinting on its pinky. Thin fingers. A gold watch.

Wrongness spider-crawls over my skin, and I want nothing more than to get out of this car *right now*. But that same thread of curiosity has me rooted to the spot, anchoring me and making my hands tremble.

I close the door.

A sleek dashboard. A polished black steering wheel with a Mustang logo in the center. The driver leans toward me, white teeth glinting in the dark. Wan orange light from a street lamp illuminates his angular face, his ash brown hair, his full lips, the liquid mercury of his eyes, and I gasp.

The shadow grins.

"Hey, hot stuff," Konstantin says, slamming the car into gear. "How about you and I go for a little drive?"

No.

I shove backward and my head cracks against the window, making me groan. If I hit my head one more time tonight, it may just do me in. Blinking through renewed fog, I fumble for the door handle, but it's locked.

"No!" I shout, but we're already prowling through the city streets.

No. I can't be in a car alone with him. I won't let him take me, too. Burning terror rockets through me and my aching body protests as I shove at the door, scrambling to find the manual lock.

For the thousandth time tonight, I wonder if I'm about to die.

"Oh, Charlotte," Konstantin drawls, glancing at me sidelong. "Do calm down."

"I'll show you *calm,*" I snarl, but there's no fire behind it. I'm tired—*so* tired—and my body would probably appreciate the break. Settling back into my seat, I inhale deeply, letting the air fill my lungs completely before I release it all at once. A strange sense of stillness trickles through me—the fire is gone, and in its place is a cool, placid lake. I let my left arm rest in my lap, finding a comfortable position that doesn't aggravate my collar bone or the ugly gashes on my forearm.

Konstantin flashes a grin, his fangs glinting. "That's my girl. Much better, isn't it?"

"I'm not your girl," I growl, wincing at the burst of pain at the base of my throat. I prod it gently, feeling the still-healing holes where an *immortui*'s fangs pierced my skin. A shudder runs through me at the memory of Konstantin in the basement—when our kiss turned, in my own words, *cannibalistic.*

What? It's not like you haven't been bitten before.

I grimace. "*Definitely* not your girl. I'd rather die, actually."

Konstantin makes a small sound of annoyance. "Because you're Tristan's girl, is that right? Do you really think he'll stick around when he finds out you murdered his sister?"

The blunt question takes me off guard; even more so the bored, matter-of-fact way he asks it.

"Thanks for sugar-coating it," I grumble, tugging on a strand of wet hair.

"I'm merely asking, love. He's going to find out at some point. I just want you to be prepared."

The warning—or rather, the *promise* is there: *It's only a matter of time.*

Swallowing through the knot in my throat, I manage a weak, "Please don't tell him."

"As I said to you over the phone, I won't." Konstantin chuckles and the unsaid words hang in the silence: *Not yet.*

I consider asking him about Golden Gate Park—about exactly what he saw that night—but I'm not sure I could stomach seeing it through his eyes. The judgment. The *amusement.*

"Why did you kidnap me?" I grind out instead, hand inching toward my knives. The leather sheath is water-logged and stained with blood, and I'm one knife short after leaving one in Enzo's ribs. "And where is Victoria?"

"First," Konstantin says, sneering, "I did not *kidnap* you. Would you believe me if I said I stumbled upon you by chance?"

"No."

He chuckles again, staring ahead where the headlights now glow through a thickening layer of fog. Rain pelts the windshield, each drop like a tiny gunshot. A heartbeat.

"Contrary to what others have told you, I am not a monster." As if to demonstrate the fact, he looks down at my arm—bloody, battered, and dripping all over my lap—then nods toward the glove box. "I'm sure those wounds have left you ravenous."

I narrow my eyes at him as I open the glove box and find a handful of blood bags. *A-negative.* Just the sight of it makes my fangs pop. Still, I don't want to give him the satisfaction.

"I'm fine," I say, but Konstantin's lips purse.

"Drink, Charlotte. I won't have you bleeding all over my car."

I'm about to protest, noting the fact that I've already bled all over his car, but his words have me reaching for a bag. Gingerly, I untie the makeshift tourniquet above my left elbow, hissing as blood rushes into my forearm, the slashes oozing. I tear the top off the bag and am guzzling it in an instant, groaning involuntarily with each swallow. The skin on my arm prickles as the blood works its healing magic, the torn edges of my skin starting to knit themselves back together. When

I finish the bag, I grab another one.

"Easy, love." Konstantin frowns, but his tone isn't unkind. "Save a bit for me, will you?"

I scoff. "Unless you do something for me, I have no intention of doing anything for you."

"I won't tell you where Victoria is," Konstantin says casually, like this is just a normal conversation. Like he didn't just kidnap my pseudo-sister. I pause mid-swig and lower the blood bag. "Not until you've frittered away all your time and forced my hand. Then, and only then"—he sighs theatrically—"I suppose I'll have to tell you where I buried the body."

I snarl and lunge across the center console, but Konstantin swerves hard to the left, throwing me back against the passenger door. Blood spurts from the bag, splattering a line of red across the windshield.

"Uh, uh, uh," Konstantin croons, his silver eyes fixed on the road. "None of that, my dear. I know how desperately you want to get your hands on me, and while I am *extremely* flattered, I hardly think now is the time."

Shifting back into my seat, I surreptitiously buckle my seatbelt.

"Glad to know you're still a disgusting bastard."

Konstantin smirks. "You wound me."

"Still a cocky son of a bitch too, I see." My fingertips brush the knives at my thigh. "What's to stop me from murdering you while I have you alone?"

A quirk of his brow. A condescending smirk. "And what, pray tell, do you intend to use?"

I try to snatch a knife, ready to attack, but Konstantin whispers, "Stop."

My hand stills, fingers twitching toward my blades. The word is quiet, but there's a command behind it that has my muscles tensing. I fight against my instincts—against the chill in my arm—but I can't seem to shake it, and I stare at Konstantin with a touch of panic.

Run.

"I said *relax*, Charlotte," he says with a crooked smile. "I'm not going to hurt you."

I inhale slowly and force my shoulders to soften, tucking my arms against my chest in an attempt to hide my growing fear. I have *got* to get out of here. But something in Konstantin's words rings true: he's not going to hurt me. Not tonight, at least.

For a few long minutes, Konstantin steers the Mustang up Lincoln Boulevard, curving around the north point of the peninsula and heading south, back down the coast. The Presidio rises on our left, the ocean to the right, miniature white caps crashing far below the cliff's edge, the water black as night. Not for the first time, dread fills my chest at the idea of plunging under those icy waves, tossed in the endless current and sucked into the darkness, out of control. Sinking. Drowning. My body healing itself only for me to drown again. And again. And again.

Konstantin steers the car toward a rocky lookout point and hits the brakes hard, killing the engine with a lazy flick of his fingers.

"You seem uncomfortable, Charlotte." He twists in his seat, eyeing me with mock concern. "As I said, I did not invite you into my car with the intention to harm you. In fact, you might say I took pity on you, bleeding out on the sidewalk like that. Exactly how did you come to find yourself so"—he gestures vaguely at me—"incapacitated?"

"If you must know, I got into it with a few *immortui.*"

Konstantin's eyes widen slightly in what could almost be alarm, but with a quirk of his brow, he looks nothing but amused. "You've lived here long enough that you should know to stay away from Fort Point. That can't have been a fun encounter."

I huff a laugh. "You know about the *immortui?*"

"Of course I do. I'm sure you've realized by now that I have been in San Francisco for quite some time."

Unable to come up with a witty retort, I just nod, scraping my teeth along my bottom lip.

"When I saw you bleeding out on the sidewalk, half-drowned and pathetic," Konstantin offers with a half-hearted shrug, "I couldn't find it in myself to leave you there."

"Oh, what a gentleman," I drawl, dramatically clapping a hand to my chest. "My heart is all aflutter."

Konstantin considers me for a few moments, eyes narrowing. "Despite what you may believe, I have grown quite fond of you, love. It truly pains me to have mixed you up in all of this."

"Oh, come *on*," I say, leveling him with a glare. "Don't think I can't see through this little charade of yours. Trying to play the good guy so I'll feel sorry for you, hmm? Am I supposed to plead to Kaleb on your behalf? If I had my way, I'd bury a silver dagger in your heart right now. Just like you did to me."

Images flash of a clear night outside Olivia's house, when I encountered one of Konstantin's fledglings on a dark, empty street. The new scar over my heart twinges.

Konstantin's left shoulder ticks slightly, his expression darkening. "If you'll remember," he bites out, "I wasn't the one who stabbed you."

"It may not have been your hand holding the dagger, but the command was yours. I see no difference."

Rage flashes in his eyes, but it's gone so quickly that I wonder if I imagined it. He leans toward me, and it takes every ounce of willpower I have not to shy away. With a slight tilt of his head, he uses a gentle forefinger to lift my chin, examining me. His lips press into a soft pout.

"You are a pretty little bird."

The words make my neck prickle, a warning dancing along my skin. I'm struck by an odd sort of *déja vu,* though I know I've never been in Konstantin's car before. Maybe it has something to do with the hungry glint in his eye or the way he grins before sliding gracefully from the car.

"Follow," he calls over his shoulder, and my heart all but stops as he crosses the street, disappearing into the swirling mist of the Presidio.

CHAPTER 28

I'M *ALONE.*

Konstantin didn't even bother to check that I was, indeed, following him. It would be so easy to run—he left the door open, after all—but something urges me to stay. To follow. To see what the hell he wants.

Slowly, I unbuckle my seatbelt.

I dart across the street, shivering in a way that has nothing to do with the cold. A huge wall of eucalyptus and cypress trees stretch into the mist-laden sky, skinny trunks supporting a too-high canopy of leaves. I've always felt small near the Presidio—like I'm nothing but a mouse scurrying through a field of ancient, tall grass.

The rain has finally stopped but the air is cool and uncomfortably damp, fog rolling over the road and soaking into my clothes. I half-run after Konstantin as he moves deftly through the trees, disappearing into the fog before reappearing again, yards away. It's like following a ghost.

After a few minutes of aimless wandering, I call out, "What are we doing here, Konstantin?"

He stops dead in his tracks and I skid to a halt, barely avoiding a collision. Slowly, deliberately, he turns to face me.

"It's a lovely night," he says flatly, motioning around us. "The car was getting a bit stuffy and I thought we might get some fresh air. But that isn't what you're asking, is it?"

"No." Mist coats to my skin, making my blood-soaked clothes cling to me. The sensation makes me shudder. I sweep damp hair from the back of my neck and Konstantin tracks the movement, his eyes dark. "It's bad enough that you found me tonight. Are you just following me everywhere now? Me, specifically? You've made yourself known, you have Victoria . . . what is the *point?*"

"Rayna," Konstantin says forcefully and without hesitation. Electricity crackles in his eyes. "Rayna is, and always has been, the point."

I jab a finger into his chest. Surprisingly, he doesn't say a word, just stares at me expectantly. "You have no claim over Rayna."

"Oh?" Konstantin inches closer, my finger still pressed to his chest. "Did Rayna ever tell you about what happened when she *left?*"

I purse my lips. "You mean after you abused her, manipulated her, and drove her away with your possessive and piss-poor seduction techniques?"

"That is not what happened!" Konstantin snarls, startling a flock of birds from their perches high overhead. Their wings flap loudly, mirroring the frantic pounding of my heart. Realizing his lapse in composure, Konstantin straightens, peering down his nose at me. More quietly, he says, "That is *not* what happened."

And then he's moving again, faster this time. Shadows and mist curl in his wake, a pale wraith moving through the night with inhuman grace.

Again, I follow. After spending a week with "Ty," I thought I knew what Konstantin would be like. I expected a cocky, over-confident man with a plastered-on smirk and a bit of a wild streak. But this man is nothing like that. He's cold, calculating, and volatile. Unstable.

A predator on the loose.

Good hell. What am I *doing?*

My flight instinct lurches into overdrive and I whirl around, ready to make a run for it, but Konstantin materializes in front of me like a vengeful spirit. He stalks forward, forcing me to take one step back, then another. His eyes—once so charming and mischievous—are dark and abyssal, irises swallowed by night-black pupils. Red bleeds into their corners and he sneers at me through his fangs.

"I don't remember giving you permission to leave, little bird."

My back bumps into the rough bark of a tree trunk and I glance up, trees rising above me on all sides. The effect is dizzying. I drop my eyes and find Konstantin standing mere inches from me. Close enough that I can feel his cool breath on my face and see the tiny white scar cutting into his upper lip.

"Do you see where we're standing?" he murmurs, walking his fingers up my arm. Cold usually doesn't bother me, but there is something about Konstantin's icy touch that makes me shiver. "This is where your little Victoria lost her fire."

I suck in a breath. The breeze stills. Even the birds seem to stop their squawking.

"She had moxie, I'll give her that." Konstantin smirks as the veins darken beneath his eyes. "So beautiful. So fierce. But abysmally out of practice. She may have once been imposing, but time proves that even the mighty swan can be broken."

My hand flies on its own but Konstantin catches it, yanking my arm sideways. The motion pulls at my collarbone and I cry out as it *cracks*, undoing whatever healing had already begun. His grip is firm and almost skeletal, squeezing tight as he traps my hand against his chest.

"Her fear was *delicious*," he says, tugging me closer. A whimper escapes me, unbidden. "Such a pathetic thing, going on and on about how her valiant Alexander would save her. The poor boy did try, but look at how marvelously it backfired."

"Victoria isn't weak," I snap, but my voice wavers. Pain shoots through my wrist and I wriggle in Konstantin's grasp, trying desperately to keep it from snapping as well. "She's strong and amazing. And if you hurt a single hair on her head I will—"

I cut off abruptly as my mind catches up to Konstantin's words, and a claw of panic tears through me.

"What do you mean, he tried? Did—" Horror makes my stomach turn. "What did you do to Xander?"

Konstantin grins, a vile, venomous thing. "I've always said that two hostages are better than one."

"No," I breathe, the word coming out as a whisper. Then, louder, *"No!"*

I thrash against him, putting all my strength into shoving him away, but it's no use. With a sharp tug, he pulls me hard against him and I wince as the pieces of my collarbone grind together.

"Oh, yes," he murmurs, voice smooth as silk. "Your dear brother came looking for Victoria earlier this evening. Impressive that he was able to track her down so quickly, but I digress." I feel him smile, a shift of his lips against my ear. "Such a waste of intelligence, that one. A pity I had to lock him up as well."

Your dear brother.

My dear bastard, betrayer, coward. The bane of my existence. The reason for so many angry tears. The voice in the back of my head chastising me for every slip-up, every bad decision, every bit of reckless fun.

Then again, he is also the reason for centuries of laughter, of sharing meals and memories and tender moments. After Rayna left, he was there for every sleepless day, holding me close as I cried into my pillow. Even when I deserved his wrath, he gave me his protection. He has always been my one constant—my fierce North Star.

Guilt claws its way through my chest, leaving behind a hollow wound where Xander should be. I should have been looking for him, but I was too angry to think clearly. Instead, I waited. I fought with Rayna, I cried to Kaleb, I fawned over Tristan.

In the meantime, Xander was searching for Victoria *alone.*

For so long, I've painted him as my villain, but part of me has always known that wasn't true. If anything, Xander is a reluctant, belligerent hero. Despite everything he has done—despite the things I said to him, broken and bleeding on the floor of Nik's living room—every fiber of my being is screaming for my brother.

"Where is he?" I ask, low and lethal, clenching my jaw to keep it from shaking.

"You're clever enough to know that I'm not going to tell you." Konstantin pulls away, a bony hand still wrapped around my wrist. He regards me with amusement. "Your big brother broke the rules, and now he and I can have a bit of fun."

"You said you wouldn't kill him!"

"Not true. I said I wouldn't kill *Victoria*. Xander, however, received no such promise."

"*Please.*" I bite back a sob, kicking myself for the weakness in my voice. My knees threaten to buckle from the sheer weight of it all, but I manage to stay upright, even though it feels like I've been doused in frigid water. Like my foundation is crumbling beneath me. My eyes burn with unshed tears. "Please don't hurt him."

If my impassioned plea does anything to soften Konstantin, he doesn't show it. His silver eyes are cold and sharp as ever, watching me with a wolfish tilt of his head.

"Your week isn't up yet, love," he says, dropping my arm. "Xander will meet the same fate as Victoria if Kaleb doesn't tell me what he did to Rayna."

"Rayna left you!" I cry, resisting the urge to swing at him again. I'm afraid if I do, he'll rip my whole arm off. Though, that might be a better alternative to the incessant fire blazing through my shoulder and my still-healing, shredded forearm. "She isn't Kaleb's *property*. He can't give her back to you. Just—just *stop*!"

"Don't play me for a fool!" The predator returns with a vengeance, black eyes wide and murderous. I shrink away. "Kaleb knows what he did, and now that Rayna has finally shown her face, it's time I take back what is rightfully mine. Why else would I be in the godforsaken city?"

"I don't *know*!" I practically shout, my frustration boiling over. "I have no idea why you're here. I don't know what you want with me, I don't know why you're tormenting us, I don't know why you won't just *let it go!*"

Konstantin makes a small sound of condescension, his mouth quirking subtly.

"You truly have no idea what happened in Belarus, do you?"

Belarus. My home. "What are you talking about?"

With a twitch of his shoulder, he tightens his grip on my wrist. "Kaleb, Rayna, and Nik would have you believe they are the heroes of this story. That I was the irredeemable monster and they were nothing but my unsuspecting victims." He leans closer, dragging a finger down my neck to the new scar over my heart. It's like being caressed by liquid nitrogen. "But the three of them are far from innocent. Rayna's powers of manipulation rival mine. Your precious Alpha has done more unspeakable things than you could ever imagine. And Nikolas?" He scoffs. "Nikolas did *nothing* to stop them."

Tension coils in my chest, knotting in my throat. I try to swallow, but my mouth has gone dry.

"What did they do to you?"

Konstantin grins, all shadow and ice. "If you want an answer to that question, you'll have to ask them yourself."

There's something accusatory in his tone. Something almost pained. It triggers an instinctual urge in me and without thinking, I reach forward and press a palm to his sternum.

Konstantin stills. My breath catches. We stare at each other for a long moment, and I'm struck by the intimacy in our shared eye contact—a connection like I've never felt before, sizzling under my skin, etching itself in every vein, in every nerve. A claim. An *invasion.* It twines around my spine and squeezes tightly, making my chest constrict.

Konstantin wets his lips.

After a slow, steadying breath, I say, "Tell me what happened."

For the briefest moment, I think he might concede. His lips part slightly, his expression open—almost vulnerable—but he slams it shut with a sharp shake of his head.

"Another time, sweetheart," he says, stepping back—away from the soft pressure of my palm. "Kaleb still has a few days to come clean. In the meantime, I need you to keep an eye on him for me."

I laugh at the sudden shift in the conversation. "Are you completely delusional? I'm not going to *spy for you.*"

"Oh, yes you are." There is a mischievous glint in Konstantin's eye, and it reminds me so much of Ty that I almost forget the fledgling character was just an act. "You'll find I can be extremely persuasive."

The tree's canopy groans in a gust of wind as I consider the implications of those words. I've only known Konstantin for a couple of weeks and I know he has only scratched the surface of what he's truly capable of doing. I'm sure there is a myriad of horrible things he could do to *persuade* me. I can't agree to this. I *can't.* But I don't really have a choice, do I?

"Whatever." I have no intention of actually being a double agent, but if it will get me away from this nightmarish encounter and into a hot shower, I'll agree to just about anything. "Now, if you're done being the world's biggest dick, can I go home now, *my liege?*"

Konstantin lifts one hand and I brace for impact, but he only presses his palm to my cheek. His thumb brushes over my lips and, for one horrifying moment, I'm afraid he might try to kiss me again.

"Careful, little bird." His expression is distant, and I get the sense that he is lost in a memory, speaking to the ghost of someone long since gone. "Someday that sharp tongue of yours is going to get you killed."

A slow breath. Another. I match them, in and out, for what feels like an eternity. Finally, he steps back and smooths both hands down the front of his black dress shirt. The emotion drains from his expression like blood from an open wound.

"Run along, pet," Konstantin says coldly. "And don't speak a word of this meeting to that pesky family of yours."

I laugh once, shakily. "You can't be serious. Of course I'm going to tell them about it."

He mirrors my laugh, but his is darker. Crueler. There's a touch of wickedness in his expression that tells me there is something more going on here—something *big*. And, true to form, he isn't going to tell me what it is.

"Oh, Charlotte." Konstantin smiles, but it doesn't reach his eyes. "You won't tell anyone about it because I forbade you. And you'll find that when it comes to me, you simply can't resist."

The memory of his lips on mine all but confirms that fact.

"Goodbye, love," he says. "I will see you again soon."

And then, with a whisper of wind against my face, Konstantin is gone.

CHAPTER 29

After what I will later describe as a cold day in Hell, I stagger up to the mansion just in time to see dawn kiss the horizon. My shoulder throbs along with my half-healed forearm and the myriad of other gashes decorating my body, sending daggers of pain through me, and I'm ready to drain every blood bag in the cellar. The same thoughts keep rattling around in my mind: Konstantin has Victoria. He has *Xander*. He knows Rayna is alive. And, for whatever it's worth, he wants to keep me alive. For now.

Wincing through a deep breath, I trudge up to the front porch and turn the knob. The door creaks open to an empty foyer. I don't know what I expected—a welcome party? A giant banner that says, "Sorry we ditched you, glad you're not dead!"? Regardless, I can't help but feel a prickle of disappointment.

This may not be the reception of my dreams, but I'm *alive*. I survived the *immortui* and Konstantin all in one night, which is more than any of my family members can say.

With a sigh of relief, I close myself inside, letting the dawn-dark house engulf me. I lean back against the door and slide to the floor with a low groan. I've never been so happy to feel the bite of cold marble through my jeans.

"Charlotte?"

My attention snaps to the living room doorway just as a golden, freckled face peeks around the frame.

"Oh, thank God," Tristan breathes, rushing toward me. He falls to his knees and smothers me in a bone-crushing hug—one that might have broken my collarbone if it weren't already in two pieces. "Thank *God* you're okay."

"Stop," I rasp, knowing full well that *okay* is a gross overstatement. "You'll get blood on you."

Tristan startles and pulls back, enough to get a good look at me. The light is dim, but I'm sure there's no mistaking the blood soaking my clothes or the battered state of my arm. He inhales sharply as his eyes sweep over me, and my skin prickles with embarrassment. I'm supposed to be a *badass*. Tristan shouldn't see me like this.

I don't *want* him to see me like this.

Mercifully, he doesn't say anything else. Resolve hardens his expression—there is no disgust there, no fear of the blood that covers every inch of me. He simply pulls me close again, more gently this time, and cradles me against his chest. His touch is so different from Konstantin's that it's almost startling: where Konstantin is skeletal and possessive, Tristan is warm and muscular and sweet. Comforting. Adoring.

Safe.

Tristan strokes my hair gently, fingers catching in a few unruly knots. "What kind of vampire's boyfriend would I be if I were scared of a little blood?"

I huff a surprised laugh, which quickly turns into a sob. Tristan's embrace breaks down the last shred of control I have, and everything hits me at once: Enzo, the *immortui,* their too-long fangs piercing my skin. The momentary belief—growing more familiar every day—that I was going to die tonight. But I didn't. I'm still here. I'm *alive*.

I sag against Tristan's chest, breathing in linen and vanilla and the metallic tang of warm blood singing through his veins. There is a touch of whiskey on him, too, and the scent of it mixed with copper and salt has my head spinning. Hunger tears through me, hot and wild, my body desperate for the one substance it needs to repair itself.

Maybe it's the fact that I know there are blood bags downstairs, or because my body isn't strong enough to fight me, but I retract my fangs with surprising ease. *I am in control.*

"Boyfriend?" I manage, smiling a little at how human the word is.

Tristan chuckles, pressing a soft kiss to my forehead. "I'm yours, Char. If you'll have me."

I press a kiss of my own to the smooth skin at the base of his throat, clinging to him for dear life. Committing this moment to memory. And, for the first time in what feels like centuries, I'm not tempted to drink.

◊ ◊ ◊

After what could have been hours or minutes, Noah sneaks up from the basement with an armful of blood bags, one of each type.

"I'm not sure which is your favorite," he says, thrusting them at me, "but something tells me you'll probably want all of them."

I'm sure I put on quite the show for the human boys as I guzzle three bags in about thirty seconds, but if they're put off by it, they don't show it.

Apparently, my disappearance set my whole family reeling. Tristan informs me that when Rayna, Pippa, and Rose returned without me, Kaleb immediately set up a search party. An actual *search party.* Like I'm some lost little lamb. It's certainly more effort than he put into finding Victoria. Or Xander, for that matter.

Xander. The brother I disowned—the one captured by Konstantin.

I bite back a pang of worry, chastising myself for caring. But disowned or not, I can't just let him *suffer.*

I inhale another blood bag before slipping away from Tristan and Noah, shutting myself in my bedroom. It takes a few minutes for me to undress, slowly peeling my sodden clothes away, careful not to aggravate my collarbone. Thankfully, the sharp pain has settled to a dull throb; the multitude of blood bags did the trick, and most of my cuts and bruises are healing nicely. The slashes on my forearm, however, have turned into angry red ridges that criss-cross my skin, making it look more like a topographical map than anything. It reminds me of Pippa's forearm, scarred after she ran into a burning building in an attempt to save her daughter. After tonight, maybe she and I will match.

The shower water is too hot when I step in—scalding—and I hiss as it practically burns off the top layer of my skin. The blood has returned some of my strength, at least, and my mind feels clearer. And though my physical wounds are healing, I have a feeling the emotional wounds from tonight are going to linger for the foreseeable future.

I hear the front door bang open, followed by Nik's deep baritone. "Charlotte?"

A rush of footsteps, then Noah says, "She's in the shower." There's a beat, then he adds in a whisper, "It was pretty bad. Like, lost-a-fight-with-a-pack-of-Rottweilers bad. But she's okay. Just a little shaken."

"Good," Nik murmurs, though his tone is edged with worry. Heavy heels click over the wood floor, and he says, "Where do you think you're going?"

"Downstairs." Pippa sighs as her footsteps move downward. "There's a bottle of vodka in the wine room with my name on it."

I take a deep breath, mentally bracing myself for an inevitable barrage of questions. How am I supposed to tell everyone what happened tonight—about the *immortui* and Konstantin and Xander? Honestly, I don't know if I want to. If I had a choice, I would climb straight into bed and lock the door in a Ferris-Bueller-level attempt to shirk responsibility.

If only Konstantin hadn't started that damn ticking clock.

Kaleb and Rose return next, followed closely by Rayna and Henry. All eight of them—Tristan and Noah included—are caught up in varying levels of anger, with Henry being zero and Nik at level ten. He and Rayna continue to be excessively rude to one another, much to the others' chagrin.

"You know," Pippa says, releasing a sound of annoyance, "I'm starting to agree with Golden Boy over here. Will the two of you just *shut up?*"

More arguing. More yelling. More accusations of who did what and who's to blame for leaving me behind. For letting me disappear. Talking about me like I can't hear their every word.

Rayna and Kaleb veer into their own conversation, voices seething with anger.

"If you would have told me the truth about where you were going," Kaleb growls, "none of this would have happened. You cannot just run amok in my city, Rayna. Charlotte almost *died* because of you."

"Enzo said she was fine when she left—"

"I don't care what Lorenzo said," Kaleb snaps. "Your history with him does not make it acceptable for you to bring him into this. You encroached on his territory, not the other way around."

I perk up, listening more intently, but Henry yanks Kaleb aside. What did Kaleb mean about Rayna having *history* with Enzo? They only met a few hours ago.

Unless Enzo was only *pretending* not to know her. Unless Rayna hoped he didn't recognize her. I make a mental note to grill her about it later.

The arguing voices fade into a distant clamor as I step directly under the shower's stream, letting it wash away the fear, the pain, the pure exhaustion. The water runs cold as I scrub the last bits of blood from under my fingernails, my lips pursed. I don't even know why everyone is arguing. Least of all, why they're arguing about *me*.

With a sharp exhale, I turn off the water, the shower handle warping under my grip. I dry quickly and wrap a towel around myself, exiting the bathroom to see none other than Tristan examining the mess that is my desk. I release a small sound of surprise and his head snaps up, eyes widening in alarm, then embarrassment. He drops his gaze and spins around, shoulders shrugged in apology.

"I'm so sorry," he says, scrubbing a hand over his neck. "I was—I didn't know if you'd need any help after—you know what, never mind."

He moves to leave, and I can't help but laugh.

"Help with what, exactly? If you wanted to join me in the shower, you could have just asked."

Tristan says nothing, but there's an audible jump in his heart rate as his neck flushes pink. And even though I mean it as a joke, my own heart can't help but echo his. Warmth blooms in me as I imagine the steam, the heat, the water sluicing over Tristan's bare skin, the press of his lips at my throat . . .

Dammit, Charlotte. Stop that.

I shake off the surge of heat in my chest and slip into my closet, dressing in an oversized sweatshirt and leggings. Tristan is sitting on my bed when I emerge, looking sheepish. He's wearing a black t-shirt and sweatpants, his tousled golden hair practically glowing against the dark color. Something about the combination makes my stomach do a little somersault.

"Black?" I ask, gingerly taking a seat next to him. "Not your usual color palette. Or rather, *lack* of a color palette."

He glances down, as though just remembering what he's wearing.

"Oh, yeah. I had quite a bit of blood on me from"—he motions at me—"you know, and Kaleb gave me some of Xander's clothes to wear. I hope that's okay."

The pang of worry is back, stronger this time. If Xander were here, he would kill Kaleb for letting Tristan wear his clothes. My eyes drop to the floor, and I notice the rolled hems on his sweatpants. I smile, just a little.

When I don't respond, Tristan shifts closer, sliding his hand into mine. His skin is warm and soft, despite the guitar-string calluses on his fingers and the white scars criss-crossing his knuckles. A permanent reminder of the aftermath of Alison's death, when he lost control and put his hand through a mirror. It's hard to imagine Tristan reacting that strongly to anything, but I have only known him for a few weeks. The truth is, I have no idea what he's actually capable of.

Slowly, Tristan lifts our entwined hands and presses a kiss to my knuckles. There's a touch of hesitance in it, like he isn't sure if it's okay. If *we're* okay. If his earlier statement was a mistake.

Vampire's boyfriend.

It was cheesy. It was adorable. And I feel almost *giddy* just thinking about it. After Konstantin killed Jason at our party, I was convinced I would never see Tristan again. Now here I am, sitting next to him, listening to his heart stutter as I let my head fall unceremoniously onto his shoulder.

We sit in silence for a few minutes while the others continue arguing in the foyer—blaming one another, still talking about me like I can't *obviously hear them*—and I find myself curling into Tristan's warmth. Somehow he has become my safe place—someone not involved with my messy family with our combined centuries of trauma. Tristan is simple. Straightforward. A breath of fresh air.

"While I would love to stay like this all day," he murmurs against my hair, "we should probably put them out of their misery. It's only a matter of time before things get violent."

As if to illustrate his point, there's a loud clatter that echoes through the foyer, followed by a chorus of annoyed exclamations.

"You're probably right," I say reluctantly. "But I'm not sure if I'm ready to talk about what happened."

Tristan squeezes my hand reassuringly. "Then don't. You don't owe them an explanation. You're home, you're safe, and that's all that matters. If anyone has a problem with that, they can go through me."

"Oh?" I sit up and meet his eyes, which are dancing with mischief. "And how do you, a human, plan to keep a gang of grumpy vampires at bay?"

Tristan smiles crookedly. "It's morning, isn't it? All I have to do is open the curtains and they'll all go running for cover."

When we step into the foyer, Tristan with a reassuring hand on my back, the conversation halts abruptly. Seven heads turn to look at us, expressions varying from pity to surprise. Kaleb opens his mouth but I silence him with a withering glare.

"Look," I say, exhaustion hanging on every word. "I know you all have questions about what happened tonight and where I've been for the past few hours. And I really don't want to talk about it."

Nik's mouth twists into a frown. "But Lottie—"

"Nikolas. What did I just say?"

Rayna's eyes widen and she casts a furtive glance at her brother, who closes his mouth with a look of concern.

"And in case you were wondering," I say, scowling, "I can take care of myself. You've all been standing here arguing about me for the past thirty minutes, like I'm not even here. Who do you think you are? Stop blaming yourselves—or *each other*," I add with a pointed glare at Nik and Rayna, "for what happens to me. I'm not a child who needs protecting. What would you all have done tonight if it were Rayna who disappeared?" My tone is calm, but every word comes out like a jab. "Or Pippa? Rose? I can guarantee you wouldn't have organized a search party so quickly. You probably would have waited a few hours, at least. Or, I don't know, *picked up the phone?*" No one says a word. Even Pippa, who always has something clever to say, stays silent. Rayna won't even look at me. "I'm over two hundred years old, for Hell's sake. Give me a little bit of credit."

The corner of Kaleb's mouth twitches. Henry fidgets with his pocket watch. Noah slides close to Nik with a look of uncertainty while Rose manages a feeble smile.

"Here's a thought." I cross my arms and Tristan slides his hand around my waist, resting it on my hip. Rayna watches closely, her eyes narrowing. "Maybe if you didn't keep so many secrets from me, I wouldn't need your protection. Maybe if you involved me in your super secret plans"—a fiery stare aimed at Rayna, then Kaleb— "I would understand the risks. Maybe I wouldn't be so reckless if I actually knew what the *hell* was going on."

I have no idea where this is coming from. It's not like I planned to make an impassioned speech to my over-protective family, but here we are.

"And next time you decide to drag me into a potentially life-threatening situation," I say to a glaring Rayna, "consider telling me the truth. I'd rather not die because my *friend*"—the word feels wrong somehow, burning in my throat—"thinks she knows better than the rest of us."

My heart thuds loudly, worked into a frenzy by my public—and quite frankly, very dramatic—speech. Ten heartbeats. Twenty.

The fridge buzzes. The hall clock ticks.

There are a few wary nods, a few murmurs of assent. Kaleb inclines his head, satisfaction glittering in his icy gaze.

Tristan looks down at me and slowly, like morning sun cresting the horizon, he grins.

CHAPTER 30

I MUST HAVE DOZED OFF, because I wake to the sound of Nik's voice.

"I still can't believe there are *immortui* at Fort Point," he says, raking a hand through his hair. Noah lounges on the sofa next to him, his head resting on Nik's shoulder. "And I can't believe they're led by that *pirate*."

We're in the living room, scattered on the collection of plush furniture, in the middle of yet another hours-long family meeting. It's no wonder I fell asleep.

"Good morning," Tristan murmurs, his fingers combing through my still-damp hair as he holds me against his chest. The soft tug on my scalp feels far too good. "You haven't missed much."

"Lorenzo does not *lead* the *immortui*." Kaleb huffs in exasperation. I notice he doesn't bother correcting Nik on the pirate comment. "They are not an army. The man has considerable experience with their kind, so he was the obvious choice to keep them in line."

"What do you mean, considerable experience?" Rose's expression is wary.

"I mean," Kaleb says, "he almost became one himself. Being a vampire stranded on a ship with other vampires has its drawbacks. While the others turned on one another, Lorenzo did not cross that line. A miracle he survived, really. Though I suppose it was because of the blood bond."

"What on earth is that?" I ask, voice rough with sleep.

"A blood bond," Rayna interjects, "is a tentative connection between an *immortui* and the vampire who feeds it. As long as it is sustained by a single vampire, he can control that *immortui*. Blood calls to blood."

Kaleb nods, and my stomach turns. Enzo had called the *immortui* his Bonded, but I didn't think much of it at the time.

"Are you saying that Enzo"—I swallow against the tremor in my voice—"feeds them his own blood? *All* of them?"

Kaleb shrugs noncommittally. "There is a reason I summoned him to be a Lesser. The man has a soft spot for the *immortui* and would rather feed them than kill them, so I told him he would be allowed to keep them alive so long as they were all blood-bound. He agreed."

Before I can ask what a Lesser is, Tristan speaks.

"Vampire cannibals," he says with a shake of his head. "Somebody call Netflix."

His fingers continue their journey through my hair. The gesture is so simple, but warmth trickles through me, nonetheless. It's been so long since I experienced this—the *butterflies*. The anticipation of waiting for him to touch me, or wondering if I should touch him first. Despite the somber tone of this meeting—despite the fact that I went through hell tonight—my heart still flutters with each new brush of his fingers.

Tristan levels a gaze on Kaleb. "Are there a lot of these *immortui* in the city? Are they—do they ever feed on humans? Or just other vampires?"

Rayna snickers and I shoot her a glare, but she barely flinches. There is something too casual about the way she leans against the mantle, as though she doesn't have a care in the world. I haven't had a chance to ask her how she got away—what happened when she ran from Fort Point, leaving me behind—but I can't really blame her. If I had found an opening, I would have run too.

My focus returns to Tristan, whose heartbeat has quickened

considerably. I suspect he is asking about the *immortui*'s feeding habits not only for his own peace of mind, but to rule them out as suspects in Alison's murder. Kaleb considers him thoughtfully and I silently pray that he won't provide any helpful information. Coming to some mental conclusion, he kicks a foot onto the opposite knee, the picture of velvet-clad perfection.

"The *immortui* prefer the blood of normal vampires," Kaleb says, choosing his words carefully, "but they have been known to feed on their own kind, as well as humans. There are only a few dozen in the city, so there is no need to worry. Lorenzo keeps a tight leash, but if they manage to break his hold..." He trails off and Henry jumps in.

"I take care of them," the boy says, his grin all teeth, but his eyes are cold and distant. As Pippa said, he may look like a teenager, but he has seen just as many horrors as the rest of us.

Tristan nods, frowning slightly. Kaleb's answer doesn't suggest that the *immortui* could be responsible for Alison's death, but it doesn't completely rule them out, either. Good. Maybe I can use that to my advantage.

Kaleb watches me, a question in his eyes: *What is he after?*

I shake my head as if to say, *Not now,* masking the movement by tucking hair behind my ear.

He nods once, just as Rayna crosses the room. She nudges his foot from his knee in order to take a seat on his lap, then leans to whisper something in his ear. Kaleb's hand snakes around her waist and Nik grimaces.

"What happened after you talked to Enzo?" Noah asks, a sparkle in his ocean-blue eyes. I glance from him to Tristan, impressed by the fact that they've taken to all of this insanity so gracefully. Barely two weeks ago, neither of them knew anything about vampires or *immortui* or an ancient bastard with a thirst for revenge. But here they sit, in the middle of our vampire family meeting, offering their own comments like it's just a normal Sunday.

The only one who seems bothered by their presence is Rayna. No surprise there. She seems to be bothered by just about everything.

"Yeah, Lottie," she says, examining the nails on one hand, the other tracing invisible shapes on the back of Kaleb's neck. "What *did* happen? Where were you?"

"I already said, I don't want to talk about it." When everyone—Kaleb included—gives me a collective look of disapproval, I sigh. "I guess it wouldn't kill me to give you the Spark Note version."

By the time I stop talking, I've woven a tapestry of lies that would make even Rayna proud. As far as the others are concerned, I ran from Fort Point by myself, not sure where I was going, and must have blacked out. I woke up in the Presidio, alone and bleeding out. I managed to find a snack nearby—"No, Rayna, I didn't kill anyone"—and it gave me enough strength to get back home.

Not a complete lie, but definitely far from the whole truth.

I fish my phone from my pocket and nervously pass it from one hand to the other. On my way home from the Presidio, I received a text and a single photo from Konstantin—one that made my stomach drop.

"There's one more thing," I say, doing a poor job of masking the fear in my voice. I swallow hard and force my hands to still, flattening my phone between my palms. "Konstantin sent me another message."

When I pause, Rayna exhales slowly. "And? What did it say?"

Apprehension spikes in the room, a chorus of too-fast heartbeats. I swallow again, making a show of opening my text messages, then read Konstantin's message aloud.

"'Your brother came for his beloved but, unfortunately, I found him first. Thanks to his little stunt, I have shaved one day off your deadline.'"

There's a beat of stunned silence, then the room explodes.

"He has Xander and you're just telling us *now?*"

"Is he okay?"

"Do you have proof of life?"

I lie, and lie, and lie.

"Is that all Konstantin said?"

"Is he keeping Xander with Victoria?"

"Are you *sure* he didn't say anything else?"

"Okay, everyone shut up!" I yell, and they do, albeit reluctantly. Tristan remains silent next to me, his hand shifting to rest protectively on my shoulder. I stare down at the grainy photo filling my phone's screen. A bare arm, palm up and bloody. The tattoo on the inner forearm—two interlocking triangles—is marred by a deep ragged gash, blood oozing from the edges.

Xander's tattoo. The one he gave himself decades ago: one triangle for me, the other for Victoria.

"Oh my God," Tristan breathes.

At that, the others rush to crowd around me, looking down at the photo with matching expressions of horror. The only one who doesn't move is Kaleb, who stays seated, staring into the middle distance. He slowly pulls a cigarette from his pocket and lights it, smoke swirling around his head in delicate tendrils.

"He has Xander," I whimper through the renewed clamor, and I find myself choking back a surge of emotion, tears stinging my eyes. It's as though telling my family has suddenly made it all real. Xander is gone—*captured*—and it's all my fault. I should never have disowned him like that. I should never have let him leave. But now Konstantin has him and who knows what he's doing to him—what kind of torture he's putting him through.

Rayna throws her hands in the air, anger pulsing from her in waves. "I'm going to kill him. I'm going to murder that manipulative son of a bitch. We're not just going to let him take Xander from us. Who does he think he is?"

"The king, apparently," Nik mumbles, backing away with an indecipherable look. The others follow suit. "And he's not going to stop, Rayna. Konstantin will take every single one of us if it means finally getting to you."

"So," Rose whispers, eyes shining, "what are we supposed to do now?"

The room descends into palpable silence as the look on Rayna's face morphs from anger to fear. And she's not the only one. The question has a sobering effect, settling over us like a heavy blanket. Instinctively, we all turn to the Alpha for guidance. But Kaleb turns to me.

"Alexander is your brother, Charlotte. What would he have us do?"

I'm about to point out that Xander and I don't exactly gossip over our preferred kidnapping contingencies when a floorboard creaks down the hall. And then everything happens very fast.

One of the living room windows explodes inward, spraying glass in all directions. I throw myself over Tristan and drag him to the ground, using my body to shield him from the debris. A few shards slice across my back and I curse loudly, looking up just in time to see Nik punch a black-hooded fledgling in the face. The force knocks the boy out and he slumps to the ground.

What the *hell?*

A dozen or so fledglings flood the room, some entering through the shattered windows, others through the main doorway.

"What is this?" Rayna snarls, sending a fledgling sprawling with a roundhouse kick. "Sparring practice?"

"Might as well be!" Pippa replies, dropping a fledgling of her own. Henry twirls next to her, a dagger in each hand, slicing through a fledgling's throat with practiced ease and a manic grin. "These ones are *weak.*"

"Stay down," I murmur in Tristan's ear, then leap to my feet, catching one of the vampires by her black hood and slamming her onto the coffee table. She yelps as I kneel over her, pinning her with a hand to her throat. My aching shoulder protests but I ignore it, staring daggers into the girl's stormy gaze.

"Please!" she croaks, clawing at my hand. "Don't hurt me!"

"You really think that's going to work?"

"Please—"

"Why did Konstantin send you here?"

Her eyes glaze over, her expression turning wicked. "Konstantin is king. He will not stop until he retrieves what was taken—"

"How original," I growl, snapping the girl's neck in annoyance. "Never heard that one before."

In a matter of minutes, we've dispatched all but one fledgling, who decides to make a run for it. Kaleb, however, has other plans. He grabs the boy by the front of his shirt, teeth bared, and hurls him through the open window. There are a few seconds of silence before we hear the *crunch* of his body landing on some unseen car.

In the stillness that follows, I survey the room: glass litters the floor, there is blood splattered on the wall above the fireplace, and bodies— either dead or unconscious—are scattered around the room. The air is thick with the sound of ragged breathing and the overwhelming scent of vampire blood. Freshly-Turned, too, by the smell of it.

How many more fledglings is Konstantin going to make? What happens when there are too many? What happens if he loses control of them all?

"Charlotte," Tristan says softly, and I turn to find him on his feet. Blood drips from a shallow cut on his forehead. "You're bleeding."

"What?" That's when I remember the flying shards of glass, and I notice the way my sweatshirt clings to my skin. I reach around and drag a hand down my back, wincing at the holes in my shirt and the sting- ing gashes underneath. Long, but shallow. "I'm fine," I say, nodding at Tristan. Reveling at the concern on his face. "I'll heal quickly. You, on the other hand, won't be so lucky."

I move closer and touch two fingers to his bloodied hairline. He winces then watches intently, his lips slightly parted, as I bring my fingers to my mouth and lick them clean. Heat dances over his skin.

"All of you, check the house," Kaleb snaps, startling us apart. The Alpha snatches his still-burning cigarette from where he dropped it on the floor—Victoria would have a fit if she saw the scorch mark it left on the rug—and stalks out of the room "This is ludicrous," he grumbles, stepping over one of the fledglings. "Absolutely ludicrous. The bastard is just taunting us now . . ."

He trails off as he disappears into the entry, heading in the direction of Xander's art studio. The look Rayna flashes him is black as pitch but, surprisingly, she doesn't protest.

"Charlotte and Nik," she barks, taking on a commanding air, "the main floor. Pippa and Henry, downstairs. Rose and I will search upstairs. And you two"—she motions at Tristan and Noah—"try not to get yourselves killed."

Without waiting for a response, she exits the room, Rose trailing with a shrug. Pippa and Henry follow suit, heading for the basement.

Noah appears next to Tristan, putting a hand on his friend's shoulder. "Maybe we should go home," he says quietly. "This is getting a little bit—"

"No!" Nik shouts, then, more softly, "No. Whether we like it or not, you two are part of this now. Konstantin knows every player in this game, and he knows every pressure point. He took Victoria, he took Xander . . ." Nik pulls Noah close. "I've suffered too much at his hand. If something happened to you, I—I don't know if I could bear it."

An old ache echoes through my chest, dredging up the memory of Nik after Rayna's death. We had been dating on and off for a few decades, but losing Rayna changed him irrevocably. Our relationship was never the same after that, and I wondered if he would ever find real love again. But there is something different in the way he looks at Noah. I can't quite pinpoint it, but I can *feel* it. One thing's for sure: Noah's a total goner. The boy looks at Nik like he was sent by God himself.

"Nothing is going to happen to me," he says, giving Nik a peck on the lips. "Not if I'm with you."

"Should we leave?" Tristan stage-whispers in my direction. "Not sure if I can stomach watching your ex devour my best friend."

Noah punches his arm and the two of them break into easy laughter.

"Come on." I take Tristan's hand and drag him from the room. I'm not sure he has any idea how literally Nik *devours* Noah, and I'm not about to educate him.

Shadows crawl from the corners as we slip into the entry, enveloping everything in a blanket of seething black. I resist the urge to turn the lights on—not to see better, but for my own peace of mind. There is nowhere to hide in the light.

I slip down the hallway toward the ballroom, Tristan following blindly, and listen for the footfalls of unexpected guests. Thanks to our vampire stealth, I barely hear the others as they search, and the house succumbs to an eerie, tense silence. If it weren't for Tristan's warm hand in mine and the steady beat of his heart, I would feel completely alone. In my giant house. In the dark.

The ballroom door whispers over the floor as I push it open. A chill settles over me, trickling down my neck, crawling over my skin. If I hadn't experienced it myself, I would never have believed that this room hosted a battle only a few nights ago. A very short-lived one, but a battle nonetheless.

Watery moonlight filters through the north windows, bathing the floor in cool white as I tiptoe inside. My hand slides from Tristan's and I turn around, reaching for him. But he takes a step back from the doorway, then another, his expression haunted.

"I—I can't," he whispers, shaking his head. He says nothing else, but I mentally finish the thought: *Not after Jason.*

I nod, heart clenching, then motion for him to stay still and quiet. He nods, pressing his back against the wall as he steadies his breathing.

Something flutters in the corner of my eye and I whirl around, staring at the white curtains that hang limply over a wall of windows. One of them shivers and my heart jumps into my throat, my frantic pulse roaring in my ears.

I dash toward the shuddering curtain and throw it open, only to find the window slightly ajar. Resting on the sill next to a deliberate smear of blood is a small figurine. I pick it up with trembling fingers to examine it, noting the smooth edges, the black varnish, the tiny cross on its head.

It's a chess piece—a shiny black king.

The piece clatters to the ground and I recoil, staggering backward.

Konstantin was *here*. It was one thing when I was here alone, but he was in my house with my entire family. With *Tristan*.

Without knowing why, Konstantin's voice rings through my head, as though he left a message just for me: *I see everything, Charlotte. Tell Kaleb what I want. Bring her to me.*

My phone buzzes.

> Did you like my little test, pet? I must say, I'm impressed that you all managed to dispatch this new batch so quickly. Next time, they'll be stronger.

Next time. My stomach lurches and the floor sways beneath me. I stumble a few steps before I gain my footing, then sprint back through the ballroom doors.

"He was here!" I shriek, seizing the hand of a bewildered Tristan. He staggers behind me as I drag him through the hall. "Konstantin was here!"

There's a flurry of footsteps, the *bang* of something hitting the floor upstairs, and we nearly collide with, well, *everyone* as we skid into the foyer.

"He was here?" Rayna snaps, her eyes alight. "How do you know?"

"Chess piece," I pant, pointing to the ballroom. "A black king."

Tristan wraps his arms around my shoulders. His steady grip grounds me, despite the way his own body trembles.

"Everyone, outside." Kaleb smooths his hair back in a show of nonchalance, but it does nothing to mask the panic building in his voice. "We're leaving."

Rose clears her throat quietly. "It's the middle of the day. Where are we—"

"*Now.*" Kaleb takes a shaky, calming breath. "Please."

Without another word, he throws open the front door and disappears into the cloudy afternoon.

CHAPTER 31

Wind screams through the trees above the Sutro Baths, whipping my hair into my face as I lock Xander's Maserati. The day is dreary and damp, carrying with it the promise of another storm, and my clothes cling to me in all the wrong places. I barely had time to grab another shirt—one without bloody slashes torn through it—before Kaleb whisked us away on what is sure to be a miserable adventure.

The Alpha slams his Mercedes door shut, surveying our bedraggled group with a bleak expression. He tallies each of us on his fingers: Rayna, Henry and Pippa, Rose, Nik and Noah, Tristan, and me.

"All accounted for," he murmurs, though worry still creases his brow. I mentally add, *All except for Xander and Victoria.* Kaleb locks eyes with me for a moment, as though sharing the same thought.

"Are we sure it's a good idea for the humans to be here?" Rayna asks no one in particular, as if Tristan and Noah aren't standing *right here*. "We're kind of in the middle of some 'family drama'"—she adds air quotes to the words—"and I'm not sure I'm in the mood to protect a couple of walking blood donors."

Tristan narrows his eyes dubiously. "Should I be offended?"

"Don't worry about her, Tristan," Pippa says, tucking a loose strand of hair into her braid. "Rayna has been away from us for far too long, and has thus forgotten her manners."

Noah snorts while Nik glares daggers at his sister.

"Don't you try anything," he warns, wrapping a protective arm around Noah's middle. "Just because they're human doesn't give you permission to eat them."

I take a step toward Tristan, who takes a sly step of his own. He removes one hand from his jacket pocket and lets it hang in the space between us. Our fingertips brush, sending a little thrill through me.

And now I'm blushing like a damn school girl.

"Besides," I say as we lock pinky fingers, "if we're going to be holed up under that cliffside for an indeterminate amount of time, then I think we all deserve to bring a plus one. You know. To keep ourselves *entertained*." Tristan's heartbeat stutters, drawing a little chuckle from Pippa and Henry. "It's safer for them, anyway."

"Are you sure about that?" Rayna's sharp tone cuts through the wind like a saber.

"Of course I'm sure," I snap back, though my voice falters, just a little. While I would rather have Tristan here, there are definitely risks involved with taking a pair of humans into a vampire-run subjugate club. What's to stop the patrons from assuming Tristan and Noah are on the night's menu?

"Ladies, ladies." Henry lifts his hands, palms forward in a placating gesture. "Is this really the best time for a squabble? I suggest we get out of this horrible weather and into the safety of the club, then you may argue to your hearts' content." He leans sideways to whisper—loudly—into Pippa's ear. "How long do you think they'll last before things get violent?"

Rose raises an eyebrow. "I bet Lottie takes the first swing."

"I'll take that bet," Pippa says, grinning. "Fifty bucks."

The girls shake hands, and I flash my middle finger with a flourish.

"Are you all quite finished?" Kaleb's tone is weary, but there's an unusual bite to it. "Konstantin could have followed us here. Do you really want to risk another attack while arguing over who is allowed inside *my club*? Anyone who is important to my family is important to me. Therefore, the humans stay." When Rayna opens her mouth to object, he says, "End of discussion. Now, if you will all follow me."

He turns heel and leads us into the wooded area overlooking the cliffside, walking with none of his usual poise. An invisible weight seems to have settled onto his shoulders, getting heavier with each purposeful step. Tristan is watching Kaleb with an unreadable expression.

"Come on," I say, slipping my hand into his. "You're not going to believe this place."

He nods absently, falling into step with me as we take up positions at the back of the group. We follow Kaleb in a shaky line, splashing through puddles and trudging through the undergrowth without bothering to hide our tracks. There's a stiffness in Tristan's shoulders that is hard to ignore, especially when his hand now has mine in a death grip.

"Are you okay?" I whisper, and I see Rayna's head angle backward. She is at the front with Kaleb, walking arm-in-arm. "Nothing is going to hurt you, you know. You've got seven vampires in your corner. Nine, when we get Xander and Victoria back."

"What?" he asks, shaking himself out of a daze.

"You seem a little tense," I say, squeezing his hand gently. "And you're cutting off the circulation to my fingers." He lets go abruptly with a mumbled apology, but I snatch his hand back. "Give me that."

Humor flashes in Tristan's eyes and his face splits into a warm grin—the one that makes him glow. The one that makes me yearn for the sun.

"I like this version of you," he says, leaning close. The butterflies stir.

"Oh, yeah? Which version is that?"

"The one who stands up for what she wants." He pulls me against his side, our steps falling into sync. "I've always been a sucker for confident women."

And there it is again: the flush of ambiguous heat creeping into my cheeks, making me want to do something unsavory and wildly inappropriate under the current circumstances.

"Also," Tristan adds with a wry smirk, "this version of you seems much less likely to run away at any sign of trouble. I still can't believe you ditched me in the middle of our first dance."

I shove him sideways and he laughs, the grin on his face gleaming bright enough to banish the shadows. For a few glorious moments, I forget to be afraid.

Tristan's laughter shatters the nervous tension surrounding our group and a few whispered conversations strike up in front of us. I pull Tristan back toward me and he boldly wraps an arm around my waist, drawing me against him with a strong hand cupping my hipbone. I return the half-embrace, sliding my hand under his jacket to tease the skin on his lower back.

Tristan startles and twists away. "God, your hands are *freezing!*"

We enter The Caged Bird through a trapdoor in the ground, a nicer—though equally creepy—entrance than the mildewed tunnel Xander, Nik, and I used last week. I can sense Tristan's apprehension as he follows me into the square hole, and he's not the only one. Anxious energy buzzes through the air as we make our way through the torch-lit hall. The only one who seems at ease is Rayna, who strides over the well-worn stone and into the *much nicer elevator* with undeniable confidence.

It seems she's been here before. Not surprising—I'm sure this is where she and Kaleb *reunited.* Though that doesn't seem to have added any warmth to their rekindled relationship. They may be hooking up and showing a nauseating amount of public affection, but they're missing some of their usual spark. I'm sure it's awkward, reuniting after so many years apart. But this is more than simple discomfort. This is a real, tangible distance—like Rayna has returned physically, but her mind is somewhere else. Somewhere dark.

The elevator spits us into a familiar marble vestibule. It's still just as gaudy as the last time I was here, with its encyclopedia-laden bookshelves, gold sconces, and gilded doors.

"Wow," Tristan whispers, his breath warm against my ear. "This place is *fancy.*"

"Yeah, you'd think so," I mumble, ears trained on the activity happening on the other side of the giant club doors.

Without warning, they fly open and we all stumble back as a bronze-skinned woman in a fitted black dress strides into the vestibule—Yara, a member of the Alpha's inner circle. Her eyes are glued to the tablet in her hands, her French-tipped nails clicking against the screen.

"Welcome to The Caged Bird," she says in a clipped Brazilian accent, swiping at her tablet. "How many are in your party?"

She glances up to see Kaleb and Henry amidst our beleaguered group, and her demeanor shifts from indifference to displeasure.

"What is this?" she asks Kaleb, waving her hand at us with a look of disgust. "What is the rabble doing here?"

Kaleb straightens, all signs of exhaustion gone. Ever the Alpha. Henry mirrors him, slipping on the cheery mask like a second skin. It's clear that the two of them are well-versed in putting on a show; they stand tall and proud, twin pictures of poise despite the hellish few days we've had.

Looking at them now—at Kaleb's cold command and Henry's calm deference—I can almost imagine Xander standing with them, his head inclined and his arms folded over his black-clad chest. The Beta.

"They are not *commoners*, Yara," Kaleb states, the words cold as winter wind. "You will do well to maintain decorum when in the presence of guests. We wouldn't want them to think I've trained my employees to exhibit such vulgar behavior."

Her smile is nothing short of venomous.

"Of course, sir," she says, shoving the tablet under her arm. "I wouldn't want to smear your glowing reputation."

"How about a drink?" I blurt out, angling my body between Yara and Kaleb. "I'll take a bottle of top shelf scotch. No less."

Yara fixes me with a snake's glare, then stomps back through the club's doors, black hair swaying behind her.

"Well," Pippa says, "ain't she just a ray of sunshine?"

"Pay her no mind," Kaleb says. "She has perfected the art of holding a grudge."

Rayna eyes him dubiously. "What did you do?"

"It hardly matters," he answers a little too quickly, shutting the question down. "You are all free to wander the Bird as you wish. The club is open to you, as are the bedrooms." He motions to a hallway on his left, then his right. "I do have some business to attend to, but I encourage you all to get some rest. We have an eventful few days ahead of us."

The mood sobers again, fear spiking in my chest. Kaleb turns to Tristan, then to Noah.

"Regarding the two of you, our family has a strict 'leave no bodies' policy, but I cannot say the same for the Bird's patrons. I would suggest the two of you not enter the main club unaccompanied."

They both nod, sharing a look of apprehension.

With a quick tug on his lapel, Kaleb pulls the gold doors open and disappears into The Caged Bird, Rayna on his arm. Henry follows, dragging a grinning Pippa behind him.

"Bedrooms, huh?" Noah wiggles his eyebrows at Nik, who swipes his tongue over his teeth. "How about we check them out?"

"Yeah, Char," Tristan adds suggestively, nudging me with his elbow. "What do you say?"

I know he's kidding—or at least, I *think* he is—but warmth still pools in my chest, trickling down into my abdomen.

Rose shakes her head with a disgusted eye roll. "You guys have fun. Meanwhile, I'm going to find the biggest, cushiest bed in this place and bury myself in it. And," she adds, lowering her voice, "I'm going to make a few calls. Maybe I'll be able to pick up on Xander's trail. You know, figure out how he was able to find Victoria."

We watch as she slips down one of the long hallways, already tapping away at her phone with a crease between her brows. It summons a twinge of guilt to my chest. Xander has always been a grounding force for Rose, starting the night Kaleb first brought her home, wild-eyed and feral. I haven't had a chance to talk to her since Xander first disappeared, and I can't help but wonder how she's doing. If she's as worried about my brother as I am.

Nik nudges Noah down the other hallway and winks as they disappear around a corner, leaving me alone with Tristan. Suddenly, I can breathe again. There have been too many people—too many *problems* these past couple of weeks, and I want nothing more than to run away from it all. Maybe I should take Tristan up on his suggestion and lead him back to what is sure to be a luxurious bedroom . . .

"Don't tempt me."

I blink up at him. "What?"

Tristan takes me by the wrists and draws me close. "If you could see the look on your face, you'd know *exactly* what I mean."

Fire blazes in his eyes as he drinks me in, his gaze snagging on the coin around my neck. He touches it softly and I hiss as he moves it aside, the silver biting into fresh, unscarred skin.

"And what is my face telling you, exactly?" The words come out as a rasp.

"That you want me." His grin is all sunshine and sultry warmth as leans in, his breath hot against my ear. "Right now."

Good hell.

I stare at the exposed column of his neck, his pulse throbbing wildly just below his skin. Pressure builds in my gums as hunger tears through me, alive and desperate and waiting.

I am in control.

Taking a slow breath, I ease my hands from Tristan's grip and bury them in his silky hair. He inhales deeply, catching his lower lip between his teeth.

"If you're right and that is, indeed, what I'm thinking"—I lift my face, my lips a whisper against his—"I should probably ask: do you want me, too?"

Our breath mingles and, for a few heated seconds, I'm afraid he might say no. But his hands tug at the hem of my sweater as he says,

"*God*, yes," and the words are practically a demand. "I've wanted you since the moment I saw you at that Halloween party. I thought you were beautiful then. But now, knowing you?" He grins against my mouth, broad hands teasing the bare skin of my lower back. "I can't get you out of my head, Char. I think about doing this"—he brushes his lips over mine, pressing soft kisses along my jawline—"every second of every day."

I arch into Tristan, fisting his hair as his kisses deepen, his hands roving wherever they can reach. My body is still sore—still healing from the night's events, but I relish every ache from my shoulder, every sharp sting from the gashes on my back. Tristan is here, holding me. *Wanting* me. Pressing me back against one of the bookshelves as he kisses his way down my sternum—

Someone clears their throat and Tristan flies backward, his cheeks flushing scarlet. Yara's head pokes out from the club doors, a look of disdain on her face.

"While we do encourage a bit of debauchery at the Bird," she says, "it is highly discouraged in the *foyer.*"

As if on cue, the elevator opens with a *ding* and a group of vampire women pours out. They look like they're ready for a night at the opera, their throats bedazzled with jeweled necklaces befitting royalty. Their elegant evening gowns shimmer in the dim light as Yara approaches them, shooing us away with a furtive flick of her wrist.

"Welcome to The Caged Bird," she says to the women as we scurry into the hallway. "How many are in your party?"

Tristan and I press our backs against the wall, and I can't help the small laugh that escapes me.

"If we would have gone much further, those women could have enjoyed dinner *and* a show."

Tristan snickers. "Wouldn't that have been something?"

"You know," I say, twisting to trap him against the wall, "I think Nik and Noah may have had the right idea about finding a bedroom."

Heat burns under Tristan's skin, darkening the flush already prevalent in his cheeks. I breathe it in—the vanilla and linen, the salty-sweet scent of blood flowing through his veins. His gaze drops to my mouth, where my fangs now peek through my gums. With one hand, he cups my cheek, gingerly touching one pointed tooth with the pad of his thumb.

"Freaky," he murmurs, his mouth curving upward. His expression turns dubious when he asks, "You're not going to bite me again, are you?"

"Maybe I will." I kiss him softly at the base of his neck, smiling when his breath catches. "You were so delicious the last time."

I freeze, replaying the words in my head.

"Sorry," I say, mortified. "I didn't mean—"

"Don't." Tristan catches my chin, angling my face toward his. "Don't apologize for what you are."

Molten gold flashes in his eyes, his pupils blown wide. He smirks at some unspoken joke, but there's something beneath that easy humor of his—something wild and bright and aching to be unleashed.

Hunger rises up inside of me, clawing at my throat while heat bubbles low in my abdomen. But the group of women in the foyer laughs, shattering the moment, and Tristan exhales slowly, gently pushing me away.

"As much as I would love to see what the bedrooms are like in this place," he says with a sly quirk of his lips, "I was thinking that this might be a good time to talk to Kaleb. About Alison."

It's like being thrown into an icy river.

"Are you two going to use a room or not?" Yara drawls, striding around the corner. "Regardless, I would ask that you kindly refrain from fornicating in the hallway."

"Oh, we wouldn't dream of it." I put a hand to my chest, fluttering my lashes in mock innocence. "Surely, Kaleb must have mentioned my glowing reputation. 'Chaste Charlotte,' they call me."

Tristan laughs, then stifles it quickly when Yara fixes him with an acidic glare.

"I need to, uh, use the restroom." He flashes an apologetic smile, touching my cheek gently. "I'll be right back."

When I nod, he goes to the nearest bedroom door and, finding it unlocked, slips inside.

I turn back to Yara with a low growl. She rolls her eyes and taps on her tablet a few times. As nonchalantly as possible, I crane my neck to see what she's doing, but she only holds the device closer.

Despite her near-constant scowl, Yara is stunning. Her skin is deep bronze and her raven hair falls past her shoulders in thick waves. Personally, I'm not a fan of the *femme fatale* look, but she pulls it off: a skin-tight black dress, nylons, and stiletto heels. If I could venture a guess, I'd say she has destroyed her fair share of men. Though, obviously, Kaleb has never been on that list. So why hasn't she moved on to fresher prey?

"Why are you here?"

Her head snaps up. "Excuse me?"

"I'm not trying to be rude," I amend, putting on a pitying air. "I'm just curious. From the few things I know about you, it seems like you and Kaleb don't get along very well. So, why do you work for him? I'm sure there are plenty of other rich vampire douchebags who need assistants."

"I'm not an assistant," Yara says through a sneer. "I've worked for the Alphas of San Francisco for eighty-five years. I know everything there is to know about this city, and then some. Men like Kaleb wouldn't survive without me."

Flipping her glossy hair over her shoulder, she strides away, her stilettos clicking like gunshots in the empty hallway.

CHAPTER 32

The woman makes her rounds.

She mingles with the patrons, moving from one group to the next with practiced ease. Soon, she thinks, surveying the room. Soon, this will all be over.

When the company is right, she shares the note.

A man takes it from her, glances at it, and flashes a wicked grin as she walks away.

The black card passes from the man in the brocade coat to a woman with diamonds at her neck, then to a girl in red satin. Slowly at first, then more rapidly as the anticipation grows.

After a few minutes, the note is returned to the woman by a girl with tight blonde braids and a scar through her eye. The woman glances out over a sea of guests—dozens of them—noting the thirteen pairs of eyes watching her carefully.

The woman nods. She receives thirteen nods in return.

And then they get to work.

She smiles to herself, smoothing her fingers over the note with its single word written in hasty silver script:

Tonight.

CHAPTER 33

I wait for Tristan in the foyer. It has only been a few minutes, but somehow I can feel his absence. Even in the midst of what might be the most horrible month of my life so far, Tristan manages to make me feel alive. Hopeful, even. Everything is darker when he's gone, even if he's just down the hall.

Closing my eyes, I lean back against the wall by the elevator, listening to the club's quiet symphony: glasses clinking at the bar, water running in one of the bathrooms, women laughing loudly at a man's unfunny joke. Somewhere in the mix, I can hear the familiar cadence of Pippa's voice as she charms her way into someone's conversation, and Rose as she answers a phone call. Nik and Noah have found a room and are, well . . . 'enjoying themselves' is putting it lightly.

The only voices I don't hear are Kaleb's and Rayna's, making me wonder if they're still inside the club at all. Maybe they're out looking for Xander and Victoria. But I doubt it.

I press my palms to my eyes and try to imagine my brother walking these halls as Kaleb's Beta. His right hand. It isn't hard to picture his shadow here, moving through the dim rooms like a wraith. When we visited this club barely a week ago, he was so confident; looking back, I'm amazed I didn't suspect something then.

With a jolt, I realize that not only have I been disrespecting my brother for seventeen years, but also the city's second-in-command—one of the most reputable vampires in San Francisco. If it were anyone else, I would have had my heart ripped out by now. But Xander put up with me, despite everything I've done to potentially ruin his reputation. Maybe I haven't been giving him enough credit.

It pains me to admit it, but I feel a touch of pride at the idea of being the Beta's sister. Xander is practically royalty, which makes him kind of a badass. By hiding that fact from me, he has denied me nearly two decades of bragging rights. The *audacity.*

Now I *want* to see him here, using his Beta privileges to boss everyone around. I want to hear his bored, judgmental voice giving me unsolicited advice. Hell, I would give anything to see him saunter around the corner and chastise me for loitering in the hallway.

I didn't realize how much I needed him until I lost him. And now I want him back.

"Dammit," I groan, just as Tristan saunters into the foyer.

"You okay, there?" he asks, all smiles. All the heat is gone from him, but I still feel the stir of butterflies when his hand twines with mine. "Yara didn't yell at you again, did she?"

I snort. "No, thank goodness. I'm just kicking myself for how I've treated Xander for the last, I don't know, hundred or so years. Just your typical existential crisis."

"Hmm." Tristan squeezes my hand. "Knowing you, you're probably overthinking it. Xander loves you. Even I, being a lowly human outsider, can see that."

"He sure does a poor job of showing it. Though," I add, fiddling with the ring on Tristan's finger, "I'm not any better."

Tristan places his free hand over our joined ones.

"Alison and I had our fair share of fights when we were growing up. You may think you and Xander are unique, but brothers and sisters are practically all the same. Just because you don't always get along doesn't mean you don't love each other. And I think you both know that."

I smile but it feels forced. It's one thing for me to love my brother. It's another thing entirely to believe that he loves me back.

Tristan hugs me tightly for a few seconds, banishing my unease before he pulls me toward the club doors. His hand is on the knob before I come to my senses, yanking him back.

"Wait. I should probably give you a bit of warning before we go inside."

I quickly explain the purpose of the club: Kaleb keeps Compelled humans here to act as subjugates for highbrow vampires in the city. Better than having them hunting for all their meals. It used to be a common practice in the vampire world, but the trend has died out over the centuries. Unfortunately, Kaleb is keeping the tradition alive.

When I finish, Tristan just stares at me, his mouth agape.

"Wow," he says finally, a hand scrubbing over his mouth. "I'm about to be very creeped out, aren't I?"

"Probably." I shrug. "But if you want to talk to Kaleb, you'll have to walk through the pit of vipers."

The inside of the club is exactly how I remember it. We push through the doors, the air thick with cigarette smoke, the burn of strong whiskey, and the reek of overlapping perfumes and colognes. Tristan coughs, discreetly covering his nose. Murmurs and quiet laughter drift through the air, and the chandeliers are dimmed, washing the lavish room in a layer of wan yellow. There are the oriental rugs, gilded paintings, and lush velvet furniture where vampires lounge in all their finery.

With them are dozens of subjugates, their necks bloody and their glassy eyes vacant.

Tristan leans close and whispers, "Thanks for the warning." His skin has taken on a greenish pallor and I squeeze his hand reassuringly.

"No one is going to touch you," I murmur, staring down the patrons who have started to gawk. One even has the audacity to lick her lips, and I snarl at her in return. "Not while I'm here."

"Psst! Lottie!"

I glance down the bar to see Rayna sitting on a barstool, facing the room with her elbows on the counter. She beckons us closer, a conspiratorial grin on her face.

"What do you think?" she asks as I take the stool next to her and Tristan claims the one on my other side. "Do Henry and Pippa actually like each other? Or are they both just really good in bed?"

I smack Rayna's arm, but scan the room until I locate the pair sprawled on one of the sofas near the fireplace, Pippa draped over Henry's lap like a swath of pale silk. A small group of vampires listens as Pippa regales them with what seems to be a thrilling story. While she speaks, Henry runs spindly fingers through her hair, pressing absent-minded kisses to the corner of her jaw, the bare skin at her collarbone. His expression shows nothing but pure adoration.

"That is the face of a man in love," I say. "Whether he knows it or not."

"More like a vicious puppy in love, but I digress," Rayna says, and we both snicker.

"Anything to drink, *amies*?"

I spin on my stool to see the handsome brown-skinned bartender drying a glass with a white towel. James—one of Kaleb's inner circle and an old lover of Nik's—grins at me, his fangs glinting.

"Miss Charlotte," he says in his deep French accent. Setting the glass down, he busies himself with another one, muscles flexing under his white dress shirt. "Kaleb mentioned you were here. And who is this golden beauty?" He smiles warmly at Tristan, who looks startled to be addressed at all.

"Oh, um, Tristan," he stammers, cheeks flushing. "I'm Tristan."

"And what can I get you, Tristan? It's on the house." James winks.

Tristan just stares at him.

"I'm not a vampire," he blurts loudly, garnering a few annoyed glares from the club's guests.

Rayna snorts. "He knows that, sunshine. What, did you think he was going to offer you a sampling of their finest O-negative?"

I'm about to snap back at her, but Tristan leans onto the bar, neck craning around me so he can glower at Rayna. "Give me a break, will you? I've only known that vampires exist for, I don't know, four days? And now I'm sitting in some blood-letting speakeasy built into a cliff-side. Excuse me for not having a clue."

Rayna makes a small sound of approval, resting her chin on her hand. "Can I assume you've never ordered top shelf liquor?"

"Technically, I *can't* order liquor. I'm twenty."

"Good Lord," Rayna says. "James, we're going to need one of everything. This boy needs a lesson in alcohol."

"Rayna," I hiss. "Are you trying to get on my bad side?"

"Actually," she whispers, "I'm trying to keep your golden retriever distracted for a few minutes. You need to go talk to Kaleb."

She jabs a thumb over her shoulder, and I glance behind her to a row of circular booths at the back of the club. The lights are dimmer there, sconces glowing on the walls and candles flickering on a few low tables. One booth is occupied and it takes a few seconds for me to make out Kaleb's familiar silhouette just as he sinks his teeth into a subjugate boy's neck.

"Why?" I ask Rayna, frowning.

"He's not okay, Lottie. It's been so long since he and I—" Her expression falls, and she picks absently at her cuticles. "I don't know how to help him anymore."

There's a helplessness in her voice that has me reaching for her hands, but I stop myself, tucking them into my lap. It's not just her relationship with Kaleb she's having to re-navigate. She and I have so much to discuss but I don't know how to approach it. I'm not sure if this new Rayna likes talking about her feelings. The old Rayna sure as hell didn't.

James sets two drinks in front of me, raising a meaningful brow. "Take the other one to Kaleb, will you? I'm worried about him, too."

I nod and snatch up the glasses, my gaze lingering on Tristan for a moment before making my way to the back of the room. Rayna is already at his side, pouring what looks like vodka into a glass. Patrons leer at me as I walk by, most likely because of my total lack of a formal wardrobe. I make a show of readjusting my t-shirt, flashing the Led Zeppelin logo to anyone who can see.

"Your Majesty," I say, sliding onto the green velvet bench across from Kaleb. "It's rather antisocial of you to be hiding back here alone."

Kaleb sighs through his nose and detaches himself from the subjugate boy. He presses one thumb to the tidy fang marks at his neck, using the other to wipe a smudge of blood from his own lip.

"Please don't call me that."

"What, *Your Majesty?*" I take a long sip of the whiskey, humming softly at the rich, woody flavor. "I think it's rather fitting. Don't you?"

Kaleb narrows his eyes reproachfully, but it lacks its usual fervor. In fact, as I watch the way he shakily lifts his glass, how his hand carelessly slides from the boy's neck, I realize that he might be in worse shape than he lets on. Ever the leader, he has been putting on airs to appear calm. Controlled. Unfazed by Konstantin's looming presence. Now, exhausted and possibly a bit drunk, I see nothing but a grayed-out version of the Kaleb I know, his edges blurred, his ice-chip eyes softened to rainwater.

"Kaleb," I say quietly, taking the drink from his hand to set it on the table. He doesn't protest, refusing to meet my eyes. "When was the last time you slept?"

He takes a deep breath, long and slow. "Does it matter?"

"Of course it matters."

A muscle feathers in his jaw as he lazily traces a finger around the rim of his glass. "Oh, it must have been a few nights ago, when we went looking for Konstantin." His hand stills for a moment before continuing. "Before that, Halloween."

Good hell. Vampires may not technically *need* to sleep—a lack of it won't kill us—but we still fatigue the way humans do. Our bodies need time to heal. To regenerate. The longest I've gone without sleeping is five days, and I truly thought I was going to die. It's no wonder Kaleb is fading.

"You've only slept once in *eleven days?*"

"Yes," he says dismissively. "But I don't need sleep."

"Technically, no. But Kaleb, you're *exhausted.* Why don't you go hole up in whatever lavish bedroom you have here and get some rest?"

"I can't do that, Charlotte."

"Sure you can. If you would just—"

"I *can't.*" His eyes blaze for a moment before guttering. "I've tried."

Frowning, I reach across the table and take one of his hands. His skin is ice cold but smooth except for a few scars on the backs of his fingers. The topaz ring on his middle finger winks in the candlelight. He squeezes his eyes shut, drawing his free hand over the beard that has surpassed his usual five-o'clock shadow.

"Kaleb," I say, "please. You're no good to anyone when you're like this."

"Stop." His eyes snap open, anger sharpening his features. "I will not accept pity, least of all from you."

"That stings, Kaleb. But it's fair."

"What I do need," he continues, "is to find Alexander and Victoria, then drive a stake through Konstantin's heart. I won't make the same mistake I did last time." Before I can ask him to clarify what the hell that means, he motions to the boy still sitting obediently at his side. "He's fresh, if you're hungry."

I grimace. "*Fresh?*"

"Yes, Charlotte. Fresh. The humans we house here are only permitted an hour on the floor each night. Connor, here, just joined us for the evening."

Connor. Of course he learns their names, just like Xander does.

"An hour per night, huh?" I say, raising a skeptical brow. "And how long has he been here?"

"Two days."

"Nice try. How long?"

"As I said, two days. We never keep them longer than a week; most are tourists, and we ensure they never miss their flights home." Hurt clouds his expression and he asks, "What kind of man do you take me for? I am not the monster that Konstantin was."

The sudden insistence in his tone surprises me. "No one said you were."

Emotion wells in my chest, unbidden. For so long, I believed he was a murderer. A traitor. I blamed him for everything bad that happened to me since that fateful night in New York, when I watched his apartment building burn to the ground while a fictional Rayna died inside.

I let my expression tell Kaleb what words can't say: *I forgive you. You were never the monster I believed you to be.*

"I see you, Kaleb Sutton," I say, taking his hand. "And you are a better man than any of us deserve."

Confusion shines in his eyes and his throat bobs. We sit in silence for a few moments, soaking in the warm embrace of the club's atmosphere. The noise has lessened since we arrived, the guests having thinned out as the day drifts into evening. Pippa and Henry are now alone on their settee, and Rayna is still at the bar with Tristan, laughing at his reaction to a shot of what looks like tequila. I notice a blue-suited man watching us intently from a chair by the fireplace, and I glare back at him threateningly. After a few seconds of uncomfortable staring, he finally shifts his gaze. Kaleb doesn't even notice. He pulls his hand from mine, thumbing moisture from the corner of one glistening eye.

Clearing his throat, he says, "Please eat something. Connor will return to his room when you're done." When I hesitate, he gives me a knowing look. "Just eat, will you? I won't let you go too far."

With a sharp exhale that says *fine,* I move to sit on Connor's other side. He smiles sweetly and the scent of his blood wafts toward me, making my mouth water and my gums prickle. Kaleb's eyes follow my movements as I examine the clear, unblemished skin on this side of his neck.

And then I say something I've never said in my entire life. "I'm really not hungry—"

"*Eat.*"

With an incoherent grumble, I unsheath my fangs, breathing in Connor's warm scent of heady cologne tinged with dark whiskey and the lingering touch of a woman's perfume. As my teeth pierce his skin, I find myself wishing for vanilla and linen.

Blood rushes into my mouth, bringing with it the familiar sensation of immediate, yawning hunger. Despite being a vampire for almost two hundred years, my hunger still hits me with as much force as it did the day I was Turned. If other vampires are to be believed, it never dulls—never fades, even after hundreds of years. We just learn to live with the constant bloodlust. We learn to hide it. To live amongst our prey like wolves in sheep's clothing.

Groaning, I pull Connor closer, bracing one hand on his nape, and allow myself to get lost in the sensation: the pulse of blood from his neck, the warmth of his body in my arms, the power, the hunger, the *control.*

Kaleb touches my shoulder, and I'm vaguely aware of a commotion rising near the bar. Still, I drink. If I stop, I have to go back. I have to remember. But I want to forget.

"Charlotte."

I am in control.

My head snaps up, a few drops of blood flying into the air as Connor sags back in his seat with a feeble smile. Kaleb catches him gently, disappointment plain on his face.

"Sorry, " I start, but a snarl cuts through the room. I whip around as the club's chatter halts abruptly, all heads turning toward the bar where a male vampire swirls a glass of wine in one hand, grinning as he reaches for a boy with freckles and golden hair.

CHAPTER 34

Pure instinct has me leaping from my chair, leaving Kaleb to clean up my mess. He calls my name but I'm already halfway across the room.

"Easy, man," Tristan says, holding up a staying hand. "I'm just—"

"Don't fight me, boy," the vampire says, his voice laced with the smooth tone of Compulsion. He stands a few inches taller than Tristan with golden skin and dark hair, and he wears a suit coat of black brocade. I might have found him handsome under different circumstances. "Shut up and let me *drink*."

Tristan's mouth snaps shut and he doesn't resist as the vampire grabs his jaw, forcing his head back—

I throw myself at the man, barreling into him like a battering ram. He lets out a sharp cry and drops his drink, wine splashing onto his coat before the glass shatters on the ground. Shards crunch under my shoes as I pin him against the wood paneling, and I clamp a hand around his throat.

"Touch him and *die*."

"Who the hell are you?" he spits, but his words are choked.

"I'm the girl who is just unhinged enough to kill you." When he only frowns, I squeeze harder, digging my nails into his skin.

"Charlotte, that's enough." Kaleb appears next to us, wrapping a firm hand around my wrist. He's watching me with a mixture of frustration and wariness, his touch more a suggestion than a command. "Tristan is fine. Let go."

I glance over my shoulder to see Rayna standing near the bar with a wide-eyed Tristan, watching the other vampires with a challenge in her eyes. Daring them to make a move. No one does.

"And where the hell were you?" I growl at her. "I thought you were keeping an eye on him."

Rayna's eyes narrow defensively. "I was only gone for two minutes."

"Two minutes too long!"

Kaleb tightens his hold on my wrist. *Control yourself, Charlotte.*

My grip loosens on the man's neck and I step back, biting the insides of my cheeks. He slumps forward, coughing loudly and rubbing at the fresh bruises on his neck.

"Kaleb, control your *dog*," he rasps, jabbing a finger at me.

"Charlotte is a personal guest and you will treat her with respect," Kaleb says, his voice eerily calm. Gone is the exhausted, broken man from a few minutes ago. In his place stands the Alpha, his words a cold command. He fixes his cuffs and straightens the emerald at his neck, pursing his lips as he sizes up the man. "And I suggest you heed her warning, Mateo. If you approach the boy again, I cannot guarantee you'll keep your head."

The man—Mateo—stares at Kaleb, a touch of anger darkening his gaze. Kaleb stares back icily for a few seconds before nodding once, a signal to the club's patrons to resume their activities. A few of them shoot wary looks my way.

"You might want to take Tristan out of here," Kaleb murmurs to me, his voice tight. "Mateo can be rather . . . persuasive."

As if to demonstrate the point, Mateo haughtily straightens his wine-stained coat and strides to the other side of the room, wasting no time as he yanks a subjugate to his feet. The two disappear into a dark corner and are swallowed by the shadows.

"James," Kaleb says quietly, his eyes fixed on Mateo, "keep an eye on him, will you?"

James doesn't say anything—doesn't even look at Kaleb—but he offers a tight deliberate nod.

I walk over to Tristan and palm his cheek, brushing my thumb over a cluster of freckles near his nose. "Are you okay?"

Without responding, he pulls me toward him and plants a kiss firmly on my lips. I inhale sharply, melting into the kiss for a few seconds before he breaks it.

"Are you trying to give Yara a heart attack?" I ask, quirking a brow. My eyes sweep the room until I find the woman, straight-backed and fuming. It's a wonder she doesn't snap the tablet in her hands.

Tristan grins. "That was either the sexiest or the scariest thing I've ever seen, but either way, the kiss was warranted."

"Why?"

He smooths a strand of hair from my forehead—the touch gentle enough to make me shiver—and his eyes turn so tender that I almost have to look away.

"Because, Char. You're *amazing*."

"Oh yeah?" I walk two fingers up his chest. "Is that all I am?"

Tristan's mouth quirks into a mischievous half smile.

"Amazing," he says, kissing my forehead softly. His lips move to my cheek. "Intelligent." My nose. "Insane."

"*Hey.*" I laugh, giving him a playful shove.

"How about," he murmurs, his lips hovering over mine, "beautiful?"

Someone clears their throat loudly, and I turn to see Pippa and Rayna watching us from the other end of the bar.

"Stick your tongue in her ear!" Pippa yells, waving a dollar bill in the air.

Tristan leans close, making my stomach do a backflip. "Maybe this would be a good time to talk to Kaleb."

The Alpha now stands at attention near the massive stone fireplace, surveying his kingdom with a sneer of distaste. Looking at him now, I would never guess that he'd barely slept in over a week, or that he may have had one too many drinks tonight. His gaze is sharp, his posture pristine. It makes me wonder just how often he puts on the same show—how many times he has had to play at being Alpha when he didn't have the strength.

Kaleb notices me watching him, so I motion to the hallway that leads to his office. He nods curtly, and I take that as a silent, *I will be there in a moment.* I usher Tristan into the hall, glad to be out of the bustling club, even though it feels like it has cleared out significantly in the last fifteen minutes or so. It's probably something meaningless, like a large party all leaving together, but a touch of warning tugs at me, urging me to slip further into the dark hall.

Tristan and I are silent until a frowning Kaleb arrives a few minutes later. He regards Tristan with feigned disinterest, but I know him well enough to see the subtle shift in his demeanor and the slight stiffening in his shoulders. Tristan shrinks a bit under his gaze and discomfort prickles over my skin. This must be what it feels like to have my boyfriend sized up by my *dad.* Sometimes I marvel that, as an immortal, I still manage to have such an array of humiliating human experiences.

Kaleb clasps his hands behind his back. "What is it?"

"I have a question for you," Tristan says without preamble, and Kaleb's brow quirks. "Earlier this year, a girl was killed in Golden Gate Park. Do you know anything about that?"

Kaleb's eyes flick to me almost imperceptibly, but he does an impressive job of keeping his expression blank. It occurs to me that I should have warned him about Tristan's question, but it's too late now.

"Yes, I remember," he says, his tone betraying nothing.

Tristan nods. "It was one of you guys, wasn't it? A vampire killed her."

Kaleb's breath stills as he contemplates the question. And while I trust him to keep my secret, my heart still stutters an uneven rhythm.

"Yes," he says carefully. After a short pause, he adds, "She was your sister. Alison Carr."

Tristan blinks, his lips parting in surprise. "How did you know?"

"An advantage of vampirism," Kaleb says easily, "is an eidetic memory. You share a last name with the girl. It was not a hard connection to make."

Tristan nods, suddenly unsure. "Well, I was wondering, since it was a—a *vampire*, if you might know who it was."

I find myself chewing anxiously on my lip. We're treading on dangerous ground here. All I can do is hope that Kaleb doesn't say the wrong thing. If only mind-reading were amongst the weapons in the vampire arsenal. Where's Edward Cullen when you need him?

"The police stopped searching for her killer months ago," Tristan continues when Kaleb doesn't respond right away. "I've been waiting for so long, and . . ." He balls his fists in his borrowed shirt. Xander would be furious if he saw Tristan stretching it out, popping a seam in the hem. "I just need to know."

Kaleb observes him quietly for a moment, the tension retreating from his shoulders. He's silent for a beat too long and Tristan fiddles with the guitar pick on his wrist. If he's waiting for a comment from me, he isn't going to get one.

"As Alpha," Kaleb says matter-of-factly, "I am privy to most information about the vampires in this city. I cannot, however, track every single one of them. More often than not, I learn about vampire-committed homicides well after the fact. In the case of your sister, I did visit the scene of the crime not long after it happened. While I can confirm the circumstances of her death"—he tugs at his shirt cuffs—"I did not see the culprit."

I lean against the wall, attempting nonchalance while my knees threaten to give out. *Let it go,* I will Tristan. *At least for tonight. Please.*

He doesn't. "Is there any way you can find out? Anyone else who might know something?"

"While I cannot guarantee I can help you," Kaleb says, "I will do what I can, though it may not be for a while, yet. The current climate in the city is a bit unstable, so I must focus my efforts on preserving what little control I have. I hope you'll understand."

Tristan nods, doing a poor job of masking his disappointment. "It's just hard, you know? Learning the truth. Until a few days ago, I believed that monsters only existed in scary stories."

Monsters. The word rolls off Tristan's tongue like it's nothing, but it burns a hole straight through my chest.

"Listen to me, sweet boy." Kaleb rests a hand on Tristan's shoulder, who balks a bit at the endearment. "While there are evil vampires in the world, most of us are just doing what it takes to survive. Many kills are accidental, committed when we are afraid, injured, or desperate. But violence is in our nature. You cannot fault a vampire for killing a human any more than you can fault a wolf for killing a rabbit. Most of us have made countless mistakes and will continue to do so, but we are trying to be better. To fight that killing instinct. And that does not mean we are bad people—it means we are good vampires."

Tristan frowns. Not a considering frown or a simple pouting lip, but a truly deep frown, like a dark cloud covering the sun.

"Yeah, well," he says, voice hard, "when I find the monster who murdered my sister, none of that will matter. I'll kill them anyway."

Surprise sparks in Kaleb's eyes and I have to fight to stay upright. I didn't know Tristan was capable of making such a threat, let alone that I would actually believe it. Nothing about his expression makes me doubt his sincerity. Kaleb shifts his weight, letting his shoulder brush mine. I'm sure he means to be comforting—reassuring, even—but it just makes me want to melt into the wall.

It's only a matter of time before Konstantin reveals the truth and paints a target on my back. One that Tristan won't hesitate to destroy.

There's a distant shout from somewhere in the club. Kaleb straightens, instantly on alert as he angles one ear down the hall, listening. In the sudden silence between us, I notice that the noise in the club has dimmed considerably—in fact, I hear almost nothing. The brush of rustling fabric, the clink of two glasses, the breath of a whisper spoken too quietly.

A creeping, eerie feeling slithers up my back as another sound finds us, this one starting as a distant murmur and growing to a dull thunder. Footsteps. Dozens of them. Not from the club, but from the end of the hallway behind us. *Kaleb's office.*

Dread pools in my stomach as Kaleb and I exchange a tense look. Confusion splinters his facade, and with each new crack in his armor, I see just how afraid he is.

The murmuring footsteps grow louder.

"There are two main entrances to this club." Kaleb speaks so softly that Tristan has to lean close to hear. "Only a handful of others know about the third—" He stops abruptly as some realization grips on him, and his pulse spikes anew, accompanied by a sneer of cold fury.

"Kaleb?" I whisper.

"Listen." His tone is low and urgent as he takes me by the shoulder. A door slams. A laugh echoes. Panic slices through me as Tristan's heart slams against his ribs. Kaleb speaks directly to me when he says, "Whatever happens next, I want you to take Tristan and get out of here. Do you understand?"

"What? If something is happening, I'm not just going to leave—"

"Promise me."

I nod, too nervous to do anything else.

Kaleb takes a steadying breath, whispers, "Stay close," and leads the way back into the smoky, silent club.

CHAPTER 35

THE LAVISH CLUB, WHICH WAS filled to bursting barely an hour ago, is practically empty, save for a group of a dozen or so vampires huddled near the fireplace. Their heads swivel in our direction and one of them—Mateo—grins.

Kaleb moves deliberately in front of us before we've taken two steps, his gaze sweeping over the group. Each one is dressed to the nines—red silk, diamonds, tailored tuxedos—and I recognize the women who we saw emerge from the elevator. They seemed innocent enough then, but watching them now, I sense a strange energy coming from them. These are no ordinary vampires, and they're definitely not fledglings. They're old. *Very* old. And based on their expressions, they're out for blood.

Tristan claps a hand over his mouth in horror, cursing under his breath. I glance at him, not sure why the ritzy vampires would warrant such a reaction, but he isn't watching them. Instead, his eyes are fixed on the body of a glossy-eyed subjugate draped over the arm of a sofa, his mouth open in a silent scream—*Connor.* And he isn't the only one. Neatly arranged on nearly every piece of furniture are all the evening's subjugates. All drained. All dead.

I swallow the bile that rises in my throat and shove Tristan behind me. My gaze sweeps over the club—no sign of Pippa, Henry, or Rayna. No James or Yara, either.

Kaleb strides across the room with his head held high, even as the ancient group of club patrons eyes him hungrily. A chill shivers through me as he dons the Alpha facade: his shoulders square, his chest fills, and he regards them with all the authority his position affords.

"Mateo," he almost growls, eyes narrowing as the man flashes a venomous grin. "Sonia." A woman in royal blue crosses her arms. "Beth." A blonde woman gives him a bejeweled wave. None of them look even remotely happy to see him. I count thirteen in all. Easy enough to fight our way through if it comes to that. I hope it doesn't.

Kaleb's nostrils flare. "Would you care to tell me why all my subjugates are dead?"

"Because we killed them," Mateo says simply. "What more of an explanation do you need?"

A muscle jumps in Kaleb's jaw. "And my other guests?"

"Oh, they've all gone home. It wasn't hard to convince them. Most didn't want to be here for, well"—Mateo spreads his arms wide—"for this."

Murmurs of excitement ripple through the room, stoking my wariness into panic. This conversation is too forced. Too calm. A memory surfaces—a night spent with a tipsy Rayna who rambled to me for hours about one of the many reasons Konstantin lives in European vampire infamy. For centuries, he was drawn to anything that gave him power: wealth, subjugates, artifacts. But most notable were the cities. Prague, Budapest, Milan, Kyiv, St. Petersburg—he collected them like a child collects shiny rocks, keeping them in his possession until they proved themselves useful.

And he didn't do it by forging alliances with their leaders or working his way into their circles of trust. He stole them. Controlled them. Took them right from under the noses of unsuspecting Alphas, dismantling their kingdoms with a few well-placed blows.

Exactly what he's doing now.

This isn't some minor rebellion with a handful of the San Francisco elite. It's a *coup*.

All the breath leaves Kaleb in a long, steady stream, his lips parted in realization. His eyes widen in alarm just as something hot and sharp nicks my ear, then there's a thud as a dagger embeds itself in the wall behind me.

"*Run,*" Kaleb hisses, and the club explodes into chaos.

The Alpha tugs me toward the exit just as a tide of black-hooded fledglings pours in from the back hallway, but I yank myself free, shoving Tristan after him instead.

"Go!" I urge. "Get out of here!"

Kaleb grabs him by the wrist but Tristan resists, fear burning in his eyes. "I'm not just going to leave you here!"

"If you stay, you're dead." The words are harsh, but they have the desired effect. Tristan recoils slightly and Kaleb drags him away, his expression furious and focused. I catch his eye. "Get him out. I'm right behind you."

With a nod, Kaleb and Tristan bolt for the doors. They almost make it.

Almost.

The well-dressed patrons overtake them, and it's all I can do to keep from screaming as they're swallowed by a sea of silk and jewels.

Rushing for the bar, I clear it in one leap and grab two bottles from the back shelf. They shatter easily against the countertop and whiskey explodes into the air, splattering my sweater with golden liquid. I vault back over the bar, ignoring the bite of the glass shards in my hands as two hooded boys barrel toward me, fangs bared. I slash upward ferociously, the glass tearing through their throats like a hot knife through butter. They collapse to the floor with gurgled moans.

Fire ignites in my shoulder and I look down to see a dagger protruding from my chest, just below my collarbone. I yank the blade free with a snarl of pain and drop the glass shards.

"Thanks for the dagger!" I yell to no one in particular, rushing for the doors. I slice my way through a few more hooded vampires and grin in triumph as fledgling after fledgling falls to the floor. They're not dead, but they're suffering. It serves them right for working for that bastard.

It takes only a few minutes to realize that, while these are only fledglings, there is no way I'm going to be able to take them all on by myself. I'm about to make a run for it when Nik bursts through the gold doors, followed by Rayna, Pippa, and Rose. Their eyes widen as a woman in pale satin rushes toward them, then Pippa lights up. She swings one leg in a wide arc, her heel catching the side of the woman's head. She crumples to the ground in a pile of shimmering ivory.

And now the fun really begins.

While Nik isn't as fast as some of the smaller fledglings, he's bigger. Stronger. He dispatches one easily as she dives for Rose, and Rose plucks the dagger from her hand. Rayna strong-arms a pair of burly boys, shoving them both to the ground with a triumphant growl.

"Charlotte, watch out!" Kaleb appears in front of me just as a woman in black sequins lunges in my direction. He slices a blade upward in a tight arc that cuts deep into her throat, coating his face in a fine spray of blood. The movement is quick and deadly, precise in a way that speaks to Kaleb's experience. The woman staggers backward, clutching her neck before slumping to the floor.

"Where's Tristan?" I ask, pitching my voice high.

Kaleb shakes his head, chest heaving, his eyes dark and his fangs out. "I don't know. He was with me one moment, and then he was gone."

My adrenaline spikes and I whirl in a circle, but there's no sign of golden hair anywhere. Maybe he managed to get out before the real chaos began. If he could be so lucky.

I take stock of the raging battle and it doesn't take a genius to know that we're hopelessly outnumbered. There are six of us to Konstantin's dozens.

"What the hell is going on?" Nik yells, appearing at my side. Blood drips from a gash on his cheek. Rayna stalks up to us, throwing a fledgling across the room in the process.

"Konstantin," she snarls, stabbing another fledgling that gets too close. "It's a coup."

Kaleb exhales sharply. "We don't know that—"

"Look around, *láska!*" Rayna shouts. "They emptied your club, they killed all your subjugates, and there's no sign of anyone in your inner circle. What else could it be?"

Nik grabs Kaleb's arm and the Alpha startles, frowning at the hopeless fear on Nik's face.

"What is the fastest way out of this place?" Nik asks, then is momentarily distracted by an attacking fledgling. He clotheslines the girl and she cries out as she hits the ground. Nik turns a wild expression back to Kaleb. "If we don't get out of here quickly, you might not make it out alive. And I won't lose you again."

Kaleb balks, but a woman's sharp voice stifles any response.

"Stand down."

The fledglings stop immediately, moving to the edges of a club like a retreating ocean wave. They're followed reluctantly by the collection of patron vamps that are still standing—nine, if I'm counting correctly. Stiletto heels click loudly in the sudden silence, and a bronze-skinned woman emerges from the shadows.

"Yara," Kaleb snarls, and the woman grins.

She steps to the center of the room, her pristine appearance a stark contrast to the blood-covered bodies surrounding her. The smile that curves her mouth lacks any hint of kindness, all venom and sharp angles. I knew I didn't like her.

"I honestly expected you to put up more of a fight," Yara says, sighing dramatically. "Some Alpha you are."

Nik bristles, but Kaleb holds up a staying hand.

"The fight was hardly fair," he retorts with lethal calm. "Was it really necessary to bring an entire army to my door?"

Yara shrugs. "No, but it was fun. Besides, Konstantin has bodies to spare."

"I'm sure he does," Rayna mutters, and Yara's head snaps to her.

"He'll be sad he missed you, *Rayna*." Surprise ripples through the room, her name repeated on the fledglings' harsh whispers. "But unfortunately, he had a more pressing matter to attend to."

Pippa scoffs. "What is more important than a literal *coup*?"

"Hush, Philippa," Kaleb says. Apprehension flickers in his eyes but he masks it quickly, glaring at Yara. "What are you doing? Where are Henry and James?"

The woman whistles once, sharp and loud. "James made the wrong choice," she says, menace coloring her words. Nik's eyes widen in horror, and I hope I'm imagining the implied threat in her words. "Henry, however . . ."

A familiar lithe figure weaves through a group of fledglings, coming to a stop at Yara's side. He surveys the room with eyes hard as raw topaz, one hand in the pocket of his crisp gray slacks while the other twirls his pocket watch on its gold chain. His hands and clothes are uncharacteristically void of blood, but there is a smudge of red at the corner of his mouth and a glimmer of mischief in his eyes.

Henry grins crookedly, fixing his attention on an unflinching Kaleb. "I made the right one."

My jaw goes slack and a sound of disbelief falls from Pippa's lips.

Kaleb locks eyes with the boy, his expression betraying nothing. No twitch of his brow, no twist of his mouth. I move closer to him and place a firm hand on his back; he's shaking, though with fury or fear, it's hard to tell.

Henry's grin broadens.

"You little son of a bitch," Pippa snarls, but Henry doesn't so much as look at her.

"Kaleb Sutton," Yara says, her voice a calm command. The fledglings and the patron traitors train their eyes on her, expectation on their blood-splattered faces. "San Francisco is no longer under your control. It belongs to me, and therefore, Konstantin. You can either leave the club quietly or"—she smirks, and the vampires surrounding her bare their fangs—"we will force you out. It's your choice."

A challenge for the Alpha's position, shoved right in Kaleb's face. My heartbeat pounds in my ears, every muscle tense, ready to jump into action at his signal. I'm itching to make the decision for him—to lunge at Yara and tell her exactly what I think of her—but I bite my tongue, balling my fists at my sides. This is Kaleb's territory. And, like the Alpha he is, it's his job to defend it.

A small cough breaks the silence. While no one else seems to notice, there's something familiar in the sound. I glance sidelong at a mirror behind the bar where I see Tristan's reflection crouched behind the counter, a dagger in one hand and a look of determination on his face.

I silently will him to stay the hell hidden.

Fledglings shuffle their feet. Fangs glint behind curled lips. I sneer back at a boy with a blond faux hawk who looks no older than me and I can't help but wonder where Konstantin found all these kids. Do their parents miss them?

Kaleb sags—just barely, but enough—and shock rattles through me. I watch him closely, looking for any indication that he's going to stay. That he'll fight. But there's nothing. Just a weary determination as he looks at each of our family in turn, his eyes lingering on Rayna for a few long seconds before settling on me.

And that's when I realize: Kaleb is going to yield.

"Kaleb, you can't—"

"I should have known you would betray me, Yara," Kaleb says icily. "But understand this: once Konstantin is done with you, he'll dispose of you like he does all his pawns. You're useless. *Worthless*. And when you're gone, I will take back what is mine. Just like I took *her*."

He jabs a finger toward Rayna, and her devil's grin burns like wildfire.

Swift as an adder, Yara attacks. She tackles Kaleb to the ground in a tangle of black clothing and for the second time, chaos erupts. Someone lands on me from behind and my knees buckle.

"Get off me," I growl, throwing my head backward. There's a sharp crunch and a groan as I connect with a nose, the scent of stale blood filling the air. I spin around and slice through the throat of the fledgling girl behind me. She collapses, and my eyes immediately search for my next victim.

Instead, I see Kaleb, eyes bloodshot and livid, slicing his way through a knotted group of patrons. Yara is nowhere to be found. And while Kaleb is strong, he's wildly outnumbered against a group of feral traitors. People he trusted. Maybe some he even considered friends. They lunge forward with blades and claws and teeth, their snarls bright and brutal. One of the women raises her arm and I see something in her hand—polished and sharp, and definitely not silver.

The woman's arm falls toward him like a guillotine, but a figure leaps to intercept it. The stake slams into a broad, blood-spattered chest, but it isn't Kaleb's.

"No!" I cry. *"Nikolas!"*

I stagger forward, knocking fledglings out of my path, panic eating me from the inside. Nik stares straight ahead, his eyes dark and distant while shadows bloom under them like bruises. For one terrifying moment, I'm afraid he's dead—that he'll crumple to the floor like a rag doll, never to wake again. But his breathing is steady, and the distance in his eyes isn't death—it's instinct. It's the animal in him, acting solely on the need to stay alive.

It's beautiful. And deadly.

In one swift motion, Nik yanks the stake from his chest and embeds it in the woman's heart. She gasps in pain and fear as the edges of the wound turn an ugly shade of gray, black veins snaking up her neck and down her arms. The stake quickly works its magic, turning her skin purple then a moldering shade of sickly gray, and she collapses with a gurgled cry as Nik reclaims the weapon. It takes him mere seconds to dispose of Kaleb's other attackers, not stopping until the two of them are standing alone. Kaleb stares at him in surprise and disbelief.

"Charlotte!" My head snaps sideways to see Rose standing near the door with Pippa. They're holding off a wave of advancing fledglings. "There are too many of them!"

"*You think?*" I turn back to Nik, but he's disappeared. In his place is an agitated Rayna yelling at Kaleb, the Alpha snapping back angrily. I don't have time to figure out what they're talking about before I relocate Nik near the far wall. He's staring down Mateo, who is holding someone in front of him like a shield. The dark hair and blue eyes are unmistakable.

Noah. What the hell is he doing in here?

I fight my way across the room, watching as Tristan's friend struggles in Mateo's grip. While the human boy looks strong—his biceps are straining, his muscular chest flexing with effort—he's no match for the vampire holding him.

"I said, *let him go*," Nik snarls, but Mateo just grins.

"Why would I do that?" Mateo tightens his hold on Noah, who winces at the arm pressed against his throat. The poor kid looks terrified, but there's a spark of fire in his eyes. "You seem to have an attachment to the boy. So as long as I have him, you can't hurt me."

"Wanna bet?" I snap, and Mateo startles. "There are two of us and one of you. I suggest you listen to Nik or we're going to have a problem."

"Shall I see what he tastes like?" Mateo turns Noah's head, *so* slightly, pressing his nose to the boy's ear. Noah stiffens as Mateo inhales through his nose. "Salt with just a *touch* of bergamot and orange," he murmurs in fluid Spanish, his fangs slipping from his gums. "Quite a delicious flavor combination."

Nik's expression turns murderous, but I'm surprised to see Noah's mouth quirk.

"Cologne from my mother," he replies shakily, also in Spanish. Mateo's brow twitches in surprise. "If I had to choose, I'd say *you* smell like tequila and cowardice. But who am I to judge? I'm sure you won't taste as good as I do."

Mateo frowns. "What?"

Noah bares his teeth and bites down on Mateo's arm. *Hard*. The vampire shouts as blood colors Noah's lips, and a few things happen at once.

Nik throws himself forward and someone slams into me from the side, knocking me flat on my face. I throw the fledgling off and scramble to my feet just in time to see Mateo wrench his arm free, face contorted in disgust. Noah's mouth is red, his smile wary, and there's something like triumph in his eyes.

Then Mateo snarls, takes the human boy's head in both hands, and twists sharply. The accompanying *crack* is deafening. Noah's smile disappears as he slumps to the floor, and I clap my hands over my mouth in horror, barely able to stifle my scream.

The sound that erupts from Nik is inhuman—a sound as angry as it is anguished—and he slams his fist into Mateo's face. The man flies backward and crashes into the fireplace, collapsing to the hearth with a low groan.

Nik curses loudly, sinking to his knees. He pulls Noah to his chest and squeezes his eyes closed, listening for a heartbeat that isn't there. Mateo's blood stains the corners of the boy's mouth.

"We have to go," I say quietly.

"No," Nik grinds out through clenched teeth.

"*Yes.*" I can feel the presence of new fledglings heading our way, and my hand tightens around my dagger. "We can come back for him—"

"Lottie, I can't leave him here."

A fledgling leaps at me but I catch him by the throat, squeezing hard. Tearing. Red explodes under my hand and I throw him aside like a rag doll.

"Nik, *please*—"

"Noah *bit Mateo*." Nik's eyes burn as he looks up at me, silver shimmering at their edges. "He bit a vampire, he ingested its blood, and then he *died*."

Oh.

Oh.

"Shit," I murmur.

"Yeah."

"Bring him," I say, and Nik doesn't hesitate. He lifts Noah's lifeless body into his arms, careful to support his broken neck, and makes a beeline for the door where the others are battling a continuous wave of fledglings.

I sprint to the bar and dive behind it. Tristan flies backward into a shelf of bottles, dagger raised defensively, but relaxes when he recognizes me.

"Let's *go*." I haul him to his feet and drag him toward the exit, rushing past Nik a little too quickly—hoping Tristan won't see the limp body in his arms.

Fledglings claw at us as we go, but they're not trying to stop us. Not really. Because Kaleb is leaving, and that's what Yara wants.

We file out of the club in a frenzy, but Pippa's gaze snags on something behind us. I turn to see Henry standing next to Yara in the middle of the floor, his clothes clean and unmarked, a deep frown marring his usually-cheery features. He meets Pippa's gaze, shaking his head slowly.

"Yara is in charge now," he says, taking a small step backward. "My loyalties lie with the Alpha."

San Francisco's new leader blows us a red-lipped kiss, and it's the last thing we see before the door slams shut behind us.

◊   ◊   ◊

Darkness, torch light, a crowded, damp elevator. We tumble through the club's lower entrance, a chorus of heaving breaths filling the dim salt-soaked tunnel. Wind howls through its opening and echoes loudly in the tight space, while thunderous waves crash against the rocks beyond the tunnel walls. The air is ripe with the scent of seaweed, and water-logged sand sucks at my feet as I stagger to a halt.

We all look about as good as can be expected. Pippa has a shallow slash over her sternum that cuts through the dark web of veins there. It bleeds down her chest in a sheet, soaking her white t-shirt. Rose doesn't look any better: blood oozes from a cut on her temple, and her hands are bruised and stained scarlet. Nik looks like he just climbed out of a vat of red paint. The scent of stale blood is cloying in the dead air.

Rayna immediately stalks out of the tunnel, uninjured and covered in a fine mist of crimson, mumbling something under her breath. And Kaleb . . . well, Kaleb is broken.

"Is everyone alright?" he asks, his voice tight. He scrubs at his face with the sleeve of his blazer, but a fine splatter of blood remains on his jaw. I watch him carefully and note the cracks in that perfect armor: a darkness in his eyes, a slight forward curl to his shoulders. He presses a palm to his ribs and winces as blood seeps between his fingers.

"Still standing," Tristan says shakily, leaning back against the tunnel wall. Despite the somber mood, I appreciate the touch of good humor in his voice. "I'm sure you were all *so* worried about me and N—" He cuts off abruptly. "Wait, where's Noah?"

Nik shifts uncomfortably, drawing Tristan's gaze. Noah is cradled against his chest, his neck bent at an odd angle. A dark smudge of blood stains his mouth. His sapphire eyes are wide open and glassy, staring blankly upward, and one of his shoes is missing. That, for whatever reason, is what finally breaks me. Emotion burns at the corners of my eyes.

"Noah?" Tristan whispers. "Is he—oh my God. Nik, is he—?"

Nik holds the boy tighter, a tear sliding down his cheek.

"No. *No!*" Tristan lunges forward but I catch him around the waist, yanking him away from his friend. *"Noah!"*

Tears fall as Tristan thrashes against my hold and I'm surprised by his strength, his muscles straining with effort in an attempt to free himself. Even so, it's a losing battle. It doesn't take long for him to tire and he sinks to the ground, pulling me with him. My knees hit the sand hard, briny water soaking through my jeans.

"Don't look," I murmur, voice shaking. Somehow, I can't find it in myself to tell him the truth: that Noah isn't dead, but that he was Turned. That his friend will wake up the same type of monster that killed his sister. I don't know if that would make it better or worse.

"Just . . . don't look."

I pull Tristan close as he curls into himself, hands clawing at his hair, and screams—a sound born of agony, pure and raw, from a boy who has lost too much.

CHAPTER 36

The crescent moon hangs low and wan over a wind-whipped ocean. We're at the top of a cliffside north of the Golden Gate Bridge, standing in the shadow of a massive house—a masterpiece of modern wood and glass nestled amidst walls of redwood trees. Behind the towering windows is an eerie black stillness that suggests the residence has been empty for ages.

I stare up at the angled roof and the stars just beginning to glitter in a twilight sky. They stare back, cold and distant. What I wouldn't give to be in my own basement right now, curled into the corner of the sectional, watching a movie while our celestial ceiling sparkles above me. Eons have passed since I first brought Tristan to that room, his eyes bright and his grin radiant. But now that boy is gone, his golden light snuffed out.

Tristan stands next to me, his hands in his pockets, staring straight ahead with bloodshot eyes. Tears stain his freckled cheeks. There's nothing in his expression but a distant numbness; he doesn't seem to notice when Nik slips through the front doors of the house with Noah, Rose and Pippa on their heels.

Kaleb and Rayna hover a few yards away, watching us with matching beleaguered expressions. Blood still seeps from a wound on Kaleb's side and Rayna frowns through a split lip.

"Where are we, exactly?" she asks, her jaw set.

"A safe house," Kaleb says mechanically. "One of Henry's, actually." The boy's name sends a sharp stab of anger through me. I swallow the urge to snarl, squeezing Tristan's arm instead. "There are a few scattered throughout the area, and I'm hoping that, since no one has visited this one for years, it will have escaped Konstantin's notice. That it will take him a while to find us."

Because Konstantin *will* find us eventually, there's no doubt about that. All I can do is pray to the demonic powers-that-be to hide us from him for at least one day. Enough time for all of us to recover from a collection of gruesome wounds, and for Kaleb to get some damn sleep.

"Speaking of Henry," I say with forced calm, "that was kind of a dick move back there."

Kaleb exhales sharply then winces, pressing the heel of his hand to his bloodied side. I almost reach for him—to comfort him, to do *something*—but decide against it when I see the hint of warning on Rayna's face.

Not now, she seems to say. *Give him space.*

"I know what you must be thinking," Kaleb says through gritted teeth, "but Henry did not betray me."

"I'm sorry, were we at the same coup?" I ask, propping a hand on my hip.

Kaleb manages to look exasperated. "He did not acknowledge Yara's self-declared position, therefore, he does not recognize her as Alpha."

"So, when he said his loyalty lies with the Alpha, he was still referring to you."

"A nifty little trick," Rayna says. "Let's hope his espionage skills are as good as they used to be."

There's a burst of icy wind that makes the trees groan, and Tristan shivers.

"You guys head inside," I murmur. "I'll catch up."

The two of them exchange an uncertain look but Kaleb nods, ushering

Rayna to the doors with a hand on her lower back. Considering what happened tonight, the two of them seem oddly calm—Kaleb especially. After having his city stolen from beneath him, I would expect him to be a nervous wreck, or maybe to put his hand through a car window. But when Rayna leans into his touch, he wraps an arm around her shoulders, supporting her as a tremor shivers through her.

Ever the protector. Ever the Alpha.

Though, I guess he isn't anymore.

With a slow sigh, I push thoughts of Kaleb aside and turn to Tristan, who is staring numbly into the middle distance.

"Hey," I say, brushing a fresh tear from his cheek. "I need to talk to you."

He blinks at that, rising from his stupor. "About what?"

"Noah."

Tristan stills, pain creasing his brow. "No. I can't . . . I don't want to talk about it."

"It's not what you think. I saw what happened. Mateo had him in a chokehold—"

"I said *no*."

"Just listen to me—"

"I can't do this right now!" Tristan yells, pitching his voice over the wind. "Two of my best friends have died in the last week. Noah is—*was* everything to me." His voice cracks and he swipes a hand over his face. "I don't know what I'm going to do without—"

"Noah isn't dead."

Tristan stops short. "What?"

"He's not dead," I say again, everything coming out in a rush. "Well, not *completely*. It all happened so fast. One minute I thought Nik was dead, then I saw him on the other side of the club with Mateo, who had Noah in a chokehold. I'm not sure how that happened—Noah shouldn't have even been in the club at that point and I know Nik would have told him to keep his distance—"

"Spit it out, Charlotte." There's a thread of deep-seated resolve in

Tristan's voice. The stoke of smoldering embers.

I snap my mouth shut. I'm rambling, which is something I only do when I'm avoiding something. When I'm trying to delay the inevitable.

"Noah tried to get away by biting Mateo's arm," I say carefully, taking a steadying breath. "Mateo retaliated by breaking his neck."

"So, he *is* dead." Tristan sighs deeply, pressing a palm to one eye. "Are you trying to give me whiplash?"

"No, sorry." I gently tug Tristan's hand away from his face, holding it to my chest. He frowns down at me with fathomless eyes. "When Noah bit Mateo, he broke skin. And if you die after ingesting a vampire's blood . . ." I swallow hard. "You Turn."

Tristan stills. "No."

"Noah is dead now, but he will come back. And he'll be a vampire."

Waves crash loudly against the cliffside below, the roar near deafening in Tristan's paralyzed silence. I wait. And wait. His face has gone completely blank and he falls a step backward, his eyes fixed on the ground. I'm not sure what to do next. Comfort him? Leave him to process? But before I can make a decision, Tristan laughs.

The sound is a cold, broken thing, like the sharp crack of a shattering mirror.

"Of course he will!" Tristan yells, his grin all ice and teeth. "Because the universe said, 'Hmm, vampires haven't already taken enough from Tristan. Killed his sister? Check. Killed his friend? Check. But let's be original with the next one. Let's make Noah a vampire himself! Then we can *really* make the guy suffer!'"

I gape at him. Of course I expected Tristan to be upset, but not like this. He throws his head back, glaring into the heavens. The dispassionate stars shimmer.

"*What do you want from me?*" he cries, voice cracking. "Just take it! I can't do this anymore!"

Something fractures deep in my heart, and it's a wonder I have anything left to break at all. This boy, the one who smiled so readily when I first met him on the Embarcadero, has been through too much in his short life. And while suffering has become a familiar companion of mine, Tristan is only twenty years old. He has had more terrible things happen to him in eight months than most humans have in an entire lifetime. Looking at him now, I can't help but wonder if he'll ever be that bright, easygoing boy again, or if everything he's been through will dim his light for good.

"Hey, it's okay." I place my palms against Tristan's cheeks, gently bringing his face down. His eyes are dark and unfocused, the fissures in his sunny demeanor deepening every day. "Look at me. Do I look like a monster to you?"

Tristan's brow furrows, and he says, "No."

"Exactly." I can still hear the way Tristan said *monsters* at the club only a couple of hours ago, but I don't have time to dwell on it now. "There will be an adjustment period for Noah, but he'll still look the same—he'll have the same memories, the same personality. His diet may be drastically different, but he'll still be the best friend you've always known."

Tristan tenses, as though rejecting the idea, then relaxes all at once. "When will he wake up?"

"I don't know," I say honestly. "For some, it only takes an hour. For others, days. There's really no rhyme or reason to it. Some say it has to do with the severity of whatever killed them, but it's not like we have scientists to study it."

Tristan nods slowly, squeezing his eyes shut.

"Noah and I have been friends our entire lives," he murmurs, leaning into my touch, "and he's stuck with me through some . . . rough times. I don't—" His voice catches and it triggers some protective instinct in me. I wrap my arms around him and he returns the embrace, burying his face in the crook of my neck. "He's so *good*, Char. I don't know what this will do to him."

◊   ◊   ◊

Tristan and I stand in the yard for a long time, well past the point when his ears and nose have turned red from the cold. I do my best to shield him from the relentless wind, but he still shivers. One con of having a vampire girlfriend is my below-average body temperature. I'm not one to rely on for warmth—physically *or* emotionally.

There is so much we could talk about—*should* talk about—but I don't think either of us is ready for an in-depth discussion about every earth-shattering thing that has happened in the past few days. Especially when the entire family is listening in.

In reality, I would rather talk to Xander. I have no idea what that conversation would entail, but he would undoubtedly come up with some brilliant way to both insult and reassure me at the same time. Since learning about his capture, every hour that ticks by makes me miss him more and more. At this point, I might even consider forgiving him for his betrayal. Maybe.

There's a rustling sound in the trees behind us—not the overhead groan of wind through branches, but the sound of hurrying footsteps crashing through undergrowth. I whirl to face the tree line, putting myself between Tristan and the intruder.

A disheveled Henry bursts into the clearing, eyes widening in surprise as he skids to a halt in front of me.

"Charlotte," he says, panting heavily, "why aren't the two of you inside? Are you alright?"

"We're fine. We just needed a little space."

Henry nods. "I know what you must be thinking," he says, holding up a defensive hand, "and before you attempt to murder me, you must know that I would *never* betray Kaleb—"

"I know," I say, cutting him off with a finger to his mouth. "Kaleb already explained it to me. Look at you, dipping your toes in the world of espionage."

"Oh, I assure you, I entered the deep end long ago." His expression turns haunted, his eyes wild as they flicker from shadow to shadow.

I touch his arm softly. "Henry, are you okay? You look like you just saw a ghost."

He sneers, fangs flashing. "Darling, my boss was just usurped, I spent the last few hours trying *not* to tear Yara's head off, and I just ran across the Golden Gate Bridge. How would you expect me to look?"

Tristan exhales sharply. "Don't you have a car?"

"Of course." Henry gives him a wry grin. "But where's the fun in that?"

"Seriously," I say. "Are you okay?"

Groaning, he slumps into a crouch, burying his face in his hands. He doesn't seem to be hurt, just exhausted. After a few steady breaths, he lifts his head.

"This is bad, Charlotte. This is *very* not good."

I glance at Tristan, who is watching Henry warily. Xander's t-shirt and jacket are doing little to protect him from the wind, and his lips are starting to look a bit purple around the edges.

"Go inside," I urge, forcing a smile. "I think you're a few minutes away from becoming an icicle."

"Are you sure?"

"I'm fine," I whisper. "Go."

With a dubious glance at Henry, Tristan turns and walks swiftly toward the house.

I chew on my lip, frowning up at the veritable boy in front of me. Henry is all sharp angles and gangly limbs, trapped forever in a body that will never reach manhood. Another vampire might have wallowed as an immortal teenager, but not Henry. He honed that boy's body into a lethal weapon: a delicate blade amongst a sea of broadswords. Smaller, more easily breakable, but twice as deadly.

"So," I say, clearing my throat, "what exactly is happening in the belly of the beast?"

Henry rises stiffly and lets his head hang back, exposing the ridges of his throat. "Yara has declared herself Alpha. Runners have already gone out to the other Lessers and their seconds."

The title catches my attention.

"Who are the Lessers? *What* are they?"

Henry's head tilts sideways. "Do you mean to tell me that your brother is *Beta,* yet he's never mentioned the Lessers to you?"

I shake my head. "No, he hasn't. If you hadn't noticed, we don't often talk about his secret day job."

"Right," Henry says, shrugging apologetically. "Well, when Kaleb became Alpha, he knew he would need help—that it would be essential to employ others he could fully trust. Once he appointed Xander as Beta, I was declared a Lesser Alpha—third-in-command, if you will— to help keep the peace with the high-brows. Shortly after, he chose Enzo to leash the *immortui,* then Mei to keep an eye on everyone in between."

I balk at that. Lesser *Alphas?* I have a hard time believing Kaleb puts so much trust in Xander, let alone three others. Henry and Enzo I can understand, but Mei? She's a stern, intimidating woman, Turned sometime in her mid-thirties, and she has never liked me. I never would have guessed she was in San Francisco, let alone acting on Kaleb's behalf.

"We report to Xander," Henry continues, "who then reports to Kaleb. It has been quite the success; from what I understand, a few other Alphas have adopted the practice. Maren in Chicago, Raphael in Paris . . . Siobhan tried in Seattle, but it hasn't gone well . . . I wonder if André ever figured it out—"

"Henry," I say, snapping my fingers. "Focus."

He shakes his head, then grins. "So sorry. My mind has a habit of getting away from me." When I say nothing more, his smile disappears. "Enzo and Mei each have a Lesser Beta, and there are a myriad of other vampires with limited power that Kaleb refers to as 'scout leaders.' I have no way of knowing who will stay loyal to Kaleb or what was actually in the messages Yara sent. She doesn't trust me enough to share that information, apparently." He laughs once, dryly. "I applaud her for her instincts."

Glass shatters inside the house, and our heads snap sideways.

There's a distant rush of footsteps and a few incoherent shouts as a snarl tears through the night—one that sends a chill straight into my bones.

The snarl of a fledgling who has just found his first meal.

CHAPTER 37

VITEBSK, BELARUS

AUGUST 19, 1824

Tick. Tick. Tick.

Darkness. A dull throbbing in my head. In my throat. A wooden floorboard beneath my cheek.

Tick. Tick. Tick.

A clock—the one in the kitchen. I have never heard it tick so loudly before. It reverberates in my ears, rattling around in my skull, deepening the ache.

I put one hand flat on the floorboards and push myself into a sitting position, leaning back against the wall.

Tick. Tick. Tick.

I blink. Again. Again. More sounds fill the air, too loud: crickets chirping outside, Natalia—our mare—whinnying behind the cottage, wagon wheels rattling by on the road beyond the field.

And my heartbeat. Pounding in my chest like a war drum, making my ears ring and my vision swim.

Tick. Tick. Tick.

The house is dark. Night dark. Strange. It was just morning . . . my birthday. Mama was making rhubarb pastries and Aleksandr was in the garden. The sky was just brightening with the first rays of dawn while I milked our dairy cow, Marya, and I came inside because I heard . . . something.

But now it's dark. So dark.

I reach up and grasp the windowsill, pulling myself to my feet. Across the room, I can make out a pale bottle of milk sitting on the kitchen table, and I notice how dry my throat is. I'm suddenly very, very thirsty. Painfully so. It strikes me that if I don't get something to drink right now, I will shrivel and die.

The room swims around me as I stagger to the table, chugging the milk in an attempt to quench the thirst, but it isn't enough. I need something else—water? If I can get to the well at the edge of the woods, I can drink my fill. Then maybe the burning, sandy feeling in my throat will ease.

I take one step and my stomach churns, nausea surging upward in a wave. I barely have time to set down the bottle before my body convulses, the milk coming back up in a cacophony of painful retching.

When my stomach is sufficiently empty, I'm thirstier than I was before. Maybe even hungry. I stumble toward the pantry, pausing only when something catches my eye near the open front door. There is a figure on the floor—a young man with dark curls and a white linen shirt. An ominous stain spreads across his front and his neck is twisted at an odd angle, his green eyes wide and glassy.

Aleksandr.

Horror unsteadies me and I stagger backward. My feet tangle in something on the floor and I fall to my hands and knees, my palms landing in something cool and sticky. I raise one hand in front of me to see a thick coating of something dark and red. I inhale sharply—

And oh, the smell.

Hunger like I've never felt before rockets through my entire body, making me double over as fire ignites in my gut. Razor-sharp pain slices into my gums and I cry out, lifting a hand to my mouth, and I unwittingly touch the sticky substance to my lips.

Copper. Salt. Sugar, butter, flour.

The hunger grows, clawing through my chest, setting my throat ablaze. Heat blooms under my skin and I'm overcome by the urge to drink.

I drag my tongue over my red-coated palm, groaning at the taste. Black circles my vision, tunneling tighter and tighter until I see nothing. I feel nothing. Just the overwhelming desire for more.

The liquid pools on the floor around me, some of it dried, some of it still viable. I coat my hands in it and lick them clean—again and again—until there is nothing left.

It is then that I notice the other form lying on the floor in front of me, blood soaking her dress and clinging to her neck. My gaze rakes her and I understand, distantly, that she is dead.

Tick. Tick. Tick.

A memory surfaces—a shadow in the house, a kitchen knife protruding from his chest, his smile cutting through the dim morning light. His shoulder ticking upward.

My eyes find the woman's face and recognition sweeps through me.
Mama.

Her blood coats my hands. I clap both of them over my mouth, but they do nothing to stifle my scream.

I FLY THROUGH the front door, not bothering to watch where I'm going. All I can hear is the sound of snarling and the pounding of a frantic heart. The polished wood floor is slippery under my feet and I stumble, knocking my head against the wall, but I can't stop. I won't stop. Because Noah is awake, and there's only one living source of blood in this house.

I skid into the night-dark kitchen and the scene comes to me in pieces.

A broken jar on the floor. Various kitchen items in disarray, knocked about in someone's haste. Tristan leans back against the counter, trembling, his hand inching toward the knife block by the stove. His hair sticks up wildly and his clothes are disheveled as he stares in horror at the hunched figure on the other side of the island.

His best friend, once dead, now risen.

Noah.

That is to say, he *looks* like Noah. The same narrow frame, the same strong cheekbones, and a messy swath of ebony hair. But this is not the soft human boy I met a week and a half ago. He's not the street artist on his five-gallon bucket or the boy who smiled at Nik like he was the most beautiful thing in the world.

This is a fledgling vampire—raw and fresh and hungry.

Noah's eyes are dark and sunken, swollen veins snaking beneath them and creeping into the whites of his eyes. His pupils have swallowed his irises entirely, creating tunnels of *nothing* in his pretty, angled face. Mateo's blood still stains the corners of his mouth, which is curled into a vicious, fanged snarl. It's all familiar, yet somehow horrifyingly inhuman. Unsettling. I fight a shudder.

He prowls slowly around the island, his teeth bared, and his eyes track Tristan's movements with hawk-like precision.

"Noah?" Tristan says carefully, shifting to keep the island between them. "Hey, it's Tristan. Just—just calm down, okay?"

Noah doesn't seem to hear him. His eyes are wide and wild, burning with feverish light. Another snarl tears from him, this one loud enough to rattle the dishes in their cabinets. Tristan recoils.

I want to jump on Noah—to catch him before he does something he might regret—but I don't want to spook him. If he gets too worked up, he'll be aggressive. *Violent.* Something I don't want to risk with Tristan in the room. Fledglings may be weaker than older vampires, but their ferocity is unmatched. They haven't learned to control their bloodlust, and everything is new to them—their heightened senses, their increased strength. I've seen good men fall at the hands of fledglings.

I assume it's why Konstantin favors them so much.

There's a thunder of footsteps behind me as the others crowd into the kitchen doorway, screeching to a halt when they see the situation unfolding. Noah twitches and tastes the air, sniffing a few times. He must sense the presence of other bodies, because a growl rumbles deep in his chest, making Tristan shudder.

Kaleb shoos the others backward. "Everyone but Nikolas and Charlotte, get out of the kitchen."

Rayna glares at him, looking like she's about to protest, then seems to think better of it. She shoves Pippa, Rose, and Henry back into the living room.

Nik's expression is miserable as he watches Noah settle into a half-crouch, his lips curled back over his newly-minted fangs. Kaleb ushers us behind him and his eyes go dark, a growl grating in his throat.

"*Noah.*"

The name shivers through me, all dominance and aggression. It's a sound I've never heard come from Kaleb—dark and dangerous, his voice resonating through his chest with thunderous force. It demands my attention in an instinctual way. A vampire responding to her Alpha.

It must have the same effect on Noah, because his head snaps sideways, his yawning gaze fixed on Kaleb. Recognition sparks in his eyes then disappears just as quickly, leaving me to wonder if I imagined it.

I look at Tristan—he's trembling, his eyes darting from Noah, to me, to Kaleb, and back again. He's positioned just right so that his exit is easily blocked by his friend, and his expression betrays his terror. My feet carry me a step forward and Noah snaps defensively, his attention still fixed on Kaleb. Uncertainty and fear war in the boy's eyes but his teeth are still bared, his shoulders tense.

"Noah," Kaleb says again, gentler this time, "can you hear me?" Noah's brow furrows and his head cocks to the side. "Good. That's good. Now, I want you to listen to me. You are safe, alright? No one here is going to harm you. I know you're hungry, and we can help you with that. But first, you need to calm down."

Noah takes a deep breath—once, twice—and some of the color returns to his eyes.

"There we go," Kaleb murmurs. "That's good. Come back to us."

And for a few seconds, I think he might. But then the scent of fresh blood wafts over me. I watch in horror as Tristan lifts his hand, having sliced a finger on the knife he's now holding. Noah's pupil's dilate, his head whipping back toward Tristan, and he snarls loudly before he leaps over the island.

I shove past Kaleb, springing into the air and slamming into Noah. We careen sideways into an upper cabinet before crashing to the floor, splintered wood falling over us like rain. Noah *screams*—it's guttural, *animal*—and I snarl back at him when his teeth snap in my direction.

"Don't you snap at me," I hiss.

Noah attempts to right himself and I wrestle him sideways, trying to get a good hold on his wrists, but his movements are ferocious and erratic. He claws at my neck, yanks on my hair, jabs a knee into my ribs as we tumble over one another. He howls again.

"A little help would be nice!" I shout to no one in particular, staving off another snap of Noah's jaws.

"What exactly do you want us to do, Charlotte?" Rayna barks from somewhere nearby. "Take a video so we can watch you humiliate yourself again later? It looks like you've got your hands full, there."

I snarl as my head *crack*s against one of the cabinets, then drive my elbow into Noah's temple. It barely fazes him.

"You are *no help*," I growl. "I'm officially writing you out of my will."

Rayna scoffs, just as I manage to catch one of Noah's wrists. I wrench it backward and Noah yelps in pain as I yank his entire arm behind him, pinning his hand to his shoulder blade. He flops onto his stomach, thrashing underneath me like a wild mustang. I pin him with a knee against his back, then plant my free hand on the nape of his neck, shoving his cheek into the stone floor.

"Don't hurt him!" Tristan and Nik yell together.

"Not trying to," I grind out, digging my thumb into the pulse point below the boy's jaw. "Noah, that's *enough*."

It takes a minute or so for Noah to still, his breath coming in ragged gasps. Then, all at once, he relaxes, blinking a few times as the colors returns to his irises. The shadows retreat from his face and his fangs slide back into his gums.

And then his eyes fill with tears.

"*Dio*—" he chokes, and it's followed by a tiny sob. "No. No, no, *no*."

I carefully ease my grip, releasing his neck and wrist one after the other. Once I'm sure he's stable, I stand, and he takes a deep breath as my weight lifts from his chest. I've barely had time to step away before Nik is on the floor next to him. He gathers Noah to his chest as the fledgling boy collapses into sobs.

I'm vaguely aware of the others watching as I dart around the island, yanking Tristan into a relieved hug. But his eyes are fixed on his best friend, anguish written plainly on his face. Nik rocks him gently as he murmurs reassuring words, Noah curling into him like a child. His tears flow freely as he buries his face in Nik's chest.

"Nik," he whimpers, his jaw trembling. "*No estoy listo para morir.*"

I'm not ready to die.

NOAH ROMERO

CHAPTER 38

Kaleb stands still as a statue with a cigarette clasped between his middle and forefinger, leaning on a railing that circles the safe house's back porch. The surrounding trees creak ominously in the cliffside wind, filling the night with the eerie ambiance of a horror movie. He inhales deeply on his cigarette, exhaling a swirl of gray smoke.

Rayna approaches him slowly, silently wishing they had met again under different circumstances. It was stupid of her to wait until now to return. Instead of a happy reunion—instead of a confident, loving Kaleb—she's stuck with . . . well, *this*.

Ruffled hair. Disheveled clothes. A beleaguered expression and hands that won't stop fidgeting. The cigarette between his fingers trembles. He's changed out of his bloody clothes and exchanged them for dark joggers and a gray henley, the ostentatious emerald at his throat looking horribly out of place. Rayna assumes the clothing came from a safe house stash—otherwise, she knows Kaleb would never be caught dead looking so drab.

Though Kaleb could make a prison uniform look like it came from Balenciaga.

"Do stop hovering, *mon coeur*," Kaleb says, gaze still fixed on the trees in front of him. He takes another drag. "If you have something to say, then say it. Otherwise, leave."

Rayna slips up behind him, wrapping her arms around his chest. "Is that any way to speak to your lover?"

Kaleb scoffs, more long-suffering than anger. "Is that all we are? Lovers?"

Rayna tries not to be offended at the cold note in his voice, choosing instead to slide one hand under his shirt, tracing the scars over his ribs. Eucalyptus and smoke fill her senses and she inhales deeply, heat simmering low in her abdomen.

"Aren't we?"

Kaleb softens almost imperceptibly, his heartbeat quickening. "I know what you are trying to do, and I don't appreciate it."

"Why not?" Rayna murmurs against his neck, pressing a kiss to his nape. He shivers. "It's been a rough night. You know it would make you feel better."

He flicks his cigarette, knocking ash onto the grass below. "I don't need to *feel better*."

Rayna makes a noncommittal noise, kissing his neck again, smiling against his skin as he melts into her, just a little. She explores his scarred torso, trailing one hand down the center of his abdomen, dipping past his waistband . . .

Kaleb catches at her wrist and curses, extracting himself from her embrace. Rayna frowns at the sudden distance between them, at the unfamiliar sting of rejection. This might be the first time Kaleb has ever refused her. She doesn't like it.

"Be serious, Rayna," Kaleb snaps, grinding the butt of his cigarette into the railing. It leaves a dark circle of smoldering black. "This is not the time for *seduction*. My world is crumbling around me and all you can think about is pleasure." He curses again, tossing a hand in the air. "Though, I suppose I shouldn't be surprised. You always were one for debauchery."

Anger flares in Rayna's chest. "I'm sorry, I think you're confused. If I remember correctly, *you* were always coaxing me into dark hallways when Konstantin wasn't looking. It's a miracle he never caught us."

"He never caught us because he couldn't imagine a world where you would choose me over him."

"And he made me believe that if I left, no one else would ever love me the way he did."

Kaleb's mouth quirks, darkness filling his expression. "He made *me* believe that I wasn't worthy of love."

A harsh silence falls between them, interrupted by a gust of wind that makes the trees groan.

"Damn," Rayna murmurs, sighing through her nose. "He really did a number on us, didn't he?"

Kaleb's gaze falls and his fingers twitch. In lieu of tugging on his buttons, he starts tying and untying the drawstring of his joggers, his topaz ring flashing. The same ring he offered to Rayna all those years ago, proposing a promise. Asking for her heart. It took four times of him asking before he finally conceded to the fact that Rayna wasn't going to marry him. Not when she knew they might have to run again. That they might have to separate, with no knowledge of when—*if* they would reunite. She couldn't promise to stay by his side only to inevitably break his heart.

With a sigh, Kaleb returns to his place at the railing. "I don't know what to do, *mi corazón*."

Rayna echoes his sigh and rests her elbows on the railing next to him. "Maybe I could offer a bit of insight. I do have considerable experience with Konstantin too, you know."

Kaleb eyes slide sideways, and in them Rayna sees two centuries' worth of fear. Of pain. Of regret.

"I can't help feeling that everything happening here"—he gestures into the dark—"is my fault. I should have ended the bastard when I had the chance. But I was *weak*. I let my emotions win that night, and we're all suffering because of it."

That night. The night they escaped from Konstantin. It was also the night when Rayna committed a ruthless, bloody betrayal—one that changed her irrevocably and forever. Kaleb may have wielded the dagger, but Rayna is the one who moved the target into position.

Even as they walked away, she knew it would be one of her deepest regrets. And now, two hundred and fourteen years later, guilt has become her constant companion. It's why she taught herself to turn off her emotions. To be cold and distant and calculating. To not let the guilt destroy her. She and Kaleb turned away from the humanity they once held onto so dearly, because they knew that emotion and regret would do nothing but make them weak.

Konstantin taught them that.

"There is nothing you can do about the past, *láska*," Rayna says quietly, threading one arm through Kaleb's. He pulls her close and she rests her head on his shoulder. "No amount of wallowing will undo what's been done. All we can do now is finish the job we started. We can't let Kostya hurt our family. Not like he hurt us."

Kaleb squeezes his eyes shut. "How are we supposed to do that, Rayna? He has taken my city from me. My resources. My *Beta*, for Hell's sake." Pushing off from the railing, he starts pacing, raking a hand through his already-mussed hair. "He's re-creating everything we did to him, but this time he's on the winning side. Who else has he turned against me? How long do we have until *he* stabs *me* in the back?"

"Hey," Rayna says softly, catching him as he paces by. "You're spiraling."

"Can you blame me?" Desperation colors his tone, and his pale eyes flash with panic. "Not only is Konstantin taking away my power, but the city is a disaster. The fledgling count is out of control. The media is having a heyday and humans are leaving San Francisco in droves. Before long, the whole Bay Area will be filled with nothing but vampires. *What then?*"

"Kaleb—"

"Kostya didn't think this through," he growls. "He's sloppy. Impulsive. If we don't stop him soon, I worry we won't be able to stop him at all."

Words evaporate from Rayna's tongue. She has had the same thoughts over the past few days but has been too afraid to voice them. From what the others have told her, Konstantin seems to be playing this game from a place of overconfidence. Like he can't lose. It could be used to their advantage, or it could be their downfall. Either way, until she sees Konstantin herself, she has no way of knowing just how far gone he is. If there is any way to bring him back.

"We'll beat him, *láska*. Just like we did last time."

"*How*, Rayna?"

In a surprising turn of events, she doesn't have an answer. A few hundred years ago, Rayna would have known exactly what to do. She wishes she knew this 2018 Konstantin, potentially so different from the man she left in 1804.

"I don't know," she says quietly, and it feels like admitting defeat. Pulling Kaleb close, she adds, "But whatever it is, we'll do it together."

Kaleb smiles sadly and brushes a gentle kiss against her forehead. It lingers a moment too long and heat slithers down Rayna's spine. He presses another kiss to her temple, then her jaw. And then his lips are on hers, hard and urgent, all despair and heartache. Rayna throws her arms around his neck, burying her fingers in his hair, yanking hard. Kaleb groans and pulls her closer.

Rayna melts into him, ignoring the fact that this is not the time for frivolity. They should be speaking with their family, making a plan to rescue Xander, and figuring out how the hell they're going to free themselves from Konstantin's skeletal grasp.

But the sound of her name on Kaleb's lips is its own type of pleasure.

She loses herself in the feeling of his body against hers, kissing him until she forgets. Until all her worries fade away. Until there is nothing but Rayna, Kaleb, and the creaking, sighing trees.

CHAPTER 39

This house doesn't have a wine cellar. I've searched the bedrooms, the kitchen, the expansive basement, but there's nothing. Well, not *nothing*, exactly. Somehow, the pantry is filled with a collection of non-perishables, which seems a bit unnecessary, considering its target demographic. I'm going to have a word with Henry about how he stocks his safe houses.

I glare down at my phone, ignoring a new text from the current bane of my existence, and text Pippa instead. She left an hour or so ago to drop Henry back at the club, then to get supplies. Whatever that means.

> ALCOHOL. We need so much alcohol.

> What exactly did you think I meant by "supplies"?

She responds with emojis of a thumbs up, a pair of clinking glasses, and a smiling devil face.

Only then do I open the unread text that mocks me with its little blue dot.

> Good morning, love. Sleep well?

I reply to Konstantin with three middle finger emojis and shove my phone back into my pocket.

Gray dawn light seeps into the living room of the secret hideout, though I wouldn't exactly call it *secret*. It's more of a contemporary cabin, complete with wooden rafters, a huge stone fireplace, and floor-to-ceiling windows that look out over the grassy yard and its sheer drop to the ocean.

Not for the first time, I sigh loudly, curling into the corner of an overstuffed sofa. Now that Noah has settled down, it seems everyone has adopted my I-don't-want-to-talk-about-it attitude. Tristan is lying next to me with his head in my lap, asleep but not resting; there's a deep crease cut between his brows that has yet to disappear. Nik is with Noah in an upstairs bedroom—I can hear the fledgling boy crying softly—and Rayna is on the back patio with Kaleb, who has been smoking for the past two hours. I don't blame him.

This is a *mess*.

I expected Konstantin to make our lives hell, but I didn't expect him to so fully break everyone in a matter of days. We're scattered, we're exhausted, and I feel like a feral cat whose tail keeps getting stepped on. My fingers trace absent circles on Tristan's neck, lingering on the thrumming heat at his pulse point—the only human pulse left.

Rose strides from the kitchen with a bottle of dark liquor in one hand, two empty glasses in the other. She raises a dubious eyebrow as she settles into a lounge chair and places the glasses on the coffee table, filling them with quick expertise.

"Where did you find this?" I ask, snatching one of the drinks. The smoky scent of bourbon meets me as I press the glass to my lips, sighing at the heat that trickles down my throat.

Rose responds with a nonchalant shrug. "Kaleb's car."

I snort, almost spitting out the drink as Tristan stirs in my lap.

"Clever girl," I say quietly, raising my glass. "I suppose I should have thought of that."

"If I know anything about Kaleb, it's that he'll never find himself without liquor or cigarettes."

We both smile, then lapse into comfortable silence. Rose's hands are tucked inside the sleeves of a too-big sweatshirt; no one bothered to pack anything before we left for the club, so we'll all be taking turns returning to our houses for new clothes. Until then, we're forced to wear what's available in the safe house, which has proved to be a collection of random shirts and sweatpants in varying shades of black and gray. It's tragic, really. Based on Henry's usual wardrobe of slim-fitting suit pants and matching waistcoats, I expected him to have invested in classier options. Like maybe a pair of *jeans*.

The bourbon is working wonders as warmth spreads through me, calming my nerves and slowing my heart rate. My collarbone still aches where it was broken, and twinges of pain echo from the phantom wounds on my forearm, back, and almost everywhere else. I rub at a barely-healed knife wound on my thigh and stare into the empty fireplace.

"Do you really think this is just about Rayna?" Rose asks, tracing her finger around the rim of her glass. The high-pitched ringing it creates is eerie in the large room, echoing through the high rafters.

I pause mid-sip. "What do you mean?"

"I don't know." She leans back in her chair, swirling her drink. "It feels like we're missing pieces of the story. There's something off about Konstantin . . . it's hard to explain. I can't quite put my finger on it."

Rose has always been the astute one in the family; she has a knack for noticing things that rest of us disregard. After a century and a half of knowing her, I've learned that if she's suspicious about something, it's best to pay attention.

"Yeah, I know what you mean." *That's not what happened!* Konstantin's voice echoes in my thoughts, sharp and wild. "Maybe Kaleb did something that really traumatized him. Maybe it has to do with what Konstantin thinks is the 'real reason' that Rayna left."

"Then why doesn't Kaleb just tell him?" Roses asks contemplatively. "Doesn't he want to get Xander and Victoria back?"

Her voice catches, just barely, and her eyes shine as she stares down into her drink. There's new tension in her jaw, her neck straining, and her fingers tap anxiously on her glass.

"Rose, are you okay?" I ask, wanting to take her hand but knowing it will be unwelcome. Rose doesn't take kindly to uninvited physical contact, even from friends. I settle for resting my hand on the arm of her chair.

"What?" she asks, sniffling, then scrubs at her damp eyes with the sleeve of her hoodie. "Yeah, I'm fine. I'm just worried about them, is all."

Before I can reply, Nik's worried voice calls me from upstairs.

"Lottie, will you come here, please?"

I angle my ear upward but hear nothing else. Rose frowns then nods toward the stairs.

"Go on," she says, motioning to the bottle of bourbon with a watery wink. "I promise not to drink it all while you're gone."

Flashing a tight smile, I set my drink on the coffee table and gently lift Tristan's head from my lap, sliding out from beneath him and tucking a pillow in my place.

"Char?" he murmurs in a voice thick with sleep, his eyes fluttering open. When he sees my look of concern he bolts upright in panic. "What is it? Is there something wrong? Is Noah—"

"Relax, Tristan," I say, touching his shoulder gently. "Everything's fine."

Tristan nods, rubbing the sleep from his eyes. "I don't think I'll ever get used to this. You know, constantly wondering if we're about to be attacked. Or if someone new is dead." He smiles grimly up at me, bitterness dimming his usual glow. "But it comes with the territory, I guess."

Unsure how to respond, I point to my abandoned glass of bourbon.

"Drinking helps."

Tristan rolls his eyes half-heartedly, then grabs the drink and drains it in two gulps. He snatches the bottle and pours another glass.

"Bottoms up," he says, raising it to Rose.

She shrugs. "Cheers."

Satisfied that I won't be leaving Tristan alone, I make my way upstairs, passing the kitchen, a lavish powder bath, and endless white walls covered in soulless abstract art. The main hall on the second floor is long and narrow, sharing one wall with the west side of the house. I gaze out the floor-length windows as I walk, watching dawn light bleed through the sky.

When I reach the single closed door at the end of the hall, I knock. "Nik?"

"Come in, *darahi.*"

Slowly, I turn the knob and slip into a large bedroom. The blackout shades are drawn, the bed is mussed, and there are four empty bottles strewn over the floor. They're all stained red, blood dripping from their mouths onto the beige carpet. Two more bottles sit on the nightstand, untouched.

The hair on the back of my neck stands on end. I try not to think about the moments after I was Turned—the confusion, the pain, the sensory overload. But most of all, the hunger. All-consuming and damn near unbearable, driving me into a bout of frenzied bloodlust that lasted for weeks.

"Charlotte." Nik emerges from the adjoining bathroom and sweeps me into a hug. "How are you doing?"

I release a long breath and sag against him, burying my face in the soft material of his t-shirt. Though the safe house clothing is musky with disuse, Nik's thick scent of alcohol and leather is still present, coating his skin like his own brand of cologne. He isn't warm, per se, but his presence is a balm for my nerves.

"Never better," I mumble, voice muffled. I look up at him. "How are *you?*"

"I'm not sure you'd like the answer."

I smooth his hair back and thumb a greenish bruise over his cheekbone. He leans into my touch, closing his eyes. The motion is so familiar—the ghost of something that was never meant to be.

Maybe if Rayna had never left, Nik and I would still be together. The idea has me balling my fist against his chest.

"I'm so sorry this is happening," I grumble. "You deserve better than this, Nikolas."

He smiles sadly. "Alas, the universe has never given much thought to what I do and don't deserve. I didn't deserve to be punished for Rayna's impetuousness, but here we are." He absently touches the scar cutting through his left eyebrow, and my stomach turns.

"Did Konstantin do that to you?"

A beat of silence. "Among other things."

I stare at him. In all my decades of knowing Nik, he has never opened up to me about the source of his scarring. We all have our fair share—hell, I've gained two more in as many weeks—but Nik's is excessive. Scars varying in color, shape, and size decorate his torso, some delicate, as though made with a small blade, while others look like they were carved into him with a jagged stone. The idea that they were all made by the same pair of frigid hands . . .

"Nik." I press my palms flat against his chest, tracing the ridges of his ruined skin through his shirt. "Are you telling me that all of these are from him?"

Nik shrugs, but the noncommittal gesture doesn't fool me. "Some, but not all. Many I've received during the natural course of my life, but others are from Konstantin. Some premeditated, some inflicted in moments of . . . *passion,* for lack of a better word. And then there was the subjugacy."

My jaw slackens as nausea roils in my gut. "He—you were his *subjugate?*"

"One of many." He hesitates for a moment before adding, "Including Rayna."

I stare at him in dull horror. It's no wonder he reacted so strongly when Kaleb first mentioned Konstantin. Why he cowered against the ballroom wall when Konstantin made his grand entrance. Why, despite Rayna's return, he seems to be drinking more than he usually does.

Konstantin is Nik's worst nightmare.

As though reading my thoughts, Nik pulls the flask from his back pocket and takes a swig. The faint tang of vodka fills the air and I frown.

"Yet another reason," I say through gritted teeth, "to rip the heart out of that miserable bastard's chest. Assuming he actually has one."

Nik clears his throat. "Yes, well," he says through a forced smile, "I didn't ask you to come up here just so we could dredge up my tragic past."

I want to press the matter but Nik's eyes shutter, a sure sign that he won't be saying anything else.

"What is it?" I ask instead.

"I need to pick up a few things from my house, but it's almost sunrise and Noah will need someone to keep him from accidentally . . . *you know*." Nik motions over his shoulder to where the bathroom door stands ajar. The room beyond is pitch black and silent. "Can you stay with him while I'm gone?"

"How is he?" My voice drops low, as though doing so will prevent Noah from hearing me. But he still can. I *know* he can. In those first few weeks after Turning, I could hear *everything*: the shuffle of footsteps inside houses, the heartbeats of rodents as they scurried by, the sound of my own blood streaming through my veins. It was overwhelming to the point of pain, and it took practice to be able to tune out all the background noise.

Noah has only been a vampire for a few hours. He can hear it *all*.

"Not great," Nik murmurs, shoulders sagging. "Though I'll admit, it's hard to tell. He has barely said anything and refuses to leave the bathroom. It's the darkness, I think. I'm worried—"

"*Stop talking about me*," Noah snarls, followed by a low groan. He says, almost to himself, "Even my *voice.*"

Nik's mouth curves into a half-smile, his eyes softening. "Did I mention he's a bit irritable?"

"I'm going to *kill you,*" Noah growls.

The two of us chuckle, and Nik's smile broadens—like the sound of Noah's voice stokes a fire in him. For a fleeting moment, I catch a distant glimpse of the man I used to know.

"You seem happy," I say. "With Noah, I mean. I've seen you with so many others"—*since me,* I almost say—"but you've never wanted to open up to anyone. Not like this. Noah is different, isn't he?"

Nik glances wistfully over his shoulder and I hear his heart skip a beat.

"Yeah, Lottie. I think he is."

CHAPTER 40

AFTER NIK LEAVES, I STAY in the dim bedroom as bright morning light bleeds around the curtains, not wanting to intrude on Noah's silence. The bed is surprisingly comfortable and I've spent the last hour or so wrapped in the down comforter. Thinking of Xander. Of Victoria.

And then there's the matter of Tristan and Noah.

Once again, I'm crippled by the knowledge that I dragged Tristan into this mess. And now Noah is involved. Inescapably.

There's a quick *buzz, buzz,* from my pocket. A text. I know it's from Konstantin before I even look at the message.

Ignoring me now, are we?

I can't help the snarl on my lips as I jam my fingers into the screen.

Don't.

Don't what?

You're trying to be clever and I want nothing to do with it. Kindly throw yourself off a cliff.

And with that, I hurl my phone across the room where it slams into the wall. I wince as Noah cries out from the bathroom.

"Could you *not?*"

"Sorry," I whisper, then bury myself in the covers again.

"Actually, Charlotte," Noah says timidly, "could you, um . . ."

The quiver in his voice has me throwing off the blankets and I hurry into the spacious bathroom, snatching up one of the blood bottles on my way. The room is windowless, pitch black after I close the door, but the tiny sliver of light peeking under it is enough to see by. My eyes slowly adjust to my new surroundings and I can just make out a shaking, huddled shape in the far corner.

"What do you need?" I ask as quietly as my voice will allow. "Are you hungry?"

"Starving," he moans, clutching his stomach. "It feels like—like there's a pit inside of me. Like I've somehow swallowed a black hole, but also like my entire body is on fire."

"That sounds about right." I pop the lid off the bottle, and the metallic scent immediately fills the room. My own throat ignites with hunger and I bite back the urge to drink the blood myself. Instead, I offer it to the boy on the floor. "Drink."

Noah growls low in his throat. His breath quickens. I crouch in front of him as his lips curl back, fangs springing out, then back in, then out again. The growl morphs into a deep groan as Noah curls into himself, hands clawing at his hair, and a shudder rocks through him.

"Please don't," he says through gritted teeth. "I don't want it."

"Yes, you do. You're a vampire now, Noah. You're never going to *stop* wanting it."

His eyes lock on the bottle. For a few seconds, I wonder if he might refuse again, but his hand shoots out and snatches it. Veins darken below his eyes as he drains the bottle in seconds, crushing it with both hands. He flings it away in disgust, then winces when its landing clatter echoes through the room.

"I didn't ask for this," he says shakily, even as he licks traces of blood from his lips. "I don't *want* this."

"Not many do."

Sighing, he hangs his head. "Tristan saved my life once, you know. We were at summer camp and I was a terrible swimmer. My canoe capsized . . ." A tear slides down Noah's cheek, mingling with the blood now staining his mouth. "I thought nothing could ever come between us. But now I'm—hell, I'm a *vampire*. I'm the same thing that killed his sister. What if he decides I'm not worth saving anymore? What if Nik only wanted me when I was human? What if—"

I deflate a little. "Noah, calm down. Neither of them—"

"Knock, knock." I whirl around to see Pippa poke her head through the door. "I couldn't help overhearing. Everything okay in here?"

She takes one look at us—at the bloodied, miserable boy—and shoves her way into the bathroom, sitting by Noah and wrapping her arms around him. I don't say anything, but settle onto my knees next to her. Watching. There is no hesitation in Pippa's touch, just a calm determination as she comforts Noah, rocking him softly. He stiffens as she smooths gentle fingers through his hair, rubs the back of his neck, scratches lightly over his spine and shoulder blades. Little by little, the tension drains from him, and he lets himself relax into Pippa's arms.

"Noah, listen to me," she says firmly, but there's a rare softness to her that pulls at me. "I know how you're feeling. You're angry, you're confused, and you're ready to gouge your ears out. And you might want to be strong—to prove that you're not a monster—but you don't have to do that. Your life just got turned on its head. It's okay to be broken for a while. It's okay to make messy mistakes. The people who love you will forgive you." She clenches her jaw. "Tristan isn't going anywhere. *Nik* isn't going anywhere."

Noah's lip trembles and he sniffs loudly.

"When I was Turned," she continues slowly, "nothing could have prepared me for the bloodlust. It was one of the most terrifying experiences of my life, coming out of it for the first time. I had a daughter. What if I had hurt her?" Noah's eyes widen in surprise and Pippa smiles softly. "But guess what, kid? You're lucky. You already have something that it takes most vampires years to find—decades, even."

He blinks wet lashes. "What's that?"

"A family," she says, and brushes a tear from Noah's cheek. "We may be a group of dysfunctional demons, but we do have hearts. Even Charlotte."

I sneer at her, but there's no weight behind it.

"Besides," I say, "if memory serves, you seem to think that vampirism is pretty sexy."

Noah huffs a laugh, fangs glinting through a wavering smile.

"Guilty." He falters, brow furrowed. "You're awfully nice for two girls who barely know me."

"Everyone is deserving of love," Pippa replies, the wisdom of centuries creeping into her voice. "And sometimes the ones who seem the strongest are the ones who need it most."

Silence fills air between us and Pippa pulls Noah closer, the boy burying his face in her pale hair. She rubs a soothing hand down his arm, adjusts the collar of his shirt, whispers sweet words in Welsh, then translates them to Spanish: *Está bien tener miedo.*

It's okay to be afraid.

The tenderness in Pippa's gaze makes my chest twist into knots. She doesn't talk about her daughter—Gwen—much, but something tells me she must have been an incredible mom.

I leave Noah in Pippa's capable hands and slip into the morning-bright hallway. Hissing, I hurry down the hall to the adjacent bedroom, then sigh as cool darkness washes over me once more.

My phone buzzes with a call and I close my eyes, willing it to stop. It does eventually, but starts right back up again.

Grimacing, I fish it from my pocket, not bothering to look at who's calling.

"You bastard." I dash to the closet and shut the door, attempting to shield myself from the house and its listening ears. There is a pile of blankets on one shelf, so I shove one over the crack in the door then bury myself in another one—anything to muffle my voice. Speaking as quietly as I can, I say, "You despicable piece of vampire trash. You staged a *coup*? Who do you think you are, Napoleon?"

Konstantin chuckles. "Always good to hear your beautiful voice, love. But why all the vitriol?"

"Because you *staged a coup*," I reiterate sharply, "and stripped Kaleb of his title. Wait, scratch that. You let *Yara* do it. What the hell are you even doing?"

"Whatever I want." The words are sharp. Final.

"You sound like a spoiled child."

"You are not entitled to my reasoning."

I exhale my frustration on a long, slow breath, forcing my voice to stay low. "Why did you call me?"

"Allow me to restate my previous point." When I don't reply, Konstantin releases a sigh of long-suffering. "Fine. I was bored."

"Of course," I say, yanking hard on a lock of my hair. "Because you were just dying to hear my *beautiful voice*. While we're here, the least you could do is explain what Yara has to do with this."

A low sound of amusement. I can practically see the smug look on his stupid face. "Yara has been invaluable to me. How else do you suppose I know so much about this city? I have been here for quite some time and have been able to discover many of its secrets on my own. However, having someone on the inside did make the job considerably easier."

I frown at the closet door. "How long have you been here exactly?"

"Eleven years."

Good hell. Here we are, thinking he's been here for eight months—a year at *most*. If he has been here for eleven years, that means he's been here since 2007, when the brand new iPhone was all the rage and the Twilight books still had humanity in a chokehold. Goosebumps crawl up my arms at the realization that he has most likely been watching us that entire time. Watching *me*. Waiting for some unknown, opportune moment to put his plan into motion.

"Well," I say, swallowing a tremor, "I applaud you for your patience."

Konstantin chuckles. "When you have been planning revenge for two centuries, eleven years passes in a blink. Besides, it has been a joy getting to know you and your little family over the past decade."

My skin crawls.

"So, Yara has been feeding you information?" I ask, steering myself out of a downward spiral. "She doesn't seem like the helpful type."

Konstantin's laugh is light and careless, as though we're discussing the weather rather than the recent overhaul of the local vampire government.

"When I approached Yara," he says smugly, "the woman practically begged to help. Apparently, she had been looking for a way to dethrone Kaleb for some time. I simply provided the opportunity and the manpower."

I snort. "Yeah, those fledglings of yours are *so* amazing. Did you know that six of us took out at least half of them before Yara said a word? You sure know how to choose them."

"Perhaps they aren't the most formidable opponents," he muses, a smile in his voice, "but they serve their purpose, for now. Even the deadliest vampire in the world cannot defeat a hundred fledglings on his own."

"How poetic. Should I be taking notes?"

There's a brief stretch of silence.

"As a reward for her invaluable help," Konstantin says, ignoring my jab, "I allowed Yara to take San Francisco, so long as she stayed loyal to me. The woman is attracted to power and, as you know, I am positively *lousy* with it."

I glare into the darkness, a snarl on my lips. "I hate you so much."

"Yes, yes, I'm crushed." There's a tense pause, and I try to picture the sneer on Konstantin's face. Or the smile. "But I can't have you berating me with every breath. Next time you answer my call—and you *will* answer—I expect you to be a bit more amicable."

"Do you know who you're talking to? What gives you the impression that I will listen to a word you say?"

"Because," he says, his voice strained, "you only have four days—strike that, *three* days until I kill your precious brother and his mistress. Not only am I extremely persuasive and devilishly handsome, but I hold their lives in my hands. I think that combination is the perfect cocktail for blind obedience. Tell me I'm right."

Until he *kills them*. Fear, bright and hot, licks at my nerves as something in my chest goes taught.

"You're right," I say. Because he is.

Konstantin laughs, and there's arrogance in it. "Now that we've established that, I'm sure you'll be more than willing to help me."

"I would rather die."

"In fact, you will tell me all your plans moving forward." A tug on that taught thread. His tone is matter-of-fact. Confident. "Knowing you lot, I'm sure there will be at least one more ill-prepared rescue attempt before Kaleb finally gives in. Your brother's was, quite frankly, pathetic."

I tense at the mention of Xander but bite my tongue. Konstantin is trying to get a rise out of me, and I refuse to give him the satisfaction.

"We'll talk again soon," he says.

I sense the finality in his words and hiss, "Wait." Konstantin is quiet, but the call stays connected. "Why are you doing all of this? What did Kaleb take?"

"He took *everything*," Konstantin replies a little too quickly, a wicked snarl in his voice. "And I am determined to return the favor."

And with those words, the line goes dead.

CHAPTER 41

I SHOVE MY PHONE INTO my pocket, resting my forehead against the closet door.

Breathe. In, out.

Three days until Konstantin kills Xander and Victoria—one day less than he originally promised. Which means it has only been three days since our fateful vampire prom. Such a short time, and yet so much has happened. It's crazy how quickly things have come undone—or rather, how quickly Konstantin has torn them to pieces.

But Konstantin hasn't actually done *any* of it, has he? Apart from his show in the ballroom the other night, he has been mysteriously absent. The fledgling attack at the house, the coup, the increased vampire activity in the city . . . that's all the work of others, with Konstantin pulling the strings. Just how far does his influence reach? And how are we supposed to stop it?

With a defeated sigh, I exit the closet, already imagining a hot shower. It won't solve any problems, but at least the scalding water might be enough to distract me for a little while.

I yank off my t-shirt and toss it onto the bed before slipping out of my safe-house-regulation sweatpants, wincing at the lingering twinges of pain pulsing through my body. When I open the bathroom door, I'm too caught up in my own thoughts to realize that the shower is already running. And that someone else is standing in front of the vanity mirror.

Tristan whirls around, eyes wide.

"God, Char," he says breathlessly. "You scared me."

I might have come back with a clever retort, but the words die on my tongue. Because Tristan is standing three feet from me in nothing but his boxers. My gaze slides down his body—over his strong shoulders, the tanned ridges of his abs—and lingers on the scar that disappears beneath his waistband.

"Are you here on purpose?" he asks with a sly quirk of his brow. Heat prickles over my skin. "Or is it an accident that you stumbled in right as I was about to take a shower?"

I frown at him, folding my arms over my nearly-bare torso. "Oh, don't flatter yourself. I could have just as easily walked in on Pippa. Or Kaleb."

Tristan grins crookedly, sending a flutter down my spine. We are alone in a bathroom, in our *underwear*. And I'm not even wearing my cute bra. I consider bolting back into the bedroom, but the damage has already been done. If Tristan didn't want me here, he would have kicked me out already. And the truth is, I would *really* like to stay. One look at the corded muscles in his arms brings a flush to my cheeks.

Tristan's eyes are intent on mine in a way that tells me he's trying *very hard* not to let them wander. It lasts all of seven seconds before his golden gaze drinks me in, moving over me slowly like a trickle of hot water. I regard him warily as he takes a step closer, touching gentle fingertips to the three parallel scars over my abdomen. Despite his warmth, I shiver.

"Where did you get these?" he asks, tracing the lines.

"A bear."

Tristan's brows shoot skyward. "A what?"

"In the Central Park Zoo. Being a vampire comes with risks. And sometimes those risks involve sneaking into a bear's cage to see if she'll let you ride her. The answer is no, in case you were wondering."

He grins, studying me like I'm the world's most ridiculous puzzle.

"Char, that's *insane*."

"I have some regrets."

Tristan's fingers move north, brushing lightly over my heart, which spasms behind my ribs. "And this one?"

I glance down at the raised scar. It's fresh enough that it twinges at Tristan's touch, the edges a sickly, glaring pink against my olive skin. I gently move his hand away, holding it between us.

"Remember the party at Olivia's house?"

"Wow," Tristan says, nodding. "I had almost forgotten about that. It feels like a lifetime ago."

"Yeah, well . . . when Olivia cut her finger, I went a little . . . *feral*, to put it lightly." I lift one hand, touching the scar gently. "I needed some fresh air, so I went outside. And then I got stabbed."

Tristan startles. "Are you serious?"

"It was one of Konstantin's people—a silver dagger through my heart, which acts as a paralytic to vampires. Hurt like hell. I was frozen for ages before Rose came looking for me."

"Oh my God," Tristan murmurs, his mouth quirking up on one side. "*I* almost went out looking for you."

"Good thing you didn't."

Tristan's attention lingers on the scar for a moment too long before his hand slides upward, sparks igniting under his fingertips. Desire thrums under my skin and I place my hand flat against his sternum, making his heart stutter and his eyes darken. The touch of his hand morphs from gentle to commanding, his thumb digging into the hollow beneath my jaw.

The air between us thickens. I breathe it in: the salt on Tristan's skin, the blood pulsing through him, the warmth radiating from his body. A pit of longing opens in me and I all but shove him toward the shower.

"At least buy me dinner first," he teases, but his breaths quicken as he fumbles for the shower door. Pausing, he drags his lip between his teeth. "Are you sure this is the best time—"

I yank him close and press a hard kiss to his mouth, filling it with every ounce of desire, uncertainty, and desperation I've felt over the past few weeks. Tristan is my pipe dream. My unattainable future. The sunshine in my dark nights, with his heartbreaking smile and his honey-gold eyes and his beautiful, annoying, *adorable* freckles. Common sense doesn't matter here.

It's my turn to take control—to take what I *want*. And right now, I want *him*.

Tristan stumbles a bit beneath the force of the kiss, but steadies himself with a hand on my bare hip.

"Have your way with me, Char," he murmurs, his lips curving against mine. "I'm at your mercy."

Yearning ignites inside me and I urge Tristan backward with a palm against his chest. His eyes turn molten as he yanks open the glass door, steam swirling around him like mist through the redwood trees. It slams shut behind us, and then it's just me and Tristan. Alone. In the *shower*.

If Pippa ever finds out about this, I'll never hear the end of it.

Tristan tugs us under the shower's stream. The water is hot, made scalding by the icy chill of anticipation pebbling my skin. I gasp as Tristan pulls me against him and fire explodes in my chest, sinking straight to my core. The last time I was this close to someone, it was nothing more than a one-night stand. It didn't *matter*. But Tristan . . .

Tristan matters.

His lips part on a gasp and my eyes drop to his mouth. I close the distance eagerly, and the world melts away.

This isn't like our kisses in Xander's Maserati or Nik's kitchen. This kiss is free and languid—born of relief and exhaustion and lowered inhibitions. I just don't *care* anymore. I don't care about the fact that Tristan is human. I don't care that I killed his sister. All I care about is the strength of his arms around me, the urgency of his lips as he devours me.

It's just the two of us, here, in the warmth. And we can just *be*.

Tristan's hands explore my water-slick skin, brushing over my hip bones, trailing up my ribcage, and his fingers tease the skin above my bra. My breath hitches and he grins against my mouth, chuckling softly when he coaxes the response from me again.

"You're such a tease," I breathe, catching a whiff of blood washing from the cut on his hand. My fangs stab through my gums and I stiffen, willing them back, pulling away on instinct.

"Don't." Tristan catches me around my waist, thumbing my parted lips. "I want all of you, not just the savory parts."

I exhale sharply, fighting the urge to recall my fangs. "Are you saying there are parts of me that are unsavory?"

"Yes."

"How romantic."

"You didn't let me finish."

Tristan takes a step toward me, guiding me backward until I'm pressed against the shower wall. There's a depth to his expression that catches me off guard—a hint of knowledge well beyond his twenty years.

"Unsavory," he murmurs, brushing his lips down my jaw, "can mean a lot of things. Of course I want you at your best"—his mouth moves down my neck and his teeth gently graze my skin; the accompanying chill has me digging my fingernails into his back—"but I will always take you at your worst. Give me your darkness, Charlotte. Show me who you really are."

I let my eyes drift shut as Tristan drags hot kisses down my neck, each more urgent than the last. Something deep inside me stirs—some ancient, primal force—and I catch a fleeting glimpse of the supernatural creature I fight so hard to keep at bay. She grins behind my eyelids, her eyes dark and veinous and bruised, her lips curled back over her fangs. She's wild. Feral. *Beautiful.*

Show me who you really are.

The change is gradual at first, but it doesn't take long for the creature to take over completely. Heat blooms under my eyes. My gums prickle. Hunger scorches its way into my throat and I let myself *feel* it:

the hollow ache, the craving for the coppery warmth of human blood.

When I open my eyes, Tristan is staring at me with his lips parted, his pupils blown wide, and his heart pounding hard against his ribs. After a tense pause, the silence filled with the steady rush of scalding water, he *grins*.

I can't help it—I grin back.

Tristan wraps his hands around the back of my thighs, lifting me with ease and pinning me against the shower wall. The motion sets his muscles flexing, his bare shoulders tan and toned and *glorious*. My legs wrap around him instinctively and he moans softly, the deep, vulnerable noise awakening something in me as desire pools between my hips. I take Tristan's face in both hands and kiss him like it's the end of the world. Yanking at his hair. Swiping my tongue along his bottom lip. He groans low in his throat, the sound reverberating through my chest and the steam-filled shower. Sweat beads on his upper lip, and my tongue burns with the taste of salt . . .

And copper.

I freeze and slowly break the kiss, staring at the smear of red at the corner of Tristan's mouth. His blood is hot on my tongue and hunger rages through me, a scorching, living thing.

"I bit you," I say, unable to form a coherent thought through the writhing hunger. "I—I'm sorry."

Tristan shakes his head and kisses me once, deeply. Pulling away, he lifts my chin with one finger. "What did I just say?"

Then he's kissing me again. I can't help but groan at the taste of his blood in my mouth. He doesn't care, so *I* don't care—*damn*, I really should—and our kiss is colored by copper and salt, longing and need. I suck on his sliced bottom lip, stoking the hunger already clawing through me, and he moans quietly, his hand knotting in my hair. His hands trace over my skin, coaxing little sounds of pleasure from me. I hold him closer, raking my fingers down his back as I press a dangerous kiss to his throat, right over his pulse point.

"Just do it, already," Tristan rasps, his breathing ragged.

"Do what?" I ask, my chest heaving in rhythm with his.

"Bite me."

I scoff, even while my fangs are inches from his throat, my hunger burning. The creature fights for control. "No."

"Come on Char. I applaud your attempt at vampiric chivalry, but we both know it's killing you."

My fangs brush Tristan's jaw. He shudders.

"What makes you think you can trust me?" I ask, my gaze fixed on the smooth column of his freckled throat. I tangle one hand in his wet hair, tugging his head to the side, enough that I can *see* his pulse. It's *pounding,* and my chest is on fire, and I slide my fangs over his skin. Scraping it.

"Because," Tristan breathes, his fingers digging into my thighs, "you may think you're made of darkness, but you underestimate how brightly you shine."

"Bright as a dying star, maybe."

"As the *sun,* Char." He kisses me then, with a tenderness that brings emotion to the corners of my eyes. "Bright and bold and so damn *beautiful.*"

"Tristan—"

"Do it," he rasps. "I dare you."

His eyes flash with a challenge and my heart jumps into overdrive. *How can I say no to that?*

Slowly—*so* slowly—I touch the tips of my fangs to his skin and flex my jaw, pressing harder, *harder,* until I feel the satisfying *pop* of punctured flesh. Tristan hisses sharply and my hunger flares to life. I latch onto his neck, a growl rumbling through my chest as his blood fills my mouth. It's bright and warm, sweet like honey and cut with citrus. Under it all, a note of the whiskey in his veins, bringing with it a hint of caramel and vanilla. The creature groans with pleasure.

My fist tightens in Tristan's hair, holding him steady. I half expect him to fight me, but he doesn't. Instead, his hips press me hard against the wall, which only strengthens the desire already burning in my core.

He frees one hand and slides it over my shoulder, tangling his fingers in the wet hair at my nape, even as he takes a ragged, shuddering breath.

Show me who you really are.

Steam billows around us, our skin hot and water-slick. The only sounds are the rushing water, the blood flowing through Tristan's veins, his muffled gasps of pain that border on pleasure. I've never fed like this before, but I suddenly understand what Nik sees in it. The trust, the instinct, the heat of blood in my mouth...and Tristan giving it *willingly.* It's intoxicating.

A frenzy builds in me, clouding my brain as I drink. And drink. Hunger, raw and bright, scrapes at my throat. I claw at Tristan's skin. More. *More.*

Then Tristan makes a small sound of protest, and my mind snaps into focus.

Control.

I throw my head back and it cracks against the shower wall as I shove Tristan away. Stars swim in my vision. My feet hit the tile with a wet *slap*. Mind racing, heart hammering, I stare at him and he levels dark eyes on me, breaths sharp and pained. Bright red blood oozes from two small cuts at the base of his neck, mingling with the water flowing down his torso.

"I'm sorry," I whisper, fighting a tremor. "That was too far. I—I should have stopped sooner."

Tristan takes a few long, shaking breaths, and wears a bewildered expression as he gingerly presses three fingers to his throat. His mouth quirks into an uncertain half-smile.

"Sooner?" he asks, still breathless. "Char, I've had nosebleeds that last longer than that."

"You—what?"

"I'm just saying."

Tristan's eyes glow with desire, making my cheeks heat all over again.

"I, uh—" I clear my throat once. Twice. It takes all my willpower to sheath my fangs, and I wipe my mouth with the back of my wrist. "We—I should go."

Tristan watches with an unreadable expression as I throw open the shower door and sprint from the bathroom, relishing the warmth of his blood pumping through my veins.

CHAPTER 42

Konstantin snarls a curse and throws yet another journal to the ground, weathered paper falling from its crumbling binding. The floor around him is littered with decades of rambling that starts in 1731— when the Vesely twins were barely ten years old. He didn't expect Nikolas to be such a terrible record-keeper. If Konstantin has to read one more entry about his infatuation with Kaleb's bartender, he might be sick.

He opens the next journal, this one labeled *January 1784 - March 1785*, and skims page after page of *nothing*. Nothing about Kaleb and Rayna, though Konstantin knows—he *knows*—they had been gallivanting for decades before that. That for the better part of seventy years, Rayna was having an affair with Kaleb right under his nose— with the only man Konstantin had ever fully trusted.

Tossing the journal to the floor, he comes to a conclusion: either Nikolas is the simpering idiot Konstantin always presumed him to be, or he's far more astute than he imagined. He filled fifty years worth of memoirs without mentioning Kaleb's relationship with Rayna *once*. And if he managed to do that, Konstantin doesn't know if he'll learn anything here after all. But no matter. He has to *try*.

April 1785 - December 1785: nothing. *January 1786 - November 1787*: *nothing*. The pile at his feet grows. Pursing his lips, he yanks a newer volume from the shelf labeled *June 1804*. An entire book for a single month.

The month Konstantin lost everything.

He flips open the leather-bound book to the first page, grimacing at the words written in Nikolas's careful hand.

June 13, 1804
Belarus

We are free.

He turns the page, but it's empty. And so is the next page, and the next. Three words is all Nikolas afforded that night, leaving the rest of the story blank. And after everything Konstantin did for him.

With a furious snarl, Konstantin turns and hurls the book across the room. It flies toward the grand piano but never finds its mark—a hand darts from the shadows and snatches it out of the air, making him stop short.

"What are you doing in my house, Kostya?"

Nikolas emerges from the shadowed hallway, the journal in one hand, a knife in the other. He watches Konstantin with wary, fearful eyes, but he shows no sign of submission. *Interesting.*

Konstantin plasters on a smile. "Catching up on our family history. What does it look like I'm doing?"

"If you're looking for answers, you won't find them here," Nikolas says, setting the journal on the piano bench without breaking eye contact. "I would never write anything down that might incriminate Kaleb or Rayna. I'm not an idiot."

"I never believed you were."

Nikolas narrows his eyes, grip tightening on the knife. "You could have fooled me."

Tension crackles in the air between them, and Konstantin takes a step forward, clasping his hands behind his back. He considers Nikolas with his blood-stained clothes, his limp hair, the tear stains on his cheeks, and grimaces. With every step closer, the scent of whiskey grows stronger, and by the time Konstantin is a few feet away, it is practically unbearable. Frowning, he lifts Nikolas's chin with his forefinger.

"Life has not been kind to you, has it, little one?"

"Don't call me that," Nikolas bites out, but he makes no effort to use the knife in his hand. Konstantin knows he won't. He doesn't have the courage.

"That's what you are, isn't it? My little plaything." Konstantin drags his finger down Nikolas's neck then cranks his head sideways, watching the pulse jump erratically at the base of his throat. "You remember this, don't you?"

Nikolas has gone still as marble, his breath stalled and his shoulders strained. With a dark smile, Konstantin leans close and puts his mouth to Nikolas's ear.

"We had such fun, you and I. A shame Kaleb had to ruin it." He looses his fangs, touching them to the other man's flesh. "Say you missed me."

Nikolas swallows hard. "Never."

Konstantin tuts then grabs his hair, viciously yanking his head back.

"Though I had no plans to kill you today," he says with forced calm, "there's nothing preventing me from doing so." His fist tightens in Nikolas's hair, who winces. "Now *say it*."

For a moment, he thinks Nikolas might resist, but his lungs empty and a tremor rocks through his body.

In a voice as feeble as a fly caught in a spider's web, he whispers, "I missed you, Kostya."

A laugh rumbles through Konstantin, accompanied by a wicked grin.

But then pain explodes in his side and he stumbles back, looking down to see a knife protruding from his ribs, buried to the hilt. Blood blooms onto his ivory sweater and it's all he can do to keep from screaming in fury. Snarling instead, he yanks the blade free, wincing as pain shoots up and into his shoulder, crackling down his left arm and into his hand. The knife clatters to the ground.

"You shouldn't have done that," he growls at a wide-eyed Nikolas, then pounces.

Nikolas cries out in surprise and takes the full brunt of Konstantin's attack, the two of them crashing to the ground. Konstantin kneels on the man's chest and throws a punch at his jaw but Nikolas deflects it, jabbing upward with an open palm. He catches Konstantin in the chin and his head snaps back, teeth clacking loud enough to echo in his ears.

"I'm surprised," Konstantin sneers as his next punch cracks against Nikolas's cheek. "I didn't expect you to use the knife." Another punch. Another *crack*. Blood spurts from a cut on Nikolas's lip. "You were always such a coward. I suppose that's why you were so easy to control."

With a roar, Nikolas grabs Konstantin by the collar and throws him sideways. He tumbles a few times and curses when his head slams against a wall, making dozens of gilded mirrors shudder above him. His shoulder screams in protest, sending a shock of pain down his arm. Numbness creeps into his fingertips.

"Not so easy now, am I?" Nikolas snarls. Konstantin rights himself, sitting with his back against the wall as Nikolas moves to stand over him. "Would you like to see what else I can do?"

Konstantin startles as he is heaved to his feet, then he breaks into easy laughter.

"Oh, would I."

With another roar, Nikolas aims a punch to his temple but Konstantin deftly twirls out of the way, jamming his own fist into Nikolas's unprotected ribcage. The man doubles over, coughing once before Konstantin grabs him by the hair and drives a knee straight into his nose. Blood spills to the floor and Konstantin grins in triumph.

"You were no match for me then," he growls, "and you are no match for me now."

Nikolas stays crouched for a few seconds, taking a few rasping breaths. But then his head snaps up, his eyes black with rage. Konstantin barely has time to gasp before Nikolas has him pinned to the floor, face contorted in fury like he has never seen.

Slam. Nikolas's right fist connects with his jaw. *Slam.* Then the left. Right. Left. Konstantin thrashes underneath him, hands clawing at whatever he can reach. But Nikolas is solid as rock, immovable as he lands another punch.

Konstantin can't see. He can't breathe. Unfamiliar panic tears through him, accompanied by disbelief. Nikolas isn't this strong. He *can't* be. But no matter how hard Konstantin fights, he can't escape.

Time for the last resort, then.

Crack. Konstantin sees stars as blood gushes from his nose, coating his mouth and chin. He cranes his arm beneath him and yanks his own dagger from its sheath, then surges upward with all his force, driving the blade straight into Nikolas's heart.

Nikolas gasps, his bloodied fists shuddering to a halt. He freezes in place for a few seconds before gravity takes over and he topples sideways, his shoulder hitting the wood floor with a dull thud. There's an agonizing moment of stunned silence as Nikolas stills completely, a single tear sliding along his bloodied nose before dripping to the floor.

Konstantin scrambles backward, not stopping until his back meets the side of the sofa. Breaths heaving and ragged, he stares at the other man where he lies paralyzed in a muddled pool of his own blood. *Nikolas,* of all people, could have just killed him. It's Konstantin's fault, of course. He underestimated his old pet. But he won't make that mistake again.

Groaning, he scrubs the blood from his eyes then snaps his nose back into place, biting back a snarl of pain. He stands shakily, his left arm hanging limply at his side, and curses at the bone handle jutting out of Nikolas's chest. This is not what he had in mind for this particular dagger. He would have preferred to bury it in Kaleb's back—it would only be fair after what he did.

"The next time you test me," he hisses in Nikolas's direction, "it won't be silver I drive through your heart."

Konstantin rises to his feet, staring at the blood spreading over Nikolas's chest. It brings back a memory he'd rather forget—one that drags fiery claws through his mind—but he fights the pull, shutting his eyes against the flash of amber hair and a red dress.

Silver? You were supposed to kill him.

The centuries-old words echo in his head as the topaz in the dagger's hilt winks up at him. Mocking him. He backs away slowly, massaging the numbness from his hand. With a final glance at his old friend's blood-splattered face, he snatches the discarded journal from the piano bench and bolts from the house, leaving Nikolas alone and paralyzed.

Maybe now he'll finally understand how it feels to be abandoned.

CHAPTER 43

I take back every judgmental thing I've ever said to Nik and Pippa about feeding on their human partners. I get it. I see the appeal.

Water drips from my hair as I exit the bedroom in damp clothes—I didn't bother drying off in my haste to get away—and my bare feet slip in the trail of droplets I leave on the wood floor. When I get back to the main level, I'm met by three amused gazes in the living room. Rayna raises her glass while Rose raises her brows, judgment etched all over her face. Pippa saunters up to me, waving a twenty-dollar bill, and shoves it into the neckline of my t-shirt.

"I think you deserve this."

I recoil, retrieving the bill and flinging it away.

"What?" She shrugs, grinning. "You put on a good show."

The other girls laugh and my cheeks flush, though not for the usual reasons. I'm silently grateful that Nik hasn't come back from his errand yet, and that Kaleb is absent—probably off on some Alpha errand. Or . . . maybe not. Because Kaleb isn't the Alpha anymore.

Does that mean Xander isn't Beta? Did I finally find out about his secret job only for him to lose it immediately?

"Yeah," Noah pipes up from the corner of the sofa, snapping me back to attention. He's in a black sweatshirt, the hood pulled low to shade his face from the light. "A *great* show. I've always wanted to hear my best friend bang someone in the shower."

Pippa snorts as Tristan emerges from the stairwell, one hand ruffling his damp hair. The cuts on his neck are smaller than I thought they'd be—thankfully—and the bleeding seems to have stopped. Mostly. The smell of it brings a flicker of heat to my chest and I hear Noah growl quietly. Pippa clamps a hand on his shoulder, fingers digging into the soft material of his sweatshirt.

Tristan pauses mid-stride, watching his friend with wary eyes. Noah stares back from beneath his hood, fangs glinting, and tucks his knees closer to his chest with one hand fisted on the cushion next to him.

"We didn't *bang*," Tristan says carefully, a smile playing at his lips. "We just . . . played around for a little bit."

The boys share a long look, then Noah says, "It's kind of hot, isn't it?"

Pippa barks a laugh and the tension between the two friends subsides, just a little.

"I bet you worked up an appetite," she says to Tristan, winking. She jabs a thumb in the direction of the kitchen, where I can see a few bulging grocery bags on the table. Next to it is a greasy white bag with the In-n-Out logo on the side. "I hope you like it animal style."

Noah actually cackles, then winces at the sound.

"Pippa, you rock," Tristan says, flashing me a smile before disappearing into the kitchen.

My phone buzzes and I bite back a sound of annoyance. Pippa, Rose, and Rayna start up a new conversation as I slip into the hallway, opening a text from Konstantin with a single kissy-face emoji. I fire back a response.

> Why are you so obsessed with me?

> Maybe I enjoy talking to you.

I find that hard to believe, given the fact that I insult you every chance I get. Dick.

See? You're delightful.

Besides, I get so bored waiting for Kaleb's answer. A man can only be alone for so long before he goes mad. Plotting revenge is so horribly isolating.

You poor thing. I'll shed a single tear for your withered heart.

Satire will get you nowhere, little bird.

"Who are you texting?"

I nearly jump out of my skin as Rayna pokes her head around the corner, her amber eyes calculating. She's wearing dark leggings and a simple white tank top that accentuates her toned arms. The deep scoop neck leaves her neck and chest bare, displaying a familiar pattern of faded white scarring at her throat.

From *Konstantin,* I realize. When she was his subjugate. I can't believe she never told me.

Smiling innocently, I lean against the wall, shoving my phone into the pocket of my sweatshirt. Hoping she can't see right through me.

"Are you trying to give me a heart attack?" I say, my mouth twisting into a frown. "Hate to break it to you, but if you want me dead, you'll have to try something else."

"Geez, relax." She saunters toward me, knocking back the drink in her hand, and smirks around the edges of her glass. Shrugging, she sets the empty cup on a dusty window sill. "It's just a question."

"No one," I say, not at all convincingly. "I'm texting no one."

"Liar."

Rayna's head tilts to the side, fire in her gaze, and the expression is so like Konstantin that I nearly turn and run. But this is Rayna. My best friend.

Though, in the past few days, she hasn't done much to re-establish herself in that role. In reality, it's almost like the real Rayna never came back at all. This is a carbon copy: all of her fox-like features, but none of her personality. No hint of those core traits that made her *our* Rayna.

Still, I find myself wanting to trust her. *Trying.*

New Rayna tucks her hands behind her back, taking one slow step, then another. The smile on her face screams *mischief,* and I move back a step in response.

"Oh, no," I say, holding up a hand to stave her off. "Absolutely not. I know that devil's grin."

Rayna's stride lengthens, her piercing eyes pinning me like a mouse in a hawk's gaze.

"I don't know what you're expecting, *darahi,*" she says sweetly, "but it isn't what you think."

Her hand darts forward, snatching the phone from my pocket in the span of a blink. And then she *runs.*

"Rayna!" I snarl, but she just laughs.

I tear after her, ignoring the confused shouts from the living room as we sprint through the front door. Rain-heavy clouds turn the midday light to a heavy gray, steeping the color from the ocean, the grass, the towering trees. Rayna disappears between two thick trunks and I follow, wicked wind whipping my hair.

"Rayna, give it back!" I cry, but she moves faster. Goading me on.

And suddenly, I'm back in Europe, racing Rayna through the cobblestone streets at midnight. At first, she was always so much faster than I was. Stronger. Stealthier. But I never let that stop me. The first time I beat her in a foot race was the most exhilarating moment of my life. I swore I would never lose to her again.

Putting on a burst of speed, I leap into the air and land heavily on her shoulders. We tumble to the ground, rolling for a few seconds before slamming to a stop against a fallen tree trunk. Rayna releases a guttural snarl. Fangs out, she fights against my hold as we wrestle in the dirt, trying to hook an arm around my neck, but I squirm out of her reach, flipping her onto her stomach. Pinning her.

I lean down, grinning at my easy victory, and whisper, "You looked back."

"You're right," Rayna says, fangs retreating. "I should have looked up."

I snatch my phone from her hand and roll off of her, flopping onto my back. The screen displays nothing but a disorganized jumble of apps, giving me no indication of whether she saw my conversation with Konstantin or not. If she did, she doesn't acknowledge it.

"What the hell was that about?" I ask, returning my phone to the safety of my pocket.

"Oh, I don't know," she says. The conifer canopy above us is dense and dark, cloaking her face in shadow, and her rose petal perfume mingles with the scents of evergreen and loamy earth. "I thought you could use some excitement that didn't involve that little damsel in distress you call your boyfriend."

I rise to my elbows, pouting. "He's not my *boyfriend*." But then I remember Tristan's declaration and I sigh, letting my head fall back. "Actually . . . maybe he is."

"Well, you sure *act* like he is." Rayna rolls onto her side, propping her head on one fist. With her other hand, she traces swirls through a pile of discarded pine needles. "You look at Tristan in a way you never looked at Nik. And I know how much you loved him."

"And how exactly do I look at Tristan?" I ask, not sure if I want to hear the answer.

Rayna chuckles, snapping tiny twigs between her fingers. "Like he hung the damn moon."

A flush rises to my cheeks and I'm grateful for the forest's dark. "Kind of like the way Kaleb looks at you."

There's a moment's pause, then Rayna sighs quietly. "He may have felt that way once, but I'm not so sure anymore."

Sadness twinges in my gut, surprising me almost as much as the vulnerable frown on Rayna's face. I shift closer, propping my head against her stomach, and she reaches one hand down to comb her fingers through my hair. Closing my eyes, I let my mind wander back to Paris, where I would lounge on the sofa with Rayna while Xander and Nik played chess by the fire. While Kaleb contemplated yet another way to ask Rayna to marry him.

"He still loves you," I say, and I actually believe it. "Even if he acts like an asshole most of the time."

Rayna scoffs. "Has he always been this way? Or have I just forgotten?"

"Always. But I think becoming Alpha made him a hundred times worse."

She nods, but her frown remains. I can't imagine being separated for almost two decades, then having to reunite and put the pieces back together. Sure, they've spoken. Sure, they know the details of one another's lives. But phone calls and texts only go so far. I wonder how Kaleb feels about it.

Rayna grimaces. "When did you start doing that?"

"Doing what?"

"*That*. Chewing on your lip."

I still, realizing that my teeth are indeed worrying at my bottom lip. "I have no idea. Why does it matter?"

"Because." She sits up, displacing me, and brushes earth from her hands. "That is a *Xander* habit. You used to be so much fun, Lottie." She gives me an exaggerated once-over, and my skin prickles under her gaze. "But you've turned into your brother."

I bolt upright. "Like hell I have. I am nothing like Xander."

"Have you seen yourself lately? You love bossing everyone around and you talk to Kaleb like he isn't your literal *Alpha*. If anyone in Santa Fe talked to me that way, I'd cut out their tongue."

She snaps her mouth shut, but the words are already out. I narrow my eyes.

"What did you say?"

"Nothing," she says in a clipped tone, picking herself up. "We should probably get back to the house—"

"Rayna." I stand too, yanking her around to face me. "I've already told you about everything happening in my life. Meanwhile, you've told me nothing about yours. What's this about Santa Fe? Are you—" My voice drops, and I stare at her in amazement. "Are you an Alpha?"

A mischievous twist of her mouth. "I might be."

That sure explains a lot.

"Holy *hell*. That may be the most idiotic thing I have ever heard."

"Watch it," she snaps, her jaw tensing. "I'm good at my job."

"Oh, I'm sure you are," I say with an incredulous shake of my head. "But you have a target on your back. I swear, you and Kaleb both have a death wish. How were either of you supposed to hide from Konstantin while in charge of entire cities?"

"Santa Fe is barely a city," she says, waving a hand dismissively. "And I don't even know if my position could be considered an Alpha. The vampire population in New Mexico is abysmal, at best. I keep everyone in line, I don't use my real name, and I have Harper to watch my back."

I frown at the name she mentioned a little while ago. "Harper?"

"My Beta."

Something tugs at my gut, my muscles tensing at the thought of someone else standing at Rayna's side. Though I've known she is an Alpha for all of thirty seconds, I can't help but wish she would have chosen me as her Beta. Maybe she would have, if I had known she was alive. If she would have *told me*.

"Your Beta?" I spit the word, my lip curling slightly.

"Betas aren't *bad*, Lottie," she says, annoyance flaring in her eyes. "They're helpful. I chose Harper because I knew I could trust her with my life. That's why Kaleb chose Xander."

"Yeah, well," I say with a wry smirk, "it seems like a lot of people are making choices without me."

"It wasn't like that—"

"I know. I do." I tug my hair over my shoulder, twisting it into a messy braid. "I just wish he would have told me, you know? I'm his *sister*. We're supposed to have each other's backs." Angry tears prick at the corners of my eyes. "I can keep secrets too, you know. I wouldn't have let anyone know you were alive. Xander should have trusted me. *You* should have trusted me."

"It had nothing to do with trust, Charlotte." Rayna takes one of my hands and my hair falls to my shoulder, the braid unraveling. Her voice softens but it carries a slight note of pity, making her words sound disingenuous. "We couldn't risk anyone else knowing. Telling Xander and Henry was dangerous enough. The more people who know something, the easier it is for the information to get out. I promise, you're making this more difficult than it needs to be."

"You don't understand, *liska*!" I shake my head, yanking my hand from her grip, and words erupt from me at full volume. "If you thought Xander was bad when you knew him before, you have no idea what he's been like for the last century. After Kaleb left and Nik crumbled, Xander stepped up and took on Kaleb's job as, I don't know, the family boss? And he's absolutely *terrible* at it. He and Nik are constantly fighting, and it's become physical more than once. Pippa and Rose act like his attitude doesn't bother them, but I know it does. And now Konstantin has him, and I don't know how to feel anymore. How am I supposed to hate him when I'm so terrified of what Konstantin will do?"

"Stop being so sensitive, Charlotte." Rayna's vixen eyes burn with cold fire. "It's time for you to grow up. You don't have to like your brother, but he's Kaleb's Beta, whether you like it or not. Stop griping and be grateful that Xander's ineptitude hasn't gotten anyone killed."

I fall back a step, recoiling from the bite in Rayna's words. "Excuse me?"

"At least it's the Beta's job to protect the Alpha with his life. Better Xander die than Kaleb."

An incredulous laugh escapes me, my lips curling into a sneer. "Funny. Only a few days ago, I defended you when Xander suggested we trade you for Victoria. We just got you back, and I wasn't about to let you go. But in the past few days, you've done nothing to convince me that you're worth saving."

Rayna balks, her expression turning murderous. Heat flares between us, fire and fury. This is exactly why I'm having a hard time trusting this new Rayna. One minute she's vulnerable—emotional, even—and the next she's spitting poison. She's leaving me in the hands of the *immortui*. She's stealing my phone and keeping secrets. Being angry with Xander is my prerogative as his sister, but I'll die before I let Rayna talk about him that way.

"You know," I say, jabbing a finger into her shoulder, "you sure changed over the last century. The Rayna I knew would never insult Xander to my face. And even if you had, I would have let it slide because I *worshiped* you. It wasn't until you left that I realized what a manipulative, conniving bitch you always were." Sneering, I add, "You're as bad as Konstantin."

Rayna's eyes widen in surprise, and maybe even a touch of hurt. Good riddance. I turn heel and storm away, tearing the silver coin from my neck and letting it fall, soundless, to the ground.

Fire flickers over my skin as I stalk through the trees, my hands fisted at my sides. After the conversations I've had with her, I'm starting to wonder if the Rayna from my memories ever existed at all, or if she was just a rose-colored version of what I wanted her to be.

I storm out of the woods and lean back against a thick tree trunk, absentmindedly scrolling through my phone. I find myself looking at the photo Konstantin sent me: Xander's forearm, tattooed and bloody.

Behind it, a blurred background, rocky and nondescript, and the distant prick of something red.

Wait. I zoom in, squinting at the shape: a rectangle, barely recognizable, but I can just make out the circular shape near the top, rimmed in weather-worn brass.

A door with a porthole window, set into a crumbling white wall. I *know* that door.

Holy *shit.*

I tear across the grass and fly through the front door of the house, drawing startled glances from the group still gathered in the living room. Kaleb has returned from whatever errand he was on and he jumps to his feet when I barrel in, expression bright with concern.

"Charlotte?" he asks, striding toward me. "What's happened? Are you alright?"

"I found them," I say breathily, waving my phone in the air. "Xander and Victoria. I know where they are."

CHAPTER 44

"What? Where?" Kaleb grabs my arm, but his grip is gentle. "How do you know?"

"Point Marea," I say, still breathing hard. "The old lighthouse, not far from here."

I can't believe I didn't notice it before. Point Marea may have once been a functional lighthouse, but it has fallen to ruin after decades of disuse. We spent a few Girls' Nights exploring the crumbling building, from the blown out lantern to the underground caverns that fill with ocean water when the tide is high. The last time we were there was only a year or two after we moved to the city, so Konstantin would never have seen us visit. Which means he has no idea that, of all the places he could have hidden hostages, this is one I would recognize.

Rose hurries over and studies the photo of Xander's arm on my phone screen, nodding in affirmation.

"She's right," she says, relief plain in her voice. "I recognize the door."

Pippa jumps up. "What are we waiting for? Let's go get them."

"Easy, darling." Kaleb's brow furrows as he pushes up the sleeves of his gray henley, looking far too casual in his safe house attire. "Even if we know where they are, retrieving Alexander and Victoria will not be an easy task."

"Come *on,* Kaleb," Pippa whines. "Konstantin could be torturing them for all we know. We can't just let them rot in there!"

Tristan catches my eye from the sofa, a question in the slight tilt of his head.

"Pippa, slow down," he says carefully, as though unsure if his comments are welcome. I nod encouragingly. "Let's think about this for a minute. If we're going to rescue them, what do we need to do first? Scope the place out to make sure they're actually there? Check for booby traps? Knowing you guys, I'm sure you have a stash of weapons you could start gathering."

He glances up at Kaleb, who regards him for a moment, looking mildly impressed.

"Well," Kaleb says, jaw working, "we'll need to—"

"What's this about a rescue attempt?" Rayna asks as she re-enters the house, her tone the epitome of nonchalance.

"*We*"—I say to Tristan, ignoring Rayna completely—"won't be doing anything. You and Noah will be staying here where it's safe."

Noah huffs derisively. "Sure, great idea. Leave the human here with the fledgling. I'm sure he'll be fine."

"He will be," Pippa says, nudging Noah's shoulder. He sneers up at her from his corner of the sofa. "Since this will most likely be a stealth mission, we won't need the entire group anyway. Nik can stay here and keep the two of you company." She stops, her brows scrunching together. "Where is Nik, anyway?"

"He went to grab a few things from his house," I say, even as a kernel of worry settles into my stomach.

Noah sits up, eyes sharp. "Yeah, but that was a few hours ago. He should have been back by now."

Silence fills the room, punctuated by the muffled sounds of quickening heartbeats. I force back a flare of panic. Maybe he got stuck in traffic or he went to more than one place—an alcohol run, perhaps. My attempts to calm myself are all in vain, however, and I see my worry reflected on the others' faces.

"Something's wrong," Rayna and I say together, which only makes it worse.

"Darlings." Kaleb's voice is calm, but he worries at the topaz right on his finger. "Let us not jump to conclusions."

"I'm not jumping anywhere," Rayna snaps. "If Nik is missing, there's only one explanation."

Kaleb's jaw ticks while Noah turns a shade of green.

"He's not answering his phone," Noah almost whines, tapping anxiously at his phone screen. Tristan takes a step toward him, concern etched on his brow, but Pippa catches him by the wrist with a subtle shake of her head.

"I'm going after him," Rayna says, turning to leave, but I grab a fistful of her tank top.

"Absolutely not."

She whirls on me and her mouth opens with an audible *pop*. "Do you think you can stop me?"

"Oh, you know I can—"

"You'll both go," Kaleb cuts in. "If something has truly happened to Nikolas, we don't have time to stand around bickering."

"I'll go too!" Noah leaps over the back of the sofa and, still unfamiliar with his newfound strength, launches himself halfway across the room. He lands in a heap on the floor, and if the mood weren't so somber, I would have laughed. As it stands, I'm not sure I'd be able to do anything but scream.

◇　◇　◇

"Can't we just . . . run?"

Noah will not stop fidgeting in the Maserati's backseat, bouncing from one window the other, his body alight with energy. I'm about five seconds away from throwing him out of the car.

"Sure, if you want to risk the sun coming out and turning you into vampire jerky," I say, and Noah swallows hard.

In reality, I doubt we have to worry about the sun coming out today. Rain clouds hang over the horizon and the scent of ozone is thick in the air, signaling yet another storm. Still, running through the city in daylight is far too risky. Midday San Francisco roads are congested with sleek cars piloted by aggressive drivers, making it nearly impossible to get anywhere quickly without being seen. Not to mention the steep hills and traffic lights at every corner. Every time I hit the brakes, Noah finds a new window to look out of, spinning in his seat, drumming his fingers against every surface.

"Noah," Rayna grinds out, "if you don't stop moving, I'm going *make you stop.*"

He freezes, then his hands start to clench and unclench in his lap. "I'm sorry, I just—I'm freaking out and everything is so *loud*. I—I can't stop moving. How do you guys live like this?"

"You get used to it," Rayna and I say together, then share an amused look, which quickly morphs into disgust. My hands tighten on the steering wheel.

Nik is fine, I keep telling myself. But even as I think the words, a heavy feeling in my gut tells me they're not true. He should have been back by now, or at least answered his phone.

Nik *always* answers his phone.

Despite the midday hustle and bustle, Jackson Street is surprisingly quiet as I turn the corner, the Maserati purring up the magnolia-lined road. Nik's Audi sits at the curb in front of his house, leaves gathering on the windshield. Dread pools in my stomach as I park behind it and kill the engine.

"Okay," I say softly. "Nik probably just got caught up in doing something. I'm sure he's fine." *Unless Konstantin found him,* I don't add, but the unspoken words hang heavily in the stifling car. I meet Noah's eyes in the rear-view mirror. "But we need to be on our guard, just in case."

He nods aggressively and the three of us slip out of the car. No one says a word as we tiptoe up the front steps, pausing on the porch to take a collective breath before we ease the door open. The lights are off, the house silent as a tomb. A chill shivers up my spine. Before I have taken two steps, Noah grimaces, nose scrunching.

"What *is* that?"

Rayna and I exchange a look of horror and we part our lips, tasting the air.

"That's blood, Noah," I say shakily. "*Vampire* blood."

Fear flashes in his eyes and something glints in my periphery. My head snaps sideways to the living room, illuminated only by the gray light leaking through the bay window. I take a slow step forward, then another, not daring to breathe.

Blood coats the floor, spatters the mirrors, drips from the corner of the sofa. I stop dead when I see the body lying paralyzed on the silk rug, the hilt of a dagger flush with his chest. Dark red pools around his too-familiar frame, coating his face, his hands, oozing over the carpet and spilling onto the hardwood floor.

I stumble backward into Rayna, who curses sharply before she, too, goes still. Her gaze falls to the floor and the color drains from her face, jaw clenching. Her voice is small when she says, "Nik?"

Noah appears at her side and recoils immediately, clapping both hands over his mouth. After a moment, he shuffles sideways and retches into a waste basket.

"It's okay, Noah," I whisper as he rights himself, even while horror roots me to the spot. "It's just silver." I focus on my breathing, trying vainly to ignore the frantic beating of my heart, the ice clawing its way through my chest.

Light catches on the dagger's hilt, reflecting the topaz stones set into a bone handle. Next to me, Rayna's breath is coming in ragged gasps. Her knees buckle and she hits the ground hard, clutching at her chest as she fights for air.

Rayna can't breathe.

Nik can't breathe.

Brushing past Rayna and a whimpering Noah, I kneel next to Nik, ignoring the squelch of coagulating blood under my knees. My hand trembles as I smooth the hair from Nik's forehead—his face is almost unrecognizable under a layer of blood and a bruised, crooked nose.

"Nik?" I murmur. "Can you hear me?

His lip twitches—just barely, but enough. I breathe a sigh of relief. He's paralyzed, but he's fine. Nik is *fine*.

"Okay, *darahi*," I say quietly. "I'm going to pull it out. Get ready." I brace his shoulder with one hand and wrap the other around the hilt of the dagger. "One . . . two . . ."

There's a puckering sound as I yank the dagger up and out. Everything is still for an endless second, then fresh blood pulses from Nik's chest, soaking through his gray shirt. After another moment, Nik sucks in a broken gasp. He coughs a few times and rolls onto his side, slowly rising to his hands and knees, his body shuddering in pain as the feeling returns to his limbs. I rest a steadying hand on his shoulder, squeezing gently.

This was not part of the deal. Konstantin wasn't supposed to hurt anyone else. He's changing the game. I almost reach for my phone—wanting to call him and *scream*—but there's so much blood, and the air reeks of death, and Nik is on the floor, broken, *bleeding*.

Konstantin can do whatever he wants to me, but I refuse to sit around while he hurts my family.

Nik groans and tucks his legs under him, deftly snapping his nose back into place without so much as a grimace. Releasing a shaky breath, I coax him forward, drawing him against my chest. His shirt is soaked with blood, and it sticks to my skin as he returns my embrace. He still smells of death and copper, tinged with the burn of silver in his veins. But underneath it all—underneath the death and pain and decades of suffering—is Nik. *My* Nik. Spice and leather and parchment paper. I close my eyes and remember: New York, promenades in Paris, the warm nights spent in quiet rooms.

Noah joins us on the floor and throws his arms around Nik's middle, and I feel a bit of the tension drain from him. The three of us sit huddled on the red-soaked floor until the trembling in Nik's shoulders subsides, until his breathing has almost returned to normal. He sits up and offers me a shaky, grateful smile, then seems to notice his sister for the first time. She leans against the sofa, her knees pulled to her chest.

"Rayna?" Nik rasps. "Are you okay?"

She doesn't respond. Her gaze is distant—contemplative—as she picks up the discarded, bloody dagger and twirls it in her hands, dragging one finger down the edge of the blade.

CHAPTER 45

"WHAT HAPPENED?" KALEB DEMANDS AS soon as we return to the safe house, a stumbling Nik in tow.

"What do *you* think happened?" Rayna snaps. She pulls the dagger from her waistband and the topaz sparkles. Kaleb blanches.

Noah has a supportive arm wrapped around Nik's ribs, but the poor boy looks like he's going to be sick again, his face ashen. Pippa rushes forward and grips Nik's other side, nodding to Noah. He gives her a grateful look and shoves away, sinking into a crouch with his head between his knees.

"It looks like a dagger," Rose says, appearing at Nik's side with a pair of blood bags. "Is that supposed to mean something?"

Nik's eyes immediately go dark and he snatches the blood bags from her, collapsing to the sofa and draining them in a few ravenous gulps. He may have cleaned himself up before we left his house, but his face is still a mess of bruises and cuts that makes my heart clench.

Something moves in the corner of my eye, and I turn to see Tristan tucked into a lounge chair, staring at Nik with mild horror. Without a word, he pours a glass of wine from a bottle on the coffee table. Tristan lifts the glass, considers it for a moment, then hands Nik the whole bottle instead. Nik responds with a crooked grin.

"Of course it means something," I say, tearing my attention from the silent exchange. "It *means* that Konstantin is a sadistic douchebag."

Rose frowns, touching Nik's shoulder. "You're sure it was Konstantin? It wasn't one of his fledglings or—"

"Oh, it was Konstantin, alright," Rayna says, flashing the jeweled weapon again. "This is the dagger Kaleb used to—"

Air hisses sharply through Kaleb's teeth, and the pair exchange a dubious glance. I look from one to the other, trying to decipher their telepathic conversation, but only manage to see a spark of scrutiny in Rayna's eyes.

"Yes, Rose," Nik says, some of the color having returned to his face. Still, his expression is distant. Haunted. "It was Konstantin. I found him rifling through my journals."

Now it's Rayna's turn to blanch. Why the mention of Nik's journals warranted such a reaction, I have no idea, but she fixes wide eyes on her brother.

"You didn't write anything about—"

"No," Nik says quickly, lips pursing. "And I told him as much."

"What was he looking for?" I ask, moving to stand next to Tristan's chair. His hand snakes up to find mine and I relax a little, taking comfort in his touch. "And why did he stab you over it?"

Nik laughs humorlessly. "To be fair, I stabbed him first."

Kaleb's brow quirks. He opens his mouth to speak, but Rayna beats him to it.

"What exactly did he say to you? Anything that might give us information about . . . well, anything?"

Nik shakes his head. "I don't think so. Kostya seemed . . . off. He definitely didn't expect to see me there, or that I would actually put up a fight."

Kostya. It's strange to hear the nickname coming from Nik—it's not like the two of them were close.

"That's because you were a pushover when he last saw you," Rayna says, sounding a bit bored. "He didn't think you had the guts to stand up to him."

"Ouch," Pippa mumbles under her breath.

"Oh, he knows I didn't mean it like that," Rayna says, even as Nik glares daggers at her.

"What do we do now?" I ask Kaleb. "If Konstantin was looking for answers in Nik's journals, he must not believe you'll actually tell him anything. Is this *truth* about Rayna really worth all the trouble he's putting us through?"

Kaleb drags a hand over his mouth, rubbing at the days-old stubble on his jaw. "I truly have no idea." He turns to Nik. "Was he looking at any specific timeframes? That might give us an idea of what he's after."

Nik shifts uncomfortably in his seat, taking another long drink before responding. "June 1804."

Kaleb and Rayna curse in unison.

"What?" Pippa asks, looking at three of them. "What happened in June 1804?"

"What do we remember about that night?" Kaleb asks Nik and Rayna, ignoring Pippa entirely. "Is there something we said that he might have misconstrued?"

"What *night?*" I ask, growing increasingly annoyed at these cryptic conversations. "What did you do?"

"It isn't so much what I did that night as what I *didn't* do," Kaleb growls.

Tristan snorts, taking a sip from the wine he originally poured for Nik. "God, you're so cryptic. Would it kill you to say what you mean for once?"

Kaleb cocks his head and Tristan cringes, like a student caught talking back to his teacher.

"Sorry," he mumbles, averting his eyes, but Kaleb actually manages to look amused.

"He has a point," I cut in, looking at Kaleb, Rayna, and Nik in turn. "If we're going to beat Konstantin, you're going to have to stop hiding things from us."

Rayna rolls her eyes. "We ran from Konstantin, he was pissed, end of story. That's all you need to know."

I glare at her.

"So, if you now know which night Konstantin is referring to," Rose muses, "can't you just tell him what happened with Rayna?"

"There's nothing to tell." Kaleb genuinely sounds confused, though his face is a mask of indifference. "He knows what happened that night. It was . . ." He inhales, touching a finger to his chin. "It was painfully obvious."

Tristan laughs quietly—incredulously—but Kaleb ignores him.

"Well," I say, clapping my hands together, "since this is proving to be a huge waste of time, I propose we move on to a new topic of discussion. Namely, rescuing Xander and Victoria. Tonight. Who's in?"

Five hands shoot into the air—everyone but Kaleb and Nik.

"I don't know if that's a good idea," Nik says, the words threaded with fear. "It could be a trap. He could have taken the photo like that on purpose, hoping you would recognize it—"

"I haven't been there in *years*," I interrupt. "I doubt he has any idea I even know the place exists."

"I'm going to have to agree with Lottie on this one," Rayna says. There's a glint in her eye, a hint of excitement that I haven't seen since she returned. If we were talking about anything else, I might be suspicious of the expression, but I'm too happy she's agreeing with me to care. "How much longer are we going to let Konstantin torture them? How do we know he'll be true to his word and let them go? For all we know, he'll behead them right in front of us just to hear us scream."

Rose pales. "Not funny, Rayna."

"Well," Kaleb says, "*I'm* inclined to agree with Nikolas. We still have a few days until Konstantin's deadline. If we waited even one more day, it would give us more time to scout the area and formulate a feasible plan. Going tonight would not only be foolish, but dangerous."

Rayna levels him with a glare. "I'm going whether you want me to or not. I'm done letting him manipulate us. It ends tonight."

The words are stern. Final. Something tells me she has more on her mind than just rescuing Xander and Victoria.

I fold my arms, carefully avoiding Kaleb's eyes. "I agree."

"Me too," Pippa says through a grin. "I've been dying to get out of this house and kick some ass."

Nik sighs, then struggles into a sitting position. "If you're all going, so am I."

"Absolutely not," Kaleb says firmly. "You need to rest."

"I'm *fine*—"

"How long was that dagger in your heart?"

Nik hesitates. "A few hours."

"Then it will be morning until you've returned to your full strength." Kaleb's tone leaves no room for argument. "I will not have you risking your life unnecessarily. We will only need a small group for this rescue—four, maximum. That will be Charlotte, Rayna, Philippa, and me. Rose, will you keep an eye on Nikolas?" Rose nods, and he adds, "Keep Tristan and Noah safe, as well."

Tristan frowns at the Alpha. "We're not totally useless, you know. I could, I don't know, drive the getaway car."

Pippa laughs a little too harshly. "No offense, but your human reflexes have nothing on mine. I would be halfway down the road before you even put the car into gear."

"You will stay here, Tristan." Kaleb sounds genuinely apologetic. "I appreciate your willingness to help, but this is much too dangerous for you to be involved. I cannot guarantee your safety."

Tristan frowns. "But—"

"Your time will come. For now, the best thing you can do is stay safe."

Though I feel a touch of pride at Tristan's willingness to help, I'm silently grateful to Kaleb for insisting that he stay behind. The last thing I need is to be worrying about him while I'm trying to stay alive myself.

Pippa claps her hands. "What's the plan?"

Kaleb squares his shoulders and sighs with begrudging acceptance.

"I suppose it will be a simple stealth mission. Get in, retrieve Alexander and Victoria, and get out. With the lighthouse as small as it is, I suggest two of us go into the lighthouse itself, while the others search the area around it. There will most likely be fledgling guards, but the area doesn't allow for too many. We should be able to fight them off and, if all goes according to plan, we will be back before sunrise."

"I'll check with Henry," Pippa says. "Make sure Konstantin will be nowhere near the lighthouse tonight."

Kaleb nods. "Good. Charlotte, I need you to search the house and find as many weapons as you can. I know Henry has a great many hidden here, if you know where to look."

I raise a brow. "And do you know where to look?"

"No."

"You're so very helpful."

"All of you, rest up," Kaleb says, ignoring my retort. "Though I pray tonight will go smoothly, I have learned never to get my hopes up when it comes to Konstantin."

We all cast nervous looks around the room. While I'm glad everyone agreed to my idea so quickly, I can't help but feel like Kaleb may have been right. Is it wise to rush into a rescue attempt without doing our due diligence? Will four of us be enough? What kind of defenses will Konstantin have waiting?

All these questions rattle around in my head, and I focus on them instead of the new tugging sensation behind my ribs.

Rayna grins, tossing the dagger into the air and catching it with a flourish. "Let's go rescue some damsels."

◊　◊　◊

You will tell me all your plans moving forward.

I snatch a bottle of whiskey from the kitchen table, doing my best to ignore the incessant tension in my chest. Ever since we finalized our plan, there's a little voice in my head that wants—no, *needs* me to make that call. The pressure is starting to hurt, making my hands shake.

Don't do it, Charlotte, I think, taking a drink of whiskey. *Don't you dare.*

But each refusal only makes the pull stronger—a thread tied to my spine, tugging and twisting until my entire chest is in knots. When I finally double over from the pressure, I know I can't ignore it any longer. I have to do it. I have to call that son of a bitch.

Clutching at my ribs, I slink down the hallway and into the powder bathroom, closing myself in. Locking the door. Everyone is scattered through the house preparing for the night's rescue, so it should be easy to escape their notice. I back into the corner and slide to the ground, breathless and trembling as I raise my phone and tap on the now-familiar number.

I am in control.

"Hello, hot stuff."

"Tonight," I blurt out, fighting to keep my voice down. "We're going to Point Marea tonight."

The pressure in my chest releases instantly, and I let out a shaking breath. What is *happening* to me? I open the bottle of whiskey and take another long swig, sighing as it warms its way down my throat.

"Mmm." Konstantin thinks for a few seconds, then says, "I'm impressed, little bird. How did you manage to find them?"

"The photo of Xander's arm. I recognized the lighthouse door in the background."

Konstantin chuckles, but it leans more toward annoyance than amusement.

"A rescue attempt," he sighs. "Why can't you all just play by the rules? Maybe I should tear your brother's heart out to teach you all a lesson."

"No!" I almost shout, then catch myself, dropping my voice to a whisper. "If you hurt him, I will *murder you.*"

Konstantin *tsks.* "Empty threats, love. You've had opportunities to hurt me, and you haven't. Why do you think that is?"

I don't know how to answer, so I stay silent, my heart racing. Hell knows I've wanted to hurt him. To make him suffer. To tear his head from his body. But when I had the chance, I hesitated, like some invisible force was stopping me.

There's a tiny sound outside the powder room door—a shuffle, barely a scrape. But it's enough to make my blood run cold. If anyone finds out what I'm doing in here . . .

"Wow, Charlotte." Konstantin's voice drones through the ear piece. "I've never known you to be speechless."

"Shut up," I hiss, my ear still trained on the door. After a few seconds of silence, my body relaxes, but my heart is now pounding in double time. "I'm not in the mood for your stupid comments."

"You know, not many who have called me 'stupid' have lived to tell about it."

"Empty threats, *love*," I say mockingly. A question comes to my mind, and I chew on the words before I say them. "And while we're on the topic, you've had ample opportunity to kill me as well. Is this really all about my relationship with Kaleb? Because I'll tell you right now, that is as rocky as it gets. You can hurt me all you want, but Kaleb isn't just going to roll over for you because of a few idle threats."

"I don't expect him to."

"Then why haven't you killed me?"

Konstantin is quiet for several long seconds and my heartbeat is a dull roar in my ears. I didn't realize how desperately I needed this answer until now—until I'm moments away from hearing it.

"Because you're important to me," Konstantin says finally, and there's a strange inflection behind the words. "There are things you can give me that the others cannot."

What is *that* supposed to mean?

Before I fully realize what I'm doing, I say, "Take me."

"Oh?" His voice deepens, turning sultry. "I would love to, my dear, but what would your little boyfriend think?"

I repress a gag. "No, dumbass. Take me in exchange for Victoria and Xander. I'll give you whatever you want if you just let them go. No one has to get hurt."

Konstantin is quiet again. I hear nothing but his slow breathing and the pounding of my own heart.

"What exactly do you think I want from you?" he asks finally.

"There has to be *something*. Otherwise I'd be dead."

A low chuckle. "All in good time, love."

"Is that all you have to say to me?"

"For now." His tone is aloof, but there's an undercurrent of frustration. "With this new bit of information, I have a lot to consider before the sun sets."

I glance up at the small window in the powder room, glowing orange with evening light. There's a rustling sound in my ear and I sense the call coming to a close.

"If you want me to keep spying for you," I say sharply, "I want proof of life."

A soft growl rumbles in Konstantin's throat, and the hair on the back of my neck rises.

"You're as bad as your brother," he says, his tone holding a warning. "Like I told him, the only demands that matter are mine. You're not tell anyone about our conversation. You will play along with Kaleb and his little plans, and no one will be the wiser. Perhaps I will see you tonight."

I open my mouth to reply, but Konstantin is already gone.

Exhaling slowly, I take a few seconds to process what just happened—and to question my own sanity. What is it about Konstantin that has me running to him with everything? I tamp down the panic screaming in my chest, trying to find a way to undo what I've done. Maybe I should tell someone else about this. Kaleb, or even Rayna. They would understand how persuasive Konstantin can be. They would be able to help me.

But something has me shutting down the idea immediately. I won't tell them. I *can't.*

Thump. There's another small sound in the hall. As quietly as I can, I stand, crossing the powder room to press my ear to the door. Listening. Waiting. When I hear nothing else, I open the door with a faint creaking noise and peer into the shadows.

There's no one there. Just a dim, lifeless hallway and the soft, lingering scent of rose petals.

CHAPTER 46

Monster. The Devil incarnate. There are many names Rayna has given Konstantin over the years, but none have ever been able to fully capture just how evil he truly is. For every kind word, there is a cutting remark. For every thoughtful action, a selfish motivation. For every bit of trust gained, there is a heartless betrayal.

And now Rayna knows that he has Charlotte wrapped around his pale little fingers.

Rayna leans against the vanity in one of the basement bathrooms, staring at her dim reflection. There are a few streaks of blood on her cheek—Nik's, no doubt—and her cross hangs crookedly at her neck, joined now by her old silver coin.

Charlotte held onto it all these years, only to discard it in the forest like a worthless trinket. Rayna touches it lightly, her fingertip sparking with heat, and frowns at herself in the mirror. Maybe she shouldn't have said those things about Xander. After all, he *has* managed to keep Kaleb safe for seventeen years. And he kept Rayna's secret. That has to count for something.

She scrubs at the blood on her cheek, rinsing it away with a splash of cold water. When they went looking for Nik earlier, she had tried to mentally prepare herself for the worst. But seeing her brother on the floor of his living room, paralyzed and bloody, was a scene straight from her worst nightmares. Two hundred years away from Konstantin had muted the memories, softening their edges and dulling the pain. But now the horror is renewed, and her chest constricts more with every breath.

Nik can't breathe.

Rayna pulls the dagger from her waistband and holds it in front of her, admiring the way light glints off the blade. It's a weapon that has found its home in many hearts, hers included. She wasn't sure she would ever see it again—not after that night in June of 1804 when they left Konstantin behind for good.

Centuries have passed since then, but she still wishes that night would have played out differently. But Kaleb had to go and have *feelings*—the one thing Konstantin told them never to give into. And look where that got them.

Rayna has been running for far too long. She is so damn *tired* of being afraid. She's tired of Konstantin's shadow looming over her every thought and filling her head with nightmares. This *has* to be the end.

I can't live like this anymore.

For the first time in a long time, she feels a step ahead of Konstantin. Rayna gathers her secrets and shuffles them in her mind, weighing them. Measuring them. Choosing which pieces to use and which tuck away for later.

She slips the dagger into her jacket, making a silent vow to the girl in the mirror.

Tonight, I will end Konstantin once and for all. Or I will die trying.

CHAPTER 47

Kaleb wasn't kidding: there are weapons *everywhere* in this house. I've found daggers sewn into the undersides of mattresses, stakes buried in flower pots, and throwing knives stashed behind the fireplace lintel. I immediately added those to my personal stash, since my own knives are back home, tossed aside carelessly under the assumption that I would be able to retrieve them. As it stands, I still haven't gone home. The house is too empty, and there are too many ghosts.

Tristan helps me scour the safe house—though his observation skills aren't nearly as keen as mine—and after a couple of hours, we have collected a small mountain of daggers, stakes, knives, and even a compound bow and a quiver of silver arrows. I watch him now where he lies on the floor, one arm fully under the sofa as he tries to yank a dagger from the wooden supports.

"You look like you're struggling a bit there."

"Not at all," Tristan grunts, frowning in concentration. "This isn't awkward or anything."

"Want some help?"

"I got it," he says through gritted teeth, upper body straining.

I hook my hand under one end of the sofa and lift it above my head, grinning when Tristan glares up at me with a look of complete and utter betrayal.

"Where was that five minutes ago?"

"I wanted you to feel useful. You don't want me to do everything for you, do you?"

With a good-natured glare, he sits up and yanks a black-handled blade from its hiding place, turning it over in his hands. I try not to stare as he flips it a few times, looking more adept than I expected. Carefully, I lower the sofa back to the floor and it lands with a quiet *thud*.

"Wielded a blade before, have you?"

Tristan stands, mouth quirking into a smirk. "Summer camp every year since I was twelve. Just don't ask me to hit a moving target. The last time I tried, Alison nearly lost a finger." The mood sobers instantly, and my chest grows heavy when Tristan's brows knit together. But then he smiles—a fond, nostalgic curve of his lips—and spins the dagger again. "She made it up to me by giving me this." He taps the tiny white scar on his cheek.

I laugh in surprise. "She stabbed you in the face?"

"Grazed me, is more what she did."

Tristan adds the dagger to a pile of weapons on the coffee table then takes my hand, his callused fingers warm against the icy skin of my palm. I step closer, wanting to soak in the warmth—to feel it radiating from him like afternoon sun.

"Let me come with you tonight," he says softly. "I'll feel better if I can see that you're safe. If I know you're not alone."

"First, I won't be alone," I say, hugging his hand to my chest. "I'll have Kaleb, Pippa, and Rayna with me."

Tristan's eyes narrow slightly. "Like I said, I don't want you to be alone."

"Tristan—"

"Listen." He leans close, pitching his voice low, as though aware of listening ears. He's learning. "Kaleb is amazing, I know. But he'll be trying to single-handedly protect all of you, which will only distract him. Not to mention how focused he'll be on Xander and Victoria when you find them. Pippa is . . . well, she's Pippa. I have no doubt she'll fight tooth and nail, but she's reckless. And Rayna . . ." His eyes flit to one side, then the other. "I don't trust her."

My stomach flips, and I'm silently grateful that both Kaleb and Rayna aren't here. They're out doing who-knows-what in preparation for tonight. I glance sideways through the living room windows, where the last of the gray twilight hangs above the horizon, and my stomach flips again.

We'll be leaving soon. I'm going to get my brother back. That is, unless Konstantin stops us.

Not wanting to exacerbate Tristan's suspicion, I force calm into my voice as I ask, "What makes you say that?"

"A lot of things, really." He frowns at a spot over my shoulder, his voice sinking into a barely-there whisper. "Despite claiming that she knows more about Konstantin than anyone, she never seems to contribute anything meaningful to our conversations. All she does is listen while everyone else talks, then makes comments that suggest she already knows everything."

As much as I don't want to admit it, Tristan is right. Rayna has been suspiciously quiet since she showed up here a few nights ago, and I'm sure we're not the only ones who have noticed. Either she's up to something and doesn't want us to know, or she has absolutely no idea what she's doing. I'm not sure which one is worse.

"Regardless," I say, shaking the thought away, "I don't want you coming tonight, even if you're just the getaway driver. Despite what you may think, *you're* the one who needs protecting."

Not only that, but Konstantin knows we're coming and I have no idea what will be waiting for us. I desperately want to tell him the truth, but no matter how hard I've tried, I can't. The words won't come. All I can do is play along and hope nothing bad happens tonight. I have a feeling I'll be hoping in vain.

"Are you saying I'm the damsel in distress?" Tristan asks.

"I'm not *not* saying that."

He meets my gaze for a few seconds, gold eyes glinting like cut topaz.

"Fine, you win," he says, "but you're going to owe me when this is all over."

"Oh? What did you have in mind?"

Pink creeps into Tristan's freckled cheeks. "I have a few ideas."

I swallow against the flare of heat in my chest just as the front door opens, revealing a frowning Rayna. Kaleb and Henry follow, each in varying states of frustration.

"He's making too many of them," Henry says, shoving the door shut. "If he keeps going on like this, it's going to become a much bigger issue than rumors of a serial killer on the news."

Kaleb rubs at his mouth. "I've spoken with Lorenzo and Mei. They're doing the best they can, but they haven't the manpower to dispose of them quickly enough."

"Wait," I say, forcing myself into their circle. "What are you talking about?"

"Fledglings," Rayna spits, crossing her arms. "Konstantin keeps Turning them, and it's becoming a problem."

"I saw something about that on the news," Tristan interjects, appearing at my side. "Not about *fledglings*, obviously. But they're labeling it 'increased criminal activity' in response to the San Francisco Vampire: muggings, missing people, 'wounds' in necks. They've warned people away from downtown at night, and there are many who are leaving the city altogether."

"I've heard the same." Kaleb's lips purse, his throat bobbing. "Excuse me a moment."

He disappears into a dark hallway and I hear the distant sound of a door opening and closing. Rayna frowns after him.

"Trouble in paradise?" I ask, and her lips curls. "Sorry, but he doesn't seem very happy right now."

Something flickers in Rayna's eyes but she hides it quickly, smoothing her expression into cool indifference. "It's nothing. Just a little disagreement, is all."

"Well, you need to get over it. We all have to be on high alert tonight, and I won't have us fail because you can't shelf it for a few hours."

Rayna fixes me with a black glare. "I'm not sure I like this side of you, Charlotte."

"Too bad."

Before Rayna can snap back, Pippa clomps down the stairs, fully-clad in black leather. She sashays to Henry and throws her arms around his neck, planting a wet kiss on his lips. Henry melts a little, hands snaking around her middle, and Tristan clears his throat loudly.

"At least Charlotte and I had the decency to keep it behind closed doors."

Pippa breaks the kiss and shoots him a wry look. "No one said you had to do that."

Rayna mumbles something unintelligible.

"It looks like you managed to find a good portion of my weapons stash," Henry says, detaching himself from Pippa with considerable effort.

"A good portion?" I ask, cocking an eyebrow. "Are you telling me there's *more?*"

Henry grins. "Darling, there is always more."

Pippa's eyes heat and she pulls him in for another kiss.

"Philippa, please." Kaleb emerges from the hallway, donning a dark jacket and . . .

I gape at him. "You own *jeans?*"

Kaleb's mouth quirks and he motions to himself with a smooth wave of his hand. "You didn't expect me to wear my best clothing on a rescue mission, did you?"

"Hell forbid you ruin your perfect clothes," Rayna says off-handedly, but I don't miss the irritation in her tone.

"*Table it*, Rayna," I hiss. "Tonight isn't about you."

The room falls silent for a few seconds, then Henry forces a cough.

"I must be getting back. Too many unexplained absences are bound to make Konstantin suspicious." He frowns with one hand on the door knob. "Best of luck to all of you tonight. I'll be doing my best to keep Konstantin occupied for the duration of your rescue. I hope that you all accomplish what you set out to do—and I expect to see all of you on the other side."

With a gentle graze of his fingertips over Pippa's cheek, he slips through the door and disappears into the deepening twilight.

HENRY ALBRIGHT

CHAPTER 48

Charlotte's call shouldn't have come as a surprise, yet Konstantin finds himself pacing the dark hallway with a snarl on his face and a tick in his shoulder. He thought that maybe—just maybe—Kaleb would have enough integrity left to honor a simple bargain. But he should have known better.

All he had to do was tell the truth about what he did to Rayna. It's the only explanation for why she would choose Kaleb over him. Before she was Turned, Rayna showed no signs of rebellion. No sign that she felt anything but love for him. They were *happy*. Therefore, Konstantin's suspicions *must* be correct.

Or maybe Rayna is a better actor than he thought.

No. Konstantin won't humor the idea. Rayna loved him. She *still* loves him. And he is determined to prove it.

There will be a rescue attempt tonight, of that he is certain. While he knows it will be a difficult task, he will not underestimate his opponent—not like he did this afternoon. His face is still sore from a plethora of fractures dealt by Nikolas. Sneering, he tears a sconce from the wall and hurls it down the corridor just as Kaleb's errand boy steps around the corner. He startles and ducks behind the wall, then cautiously reappears.

"Konstantin?" He slowly makes his way down the hall, accompanied by a young vampire woman in a lacy white dress. "I have a few questions from Yara—"

"No." He spits on the floor, flashing the boy a look of disgust. "Yara means nothing. I have no interest in her."

The boy's eyes widen but he nods. "Yes, sir. In that case, I have—"

"You have nothing." Konstantin strides toward the boy and stops less than a foot from him. Too close. Cool breath mingles between them as Konstantin says, "I, on the other hand, have a job for you. For you, as well," he adds, turning to the young woman.

She flashes a dainty, fanged smile, her chestnut ringlets bouncing. "Anything for you, Kostya."

Taking a step back, he inclines his head at the boy and says, "Meet me in the lobby in ten minutes. We will discuss it then."

The boy hesitates for a moment then nods again. He slinks away, and Konstantin waits until his footsteps disappear before he speaks.

"Gather sixty," he murmurs to the girl, and she nods eagerly. He leans closer, his lips at her ear. "And if the boy behaves as you predicted, you know what to do."

A small laugh escapes her, like the tinkling of tiny bells, and she presses a single finger to her blood-red lips.

CHAPTER 49

I'm a bit disappointed when we arrive at the lighthouse. Not only because of the location itself, but because I don't see a sign anywhere that says, "Charlotte, go this way!" That would have made everything so much easier.

But alas, Konstantin had to go and be dramatic. Rescuing Xander and Victoria from this place looks about as easy as rescuing a kitten from a storm drain. Luckily, I've spent time here and I know the building's secrets. And Konstantin has no idea.

The Point Marea lighthouse is nothing special: maybe forty feet high with rust-stained metal panels, resting at the foot of a cliff that towers over the Pacific Ocean. The glass dome on its head has long-since shattered, leaving the inactive lantern open to the battering wind and corrosive sea spray. Due to its perilous location—and the fact that its rocky foundation is crumbling beneath it—the lighthouse has been out of use for decades, slowly falling to disrepair.

The perfect place to hide two vampire hostages without fear of being found.

Kaleb, Rayna, Pippa, and I sneak down the switchbacks leading to the lighthouse, our feet light and our breaths held. Wind and rain buffet the cliffside, making my eyes water as I check my weapons for the thousandth time: throwing knives at my hip, a dagger in each sleeve, a serrated blade in my right boot. In addition, two blood bags tucked into a drawstring backpack. Chances are, Xander and Victoria are going to need them.

As far as I can tell, we're the only ones down here, but with Konstantin, I've learned we can never be too careful—especially when he knows our plans. When I *told him* our plans. My neck prickles with unease and I whip my head around, scanning the cliff behind us, but I see only black rock and scraggly brush.

Get in, get Xander and Victoria, and get out. That's all we have to do. I just hope we can do it before Konstantin shows up.

We reach the outcropping that juts into the ocean, the lighthouse cutting a jagged outline against the storm-dark night. Rayna makes a few gestures with her hands, indicating that Kaleb and I should go into the lighthouse while she and Pippa search the surrounding area. Kaleb narrows his eyes at her but ultimately nods, motioning for me to follow. With an encouraging nod to Pippa—and a pointed glare at Rayna—I make my way down the muddied dirt path to the lighthouse's familiar door.

Kaleb, soaked to the skin, touches a finger to his lips before pushing open the rickety red door. Strange, the last time we were together in the rain was barely a week ago in Golden Gate Park, when he told me that Rayna's death had been her idea all along. If only I had known then that in just a few days, I would be watching a very alive Rayna slowly picking her way over a pile of jagged rocks, a distant, distracted expression on her face.

But I don't have time to worry about that right now. *Get in, get Xander and Victoria, get out.*

The lighthouse's interior is drafty and empty, water stains oozing down once-white walls. A rusting spiral staircase twists up through its center. I cover my nose at the reek of mildewed wood and grimy water, and under that, something stale and metallic—*vampire blood.*

Above us, three floors stretch between the main level and the lantern. Pippa and I once spent an entire evening trying to go up and down without touching the stairs themselves, so I became intimately familiar with the lighthouse's structure, remembering every foothold and rusty nail that juts from the walls and floors.

I nod to Kaleb and motion to the stairs; he takes them two at a time, leaving me to explore the barren main level on my own. Rain pounds overhead, wind howling, waves crashing against the outer walls. A cacophony of sound that manages to mask any hint of another's presence. Still, I close my eyes, forcing the roar into the background—listening for something, *anything* that will tell me where Xander and Victoria are hidden.

But there's nothing. Just the sound of my heart pounding in time with the waves.

On the side of the lighthouse that faces the ocean is a small door that leads into a crumbling storage room. From what I remember, it's dark and drafty, but might be the perfect place to stash hostages.

They have to be there. Otherwise, all this will have been for nothing, and Konstantin might just kill us for it.

"Xander," I murmur, scrubbing hot tears from my eyes, "where are you?"

I hear something, then. A name, barely a whisper over the raging storm. I train my ear toward the sound, and I hear it again.

"Ksusha?" the voice rasps. "Ksusha, we're down here."

Down. *Down.* I drop to my knees, pulling at floorboards, searching for the edge of the trapdoor. I only opened it once, but it was enough. Even when Pippa dared me to go inside, I refused to leap into a dark cavern filled with ocean water. But if my brother is down there . . .

My hands scrape at loose nails, and I bite back a cry as one stabs into my knee. Just when I'm about to give up, a floorboard shifts, taking the nearby planks with it. *The door.*

"Kaleb!" I hiss. "I found them!"

I claw at the wood until my fingers find purchase and the door clatters open, revealing a square of pitch black. Bracing myself, I slide my feet into the opening as Kaleb reappears.

"Be careful," he whispers and I nod, lowering myself into the dark.

A metal ladder is anchored to one side of a hollowed-out hole through the lighthouse's foundation, leading down through a column of rough-cut stone. I move quickly but carefully, doing my best not to slip on the slimy rungs. Once inside, the deafening noise turns into a dull roar, the light swallowed up by blackness. Kaleb climbs in after me and for a few moments of torturous silence, I wonder if Konstantin will appear above us and slam the door shut, locking us in.

But the opening remains clear as we descend, and descend, and descend.

"Take it out," Xander groans, voice rough as sandpaper. It's louder now, accompanied by the clear, crisp rush of water. "*Take it out.*"

I sense the shaft widening as we descend, and then . . . the ladder ends. The scent of blood is so strong that I nearly gag—stale and cold and decaying, mixed with salt and seaweed. I pull out my phone and wake the screen, offering just enough of a glow to see by. I blink a few times as my eyes adjust, and my heart drops into my stomach.

Below us, standing chest-deep in foamy, rushing water, are Xander and Victoria. Each has their hands bound above them, blood oozing from their wrists where silver wire cuts into their skin. Xander squints against the light, sneering through cracked, bleeding lips.

I wedge my phone into a crack in the wall and drop the remaining distance from the ladder, icy water biting through my clothes and soaking me up to my armpits. A barbed silver wire is wrapped around Xander's neck, more blood leaking from blistering wounds and soaking into his collar. Horror makes my stomach heave, and I reach for one of my knives just as Xander makes a sound of protest, looking down at me with an opaque gaze.

"*Take it out.*"

I freeze, giving him a once-over. "Take what out, Alexander?"

"Victoria," he wheezes. "The dagger. Take it out."

Kaleb splashes down next to me as I look to Victoria, who has yet to say a word. And when I see the dagger's handle protruding from her heart, I understand why. Her eyes are frozen wide in terror and pain, tears leaking down her chapped cheeks.

Without hesitation, Kaleb's hand closes around the dagger and yanks it from her chest, making quick work of freeing her wrists. After a few seconds, her lungs fill with a tortured breath and she moans, letting out a few coughs that morph quickly into choking sobs.

"Steady, darling," Kaleb whispers. "I've got you."

"Victoria—" Xander starts, but I stop him.

"She'll be okay. Now hush so I can help you." I reach into the frigid water and slide the serrated knife from my boot, taking a deep breath to steady my hand. I raise the blade and slide it carefully under the wire around Xander's neck, sawing carefully with the jagged edges. I focus on the action of loosing the cord, distancing myself from the blood, my brother's ashen skin, the panicked, too-fast breaths coming from Victoria. The wire snaps and Xander hisses in pain and relief, letting his head hang.

"Every day," he says, almost to himself, "the tide comes in. And we're trapped here. The water . . . it fills the shaft—"

"Shh," I hiss, forcing myself not to dwell on the words. I move on to his wrists, his skin slick and coated in red. Xander's sleeves are rolled to his elbows, revealing the slashed tattoo on his inner forearm. It hasn't healed at all, suggesting that Xander has lost a lot of blood—and that Konstantin hasn't been feeding him.

The wire around Xander's wrist gives way and my brother crumples. I catch him against me before he can sink beneath the waves and I stumble slightly under his weight, sighing in relief. It's followed by an immediate and startling bolt of anger.

"Don't you *ever* do that to me again."

"Do what?" he rasps.

"Run away!" My voice pitches upward, but I reign it back in, dropping it to a whisper against Xander's chest. "I was so *worried,* Alexander." I bite back a sting of emotion. "I thought I was going to lose you."

Xander is still for a few seconds before he tightens his hold around me, fisting my jacket in his hands.

"I didn't think you would come for me," he says, his voice wavering. "I thought—"

I pull away and catch Xander's face in both hands, brushing away a tear with my thumb. A few days ago, I thought I wanted him dead. I wanted him to suffer just like I did—like *Nik* did—for the last century. But I didn't want *this*. Because this is worse.

This is *so much* worse.

"Charlotte," Kaleb murmurs, and I blink tears from my eyes, turning to the Alpha. He stands with one hand on the ladder's bottom rung, clutching a barely-conscious Victoria to his chest with his other arm. A small whine escapes Xander's throat. "We need to go. Quickly."

"Do you need help?" I ask my brother.

He shakes his head, wincing as the movement tugs at the wounds on his neck. "I can manage."

I usher him up the ladder after Kaleb, who deftly carries Victoria while climbing with only one hand. I bring up the rear, the bitter tang of Xander and Victoria's blood still bright in my nose. Xander is unsteady above me—he seems to be favoring his arms, putting no weight on his right foot—but I silently urge him forward, upward, out from the blackness and into the drafty old lighthouse.

The storm has intensified by the time we push through the rickety red door, frigid north wind blasting us sideways, making Xander stumble. He bites back a cry of pain and I catch him by the arm, throwing it over my shoulders.

"You're hurt," I say as I take some of his weight, swaying under his tall frame. "There's a blood bag in my backpack."

"Victoria—"

"There's one for her too."

Xander hesitates then retrieves the bags, handing one to Kaleb and tearing the top off the other with his teeth. He guzzles the blood in a few deep swallows before tossing the bag to the ground, hissing as a few of his cuts zip closed.

We trudge on, back toward the cliffside, and I try to ignore the gnawing feeling in my gut. This is too easy. *Far* too easy. There's no way Konstantin knew we were coming and chose not to do anything. If he loses Xander and Victoria, then he loses the only leverage he has against Kaleb. But, with how much I *don't* know about their relationship, I wouldn't be surprised if there were a multitude of things that Konstantin could hold over his old friend.

Pippa appears from behind a pile of boulders, her face paling when she sees Xander and Victoria. She sprints to us, platinum hair streaming behind her like a jet trail.

"Are you two alright?" she asks, hands fluttering uselessly over Victoria's bloodied chest. "What did he do to you?"

Kaleb shakes his head. "Now is not the time. Let's focus on getting to safety, then you can ask whatever questions you want."

I glance around, frowning. "Where's Rayna?"

Pippa shrugs. "I don't know—"

She cuts off as a small, bright voice—like the pealing of tiny bells—pierces through the raging storm. Icy rain bites my face but I barely feel it, focusing instead on that lilting sound. A voice—no, a *laugh,* I realize, that touches a memory, ancient and buried in the back of my mind. I glance up at Xander, whose eyes are bright and intense as he scans the landscape. His back straightens and his lips part as he tastes the air, the same flash of familiarity burning in his gaze.

Another laugh. Louder this time, but still soft. Sickly-sweet. I blink and a young woman appears at the base of the cliff, in the middle of the path that leads to safety. She is thin and delicate, with a round face and a head crowned in sopping chestnut curls, giving her the appearance of a living porcelain doll. Rain soaks her white dress, turning it translucent, and she regards our bedraggled group with a deliberate tilt of her head.

Two fangs, like tiny pearls, peek out from behind an unsettling grin, and I catch a whiff of rich chocolate and cherry blossoms on the salt-soaked wind.

Recognition shudders through me: a beautiful girl in Belarus, her chestnut hair shining in the summer sun. The cloak of deep burgundy that she wore every day during the winter, and the wolf-skin muff she wore on her hands. The light, shimmering laugh that echoed through the garden when Xander caught her in a dance, and the enamored look on my brother's face when he laid eyes on his new fiancée.

Mira.

"Hello, Alexander," she says in lilting Belarusian, her eyes sparkling. "Have you missed me?"

Xander takes a faltering step, then another, disbelief apparent on his face. It takes me a few seconds to find my feet, but then I lunge forward, yanking Xander to a halt. This is wrong. I can hear it in the tone of her voice, see it in the bird-like twitch of her head.

"Mira," I say carefully, forcing a small smile. "It's been so long. Are you—how are you here?"

Xander's ex-fiancée narrows her eyes, but the smile doesn't leave her lips as she slips into English.

"Hello, Ksusha."

"Actually, it's Charlotte now."

"I know."

Pippa murmurs something to Kaleb behind me, but I don't hear it. I'm too focused on the second ghost from my past that has visited me this week. Never in a million years did I expect to see Mira again, let alone on a rain-battered cliffside with a bleeding Xander next to me. And never—*never*—could I have imagined that she would be a vampire. Turned not long after we were, if I'm not mistaken. She looks like she would have when she returned from her trip to Sweden—when she promised to bring me a piece of Swedish chocolate for my birthday.

"Alexander," Mira purrs, stalking forward with a coy smile. "You don't look well, *majo kachannie.* Let me have a look—"

I throw up a hand between her and Xander, even as my brother's expression softens, just a little.

Another figure appears at Mira's side, and I force a mask of neutrality as Henry steps into view, one hand in his pocket, the other spinning his pocket watch on its chain. Pippa stiffens next to me, her heart rate doubling, and I furtively reach back to squeeze her hand.

"I'd be careful if I were you, Charlotte," he says with an air of cheerful arrogance, looking down his nose at me. "Mira has been known to bite."

His hazel eyes are hard as amber, his mouth quirked in a superior half-smile. If I didn't know any better, I might actually believe that he had truly switched to Konstantin's side. Hell, even knowing the truth, the glint of his too-long fangs sends a shiver down my spine.

"She always was a bit fiery," I reply with a half-hearted shrug. "That doesn't surprise me one bit."

Humor flashes in Henry's eyes, but he hides it quickly.

"Mira," I say again, turning back to my almost sister-in-law. "You didn't answer my question. How are you here?"

Mira stops mid-stride and gives me a pitying look. Tutting, she says, "Little Ksusha, always asking the wrong questions. It doesn't matter how I'm here, but *why.*"

With that, she raises a manicured hand in the air, palm to the sky, and snaps her fingers once, the sound cutting through the storm with surprising force. For a few tense seconds, nothing happens. Still, dread settles like a stone in my stomach when I see the quirk of Mira's lips— at the same time Henry's face goes white as death.

Lightning flashes and the cliff behind Mira shudders, like the rocks are coming to life, tumbling toward us in a blur of black and gray—but they're not rocks. Crawling down the cliff face, black-hooded and feral, are dozens of brawny fledglings, filling the path to the switchbacks, blocking our one and only way out.

CHAPTER 50

Kaleb curses sharply as fledgling after fledgling streams down the cliffside, barely more than shadows in the storm. I try to count them but they're moving too fast for an accurate number; there has to be at least fifty, maybe more. The last time Konstantin sent fledglings to attack, they were all young. Weak. But as these vampires move closer, I realize they are anything but.

There are middle-aged men with chiseled faces, tall women with toned muscles. If I had to guess, they are fighters, athletes, wrestlers, military. Interspersed are some softer faces, but the cruelty on them more than makes up for their apparent age or strength. Against the six of us—two on the brink of death—it won't even be a contest. They're going to annihilate us. Especially since Rayna is still suspiciously absent.

Mira watches us with that sickly-sweet grin, eyes alight with excitement. Her hand is on Xander's chest before I can stop it.

"It is so good to see you," she croons, pressing close. Her lips hover over his, sending a shudder through him. "I do hope you live through this so we can get reacquainted properly."

Xander's eyes close as she vanishes into the rain-streaked shadows, leaving him reaching for open air.

"Come on!" I yell over the storm, wincing as a crashing wave showers us in seawater. I grab Xander's arm, ushering the others forward.

"The only way out is through!"

Kaleb murmurs something to Victoria who nods, and he gingerly sets her on her feet. She wobbles for a few seconds before Xander catches her, though it's more of a reflex than anything. His eyes are still fixed on the spot where Mira disappeared, an unreadable expression on his blood-drained face.

"The three of us," Kaleb says, looking from me to Pippa, "will cut a path through the fledglings, allowing Alexander and Victoria to follow safely. Understood?"

We nod, then Pippa asks, "What about Rayna?"

Kaleb's lips press into a tight line. "Rayna can take care of herself."

Pippa and I share a questioning look, but my attention snaps away when a fledgling leaps toward us, landing on the path barely three feet in front of me. The woman's lip is curled, her pale eyes manic. She lunges forward with a murderous snarl, and I snatch a knife from my hip, swinging my arm in an upward arc. With a snarl, she darts out of the way, crouching under my blade before landing a jab to my side. Grunting, I snatch her wrist with my free hand and bury my knife between her ribs. She cries out in pain as I yank the knife out, shoving her backward where she collapses onto her knees, clutching her stomach.

"Hurts like a bitch, doesn't it?"

Within seconds, fledglings have surrounded us. A burly boy in his mid-twenties barrels toward me and I veer out of the way, barely avoiding the meaty fist he aims at my jaw. His other hand doesn't miss. He drives a punch into my gut and I stagger backward, fighting for the breath that's been knocked out of me. The boy lunges again but he's knocked sideways by a blur of black and red.

Xander.

"Get back!" I yell at him, but he doesn't so much as acknowledge me as he lifts the boy by his collar and throws him over the cliff's edge. I watch, wide-eyed, as the fledgling tumbles into the ocean. "You're supposed to be back with Victoria!"

"She's fine," Xander pants, just as I hear a growl tear from her throat.

Black-eyed and white-faced, Victoria snarls again as a fledgling leaps at her. She may be weak, but her ferocity is, as always, deadly. The fledgling goes down with a *thud,* and Victoria whirls to the next one, mouth and hands streaked with red. Pippa lets out a whoop of triumph, even as another wave of fledglings descends upon us.

Bright orange flashes in the corner of my vision, and I look to see Rayna, her hair a blazing beacon, making her way down the cliffside. Why she was at the top, I have no idea. But she seems to be thinning the horde a bit, landing expert punches and a few well-placed jabs with a dagger. Fledglings fall quickly, and I'm silently glad she's on our side.

There's a cry to my left, and I turn to see Xander locked in a battle with a stocky fledgling boy. My brother is taller, but he's still weak from the effects of the silver, the blood loss, and what looks to be a badly-injured foot. The fledgling lands a powerful punch to Xander's ribs and he staggers backward, spitting blood.

I adjust my grip on the knife in my hand and fling it at Xander's attacker. It lodges in his shoulder and the boy cries out, turning to me with a frustrated snarl. He throws a fist and I avoid it easily, returning with a punch of my own. My knuckles scream as they connect with his jaw—he stumbles backward and his back connects hard with a metal railing along the pathway. I finish him with a jab to the ribs and a hard elbow to the temple, and he collapses to the ground, unconscious.

"That's what you get for hurting my brother," I snarl, yanking the knife from his shoulder.

"Charlotte." Xander appears at my side, wiping blood from his mouth. There's a hardness in his eyes that usually precedes chastisement, and I brace myself, *really* not in the mood. But instead of berating me, Xander just says, "That was badass."

I stare at him and bite back a bewildered grin. "Did you expect anything less?"

Xander snorts and puts a hand on my shoulder. Something

unspoken flickers between us—an understanding, almost. Regret is a stone in my chest. After all, there's a lot for me to feel bad about: everything I said to him at Nik's, practically disowning him in front of our entire family. Fighting him at every turn. Spending the last century acting like a belligerent teenager, just because I could.

I've been so angry with him for so long, and I don't even know *why*.

Buried deep under the anger and betrayal are memories of my brother at his best: grinning in his garden under the warm Belarusian sun, charming his way into parties in Paris, skipping stones in Lake Michigan. And he always—*always*—kept me by his side, despite the fact that I *did* deserve all the yelling and chastisement. Even on my worst days, when I broke rules and bones and hearts, he stood by my side. Sometimes looking down on me, but always willing to lift me back up.

Xander is my brother. My blood. I look at him now, battered and bloody and red-eyed, and realize how close I was to losing him. A few days ago, I wanted him dead. But now, I've never been so happy to see him alive.

"I'm sorry," he says, his brow furrowed. "I'm so sorry, *siastra*."

Tears burn at the corners of my eyes, and I'm aware this has to be the absolute worst time for an emotional revelation. The sounds of battle are all around us, but all I can think about is what a horrible sister I've been.

I open my mouth to reply but I'm interrupted by a string of colorful curses.

"Where were you?" Kaleb snaps, and I turn to see Rayna standing in front of him. He's staring at her with a snarl of unbridled fury. A nearby fledgling lunges at me but I shove him aside, attuning my ears to the lovers' conversation.

"None of your business," Rayna grinds out, slicing at the neck of the nearest fledgling.

Kaleb glowers. "Isn't it just like you to work behind my back for your own purposes."

"I didn't work behind your back." Rayna hesitates. "In fact, I hardly did any work at all. I had certain expectations, and I miscalculated."

"*Magnificently.*"

"Rayna!" Pippa shouts, shoving through a knot of fledglings. "Will you stop arguing with everyone and help get us the hell out of there?"

And then I see it: a gap in the horde. A way out.

"There!" I yell, pointing back the way we came. "Let's go!"

Kaleb takes Victoria's hand and I keep a firm grip on Xander's elbow as we hurtle toward the opening. The fledglings notice their mistake as we sprint up the switchbacks and they converge on us from every side, fury in their eyes and snarls on their lips. By the time we reach the top of the cliffside, we've sent a few of them tumbling back down, their bones cracking on black rocks.

My lungs burn, my likely-fractured ribs screaming with each heaving breath. Xander stumbles as the ground levels out but quickly finds his feet again. *We did it,* I think, nearly sagging with relief. *We're getting out of here.*

A tall figure appears in our path and I cry out in surprise, then relax as I recognize Henry. Pippa rushes to him, going in for an embrace, but he catches her by the shoulders.

"No," he hisses, eyes fixed behind us where the fledglings are inevitably following. "You need to get out of here. I'll hold them off."

Kaleb frowns. "Henry, you don't have to do this."

"Yes, I do," he says assuredly, winking. "They think I'm on their side. I don't have to fight them, I only have to say something that will delay them long enough for you to get away."

"Henry," Pippa whispers. "Listen to Kaleb."

"Really, *cariad,*" Henry says. An endearment in Welsh, Pippa's native language. *My love.* "I'll be fine."

"Where is he?" Rayna stomps forward, marching into Henry's space. He startles back a step. "Where is Konstantin?"

"I—I don't know," he stammers. "Not here. He ordered Mira to bring me on this 'mission,' and by the time I figured out where we were going, it was too late. I had no time to warn you about the fledglings. Mira has been watching me so closely—"

"I don't care about *Mira*," Rayna sneers. "Why isn't Konstantin here? If he knew we were coming, why wouldn't he show up himself?"

"How *did* he know?" Pippa asks, concern in her eyes. "We should have been able to do this without a problem."

Because I told him. Guilt sears through my chest, but what's done is done. What matters now is getting out of here with no casualties. I listen for approaching fledglings—footsteps, snarls, and the clatter of falling rocks—but there's nothing. Just the ever-present roar of the ocean and the storm. Unease crackles through me like lightning.

"He should have been here," Rayna says almost to herself, then glares at Henry. "What kind of spy are you, anyway?"

Hurt flashes in the boy's eyes. "It isn't easy, you know. I'd like to see you try—"

Crunch.

Henry jerks forward, confusion clouding his gaze. He blinks a few times and his eyes drop to the delicate hand protruding from his chest, his heart clutched in its fingers.

I clap my hands over my mouth, battling a surge of nausea. Of horror. Of guilt, writhing and wicked.

Pippa screams.

There's a sickening *squelch* as the hand withdraws sharply. Henry's jaw trembles, his eyes lift to meet Pippa's, and he sinks to his knees before slumping to the ground.

In the darkness behind him, a pale figure stands: a girl in a white dress, her wet hair pinned back with pearl clips, Henry's heart glistening in her hand. Blood oozes from it, sliding down her forearm, dripping from her elbow and onto the rain-soaked dirt. She examines the heart with the rapt curiosity of a child with a new toy, rotating it in her dainty grasp.

"I *had* hoped Konstantin was wrong about this one," Mira says, a pitying frown twisting her mouth, "but, oh, I do so love the sound of a weak heart breaking."

Without another word, she vanishes back into the shadows.

"Henry!" Pippa's anguished cry slices through the storm, and she throws herself onto the ground next to him. "No," she whimpers, her hands fluttering over his face, his arms, the gaping hole in his chest. "No! Please, don't leave me!"

Kaleb is at her side in an instant, the picture of calm, but I don't miss the pain in his eyes or the way his lip quivers. "Philippa, we have to—"

"Don't touch him," she snarls. "I won't leave him!"

Xander approaches and carefully lifts Henry's body into his arms; the boy's long limbs dangle in the air, his hazel eyes glassy and unseeing. His fangs, bright and sharp, peek out from behind slack lips. Victoria makes a small pained sound behind me, and my heart gutters.

Henry is dead. He's *dead,* and it's all my fault.

"You!" Pippa barks and I shy away, sure she can see my guilt, but she isn't pointing at me. "This is all your fault!"

Rayna balks, eyes narrowing on Pippa. "Me? Why me?"

"You just proclaimed to the whole world that Henry is a *spy!* We're surrounded by Konstantin's people. You didn't even think!"

"Pippa—"

"No!" Tears stream down Pippa's furious face. "I don't want your excuses. I've been trying to give you the benefit of the doubt, I really have. But you've been nothing but trouble since you came back. And now, because of you, my Henry is *dead.*"

She chokes on the last word and whirls away, wrapping her arm around Victoria and pulling her along, back up the path.

Rayna freezes. Lightning cracks over the ocean, cutting harsh lines over her face. For a fleeting moment, her eyes flash silver.

"Come," Kaleb says to us, pointedly ignoring Rayna. "The longer we're here, the more vulnerable we become."

Silently, he turns and stalks away, followed closely by a limping Xander carrying Henry's body. I move to join them but Rayna grabs my arm, yanking me off the path and into the trees.

"Why did you tell Konstantin our plans?" she demands, fingers digging into my bicep.

The question stops me in my tracks. There *was* someone listening at the door; when I smelled her perfume lingering in the hallway, I had attributed it to her general presence in the house, not that she was actually eavesdropping on my phone call with Konstantin. I had hoped it was a coincidence—that she had simply walked by—but nothing is a coincidence with Rayna.

She heard the whole thing.

"Are you working with him?" she continues, her tone almost urgent. "Do you know where he is?"

I open my mouth to reply, but the words don't come. Even when I try, I can't get myself to explain.

Instead, I say, "If you heard my phone call, why did you agree to come tonight? Why didn't you tell everyone and postpone?" When she doesn't answer, I narrow my eyes suspiciously. "You wanted him to be here, didn't you?"

Rayna hesitates a beat too long. "No."

"You would have us all risk our lives so you could, what, exact your revenge? At what cost, Rayna?" I laugh once, humorously. "Wait, I guess we know the cost, don't we?"

Henry's life. The words hang between us, unsaid, and I think I almost see a hint of remorse in Rayna's eyes.

She banishes it quickly. "None of this would have happened if you hadn't spilled everything to Kostya."

"Yes, it would have." I cross my arms, my rage sharpening into a red-hot dagger. "Because if he didn't already know, I'm sure you would have figured out a way to tell him yourself."

Rayna clenches her jaw, her gaze turning black. "He hurt Nikolas."

"He's hurt *all* of us!"

"The only way to stop him from hurting anyone else is to end him, once and for all."

"And you thought you could do that all by yourself?"

Rayna's jaw clenches. "This is *my* fight. I *have* to do it by myself."

I bite back a scream of frustration. Every word that comes out of her mouth, every explanation she offers only makes her more flustered. More belligerent. For whatever reason, I couldn't tell my family that I shared information with Konstantin. But Rayna? She could have. But she didn't.

I wanted to believe in her. I wanted to trust her again. But she has been keeping secrets for centuries, lying and manipulating to maintain control of her narrative, and she shows no sign of changing. Poor Rayna, with her tragic story of love and loss, valiantly surviving against all odds. Saving her family. Exacting her revenge.

She's no better than Konstantin.

"You are, without a doubt, the most selfish, inconsiderate—"

"Lottie." Rayna exhales sharply, eyes boring into mine. "Do you know where Konstantin is or not?"

"I'm right here, darling."

Fear ignites in my chest as a pair of silver eyes appears over Rayna's shoulder and a wiry arm wraps around her ribs. Konstantin touches a dagger to her throat, a wicked grin on his face.

"Run along, Charlotte. You saw nothing here."

His words hit me like a blow to the chest. I stagger back, feet catching on loose rocks, and the last thing I see before I run is a drop of blood blooming on Konstantin's blade.

CHAPTER 51

THE GLOW OF FIRELIGHT. A red dress. Light reflected on metal and the gasp of surprise against her lips.

It was the last time Rayna saw Konstantin—a moment burned in her memory, haunting her nightmares for the last two hundred years. She knew it was only a matter of time before she saw him again, and she thought she was prepared.

She was wrong.

Konstantin presses close to Rayna and she shudders, the feeling of his body both familiar and foreign, sultry and sinister. His scent swirls around her—ash and ozone, like he carries electricity inside him—filling her with an ache that quickly turns to nausea. It transports her back to dark rooms in Europe, to commanding lips and bruising fingers.

To the way he held her close and promised her the world. And the way he stole it all back.

The old pull is still there, that deep-seated yearning that twists Rayna's stomach into knots, but it's dampened by two centuries of separation. Still, it scorches through her like lightning finding a metal rod.

He was good, once.

"Hello, little bird," Konstantin purrs, grinning against her ear. "I hear you've been looking for me."

"Have I?" she asks, trembling under his blade. Her hand twitches toward the dagger at her side but he snatches her wrist.

"There's no need for violence, my dear."

"Then explain to me why you're making *fledglings,* Kostya."

His breath stills at her use of the nickname, and Rayna swears she feels his heart stutter.

"Rayna," he murmurs, a drop of heat in his voice, "you know why."

Rayna's cheeks flush as her name resonates in his chest, falling from his lips like a caress. More memories join those already dancing in her head: passionate kisses, warm smiles in the firelight, silver eyes bright with mischief and adoration.

He was mine, *once.*

"I am an open book, *dragoste,*" Konstantin continues. *Love.* An endearment in his native Romanian that he reserved for her, and only her. Warmth trickles down her spine as he presses a cool kiss to the shell of her ear, sliding the flat side of his blade along her throat. "Everything I've done, I've done for you—but my patience is wearing thin."

Konstantin releases Rayna's wrist, dragging his fingertips up the outside of her thigh. The response it elicits is startling and completely unwanted, but it's a response, nonetheless. Rayna's breath catches in her chest and heat flickers in her, drawing a small sound of amusement from Konstantin's throat.

"Missed me, have you?"

Yes, she almost says, and the thought startles her. Why the *hell* would she have missed him? He has done nothing but terrorize her and her family for hundreds of years.

She takes a slow breath. Another. "No."

"Your hesitation betrays you."

Konstantin's hand slides from her thigh to her hip, then settles over her navel, drawing her back against him. The motion sends a bolt of heat through her abdomen and she glances over her shoulder, just enough to see his eyes, molten as mercury and glinting with promise.

"You've been using Charlotte," Rayna says, though her words

sound less menacing than she had hoped. Every instinct is telling her to run, but Konstantin's proximity is making her head swim, her body steadily going soft. Malleable. "Why?"

Konstantin sighs. "Really, it should be quite obvious. It's a wonder Charlotte hasn't figured it out yet." His voice drops and he sways slightly to the left, then to the right—the suggestion of a dance that has Rayna squeezing her eyes shut, moving with him. She places a hand on top of his and his grip slackens, just a little. "Though, it would seem you've been using her as well. Tell me: how long have you known?"

"Known what?" Rayna murmurs, lost momentarily in his embrace.

"That Charlotte has been spying for me."

Her eyes snap open and she brings their swaying to an abrupt halt. "Does it matter?"

"To me? No. But to your family?" He pauses to press his lips to her nape, even as the blade still kisses her throat. "A bit of a betrayal, isn't it? Knowing very well that they might walk into a trap, but letting them come here, nonetheless."

Rayna swallows, her Adam's apple bobbing against the blade. "It isn't a betrayal."

Konstantin shifts and seizes her hand, drawing it upward to press a slow kiss to her palm. He shifts closer, fitting the hard angles of his body against hers, and heat courses through her—a deep longing that makes her dizzy.

"What of your dear brother?" he murmurs condescendingly. "You 'died' to protect him, didn't you? Hid away for all these years, only to return and betray poor Nikolas once again."

The sound of her brother's name is like a splash of frigid water.

"Don't you dare bring Nik into this," Rayna growls. "It has nothing to do with him."

But Konstantin continues. "Imagine how Kaleb will feel when he learns you never intended to help him at all."

"Stop!"

Rayna whirls on Konstantin but he holds tight, and there's a loud *crack* as her wrist snaps in his hand. She shrieks in pain but he doesn't falter, snaking his arms around her. They stand face to face now, breath mingling, and hunger alights in his eyes as they drop to her mouth. There are remnants of freshly-healed cuts on his brow and lip, and slight smudges of fading purple rimming both eyes.

A breath hisses through Rayna's teeth. He's still so *beautiful*.

"Did Nik do that to you?" Rayna asks through a pained breath, feeling a touch of triumph when Konstantin's expression darkens, his mouth twisting into a dangerous frown.

"What was it all for, hmm?" His hand tightens around Rayna's injured wrist and she cries out again, black swimming at the edges of her vision. "So you could come here on your own, corner me, and kill me yourself? Did you really think it would be so easy?" Konstantin shakes his head sadly. "Though it seems you learned your lesson after the last time, when you entrusted the job to someone else."

Silver? You were supposed to kill him!

Rayna exhales shakily. "If you want something done right, you have to do it yourself."

Konstantin drags his bottom lip between his teeth, a motion that would have made a younger Rayna swoon. And maybe this Rayna is swooning, too. Just a little. "We both know you don't want to kill me, little bird. Otherwise you would have done so already. I was at your mercy that night in Belarus." He rolls his left shoulder absently, and Rayna locks onto the movement. "But you let me live."

"I am not your little bird," Rayna snarls, sliding a hand behind her back.

"What are you then?" Konstantin chuckles. "A traitor? A coward?"

She grins. "I'm the last face you'll ever see."

Rayna yanks the stake from her jacket and raises her arm high, plunging it straight toward Konstantin's heart. Adrenaline rockets through her as she drives the stake home, eyes widening in disbelief when she meets resistance.

Time slows. The howling storm fades away, reduced to a dull roar in Rayna's ears. Konstantin's hand is wrapped firmly around hers, his whole arm trembling as he holds the weapon at bay. The pointed tip is pressed into his chest, just barely, and a trickle of blood soaks into his shirt. He stares at their joined hands for a few seconds before he meets her eyes with a frigid glare.

Rayna curses inwardly, but then she sees it—a flicker in his expression. A tiny crack in his armor.

Alarm.

"I'm still faster than you are, it seems," Konstantin says drolly, but Rayna doesn't miss the tiny tremor in his words. "Isn't that a pity?"

Rayna yanks her hand from his grip and whirls out of his way before she strikes again. He blocks her. Again. Her movements aren't born of skill and care, but of frustration and anger. Panic grows with each blocked blow, but Konstantin seems completely unfazed. Unaffected. She can hear his heartbeat, smooth and slow, as if he were doing nothing more exciting than watching grass grow. Rayna realizes— too late—that this may have been a terrible mistake.

It's been two hundred years. And while Rayna's skills have improved, so have Konstantin's.

"What's wrong, my love?" Konstantin croons, parrying a jab toward his ribs. "Did you miscalculate?"

The heel of his hand connects hard with Rayna's shoulder, sending her staggering backward as he snatches the stake from her and hurls it into the trees. Cold fire sparks in his eyes.

"A valiant effort, but the time for games is over." He holds a hand out in front of him, palm up. Beckoning. "Come with me."

Rayna glances one way, then the other, searching for a way out. But Konstantin is faster than she is. Stronger. Even if she tried, there's no way she would outrun him. The amusement in Konstantin's eyes tells her he has come to the same conclusion.

"Come with you?" She laughs, attempting nonchalance as she cradles her injured wrist. "Why would I do that?"

Konstantin's mouth quirks. "You care for your little family, don't you?"

Rayna nods, taking a hesitant step toward him. His shoulder ticks.

"And you want them to be safe," he continues. "Nikolas, Charlotte . . . Kaleb."

Another step. Another tick. "Yes."

"Rayna." His voice is almost a whisper now, rough and imploring. "Come with me and your family will live. We both know you never really loved Kaleb."

Rayna turns slightly, walking a slow circle around him. He doesn't move. Doesn't react. He simply allows her to size him up, all the while caressing her with his bright gaze. Her skin prickles with the heat of it. Taking a slow breath, she presses up behind him, wrapping her arms around his chest.

"Kostya," she murmurs, and she doesn't have to manufacture the touch of longing in her voice. His chest rises and falls against her, his heartbeat jumping slightly as her lips whisper down his nape. "I was enamored with you the first time you touched me. Do you remember?"

Konstantin sighs quietly. "Prague."

"Mm-hmm."

Rayna slides her good hand down his side, snaking under the hem of his sweater, and he moans softly as she strokes the column of his spine, tracing a curving line up his back. When her fingers graze a knot of scar tissue behind his heart, he gasps sharply and his shoulder snaps upward.

"Did that hurt?" Rayna asks, pressing a gentle kiss to the corner of his jaw.

Konstantin hums a laugh, though it comes out strained. "Everything you do hurts me."

"Then this will be no surprise to you." Thunder rumbles through the sky as she touches her lips to his ear and says, "I never loved you. Kaleb had my heart from the first time I laid eyes on him. And there is nothing you can say or do that will *ever* make me come back to you."

Konstantin's shoulders tense, and Rayna feels the snarl before she hears it.

"*Liar.*"

"You wish."

"What did Kaleb do to you?" Konstantin growls, a note of urgency in his voice. Rayna feels his heart begin to pound. "I know he's the one who Turned you. He *Sired* you. It's the only explanation for why you left me—"

Rayna laughs in disbelief. "*That's* what this is about? Is that the mysterious *truth* you've been after this whole time?" She drags her fingers over the puckered scar on his back, drawing another pained gasp. "I'm sorry you've believed that for all these years, but it wasn't Kaleb who Turned me."

Konstantin stills, his lip curling. "What?"

Grinning, Rayna whispers, "I Turned *myself.*"

"Liar!" Konstantin snarls again, his tone rising with each word, with each frantic beat of his heart. Lightning strikes. Thunder crashes. "He Turned you! *Tell me the truth!*"

"That *is* the truth." Rayna's grin turns wicked and she laughs again at the sheer absurdity of it all. "When you refused to Turn me—when I could no longer *stand* to be your subjugate—I took matters into my own hands. All I needed was a drop of your blood and a bone-handled dagger."

Konstantin wrenches himself from her embrace and Rayna zeroes in on the movement, noting the way he favors his left side. The stiffness in his hand. As he lunges for her, she twists out of his reach and slams her fist into the knotted scar on his back.

And then she runs.

CHAPTER 52

Pain.

White-hot. Blinding. Incapacitating.

A red dress. Pale eyes. A fire-lit parlor. The flash of a blade.

Fire scorches through Konstantin's veins. He screams as his left arm seizes at his side, his hand going numb and contorting into a claw. The pain sucks the air from his lungs and blackens his vision.

He folds forward, his forehead kissing the muddy ground as he breathes through the agony. Waves of it. Massaging his left hand, he tries desperately to dispel the stiffness, but to no avail. Weakness surges through him, accompanied by nausea and a burst of fierce hunger that claws at his throat.

Control, he thinks. *Control yourself.* But when he tries to sit up, the nausea intensifies, the hunger strengthens. His shoulder twitches. His head ticks.

He's slipping.

Konstantin squeezes his eyes shut and curls into himself, willing his seizing muscles to relax. Everything *hurts* and his mind is fogged. He can't *focus*.

He's furious.

Burning.

Livid.

His head snaps up and he shoots back onto his heels, watching Rayna's retreating form. Lightning crackles through Konstantin's veins, and he screams again.

"*SHE DOESN'T LEAVE,*" he roars, and he grins through the pain as a mass of shadows spills from the trees behind him.

CHAPTER 53

RAIN PELTS MY FACE AS I sprint away from the cliff, blurring my vision and biting at a split on my eyebrow. My heart hammers in my chest, beating in time with my rapid footsteps. I'm running and running from . . . something.

Something I can't remember.

My steps slow as I fight to recall the last few minutes, but they are infuriatingly blank. We had escaped the fledglings on the cliffside, Rayna and I were arguing, and then . . . nothing.

Silver sparks in my mind just as I collide with someone running in the opposite direction, and we tumble to the ground in a heap of black and gold. A jagged rock cuts into my palm as I catch myself and I wince, looking up to see Tristan push himself up to his elbows with a groan.

"*Tristan.*" I scramble toward him, rocks jabbing into my knees, and he rubs at a red lump that's sprouting on his forehead. "What the hell are you doing here?"

"Hello to you, too." He smiles, but it's all sharp edges. "It took about fifteen minutes for us to lose our minds—Noah, Nik, Rose, and I—so we followed you, just to make sure you had backup if you needed it."

"You're not backup!" I cry, flinching at my shrill tone. "Tristan, you're *human*. You're going to get yourself killed if you keep showing up to vampire battles."

"Maybe I have a death wish."

I smack his arm. "Don't even joke about that."

"I had to make sure you were okay."

My chest warms a bit at that, but unease still nips at my heels.

"Come on," I say, standing and offering Tristan a hand. "Before the fledglings catch up."

"What about Rayna?"

Ice forms in my chest, biting into my lungs. "What about her?"

Tristan eyes me warily, rain dripping from strands of his golden hair and onto the front of his black sweatshirt. "Everyone else got back to the cars, but you and Rayna weren't with them. I came to investigate."

I throw up my hands in exasperation. "Why wouldn't you let someone else do that? What did I just say about getting yourself killed?"

He only shrugs.

I turn back toward the cliff—back to the shadow-shrouded trees—and my unease intensifies. Something happened back there. I scan my memory, searching for anything that stands out, but there's nothing. Just a blank slate. I was at the cliff, and then I was here. I was running.

A warning bell chimes in the back of my mind.

"Stay here," I say to Tristan. He raises a challenging brow but I take his hand, injecting sincerity into my words. "Please. I have a bad feeling about this, and I don't want you to get hurt. I—I care too much about you."

Tristan steps closer, one hand sliding into my sopping hair. A playful smile dances on his lips.

"Say that again."

I swallow against the rising heat, forcing myself to meet his eyes. They shine like gold coins, even in the storm—pinpoints of warmth in the darkness.

"I care about you," I murmur. "It's kind of stupid how much I care about you."

Tristan laughs softly, leaning to press a lingering kiss to my lips. My stomach flutters.

"I'll stay here, if only because I know how hard it was for you to admit that." He smirks, brushing a callused thumb over my cheekbone. I pull away, barely catching his next words before they're swallowed by the screaming wind. "Come back to me."

I will. I leave the words unsaid, turning away from my glowing golden boy and slipping into the seething shadows.

Part of me feels like I should run, but there's another much stronger part of me that knows I should be stealthy. I sneak through the underbrush, avoiding the main path altogether in case I'm met by something unsavory—like a horde of fledglings. Darkness closes around me and while I can see fairly well, I let my other senses take over. The scents of salty rain and peaty earth engulf me, my attention focused ahead to catch any warning sounds.

It's a minute, maybe two, before I hear the faint murmur of voices, one male and one female. After a few seconds, I recognize the woman as Rayna, and the man . . .

The man is *Konstantin.*

When did he get here? *Why can't I remember?*

"Did that hurt?" Rayna murmurs at some unknown gesture.

"Everything you do hurts me."

Thunder booms overhead, loud enough that I jump as it reverberates off the cliffside. The next part of their conversation is drowned out by the noise, then I hear Rayna's voice, sharper than it was before.

"I'm sorry you've believed that for all these years, but it wasn't Kaleb who Turned me."

"What?"

Then Rayna whispers, "I Turned *myself.*"

My jaw drops. There's another flash of lightning. A peal of thunder, absorbing their words again. I take a step forward and peer around the trunk of a narrow tree. The pair comes into view just as Rayna slams her fist into Konstantin's back, right behind his heart.

He *screams,* and I've never heard such a sound—at once tortured and frenzied, ripping a hole in the fabric of the night. Even the storm seems to cease its roaring, the wind and rain ebbing for one tense moment. Konstantin's back arches in agony and his knees hit the hard ground with an audible *crack.* Then Rayna, eyes wide and aghast, takes off running.

I tear after her as Konstantin roars, *"SHE DOESN'T LEAVE!"* and the night fills with the ominous thunder of footsteps.

I barely register where I'm going as I follow a fleeing Rayna, tripping over rocks and swatting branches out of my path. We emerge into the open parking lot to see Kaleb standing outside his Mercedes, eyes snapping wide when he notices us. The sound of approaching fledglings increases, snarls accompanying the snapping of twigs and the slapping of shoes in mud.

"Get in!" Kaleb calls, leaping into the driver's seat and revving the engine to life.

Rayna flies into the backseat but I skid to a halt, my neck prickling at some sixth sense. I turn slowly to face the trees.

Konstantin stands with a struggling Tristan in his arms and a manic grin splitting his face.

"If you're not going to play by the rules," he snarls, "then neither am I."

And then he dissolves into darkness. The last thing I see is Tristan's fear-bright eyes extinguishing as Konstantin drags him into the shadows.

"Tristan!"

Terror, hot and urgent, sends a bolt of white across my vision. And then I'm running. Again, running. But not away from something this time—toward something. Toward *him.* To the golden boy with too many freckles. To the hope of a future I long to have.

To the creature who would take that away from me.

"Charlotte, *no!*" Xander shouts as my feet pound the pavement, but I don't stop. I don't slow. All I can do is silently pray that my family gets away before the fledglings catch up to them. We already lost

Henry. I won't let Konstantin take anyone else from me.

I plunge into the trees, following Tristan's salty-sweet scent as it veers south, skirting the cliffside as it retreats farther, *farther.*

Come back to me. Tristan's words ring in my head like a plea, a promise, a beacon in the storm.

I'm coming, Tristan. Wait for me.

It isn't long before the trees thin and I find myself hurtling over open ground, straight toward the cliffside. I screech to a halt as the ocean fills the horizon, mud and grime splashing in my wake. My jeans are covered in it, the icy sludge bleeding through the fabric, but I don't care. I *can't.* Because standing right at the cliff's edge, with nothing but a crumbling stone barrier separating him from a hundred-foot fall, is Tristan.

Startling, he throws a frantic hand in my direction. "Charlotte, don't! It's a trap—"

"Not another step, darling."

My steps slow at the sound of Konstantin's voice and fear prickles through me. I want to go to Tristan—to grab him and *run*—but I come to a stop a few yards away, my feet rooted to the spot.

Footsteps splash through the mud and Konstantin appears in a swirl of shadow and mist, head tilted to the side. There's a slight hitch in his gait, adding another level to the already-manic air about him.

Tristan frowns at me, brow furrowed in confusion. Something like anger sparks in his eyes and he turns a scowl on Konstantin.

"What are you doing to her?"

"Nothing you need concern yourself with," Konstantin says simply. His mouth slides open into a devilish grin as lightning flashes, igniting sparks in his eyes. There's something unsaid in the sharp tilt of his mouth that sends dread pooling into my stomach.

Tristan's lip curls. "I have *plenty* I need to concern myself with. First of all, the fact that you killed Jason. You tricked him into being your friend, and then you killed him."

"Don't be stupid," I hiss in warning, but my words are swallowed by the wind.

Konstantin laughs sharply, the sound like a blade against stone.

"It wasn't a *trick*," he says. "Just a touch of Compulsion. And your little friend served his purpose well. I must thank him for making my entrance such a grand one."

Tristan's expression turns murderous.

"My offer still stands," I interject, drawing Konstantin's attention. I square my shoulders in a fruitless attempt at bravado. "Take me and leave Tristan out of this."

Konstantin laughs again, but this time it's darker. Deeper.

"Oh, little bird," he muses, raising his chin, "we are well past the point of making deals."

Little bird. That stupid endearment. I know it's important—I know there's a reason it keeps rattling around in my head—but I still can't seem to place it. Tonight, it forces a touch of fear as amusement and hunger swirl in Konstantin's eyes.

"Please." I hate the word as soon as it comes out of my mouth. The last thing I want to do is plead with this man, but I can't move. I can't do anything but beg for Tristan's safety, even if it costs me my life. I'd gladly give it up if it meant he would be safe. If it meant my entire *family* would be safe. "Please, Konstantin. I'll do whatever you want. Just don't hurt him."

Lightning flashes again, etching Konstantin in electric white. An ominous peal of thunder mingles with the deafening roar of water crashing against the cliffside below.

"I do love when you say my name," he says, that cocky smile still playing at his lips.

"Does that mean you'll accept my offer?"

Konstantin considers me, then says, "Come here, my girl."

A tug behind my ribs. I stride forward, catching myself with my palms flat against his chest. I blink in surprise as Konstantin's hands settle on my hips, and I feel myself sinking into his embrace.

Come here, my girl.

"She's not your girl," Tristan growls—literally *growls*. I can't help the little shiver that trickles down my spine, because that sound coming from Tristan might be the most beautiful thing I've ever heard. Even so, my body stays close to Konstantin, his thin fingers digging into the spaces above my hip bones.

"That's where you're wrong, boy." Konstantin smiles down at me, something like affection coloring his words. He runs two fingers along my jaw, capturing me in his predator's gaze. "Charlotte is mine. She always has been."

Fear rocks me as Konstantin's fangs flash. I try to pull away, but his hands are unyielding. Hard as stone, cold as ice. Here I am, standing inches from the man who forced Rayna, Kaleb, and Nik into hiding. Who scared Rayna to the point of faking her own death just to escape him. And while he may still look like an arrogant frat boy, I can sense something sinister brewing just below the surface.

"Why are you doing this?" I ask quietly, blinking away the threat of tears. "Rayna is *gone*, Konstantin. You could have just let her go."

Konstantin's smile fades, misery flooding his expression. "Rayna left her mark on me." He presses one palm flat against his heart. "I can never let her go."

"You're pathetic," Tristan scoffs, and Konstantin stiffens.

"Don't move," he murmurs to me, then stalks toward Tristan with murder in his eyes. Lightning flashes again and is accompanied by an immediate and deafening clap of thunder. His shoulder twitches.

"Don't hurt him!" I beg, my feet rooted to the spot. *Don't move.*

Neither of them seem to hear me. Tristan recoils as Konstantin approaches, but he can't go far. His legs bump up against the stone barrier and he sucks in a sharp breath as he teeters for a few seconds, his body swaying dangerously. He catches my eye over Konstantin's shoulder, then slowly mouths a single word: *Run.*

I shake my head. *I can't.*

"There are billions of other women in the world," Tristan says bravely, even as his voice wavers. They're almost nose-to-nose, though

Konstantin is slightly taller. Thinner. "Yet you've devoted your life to the only one you can't have. It's sad, really. Most humans learn to move on from heartbreak in a few months. A few years, at most."

Konstantin studies Tristan, his eyes sweeping down to his feet and back again. Then, his mouth twists into a wry smirk.

"Do they, now?" he asks with an air of over-confidence. "I suppose humans' lives are so pathetically short, it serves them best to push aside their heartbreak in pursuit of something new. But"—he stares out over the ocean, as though deep in thought—"what if a human were to learn a secret about his beloved—something that would shatter the ground he walked on? How long would it take to recover from that heartbreak, do you think?"

My breath catches as dull horror sweeps through me. He wouldn't.

"Don't," I say quietly, but Konstantin only smiles.

"You see," he says, pacing slowly in front of Tristan, "I have spent the past eleven years observing dear Charlotte and her little family. And, as such, I have learned quite a bit about her. The relationships she cherishes." He pauses mid-stride, emphasizing his next words. "The sins she has committed."

Tristan frowns, eyes jumping warily from me to Konstantin. "What are you talking about?"

"I believe you remember a little text I sent you a few days ago—the one about your sister."

Ice fills my veins as I remember the look on Tristan's face, the pain in his voice when he told me what happened to Alison. When he showed me the text in the back of Xander's Maserati: *Would you like to know who killed your sister? The answer is closer than you think.*

"Konstantin," I whisper. "*Please.*"

He ignores me, choosing instead to focus on Tristan, who is hugging his arms to his chest. Waiting for the bomb to drop. Konstantin leans close.

"I wasn't lying," he murmurs, "when I said the answer is closer than you think. So close, in fact"—his eyes slide to me—"that you can almost touch her.”

Tristan huffs a laugh, but there’s a touch of wariness in his expression. “You’re lying.”

Konstantin chuckles and straightens, thunder crashing again as his smile turns triumphant. “Tell him, love. Tell your little plaything who’s to blame for his sister’s death.”

No. *No.* I can’t let Tristan find out this way. Not with Konstantin watching. Not while we’re precariously perched at the edge of a cliff, a hundred feet above a potential watery grave. When I tell Tristan about Alison—*if* I tell him—I want to do it at the right moment. When he will have time to process. To grieve. To yell and scream and run away, if he wants. But there’s nowhere for him to run. There’s no time. And the sharp tug in my chest grows stronger—more painful with every breath.

Tristan will never forgive me for this.

I stare at him, memorizing him—the flecks of green in his eyes, the freckles dotting his cheekbones, the way his sandy hair falls perfectly over his forehead. The smooth curve of his lips and the scar on his cheek. The tiny lines at the corners of his eyes—the ones that crinkle when he smiles. Even in the pouring rain, fear etched in every line of his face, he’s beautiful. He’s perfect.

And now I’m going to lose him. But that’s the curse of immortality, isn’t it? Forever doomed to lose the ones I love.

The words pour out of me like water—like they’re drawn from my throat by an invisible force. I can’t stop them. I barely even try.

“It was me,” I say in a wavering whisper. “I killed Alison.”

Agony bleeds into Tristan’s expression—slowly at first, then the full force of the confession hits him. His eyes widen, disbelief and anger replacing the fear that was so prevalent only seconds ago.

“Is this some kind of sick joke?” he asks, pinning Konstantin with an acerbic glare. “Are you making her say this?”

Konstantin considers him for a too-long moment. “In a way. But I assure you, she speaks nothing but the truth.”

Tristan releases a slow breath, his gaze dropping, and I can practically see the wheels turning in his head. The memories he's reliving.

My reaction when he told me about Alison at the Land's End Labyrinth. My hesitance when he asked for my help with finding her killer. The way I carefully steered our phone call with Konstantin. The way Kaleb skirted around his questions and offered excuses instead of answers.

The answer is closer than you think.

Tristan's eyes snap up, boring into me with white-hot fire. "Tell me you're lying. Tell me—" He chokes on the words, eyes glistening. "Tell me it was Xander or Nik or Pippa. *Anyone* but you."

My eyes blur as tears mingle with the rain streaming down my face, each one a different emotion: desperation, fear, guilt. Loss.

Lip trembling, I whisper, "I can't."

Tristan groans and sinks into a crouch, fisting both hands in his hair. "Don't do this to me, Charlotte." I open my mouth to speak but Tristan exhales a sharp, incredulous laugh. "You—you started acting so weird after I told you about Alison at the Labyrinth. That's when you realized, wasn't it?"

Unable to form any words, I nod.

"Oh my God." Tristan's voice wavers and he brings a hand to his throat, his fingers shaking as they brush the still-healing bite marks on his neck. His face turns a pale shade of green. "Oh my *God.*"

All at once, the fragile hope of a future with Tristan explodes like a shattering mirror, a million jagged pieces burying themselves in my chest. Tearing me apart. *Destroying* me.

Konstantin chuckles low in his throat, the sound oozing arrogance. "See? Isn't that better, now that the truth is out in the open?"

"Why are you doing this?" Tristan cries. "*Why are you torturing me?*"

"I assure you," Konstantin says, "I am doing no such thing. You should be thanking me for showing you Charlotte's true nature before you fell in love with her." Tristan stills, jaw working, and Konstantin grins smugly. "Or am I too late?"

Tristan is quiet for a long moment, and I wonder if maybe—just maybe—he'll give me the chance to explain. But then he straightens and snatches a handful of Konstantin's red shirt, yanking him close.

"I'm going to *kill you*," he growls, their noses almost touching. "I don't care if it takes the rest of my life, and I don't care if I die in the process. You're nothing but a sad, pathetic little man and you deserve everything that is coming to you."

To Tristan's credit, Konstantin actually seems surprised by the outburst, but it only lasts a few seconds. Recovering, he clamps an unyielding hand around Tristan's throat. His eyes widen in alarm and he claws at Konstantin's arm, fighting for air as his feet lift a few inches off the ground.

"*No!*" I scream, trying to surge forward. To help him. But my feet still refuse to move. "Leave him alone!"

"You're becoming quite the nuisance, aren't you?" Konstantin snarls at Tristan, his hackles rising. "Why is that, I wonder? Even now, do you really love this little bird so much that you'd risk your life for her?"

Tristan's eyes flicker to me as Konstantin leans him backward over the barrier, his expression empty. Wind tears at Tristan's hair and pelts him with rain. The ocean is black behind him, and I can hear the waves crashing against the cliffside below. It's a low, thunderous sound, making the ground below us shake, and I watch helplessly as Konstantin's fingers dig into Tristan's neck.

"I think I've had enough of you, *golden boy*," he says through a sneer, "but it was fun while it lasted." He pulls Tristan close, his mouth at his ear. "Give my regards to Alison."

And with a wolfish grin, he hurls Tristan over the cliff's edge.

Time slows as images flash before me: Tristan's hand outstretched, the pure terror on his face, the wild gleam in Konstantin's eye, a spider-web of lighting splitting the midnight sky.

And then Tristan is gone.

I scream, collapsing to my knees. *"Tristan!"*

Konstantin peers after him with an impassive expression, then stalks back to me, his gait hitching. He grabs me roughly by the arm and hoists me up, holding me to his chest.

"This," he murmurs, stroking my hair a little too roughly, "is what happens when you don't follow the rules. This is *my game*. And if you try to change it, then I have no choice but to dole out the appropriate consequences." He brushes his knuckles down my jaw, his touch like ice, even in the freezing rain. "Remember, you're the one who decided to come here tonight. You should have kept a better leash on your pet."

My whole body is shaking. I can't tear my eyes from the space above the railing where Tristan disappeared, now dark and empty as a black hole. He isn't dead. He *can't* be dead.

"I'm going to kill you," I snarl, still staring into the darkness, "if Tristan doesn't get to you first."

Konstantin releases me, slicking his hair back with one hand. The rage is gone from his expression, replaced with bemusement.

"He won't live long enough to try." He pauses, then says, "Go after him if you'd like. But know this: you have taken my leverage away from me. Rayna"—his voice sharpens on her name, turning almost bitter—"has revealed the truth. As far as I'm concerned, there are no rules anymore. There is nothing stopping me from killing every last one of you."

The invisible shackles on my ankles lift as Konstantin melts away with a tick of his shoulder, his usual swagger replaced with stiff fury.

I fume in place for a few seconds before reality slams into me.

Tristan.

I spin around and race for the cliff's edge, climbing to the top of the barrier. The water below is rough and dark, slamming against the cliffside with tremendous force. Nausea heaves in my stomach and the ground seems to tilt beneath me. This is my nightmare. Not only is Tristan lost somewhere in the waves, but he might not even be alive, and that scares me more than I'd like to admit—more than the idea of jumping into a violent sea. More than getting tossed in the icy waves.

More than sinking, lifeless, into the yawning void.

The ocean may be a soulless bitch, but Tristan is *mine*. And I won't let her take him from me.

Taking a deep, steadying breath, I close my eyes and jump.

CHAPTER 54

There's a moment in every one of my nightmares when I fall.

I'm not sure where the fear comes from—it's not like I have a habit of falling from things—but it weaseled its way into my subconscious decades ago and refuses to leave.

In my nightmares, I always wake up *just* before I hit the ground. Some kind of adrenaline response, I think. My mind knows it doesn't want to die—doesn't want to feel the snap of bones or the splat of my body hitting the pavement—so it always kicks me out of the dream before that last, fatal moment.

But I'm not dreaming now. And when I slam through the surface of the ocean, I almost wish it had been concrete. Because even death would be better than this.

Tumultuous darkness swallows me whole. The water is *freezing*, surging around me in an unyielding current, tumbling me head over heels, then again. I can't seem to right myself—I see only the black ocean stretching endlessly around me, hear only the dull roaring of the storm-tossed waves. Panic flares in my chest as my arms and legs thrash uselessly, and the salt water burns my eyes as I search for any point of brightness that might lead to the surface—

There. A shimmer, like moonlight through the trees. I kick toward it, straining against the current, but the waves hold me in icy claws, tugging me down, down . . .

I cry out in fear, emptying my lungs of whatever air was left in them. And now my panic has cranked up to an eleven.

You can't die, Charlotte. You're already dead.

My muscles ache and my lungs burn as they strain for air. *You don't need it.* But the reflex is there, my instincts screaming wildly that I need to breathe, breathe, *breathe.*

I inhale sharply, and my lungs fill with ocean water.

This is worse than Hell. This is purgatory.

My insides are on fire but my skin has turned to ice. Silver sparks swim in my vision but I shake them off, keeping myself from passing out through sheer force of will. If I were a human, I would already be dead.

How is Tristan going to survive this?

Pain cracks through my skull as I'm thrown against something hard and unforgiving: *the cliffside.* Thank the demonic powers-that-be. My head throbs as I dig my fingers into the rock, clawing my way up, up, up . . . and out.

I break the surface and gasp for air, only to immediately vomit up a lungful of water. The salt scorches my throat, but after a minute of painful coughing and retching, I finally draw breath.

It's like breathing fire instead of air.

"*Tristan!*" I scream, my voice hoarse and raw. "*Tristan, can you hear me?*"

But I can barely hear myself. For a few seconds, there is only the howling of the wind, the roar of the sea, the deafening thunder of the waves as they crash against the cliffs. One slams into me and nearly knocks me loose, my arms and legs screaming with the effort to hold on.

I'm exhausted, I'm terrified, I'm never going to find him—

And then I hear it. A small cry, barely loud enough to cut through the storm—but loud enough for me.

My head snaps toward the open ocean, my eyes searching through the dark until I see him: a distant figure, being pulled out to sea.

After a few deep breaths, I shove off the cliff. I'm prepared for the waves this time, but they're no less threatening, no less eager to drag me down. They crest and surge at random intervals, throwing me off course, burying me over and over as I swim. Familiar fear screams in my chest, and I try not to think about the expanse of *nothing* beneath me or what might be lurking in the vast emptiness.

I focus instead on Tristan, who is still too far away. Who just disappeared beneath the waves. Who hasn't resurfaced.

I swim faster, dread driving me forward. When I reach the place where Tristan disappeared, I dive, my eyes screaming in pain as I search through the salty darkness. This may be terrifying for me, but I can't imagine how Tristan feels. I have to find him. I have to *save him*.

Something brushes against my foot, and I look down to see a pale hand sinking into the abyss. I scramble down and catch his wrist, fighting the icy current, but he's too heavy. His sweatshirt is waterlogged and does nothing but weigh us down, so I wrestle it from him and let it sink into the depthless dark.

"Tristan?" I yell as soon as we hit air. "Hey! Are you okay?"

Silence.

"No way," I growl, riding a wave as it surges beneath us. "You're not getting off that easy. If you die, I will *kill you*. I know that doesn't make any sense," I add through a heaving breath, "but you're just going to have to trust that I will find a way."

How did the shore get so far away? And did the waves somehow get *bigger*? They're practically mountains at this point. The current is relentless. My muscles are failing. I don't know how much longer I'll last.

Is this how Tristan dies? Drowned at sea because a pathetic little vampire girl couldn't save him?

After what could have been minutes or hours of frantic swimming, I finally look up to see the looming cliffside. With more effort than it should take, I manage to drag myself a few yards up the rock, pulling Tristan onto my lap. I jam my feet into a crevice to keep us from sliding back into the icy water then look down at Tristan, pressing a hand to his chest.

He's not breathing.

"Tristan?" I brush wet hair from his forehead and tuck him against me, doing my best to shelter him from the rain. His freckles are dark against his pallid skin. His lips are blue.

I wrack my brain, trying to *think*. Do I even know how to do CPR? If I tried, would I just make it worse? I've never had to save someone's life before. Vampires are malleable, after all—we get hurt and we bounce back. But humans? Bend them and they break.

"Tristan, I don't know how to help you," I whimper, giving him a little shake. My voice is still raw, and I can't seem to catch my breath. "Please don't die on me."

He *can't* die. Not after everything that has happened. I won't let my confession be the last thing he hears; he deserves better than that. He deserves to *live*.

All at once, Tristan's body convulses and he coughs violently, water streaming from his mouth. I choke out a sob, holding him steady as he rolls to his hands and knees, emptying his lungs of sea water.

He's alive.

Air rattles through his lungs as he takes a deep, ragged breath. When he finally lifts his gaze to mine, it's dark. Empty.

"Why did you do that?"

I frown, blinking rain and relieved tears from my eyes. "Do what?"

"Why did you save me?" Tristan stares down at the rock beneath him, rain dripping from his hair, his nose, his trembling jaw. "You should have just let me die."

"Don't joke about that—"

"I'm not joking, Charlotte." He ends my name with a hard *T*, sneering through every syllable. A shudder ripples through him, his teeth chattering behind blue lips. Without his sweatshirt, he wears only a gray t-shirt; he must be *freezing*. "You've already killed one Carr sibling. Why not make it a matching set?"

My jaw sags, taking my shoulders with it. "Tristan, I—that's a horrible thing to say."

"Well, you're a horrible person. It all evens out."

Grimacing, he collapses onto the rock, curling into a ball—and away from me. Another spasm shudders through him and I touch his shoulder, willing his body to relax. He recoils.

"Tristan," I say, shoving back my emotion and replacing it with practicality. "The ocean may not have killed you, but if we don't get you somewhere warm, hypothermia still might."

Tristan chuckles dryly, fighting another tremor. "Let it."

I take quick stock of our surroundings. From what I can tell, we climbed ashore about a hundred yards down the coast from the lighthouse. I try to stand but my legs refuse to cooperate. It's like this cold rock is seeping all the strength from me, taking my determination with it. I slump back down with a groan.

The cliffside isn't as steep here, but it's still quite the climb to get to the top. I'm not sure I'll be able to make it, seeing as all my muscles currently feel like jelly. I check my phone—which is still, miraculously, in my pocket—but it's waterlogged. Useless.

I'm useless, we're stranded, and Tristan's heartbeat is too slow. His eyelids droop.

"Hey," I say, patting his cheek a few times. His eyes flicker open in annoyance. "You can shun me later. Right now, I need you to stay awake."

His brow furrows, his lips pressing into a hard line. "Leave me alone."

"Stop it." I yank on Tristan's shoulder and he flops onto his back with a belligerent scowl, squinting against the pouring rain. "You may have a death wish, but I'm not just going to let you die here."

"You don't have to *let* me do anything. I can sleep if I want to."

"Absolutely not. I'm not well-versed in the human body, but I'm pretty sure I'm not supposed to let you fall asleep if you're a breath away from dying."

Tristan snorts, then squeezes his eyes shut anyway. "Your bedside manner is truly remarkable. They should give you a medal."

A familiar metallic scent touches the wind. Just a hint, but enough to stir something in my chest. Warmth, copper, a touch of salt . . .

Hunger slams into me with surprising force, my body curling in on itself. With dull horror, I notice the blood seeping into Tristan's hair from a hidden head wound. Fire screams in my throat and works its way to my cheeks, pooling beneath my eyes and in my mouth as my fangs slice through my gums. Raw, animal instincts threaten to take over, so strong—so *violent*—that pain rockets through my body.

On another night, I might have been able to fight this. But tonight's swim would have easily killed me if I were still human, which means my vampire body is weak. Desperate to heal. And in order to do that, I need *blood*.

My lungs are screaming, each breath like the twist of a dagger. I clench my teeth together. The hunger is strong, and I'm *weak*, and Tristan is lying in front of me, alive and bleeding. My hands clutch at the fabric of his t-shirt and I tense when I see the pulse slowly thrumming at his throat.

Just one taste. Just enough to bring the feeling back to my legs. I'm hungry—*starving*—and Tristan is *right here.*

A little growl rumbles in my chest, making Tristan's eyes snap open. My body shakes as I fight my instincts, holding the hunger back with every ounce of strength I have left.

"You're hungry, aren't you?" he asks. I expect to hear fear in his voice, but the bite in it is dulled by exhaustion and cool annoyance. "You're hungry and you're about to lose control. Is that what happened with Alison?"

"Not the time," I snarl, the words deep and vicious, and I finally see that flicker of fear in his eyes. I exhale a sharp laugh. "Something tells me you don't want to die here as much as I don't want to kill you."

Tristan stares at me for a long moment then winces suddenly, his face contorting in pain. He clutches at his side with a grimace.

"Tristan?" Panic surges through me, hot and wild, and it's enough to tame my hunger, if only for a second. His skin is pale, all the golden warmth drained away. Blue veins pulse at his temples. "Tristan?"

His eyes close. His breathing slows.

"Hey!" I pat his pallid cheek, but his eyes don't open. "Hey. Come on, freckles. Come back to me."

Nothing. Just the ever-slowing beat of his heart.

I smooth the hair from his forehead, memorizing every line of his face, every freckle. My legs are completely numb now, a combination of cold and exhaustion, and I gather Tristan against me, burying my face in his hair.

This wasn't supposed to happen. We were supposed to save Xander and Victoria tonight—in and out, simple as that. In hindsight, I may have oversimplified it, but *still*. Tristan wasn't even supposed to be there. He shouldn't have come anywhere near this hell-forsaken place, much less when Konstantin knew about it.

Because I told him. Because I *had* to tell him.

Why can't I say no to that ancient bastard?

A voice slices through the storm and my attention snaps to the top of the cliffside. Trees loom over the distant edge like a storm cloud, and I stare into their darkness. Waiting.

"Charlotte, where are you?"

Xander.

"Down here!" I croak, scrambling into a sitting position. "We're down here!"

I stare at the trees for a few agonizing seconds before my brother's worried face peers over the cliff's edge. He curses loudly and holds up one finger before disappearing again.

"It's Xander," I breathe, not knowing if Tristan can even hear me. "Xander found us."

But then Tristan exhales shakily, his heart jumping at the words.

"Oh, thank *God*," he murmurs. "I really don't want to die."

Less than a minute later, Xander is skating awkwardly down the cliffside with Kaleb close behind, and I'm surprised my brother even has the strength. But as he draws closer, I see the resolve set into his brow, the rigid set of his shoulders as he skids to a slippery halt on the rock next to us.

"What the hell happened?" he asks, stooping to pick me up. He cradles me to his chest like a damn baby, but for once, I relish in it. Xander's arms are strong and all-encompassing, and I let myself curl into him, chuckling against his chest. "What's so funny?"

"I came here to save you tonight," I rasp, exhaustion sweeping over me, "but here you are, my big brother, coming to the rescue."

"We saved each other tonight," he muses, but his frown only deepens. "Poetic, isn't it?"

I don't respond. I don't even nod. I'm vaguely aware of Kaleb delicately lifting Tristan into his arms and I almost call out to him, but my energy is spent. There's a strange sort of numbness seeping through me, making me dizzy. Like I exist somewhere outside my body. Xander's grip is firm as he makes his way up the steep incline, his movements surprisingly steady. He winces when he slips on a smooth bit of rock, and I look up at him—at the blood still oozing from the wounds on his neck.

"You're hurt," I murmur.

"Am I? I had no idea." Xander almost smiles, keeping his attention fixed on the rocks in front of him. "You don't look much better."

"What—" I touch a twinging spot on my forehead and my hand comes away red. "I'm bleeding?"

He rolls his eyes. "I would ask if you hit your head, but that much is clear."

My body feels like it's shutting down—shutting me out. Black spots hover at the edges of my vision.

"Lottie?" Xander says, his voice sharp. "Hey, stay with me, okay? Stay here."

I nod. *I'm here.*

And then the world goes dark.

CHAPTER 55

Hot air blasts against my face, making needles dance over my skin. My eyelids feel like lead, but I manage to crack them open—just enough to see Kaleb next to me in the driver's seat of a car, his knuckles white on the steering wheel. Trees rush by in a steady blur through the window, fog shrouding them in a blanket of churning gray.

"Hang on, Tristan," Xander murmurs from the backseat, his voice tight with worry. "How much longer?"

Kaleb glances at his phone. "Ten minutes."

"Drive faster."

The engine roars.

◇　◇　◇

Voices hover like a cloud around me. They pulse in and out, some clear, others muffled. I reach out through the fog, catching nothing but snippets.

"What happened?"

"—both been out cold—"

"Charlotte, darling, can you hear me?"

"I'm going to need every blanket you can find."

A pair of strong arms lifts me from my seat and I breathe in the scent of whiskey and leather.

"Nik?" I rasp. My throat burns. "Is—where's Tristan?"

"Shh, shh," Nik soothes, carrying me inside a room that's warm and dry. My clothes feel suddenly frozen.

◊   ◊   ◊

"—and he doesn't want to see her."

A muffled curse. "He knows?"

I'm lying on something soft and there are blankets *everywhere*. Someone sits next to me, a gentle hand smoothing over my hair. I inhale the scent of sea spray and drying blood and inky shadows, relaxing under the gentle touch.

"Is she going to be okay?"

I don't hear an answer.

Everything is fine, I think. Then everything disappears.

◊   ◊   ◊

She is mine. She always has been.

My eyes snap open, my heart hammering, and I'm immediately aware of two things: first, I have no idea where I am. Second, I am *starving*.

It's not the kind of hunger that simmers low in my abdomen, ever-present, waiting for an opportunity to strike. This hunger is writhing, all-consuming, burning through me like acid. I cough against the sandpaper feeling in my throat and my lungs scream in protest. It's like my entire body has been sucked dry—like the ocean isn't just a soulless bitch, but her own sadistic breed of vampire.

I blink a few times, blearily, and recognize the beige furniture and the soulless art on the walls from the safe house. A lamp shines next to me, casting a dim yellow glow over the room. It sits on a nightstand that holds a handful of water bottles, all filled with something dark and red.

"Thank *hell,*" I groan, tearing the lid off one of the bottles to chug what might be the best meal of my life. Somewhere in my mind, I'm aware that the blood is, in fact, room temperature—*very* tepid—and has probably been sitting here for hours, but I'm too hungry to care. When I finish the first bottle, I snatch up the second one, then pause.

How did I get here? And why am I so *hungry?*

My mind works for a few seconds before it all comes crashing back: Konstantin, the cliffside, the wind howling over the stormy ocean. My confession. The deep, long dive into suffocating blackness.

Good hell. *Tristan.*

I shoot to my feet, then sway as the room swims around me.

"Easy there, Lottie." Nik's voice startles me backward. My legs hit the edge of the bed and I sink down onto the comforter, my eyes scanning the room as I set the bottle down. I find him lounging on a recliner in a shadowed corner, a smirk on his lips.

"You scared me, Nikolas."

"Yeah, well, it's only fair." He crosses the room and sits next to me, wrapping his arms around my shoulders. "Watching you run after Konstantin was the most terrified I've ever been. Never do that again."

I snort. "Believe me, I don't plan on it."

"I'm serious, Lottie. He could have killed you."

Come here, my girl.

"But he didn't." It's all I can say. Even though I know Konstantin is dangerous—that he could kill me in an instant—something about him leaves me feeling safe. Protected, even. Like he won't hurt me—like I'm part of some bigger plan. I just wish I knew what it was.

"Thank goodness for that," Nik murmurs, crushing me to his chest. "And thank goodness he didn't kill Tristan the easy way."

I think of the sound of Jason's neck snapping, and shudder.

"Did—what did Tristan tell you?"

Nik sighs, rubbing the back of his neck. "He woke up a few hours ago and, um . . . he told Noah and I everything."

"By everything, do you mean—"

"*Everything,* Lottie." He hesitates, touching my knee softly as the blood drains from my face. "Is it true, then? Was the girl in Golden Gate Park really his sister?"

Shame slices through my gut as I murmur a tiny, "Yes."

Nik is still for a few tense seconds, and I worry that he might just walk away. Instead, he asks, "Why didn't you say anything?"

"Would *you* say anything if you suddenly found out that you killed Noah's sister?"

Nik frowns. "I guess not."

"Are you and Noah the only ones Tristan told? Or . . . ?"

"Oh, no," Nik almost laughs. "Tristan wasn't exactly quiet about it."

"Right. So everyone knows."

"Yeah."

I groan, pressing my palms to my eyes as I flop back onto the bed. "At least Xander and Kaleb already knew. I'm not sure I'd be able to withstand their scrutiny in the midst of everything else."

"You told Kaleb?" Nik says, almost offended. "Xander, I understand, but *Kaleb?*"

"Not exactly." I let my hands fall to my sides. "Xander got the brunt of it when I figured it out myself. Kaleb is the one who cleaned up after it happened, so it was only a matter of time before he put two and two together."

"Hmm," Nik murmurs. "I heard Tristan yelling at Kaleb earlier. I guess that explains why."

A smile tugs at my lips as I imagine Kaleb getting a dressing down from a *human.* I would have paid money to see the look on his face.

"Yeah, Kaleb and I both told him we would help find Alison's killer." I shrug, feigning indifference. "Oops."

Nik lies down next to me and we are silent for a few minutes, staring up at the unmoving white blades of a generic ceiling fan.

"How are you doing, by the way?" I finally ask, propping myself up on one elbow. My vision blurs as pain throbs behind my eyes, signaling an impending ocular migraine. I blink a few times to clear it and retrieve another blood bottle from the nightstand. I'm not sure how much more abuse my head can take this week. "You and Kaleb? After the"—I gesture at the empty air—"you know. The Rayna thing."

Nik's brows knit together and he laughs coldly. "Honestly, I don't know how I feel. Kaleb has been enemy number one for so long, but now that I know Rayna is alive, I'm starting to look at things differently."

"Oh?" I ask, taking a long drink from my bottle. "How so?"

"Well . . . " He twirls a strand of my hair in his fingers contemplatively. "Last week when we went to The Caged Bird with Xander, it was the first time I'd actually spoken to Kaleb since the night Rayna 'died,' and I—I couldn't help myself. I lost control. I know I shouldn't have attacked him like that, but did you notice how he didn't fight back, even a little bit? He just sat there and let me pummel him. He didn't even seem angry, just . . . tired. Accepting."

I frown down at him. "Actually, yes. I did notice that."

"The more I think about it, the more I realize how matter-of-fact he was about everything." Nik's jaw works in a few slow circles. "I *knew* Kaleb, and I knew my sister. Their relationship was volatile, yes, but there was a level of connection there that I had never seen between anyone else. If Kaleb had actually killed her, it would have torn him apart. Look at him now—just the thought of Konstantin harming any of us has him coming apart at the seams.

"That night in New York," he continues, "when he told us he had killed Rayna, it felt forced, somehow. I should have suspected something then, but I was too blinded by anger and grief to examine it closely. Maybe if I would have taken the time to really think about it, I would have realized how ridiculous it all was. Kaleb would *never* have killed Rayna. He loved her more than life itself.

"And now . . ." Nik sighs, dragging a hand over his face. "Now I feel like a fool. Like I've wasted an entire century of my life hating one of the few people in this world who I truly care about."

"Yeah," I say on a slow exhale. "I know what you mean."

While I don't think Kaleb should have taken the blame for Rayna's death—or *disappearance*, rather—I understand why he did it. He was so desperate to protect us that he willingly let himself suffer to ensure our safety. And Nik is right. If we wouldn't have been so quick to paint Kaleb as the villain, maybe the last hundred and twenty-one years would have been different.

Maybe I would have realized that Rayna was the mastermind all along.

"Have you talked to Xander?" I ask, then immediately regret it.

Nik stills, his expression turning fierce. "Yes."

"And?"

"And nothing. We talked, we didn't kill each other, end of story."

"Nik—"

"We're fine, Charlotte." Nik sits up and his eyes lose their fire, a sure sign that the conversation is over. I purse my lips but say nothing else. The two of them will have to work through their issues on their own.

Sighing, I switch tactics. "What about Pippa?"

The sound of her agonized scream still rings in my ears, accompanied by the memory of Henry's heart oozing in Mira's hand. Acid rises in my throat and I swallow against the burn.

Nik makes a pained noise in his throat. "She's been in with the— with *Henry* since we got back. So far, she has refused to talk to anyone."

"How long has that been, exactly?"

"We got back around two in the morning, and it's nearly nightfall again."

Good hell. I've been asleep for *that long*?

"Where is she?"

"Lottie, she's really not in a good place—"

"Nik."

He sighs in resignation, gesturing vaguely downward. "She's in one of the bedrooms in the basement. But be careful," he adds as I make for the door. "We've all tried. Rose, Kaleb . . . even Tristan. She practically bit the poor boy's head off."

Warmth sparks in me at the thought of Tristan, battered and bruised, attempting to console a feral Pippa. Under different circumstances, I might find it funny. But now, it's only sad.

◊   ◊   ◊

Knock, knock.

"Pippa?" Silence greets me and I knock again. "Pippa, it's Charlotte. Can I come in?"

There's no response, just the quiet rustling of blankets. I take her lack of answer as acquiescence and ease the door open.

Hallway light slices into the windowless bedroom, cutting a jagged rectangle on the bed. Henry lies in the middle of it, eyes closed, a crisp white henley replacing his ruined clothes from last night. His comfortable pose suggests he could be sleeping, but his pale skin has taken on a gray, waxy pallor, and his body is too rigid. Still, there's a softness to him, reflecting not the centuries-old features of a vampire, but the gangly youth of a sixteen-year-old boy.

If I hadn't seen it myself, I would never know there was a gaping hole where his heart should be.

Unexpected sorrow grips me, squeezing my lungs like a vise. Such a peculiar, terrifying, wonderful boy—so much enthusiasm extinguished in the span of a breath.

Curled at Henry's side, her head on his chest, is Pippa. I assume she's the one who changed Henry into fresh clothes, but she didn't bother doing the same for herself. Her leather jacket is crusted with blood and grime, and there is dried blood caked into her hair. She doesn't move when I enter, just curls more tightly into Henry, her body trembling.

"Pippa?" I sit next to her and lightly touch her arm. "I'm going to get you some clothes. You can't be comfortable stuck in all that leather."

"Go away," Pippa growls, her voice muffled against Henry's chest.

"Unfortunately," I say with a soft pat of her arm, "since you've already turned everyone else away, you're stuck with me."

"*Go. Away.*"

"No. I'm nothing if not a stubborn ass."

A small tremor moves through Pippa. After a few seconds of ornery silence, she turns her face toward me, revealing mascara-stained cheeks and red-rimmed sapphire eyes that shimmer with tears.

"I don't want to leave him."

The grief in Pippa's voice sucks the air from my lungs.

"We won't go far," I reassure her. "Just the bathroom, only a few steps away."

Frowning, she kisses Henry's gray cheek then reluctantly peels herself away, careful not to disturb him. She smooths his makeup-stained shirt where her face was resting, taking a few extra seconds to brush an unruly curl from his forehead. The touch is so tender that I almost look away, but then she stands, holding her arms out in surrender.

"Do what you will, you stubborn ass."

I find a t-shirt and a pair of sweatpants in the dresser then steer Pippa into the bathroom. It's almost identical to the others in the house, with clean white tile and marble countertops. Pippa hisses when I flick the light on but doesn't protest further, just obediently adjusts her stance accordingly as I help strip off her ruined clothes. I don't bother asking before I toss them in the trash can.

Pippa watches as I turn the shower on, arms folded tightly over her bare chest. The black veins on her torso are stark against her too-pale skin, snaking from her jaw down through her heart and all the way to her left hip bone. That night feels like a lifetime ago, when we tried to outsmart Konstantin. When one of Henry's hawthorn-dipped daggers broke off in Pippa's chest. When Kaleb was able to remove it just in time—before the wounds festered and killed her.

I had been so furious with Henry then. Everyone had. But it all seems so silly, blaming him for what happened. He was only trying to help. Haven't we all done something stupid in the name of helping our family?

By the time steam is billowing from the shower, Pippa's sour mood is losing its flavor. Even her hair seems to be affected, the usually-voluminous platinum strands hanging limply over her hunched shoulders, and the first traces of black roots are showing at her scalp.

"In you go." I motion to the shower but Pippa doesn't move. "Come on, baby girl. Let's get that blood off of you."

Pippa blinks as though waking from a trance, then mechanically makes her way into the shower. The door closes with a magnetic thud and I release a shaky breath, my nerves easing as I take a moment to examine my reflection in the mirror.

I could use a shower myself. Someone dressed me in safe house clothes while I was unconscious, putting me in a white sweatshirt that somehow makes my skin look gray. Blood from a healing gash on my forehead plasters hair to one side of my head, a blackish bruise blooms on my jaw, and the salt-burn on my cheeks could almost be mistaken for a sunburn. If I look this bad, I don't even want to know what that swim did to Tristan.

Something hollow clatters to the shower floor.

"Pippa? You okay?" I peer through the steam-fogged door to see Pippa standing under the shower stream, eyes fixed on the green shampoo bottle that rests at her feet.

"I—I didn't—it was slippery, and I couldn't hold on." Each word comes out faster. Louder. "I could have stopped it. Why couldn't I stop it?" She lets out a choked sob. "*Why couldn't I save him?*"

Pippa claps both hands over her mouth and I walk straight into the shower, clothes and all. I catch her as her back hits the wall and we slide to the floor together, her shoulders shaking, her breath quickening. Sobs wrack her body, growing in intensity until she's all but hyperventilating. I hold her tightly as she releases an agonized wail that echoes in the small space, ringing in my ears, cutting deep into my bones.

Tears stream down my cheeks, slow and steady. I hold her until the water runs cold. Until her screams become sobs, then her sobs turn to weeping. And when she finally finds her voice, my heart breaks all over again.

"Why, Lottie?" Pippa whimpers. "Why am I destined to lose everyone I love?"

CHAPTER 56

Xander's voice drifts through the safe house, caught up in an unintelligible conversation with Kaleb. I make my way toward them begrudgingly, knowing that I can't avoid this confrontation forever. We may have had a brief emotional breakthrough at the lighthouse, but I still have so much I want to say to him—and so much I want him to say to me.

I finally find the pair in a secluded corner of the house and their rough whispers shiver into clarity. Kaleb makes a sound of disapproval and I pause around the corner, listening with anxiety bubbling in my chest.

"When was the last time you ate?" Kaleb asks, all concern and frustration.

"It doesn't matter," Xander replies softly, but quickly acquiesces. "At the lighthouse."

There's a muffled slap, and I can only assume Kaleb hit Xander in the arm. "Dammit, Alexander. Stop torturing yourself."

Xander sighs, then brushes fingers through his hair. "I've made too many mistakes, Kaleb. I tried to save Victoria and only made it worse for her. And Charlotte—" His voice catches, making my heart twinge. "I don't think she'll ever forgive me."

"*Moj siabar.*" *My friend.* Kaleb's tone is firm but not unkind. "If

Charlotte has it in her to forgive *me*—someone who is, quite frankly, not worthy of forgiveness—then you have nothing to worry about."

Xander murmurs an acknowledgment but doesn't sound convinced. With a steadying breath, I push off from the wall and swing around the corner to see the two of them standing in a dead-end hallway by a single closed door, Xander frowning with Kaleb's hand on his cheek.

I clear my throat and they both jump, Kaleb's hand falling to his side. He raises an eyebrow in silent question.

"Give us a minute," I say.

Kaleb shoots a furtive glance at Xander before pulling me into a bone-crushing hug. I return it readily, wrapping myself in smoke and ice.

"If you ever go after Konstantin alone again," he growls into my ear, "I will hunt you down and kill you myself. Do you understand me?"

"Yes, Your Majesty."

He hangs on for a second too long, then releases me with a weary glare and strides around the corner, leaving me alone with San Francisco's Beta.

Xander looks *awful*. The wounds on his neck are a festering bright red, blood oozing into the collar of his safe house gray sweatshirt, and a few of his earrings look like they were ripped from his ears. All his weight is on his left foot—the right one is bent at a strange angle—and there are blackish bruises on his jaw and beneath one eye. The dejected, hopeless expression on his face is terribly foreign.

I swallow hard. Konstantin had no intention of letting Xander go easily. Instead, he strung him up in that cavern next to Victoria, then put a silver dagger through her heart. Every day the tide would rise, filling the small cavern completely, drowning the two of them over and over again.

The ocean tried to drown me *once* last night, an experience that will likely be one of the top five worst of my life. I can't imagine the agony of having to go through it for hours on end.

Konstantin tortured both of them for *days*. And he barely lifted a finger.

"You look like shit," Xander says, startling me from my thoughts.

I scowl. So much for emotional breakthroughs. "Have you looked in a mirror recently?"

Xander crosses his arms but the movement makes him wince, taking the edge off his own scowl. I want to reach for him—to take the weight off what is obviously a shattered foot—but I'm not sure if I should. If he would appreciate the offer or shove me away, like he always does.

And I'm not sure I could handle his rejection right now.

"Xander, listen—"

"No, *you* listen." My mouth snaps shut and Xander flinches at the harshness in his words, dragging a hand over his face. "I'm sorry, I just—" He sighs. "I'm exhausted."

"Maybe you would feel better if you weren't *starving yourself.*"

His expression hardens into a glare. "What I do or don't eat is none of your business."

I close my eyes, swallowing the sting, and throw my hands up in defeat. "*Niama.* You know what? Never mind. I knew this was a bad idea."

When I turn to leave, Xander catches me by the wrist.

"Ksusha, *wait.*" All the bite is gone from his voice and when I turn back to him, silver rims his eyes. "Don't go. Please."

Frowning, I pull my arm away, watching him warily as he tugs at the hem of his sweatshirt. The nervous tick has always made him look young—like a child waiting to be scolded. Tense silence stretches between us and I watch him closely, noting the uncharacteristic hunch in his shoulders, the way he carefully avoids my gaze.

Xander is *scared.*

"I never trusted Rayna," he says quietly. Cautiously. "Not really. I watched her gaslight you and Nik for decades. She never took the blame for anything, even when it was clearly her fault. And when she dragged the two of you into trouble, she played the hero by dragging you back out." His brow furrows, his attention glued to the floor. "When she died, I was . . . hell, I was *relieved*. I thought it meant you would finally be free of her. But then Kaleb told me the truth—that she ran away under the guise of protecting us—and I was *livid*."

Xander hugs his arms more tightly to his chest and I feel the urge to reach out to him again. Instead, I stay still. I stay silent.

"We knew that if we told you or Nik what really happened, you would go after her. And I—I couldn't let you do that. I truly believed that you would both be happier without her."

"Well, we weren't." There's no anger in my voice, just cold indifference.

"I know." A tear shimmers at the corner of Xander's eye and he gruffly wipes it away. "And to make matters worse, Kaleb was miserable. Every time I spoke to him, it was obvious how depressed he was—how broken. He missed our family so much. And it was *killing* me, Lottie, knowing how much my brother needed me. So when he asked if I would be his Beta—"

"You said yes." The image of Kaleb alone and heartsick ties my chest in knots. I can't help but think that if I knew the truth—if I knew how much he was hurting—I would have run to him, too.

Xander nods. "I didn't even hesitate. I wanted to tell you why we came here, I *really* did. But everything was so complicated with you and Nik and Kaleb . . . I didn't want you getting involved. I see now just how stupid that was.

"And I'm not sure if—" His voice wavers. "I know I don't deserve your forgiveness, but I need you to know how much I loathe myself for keeping this from you. For the way I've treated you for the last hundred years."

Slowly, I lift a hand to Xander's face. He recoils slightly, as though bracing for a blow, but I only brush a tear from his cheek. Seeing him cry is as rare as seeing lightning in a cloudless sky. For our entire lives, he has always been the strong one. He didn't even cry when we buried Mama or when we left Belarus—and Mira—behind for good.

But here he is now, crying over *me*.

I slowly wrap my arms around Xander's neck, ignoring his grunt of pain and surprise. He still smells like ocean water, like mildew and blood and burning silver. Hesitantly, he returns my embrace, hands fluttering awkwardly before settling on either side of my spine.

"I don't blame you for keeping secrets," I say against his chest. "Kaleb should never have asked that of you. Ideally, Rayna should never have faked her death in the first place."

Tears well in my eyes and I let them fall, soaking into Xander's sweatshirt. For a few terrifying days, I wondered if I would ever see him again. If I would ever be able to tell him how much I need him.

When I look up, I find Xander staring down at me, his emerald eyes guarded, and I can't blame him for being wary. Two hundred years have left us broken—mere ghosts of the carefree siblings we once were. But deep down, I'm still that little girl in Belarus who would do anything to make her big brother proud. And after all this time, despite my endless belligerence, he's still here. Strong and brave and more amazing that I give him credit for.

"I'm still pissed at you," I grumble, "so don't be surprised if this becomes a trump card in every argument for the foreseeable future. But you're my brother, Alexander. I'm never going to stop loving you no matter how much of an ass you are."

Every ounce of tension melts from my brother's body and his hug goes from hesitant to smothering. He releases a shuddering breath, burying his face in my tangled, salty hair. We hold each other for a few healing minutes, and I distantly realize that this might be the longest hug we've shared in a *very* long time.

"I love you so much, *repa*," Xander says quietly, squeezing me for emphasis. "I know I don't say it enough, but I thank the stars every day that we were Turned together. I don't think I would have been able to live in a world without you in it."

"Gross," I say, shoving away from him as I swallow a too-strong surge of *feelings*. "What is this, a soap opera?"

Xander stares at me for a few seconds before his mouth quirks into the barest hint of a smile.

"No chick flick moments?" he asks wryly, drying his face with the hem of his sweatshirt.

I feel a rush of fondness and grin at him, scrubbing my tears away. "Absolutely not."

The wall I built between us cracks, just a little.

"So tell me." Xander clears his throat, forcing the emotion from his voice. "Why are you talking to me right now?"

"What kind of question is that?"

One brow quirks and he leans back against the wall. "Well, after listening to Tristan rage through the house for an hour, I thought you might be groveling at his feet."

Dread gnaws at my gut and I cringe. "That bad, huh?"

"Kaleb isn't the only one he screamed at."

I groan and step forward, letting my forehead *thunk* onto Xander's chest. Tristan's words ring through my head: *You should have just let me die.*

"I'm not sure if I'm ready to face him."

"He doesn't have to stay here, you know." Xander tentatively strokes my hair. "Just say the word and I'll put him on a plane home to San Diego."

"It's a tempting offer, but he would never take it. He won't leave Noah."

Xander nods. "Do you want me to Compel him?"

"*No.*" The word comes out more forcefully than I intend it to, and I straighten. "The cat is already out of the bag. I don't want to shove it back in, knowing it will inevitably come out again. I can't watch Tristan go through that twice."

He nods again, frowning. "Then how can I help?"

The sincerity in his expression nearly makes me cry again, but I shake the feeling away, swallowing against the knot in my throat.

"You can talk to me about Mira instead."

Now it's Xander's turn to groan, and he slides a few inches down the wall. "I have nothing to say about Mira."

I glance at the closed door next to him, where I can hear Victoria's deep, even breaths.

"I saw the way you looked at her," I whisper, "when she appeared at the lighthouse. You must have *something* to say."

"Fine, but you asked for it." The dull anger is back in his voice, and when he looks at me again, his eyes are hard. "I never expected to see Mira again. Why would I? It's not like vampirism is *common*. But somehow—*somehow*—she's here and she's working for *Konstantin*. What the actual hell, Lottie?"

I open my mouth to reply, but he keeps ranting, growing more agitated by the second.

"The minute I caught her scent, I thought I was going crazy. And then she appeared, looking so damn feral—so *beautiful* . . ." He laughs derisively, raking a hand through his hair. "When I saw her, I forgot all about Victoria, half-dead and bleeding in Kaleb's arms. What does that say about me?"

"That you're the scum of the earth," I quip, and Xander balks. Awkwardly, I tug at my hair. "Relax, I was only joking."

"Well, don't. You're bad at it," Xander says, then his eyes flash with fury. Maybe I shouldn't have brought up Mira after all. "Oh, and one more thing. Let's not forget the fact that the girl I once loved just punched the heart straight out of Henry's chest."

Henry. I picture him lying in the bed downstairs, his youthful face ashen, and sorrow grips me all over again.

Before I can reply, there's a sudden sharp gasp in the bedroom, like someone coming up for air. Xander's anger dissipates immediately, replaced by worry as he throws the door open. Victoria is tangled in the bed's white comforter, thrashing wildly, and my brother rushes in to free her, grabbing her by the shoulders as she claws at her chest, right over her heart. Her eyes dart around the room, wide and panicked.

"Victoria," Xander says, gently rubbing her arms. She flinches sharply, breath coming in ragged gasps. The miserable expression on my brother's face almost has me sinking to the floor. He pulls Victoria onto his lap, even as she fights against him, and he murmurs calming words into her ear. "Sweetheart. *Bǎo bèi.* I'm here, my love."

The moment feels too intimate to warrant an audience. Xander nods as I give him an apologetic smile, then I turn and slip quietly from the room.

"Alexander?" Victoria whimpers, then she sinks into broken sobs as the door clicks shut.

CHAPTER 57

SAN FRANCISCO, CALIFORNIA

MARCH 2018

"Alison? Alison, are you there? *Alison!*"

The phone-muffled voice snaps me into focus and I release the girl a little too quickly. She slumps to the ground, her knees cracking against the rain-splattered cobblestones. Pain contorts her face and she releases a choked sob, hands scrabbling at her neck. On a normal night, the bite would have been cleaner—two simple punctures—but I went too far this time. I lost control. And there's a huge open wound on the side of her throat.

Rayna would have stopped me—she would have made sure this girl stayed alive. But Rayna died a hundred and twenty-one years ago. She can't save me anymore. Two words ring out in my head—words that I have barely acknowledged since 1897. Nullum corpus. *Leave no bodies.*

Damn that stupid phrase. Remembering it now, I feel a sudden spark of fear. Kaleb is going to kill me when he finds out about this— his little Charlotte, breaking all the rules. Further proof of the stunning disappointment I've become. I haven't seen the bastard in a century, and I pray he never finds out about what I've done here tonight, though I know he will. It is his *city, after all.*

The girl groans from where she lies at my feet, blood streaming from her neck as she takes slow, pained breaths. Red mingles with rainwater, swirling in eddies around her. Maybe I should finish her off—make it quick and painless—but something like remorse gnaws at my gut, telling me to help her. To fix this. I grimace at my inner voice, wishing she hadn't been trained by someone like Kaleb Sutton.

Steeling myself, I kneel next to the dying girl. Her orange curls are limp and sodden, having come loose from the green bandana tied around her head. I brush the hair back from her face and she stares up at me with terrified gold eyes.

"Please," she whimpers, her voice a rasp. "Please don't kill me."

"I'm not going to kill you," I lie, not wanting to tell her that she's already dead. "I'm going to help you. It's Alison, right?"

She nods weakly—reluctantly—as I take one of her hands.

"Look at me, Alison." My gaze captures hers and I zero in, focusing on my words. Making myself believe them. "You're going to be okay. In fact, it doesn't even hurt."

Alison shudders as the Compulsion sinks in, then her face relaxes into an expression of pure relief.

"You're right," she breathes. "It barely hurts at all."

I contemplate dialing 9-1-1 on her phone, but I've been here before. I've killed before. And I know that no ambulance would get here in time. She's lost too much.

The thought makes me squirm in discomfort, confused by the way my heart twinges in my chest. This is just a random girl who happened to be in the park tonight. Still, there's something about her that tugs at me, urging me to save her. But I can't. And the knowledge feels like salt in an open wound.

"Your painting is beautiful," I say to Alison, even as the rain washes colors from the canvas.

She smiles weakly. "Thanks. I'm about to graduate from art school."

"That's more than I've ever done."

"You still have time."

"Believe me, I know." My shoulders sag under the weight of it. "I have all the time in the world. Though I think you deserve it more

than I do."

"No," the girl says, shaking her head feebly. "Don't say that. You're so nice. My brother always says that's the best thing anyone can be."

I scoff to cover a stab of guilt. "Your brother is obviously an optimist."

"The opposite, actually. He thinks he's unlucky—that the universe is against him, when it seems like everything has fallen into place for me. My secret is that I make my own luck." She beckons me closer and I lean in, breathing in the scent of her blood diluted by rainwater. "But you know what? I was lucky tonight, because the universe gave me you."

Regret knots behind my ribs, writhing in a way that makes it feel like my entire chest cavity might cave in. You're so nice, she said. But if I were nice, she wouldn't be lying here in a pool of her own blood. She would be going home to eat crappy Chinese food with her brother and finish up her last few months of art school. The universe may have delivered me to her, but that was anything but lucky.

Because I'm the monster from the storybooks, and I just killed a girl in cold blood.

Alison's breathing slows, the space between each inhale stretching longer than the last, her once-strong heartbeat now barely an echo in my ears. I stare at the girl in my arms, my appetite gone, my heart like a stone. She has freckles that cover her entire face—a feature I hate on my own skin, but one that only makes her more beautiful. More human.

The wind calms for just a moment, leaving nothing but the sound of splattering raindrops and the distant, high-pitched whine of an approaching siren.

And then, with a final, shuddering breath, Alison goes still.

WITH ANY LUCK, I'll find a bottle of something dark and mind-numbing in the kitchen. I shuffle through the house, massaging my temples in an attempt to banish the last traces of a migraine, but it returns ten-fold when I enter the living room. Everyone—sans Xander and Victoria— are huddled on the furniture, speaking in hushed tones. The conversation grinds to a halt and a familiar feeling prickles over my skin.

"Are you guys talking about me?"

"No," Nik and Noah say in unison, while Rose doesn't even bother hiding her guilt. Kaleb's expression is a carefully-crafted mask of neutrality, as usual, and Pippa doesn't seem to be paying attention. She's curled up next to Noah with her head on his shoulder, and he's holding tightly to one of her hands.

At the far side of the room by the wall of windows, Rayna sits sideways with her legs kicked over the arm of a chair, a bottle of wine in her hand. She watches me with scrutiny, her amber eyes bright and penetrating. There's a question in them, but also a touch of I-know-something-you-don't-know. I glare at her, but she only smiles.

"We were, actually," she says. Nik shushes her loudly, but she doesn't acknowledge him. "It seems like you and Tristan had quite the adventure with Konstantin."

Her gaze slides to something behind me and I turn to see Tristan enter the room, halfway through tugging on a black t-shirt. He does so quickly, but not before I catch a glimpse of the huge mottled bruise that covers his entire right side. More bruises decorate his throat, a reminder of Konstantin's choking hand. It's a miracle his neck isn't broken.

It's a miracle he's alive at all.

"Tristan," I say before I can stop myself. "Are you okay?"

He jumps at the sound of my voice then winces, fixing me with an acerbic glare. "I was thrown off a cliff, Charlotte. What do you think?"

Tension thickens the air, making it hard to breathe, and the look on Tristan's face is nothing short of hostile. It's wildly at odds with his usual easy demeanor. Even after the party when Konstantin killed Jason, he was more devastated than angry. But now, with his mussed hair, his fresh cuts, and the sneer on his cracked lips, he looks less like a golden human boy and more like . . . well, like a *vampire.*

Rayna takes a swig straight from her wine bottle, then glances slyly at Tristan.

"Is it weird," she asks, kicking her legs lackadaisically, "to be in love with your sister's murderer?"

Tristan's eyes snap to her, and if he *were* a vampire, I imagine he would be going for her throat. Instead, he takes a deliberate step away from me and I feel his absence like a missing limb. Like someone has snuffed out the sun.

"Rayna," Kaleb chides. "That is quite enough."

She shrugs. "What? I'm sure Lottie will just Compel him later, anyway."

Tristan recoils.

"You shut your mouth," I start, but Tristan cuts me off.

"Oh my *God,*" he says to Rayna. He lifts both hands, palms out, and shakes his head incredulously. "You have to be, without a doubt, the most horrible person on planet Earth. Well—" He glances at me, and he might as well have shoved a knife into my ribs. "No. You know what? I don't want to do this right now. I need some air."

Tristan blows past me, nearly stumbling in his haste. He throws the door open, stomping into the gathering dark, and the room goes silent.

I press both palms over my eyes and stifle a groan. For the past few days, I had almost started to believe I could make things work with Tristan, despite everything. But I should have known that I was only kidding myself.

I killed his sister, after all. And if Xander ever died, I wouldn't fall in love with his killer. I would murder them.

"Hey, moon girl." Rayna appears at my side, her rose-petal scent wafting over me. It makes me gag. "I'll Compel him if you don't want to. I have no skin in this game."

"None of this would have happened if it weren't for *you,*" I snarl, and Rayna actually flinches. "Do you know why I was in Golden Gate Park that night? It was the anniversary of the day I met you. I couldn't stop thinking about how much I missed you, how mad I was at Kaleb, how *desperate* I was to see your face just one more time. Tristan's sister—" I clamp down on the words. "*Alison* didn't deserve what was coming to her. And if it weren't for you and your selfishness, she would still be alive."

"Darling," Kaleb warns. "You're not being fair—"

"Don't chastise me, Kaleb."

"No, he's right," Noah says, surprising me into silence. There's a darkness in his expression I haven't seen before. "It *isn't* fair. You can't blame Rayna for Alison's death. You're the one who killed her. *You're* the one who lost control. Take some damn responsibility and go throw yourself at Tristan's feet. I would wish you luck, but he doesn't believe in it."

Stunned silence greets his words and everyone's attention collectively shifts to me. Embarrassment brings a flush to my skin and I'm suddenly burning in my hoodie. I almost forgot that Noah likely cared about Alison as much as he cares about Tristan, which means I might need to beg for his forgiveness, too.

Rayna releases a low whistle. "You sure know how to pick them, Nikolas."

I smack her arm then glance out the window, but Tristan has disappeared. I should go talk to him—I *need* to—but the idea ties my stomach into knots. What am I supposed to say to him? *Sorry I killed your sister, do you still want to be my boyfriend?* I'm sure that would go over *really* well. Leaving him out there alone, however, is only going to delay the inevitable.

Time to rip off the Bandaid, I guess.

"I'm going to go talk to him," I say, trying to sound more confident than I feel. "No matter what happens, I'm not going to Compel him. I expect the same from all of you," I add, my gaze sweeping the room. "If you so much as think about messing with his head, I will string you up by your entrails. Got it?"

They all nod hesitantly and I storm out of the house, following

Tristan into the darkness.

"Tristan?" I call, bracing myself against the chilly wind. The night is blustery but clear, stars glittering in the sky like fireflies. I start across the expanse of patchy grass separating the house from the cliffside, grimacing at the way the damp earth squelches between my bare toes. Trees loom on either side of the yard, tall and imposing, and I stare between them, hoping Tristan didn't wander into the woods alone.

As much as I hate to admit it, Noah was right. Alison's death was my fault, and mine alone. And instead of ending things with Tristan the moment I found out who he was, I was selfish. Stupid. I should have let him go. But then he did that thing he does where he makes me fall in love with him, just a little.

It's ridiculous, really. I've barely known him for two weeks, but I let him carve out a little corner of my life—of my *heart*. And I shattered his in the process.

Nik is the only other person I've truly fallen in love with. But while that love was wild and passionate and reckless, what I have with Tristan . . . it's more. It *was* more.

And now it's nothing.

Movement catches my eye and I spot Tristan sitting on the edge of the cliff, his feet dangling over the side. The pale crescent moon paints him in a rim of silver, his shoulders hunched forward and his face buried in his hands. He doesn't move as I approach and I keep my distance, sitting down a few yards away. I kick my legs over the edge and stare out over the ocean for a few minutes, my chest writhing with apprehension as I watch the waves surge and break beneath us.

"Tristan," I say finally, my chest tightening. He doesn't even acknowledge my presence—just keeps his face in his hands while the wind stirs his hair. "I'm so sorry."

Tristan's voice is muffled but there's an edge to it. "You tore my sister's throat out, Charlotte. Sorry isn't going to cut it."

Ten seconds in and Tristan has already dealt the fatal blow. I sigh through my nose, beating back a fresh wave of guilt. Tristan retreats further into himself, tucking one knee to his chest, and he looks so young, curled up like this. Angry. Broken. All because of me.

"It was an accident," I say quietly, and Tristan scoffs.

"Like that girl on the wharf was an accident?"

My heart trips over itself as I remember the day I met Tristan on the Embarcadero—when the sun made an unexpected appearance and had me cowering in the shadows of a trendy coffee shop. The poor nurse who stopped to help me never saw it coming.

I wince. "How did you know that was me?"

"Because I'm *smart*." Tristan lifts his head and glares at me, his eyes damp and red. "And it was obviously you in that video. I can't believe I didn't see it before."

Right. The *video*. The one that showed me *very clearly* killing that girl. The one that Konstantin most likely captured himself. I shudder.

"Why didn't you say anything?"

"Frankly, because it was none of my business," he says, his voice thick with accusation. "I'm not naive enough to believe you've never killed anyone. You're a *vampire*. I'm just grateful it wasn't me you decided to emaciate that day."

My face falls, my chin hitting my chest. This conversation is turning out to be just as bad as I expected. Worse, even.

"Look," I say, more than a little exasperated. "I don't expect you to forgive me, but we're going to have to be civil. You're part of this now, and as long as Konstantin is still out there, you're in danger. I'm not going to let you out of my sight."

"Is that supposed to make me feel better?"

"Yes."

Tristan stares down at his lap, fingering the guitar pick at his wrist with its tiny inscription: *Make your own luck, Lemongrass.* The misery in his expression brings new tears to my eyes; gone is the sunshine, the warmth, the carefree disposition that once radiated from him. All that's left is an emotionless gray sky.

"Would you really do it?" he asks softly.

I frown. "What?"

"Compel me. Would you—" Tristan sucks in a breath. "Could you make me forget that it was you?"

Shock shivers through me, followed by distant horror. "No, Tristan. Never."

He laughs scornfully and looks out over the ocean. "Figures. The vampire murderess has grown a conscience. That sure would have been handy the night you killed Alison."

"Shut up," I snarl, startling myself. "Don't presume to know *anything* about what happened that night."

"Then tell me," Tristan says on an exhale, sounding almost reluctant.

Alison's gold eyes flicker in my memory. She was so beautiful, lying on the cobblestones surrounded by a halo of orange curls. And her smile . . . warm and fleeting, like the last dying rays of an autumn sunset.

The universe gave me you.

"I really don't think that's a good idea." My voice is thin. "It wasn't—"

"*Please.*" The word scrapes through Tristan's throat, like the act of saying it causes him pain. "I've waited so long, Char. I have to know."

The rawness in his voice destroys what little conviction I have. Sighing, I press my palms to my eyes, not daring to look at him while I recount the details of his sister's death.

Golden Gate Park. A spring storm. The crash of thunder that made Alison jump, and the knife that sliced across her palm. The tang of her blood in the air. And the hunger that overtook me, stealing all rational thought.

"I—I acted on pure instinct." I force the words out, hating myself more and more with each stunted syllable. "I would have killed her outright if I hadn't heard your voice through her phone. You snapped me out of it, somehow. Alison was still alive but . . . I knew she wasn't going to make it. So I Compelled her. I told her that she wasn't in any pain and that everything was going to be okay. "

I drop my hands, letting my head fall backward. The stars stare down at me impassively. A lump forms in my throat as I turn to face Tristan, who gazes at the distant horizon with an unreadable expression.

"Were you there when—" His voice catches, eyes shining. He clears his throat. "When she died?"

The moment comes back to me in a rush, and I can practically hear the soft sigh of Alison's last breath. I nod, yanking on my hair, twisting it into a braid only to let it unravel.

"She said I was *nice* to stay there with her. I didn't have the heart to deny it." I chew on the insides of my cheeks, then add, "You told me once that Alison and I might have been friends if she were still alive. I can't help but wonder if, for a few minutes that night, we were."

Tristan claps a hand to his mouth and hoists himself to his feet, striding purposefully toward the house, then back. He looks down at me, a touch of wildness about him.

"Compel me."

I stand too, fighting back a flare of panic. Tristan paces in agitation, creating ruts in the grass with his bare feet. With the wind, the damp earth, and Tristan's short sleeve shirt, he must be freezing.

"No, Tristan. I'm not going to do that."

He pauses mid-stride. *"Please."*

I want to go to him. I want to wrap my arms around his chest and tell him it's going to be okay, like I did with Alison. But I can't. Instead, I ball my hands into fists.

"You're not thinking straight," I say, tamping down my anxiety. "I'm not going to erase your memory."

Tristan snarls, throwing his hands in the air. "Oh, come on. You've done it before."

"Why is this so important? Why do you want to forget?"

"Because I'm *falling for you,* Char!" Tristan cries, all anguish and despair. "And *God,* I'm falling hard."

Groaning, he strides forward and takes my face roughly with both hands, his fingertips digging into my skin, his touch like fire. I seize his wrists, holding him tight, and swallow a sob as he presses his forehead to mine, too hard. Like he knows it will be the last time. Moonlight glints in the tears that stream down his face. I ache to brush them away—to kiss the salt from his cheeks and smooth the deep crease from his brow.

Here, in the dark, our little world is crumbling around us—the one far-removed from reality. Where it's just the two of us. Where we can just *be*.

But I've been kidding myself this whole time. There is no world for me and Tristan. Just my world . . . and his.

"Please," he whispers. "I can't do this. There's a part of me that wants to tear your heart out, and another . . ." He exhales sharply, almost a laugh. "Another part of me wants to kiss you into oblivion."

I laugh once, dejectedly, daring to wrap my arms around Tristan's chest. He doesn't pull away but he stiffens, his breaths shallow and rough.

"I'm so sorry," I whimper, palming his cheek. Brushing my thumb over his lips. Smoothing my hand over his hair, then tangling my fingers in the silken strands at his nape.

Tristan releases a strangled sob and squeezes his eyes shut, taking a shaky breath before he yanks himself away. Freezing wind buffets his hair as he stalks back into the house without another word. It's only a few seconds before my legs give out and I slump to the ground.

Tristan's voice is quiet and desperate as he pleads with Rayna to Compel him. She says no—and so does everyone else. Even Noah.

I watch through the floor-to-ceiling windows as he climbs the staircase and storms into a bedroom, slamming the door behind him. There's the sound of breaking glass, a thump, an anguished scream. And then everything goes quiet.

◊　◊　◊

I kneel on the damp ground for what feels like hours. Long enough that my feet fall asleep and I no longer notice the wind. The stars are still watching me, twinkling dispassionately, reminding me of how small I am in the grand scheme of things. How little I matter.

It's amazing how someone so small and insignificant can ruin so many lives.

The memory of Alison's death is playing on a never-ending loop in my head, and I do nothing to stop it. I simply relive that night over and over—the scent of her blood, the uncontrolled hunger, the bite of cold rain against my skin. Alison's pleading voice, then the sigh of relief as I absorbed her pain. As I internalized it, held onto it, and let her die in the comfort of a kind stranger's arms.

Blessed by the universe, she said. But me? I was cursed by it.

CHAPTER 58

WHEN I FINALLY GET THE nerve to go back inside, I find Noah alone in the living room with a laptop balanced on his knees. He pauses what he's doing long enough to glare at me, and I offer a hesitant smile. Glowering, he makes a show of hiding his face behind the edges of his hood.

Low voices from the kitchen catch my attention and I follow them, walking in on a hushed conversation between Kaleb and Xander.

"Who do you think will show up?" Xander asks, arms crossed over his chest. His neck is still oozing slightly, but he does seem to be putting more weight on his foot. Maybe he finally decided to eat something.

Apprehension creases Kaleb's forehead. "We have no way of knowing until we get there."

"Get where?" Their heads whip in my direction as I saunter into the kitchen, skirting the pile of splintered wood left over from my tussle with Noah. I retrieve a blood-filled bottle from the fridge and toss it to Xander, who ruefully snatches it out of the air. "It sounds like the two of you are going on a secret mission that no one else is supposed to know about. Am I right?"

Kaleb and Xander share a sideways glance, brows quirking in silent conversation. The exchange is effortless. Practiced. It seems that seventeen years of working together has honed them into a well-oiled machine. Knowing the truth about their relationship paints them in a whole new light: I'm not just looking at my friend and my brother, but the Alpha and Beta vampires of San Francisco. The thought of it sets my nerves on edge.

"We have a meeting," Kaleb says, "with the Lesser Alphas."

"We're trying to gauge who is still on Kaleb's side and who has defaulted to Yara." Xander sneers through her name, and I take it he's been informed about the coup. Metal and salt fill the air as he twists the top off his bottle and takes a long drink, and I practice keeping my fangs sheathed. "As far as we can tell, she still has a lot of dissenters. The underground is restless."

I smirk, hopping up to sit on the island. "Diving right back into our courtly Beta duties, I see."

Xander presses his lips together. "It's my job, Lottie."

"Kaleb wouldn't give you a bit of sick leave?"

Xander just scowls, but Kaleb narrows his eyes.

"Believe me," the Alpha grumbles, "it wasn't from lack of trying."

Another silent exchange between the two of them, their expressions both frustrated and bemused. They're doing nothing to hide their camaraderie now, and it's like a bit of weight has been lifted from Xander's shoulders. He's been hiding this part of himself for so long—the part that still cares about Kaleb; the part that *works* for him—and I can only imagine the relief he must feel, not having to hold back anymore.

"So," I muse, kicking my heels against the cabinet below me, "when do we leave?"

Kaleb frowns. "We?"

"Yes, *we*." I jump off the island and square my shoulders. "I'm coming with you, obviously."

Xander nods. "Okay."

"I know you don't want me there," I say with an exasperated sigh, "but I think you two owe me after—" The words die on my tongue. "Wait. What?"

"Okay." My brother's mouth twitches.

"We leave in twenty minutes," Kaleb says without hesitation, looking from Xander to me with a surprising amount of warmth. "Arm yourselves accordingly. We have to assume the worst: this could very well turn into an ambush."

He strides out of the kitchen and I turn to Xander, who stares after Kaleb with a pensive expression.

"You actually want me to come?" I ask quietly.

"I'm your brother, aren't I?" Xander pauses for a beat before pressing a quick kiss to my hair. "It's time I start acting like it."

And then he follows Kaleb out of the room, leaving me alone with my jaw on the floor.

◇　◇　◇

Knowing Kaleb, I expected this meeting to be somewhere fancy, like a hotel ballroom or a theater—maybe even the Majestic, where he holds his annual Halloween party. But we're stuffed into the lowest level of an abandoned parking structure, surrounded on four sides by oozing concrete walls. It could probably only hold about twenty cars, its size and its uncomfortably low ceiling triggering a bout of claustrophobia. The only light comes from a dim emergency bulb in one corner, the two exits shrouded in shadow, and I cough at the nauseating scent of grime and mold.

Though Henry did tell me a few things about the Lesser Alphas, I still didn't know what to expect when we arrived. He only mentioned two other Lessers, but there are six vampires here. Five are strangers, but one familiar face stands out, her black hair chopped into a severe asymmetrical cut: Mei Feng, an old acquaintance from New York, wears a pair of gold silk palazzo pants with a red halter top, and her slanted eyes meet mine with open hostility. I offer a hesitant smile but she doesn't return it.

"Why didn't you tell me Mei was in San Francisco?" I hiss at

Xander, still trapped in Mei's narrow-eyed stare.

Xander leans close. "I didn't think it was necessary."

"You do remember the *baijou*, don't you?"

"Ah yes," he replies with a snort. "How could I forget? Destroying her precious liquor cabinet was not one of your proudest moments."

"And Mei has never let me forget it." I glance back at her, eyeing the girl at her side. She's dressed in fitted black clothing with her dark hair slicked back into a tight ponytail, similar to looks I've seen Victoria don. "Who is that?"

"Jia." Xander murmurs. "She's Mei's second."

I nod. "And the others?"

"Scout leaders. They don't have authority, per se, but they help keep an eye on things." He motions toward a brown-skinned woman with the bone structure of a goddess talking to a handsome red-haired boy. "Farrah Eyoh and Robbie Shields. They watch Midtown and the Sunset District." He nods to another pairing: a tan boy with two-toned hair and a petite blonde girl with too-big eyes. "Rhett Babineau and Abigail Dupont—they're practically a matching set. They live in Berkeley, near the university."

"It sure seems like Kaleb needs a lot of help." I mean it as a joke, but Xander frowns.

"There are twelve scout leaders. Which means—"

"Eight aren't here."

A knot forms in my throat and I swallow to dislodge it. Until now, I hadn't given much thought to the idea of Kaleb's allies turning against him. But if Konstantin can get Yara to do his bidding—a woman who has been working for Alphas in the city for eight decades—then it wouldn't surprise me if others have defected as well.

After all, I've been doing everything Konstantin asks. And I don't even *want* to.

"Is anyone else coming?" Xander whispers to Kaleb, who regally surveys the small gathering in a blazer of charcoal velvet. No jeans tonight, it seems.

"It's hard to say," Kaleb responds, inhaling deeply. "I thought—" He stops himself, biting down on the words. "It hardly matters. I will take what I can get."

"So sorry I'm late!" A deep voice echoes through the garage and I turn to see Enzo stalking toward us, an *immortui* in tow. Just the sight of the white-haired boy makes my skin crawl, his pale face looking especially gray in the dim light. I rise to my toes, ready for a fight, but he stays close to Enzo's side as they stop near Rhett and Abigail. The *immortui* boy scans the room slowly, taking everything in, and I fight the urge to hide from his insidious black eyes.

Kaleb exhales through his nose, his shoulders relaxing slightly. The movement makes the velvet of his blazer shimmer. "Good of you to join us, Lorenzo. Diego."

Somehow, giving the *immortui* a name humanizes him more than I'd like.

"Always a pleasure, my liege," Enzo says, bowing with a flourish.

Enzo looks less like a pirate tonight and more like the hero in a romance novel. He's wearing dark jeans with a brown leather jacket over a white t-shirt, his hair tousled and his beard freshly trimmed. Even his accent seems less prevalent, like the version of him we met at Fort Point was nothing but a kid playing make-believe. I do notice, however, that he has an ancient-looking revolver holstered at his hip. He gives me a little thumbless wave and I tense, worried he'll try to retaliate after I shoved that knife through his ribs, but he only grins when I respond with two enthusiastic thumbs up.

"I suppose we should get started," Kaleb says, clapping his hands together. Whispers cease as all eyes fix on the Alpha. "As I'm sure you're all aware, there was an insurrection a few nights ago, led by Yara Carvalho."

Farrah scoffs, her afro bouncing as light catches the glitter on her indigo blouse. Something about her is familiar, but I can't put my finger on it.

"Doesn't surprise me," she says. "That woman has been after your position for years."

"If only it were that simple." Kaleb tucks both hands in his pockets to hide the tiny tremor in them. "The coup may have been led by Yara, but it seems she has been in Konstantin's employment for quite some time."

Murmurs ripple through the group, and a few of them exchange knowing glances.

"What does that mean?" Robbie asks, fixing Kaleb with a hard glare. "Is *Konstantin* Alpha now?"

Farrah rolls her eyes. "Like you care, Robbie. You've hated Kaleb from the beginning. Why does it matter which asshole is bossing you around? They're both assholes either way."

"Robbie, Farrah, *please*—" Kaleb starts, but Mei interrupts.

"You should show your Alpha more respect," she snaps, eyeing the two belligerent scout leaders. "Do you think *Yara* will provide you with better opportunities than Kaleb? Do you think Konstantin will continue to grant you any kind of power?" Robbie sneers while Farrah opens her mouth, but she closes it again, both of them settling into uncomfortable silence. Mei nods sharply. "That's what I thought."

"I, for one, think you are a *fabulous* Alpha," Enzo chimes in, all bravado. "I am, and have always been, your humble servant."

"Can it, Enzo," Xander snaps. "No one cares what you think."

I bite back a laugh, but it seems I'm the only one with a sense of decency. The other vampires—even Mei—snicker at Xander's comment. Enzo's expression darkens.

"Alexander," Kaleb chides, but Jia steps forward.

"Where is Henry?"

Kaleb stills, taking a moment to compose himself before speaking. "Henry was killed last night."

There are a few shocked gasps and Jia falls back a step. I squeeze my eyes shut for a few seconds. Hearing Kaleb state it so bluntly feels a bit like getting stabbed with a hot poker.

"What happened?" Mei asks quietly, and I think I hear a touch of sadness in her impassive tone.

"Konstantin happened," Xander growls, absently bringing a hand to his throat. The others track the movement, Rhett's gaze lingering a bit too long on the angry red wounds above his shirt collar. "He sent one of his people to facilitate an ambush, and she—" He swallows hard, unease sparking in his eyes.

"It doesn't matter exactly what happened," I say, burying thoughts of Mira, "only that Konstantin was behind it."

"Who are you to speak here?" Rhett asks, crossing his arms in disdain. "Did Kaleb take mercy on another stray?"

My hackles rise, but Kaleb puts a staying hand on my shoulder.

"This is Charlotte," he says in a warning tone. "She is Alexander's sister and an integral addition to this council. Speak to her that way again and you'll lose your tongue."

Kaleb's words bring a flush of warmth to my chest. *Integral,* he said. If I had a nickel for every time someone called me *integral,* I'd have . . . well, I'd have one nickel. But it's more than I had yesterday.

Rhett stares back at Kaleb defiantly, but he recoils slightly under his Alpha's gaze. Abigail sends a scrutinizing look my way and I waggle my fingers in greeting, her eyes flashing with sharp amusement.

Kaleb straightens, his emerald sparking as he reclaims the conversation. "Yara has declared herself Alpha, but we must assume that she is under Konstantin's influence. All of you understand the implications of this."

The scout leaders murmur to one another warily but the Lessers retain their poise. Enzo rests a hand on his revolver while Mei's dark eyes flicker between Kaleb and Xander.

"He has been Siring fledglings to do his bidding," Kaleb continues, "and their numbers are increasing exponentially. It is becoming a problem not only in the vampire community, but for the humans as well." He pauses, a touch of trepidation in his expression. I wish I could help him, but I can only watch as he grasps at the last fragile pieces of his carefully-built world before it crumbles around him.

"Yeah, let's talk about the fledglings," Farrah says. "I've found fourteen in the last week alone. And that's just in Sunset!"

Rhett snorts. "You think that's bad? I live on a college campus. Vampirism is spreading faster than an STD."

Enzo chuckles, Diego following suit. There's a strange kind of mirror effect between the two: every time Enzo shifts—even slightly— the *immortui* does it too. Like he's Enzo's pale shadow. I suppose that has to do with the creepy blood bond Kaleb told me about.

"So, the fledglings are Turning others now? It isn't just Konstantin?" I ask. I find myself leaning forward, desperate for information. Wanting to know *everything*. "Why aren't you all teaching them how to, I don't know, *not* to Turn people? Xander does it all the time."

"It's easy when we only have to deal with a few rogues every year," Abigail says, grimacing. "We can barely keep track of this many at once, let alone train them before they have the chance to Turn anyone else."

Kaleb scrubs at his jaw. His line of sculpted stubble is almost long enough to be considered a beard, and it makes him look about ten years older. I'm not sure if I've ever seen him with more than a five o'clock shadow.

"If Konstantin doesn't turn the fledglings himself," he muses, "they aren't Sired to him. Therefore, many are still malleable. We could use that to our advantage."

"Possibly," Farrah says. "But the media has caught wind of it and they're labeling it as a disease. An epidemic. People are already leaving the city in droves and there are whispers of setting up police barricades on the main highways in and out of the Bay Area."

"Barricades?" The idea has me raising an eyebrow. "Do they really think that will keep the fledglings in?" If anything, it will make them more eager to get out. Fewer humans means less blood, which means fledglings may get desperate and start feeding on other vampires. I would rather deal with a thousand fledglings than a small horde of *immortui*. Enzo seems to have the same thought because his expression sours, his mouth turning down.

Farrah continues. "A few people at the station are throwing around the term 'zombie apocalypse.'"

The *station*. That's where I've seen her before. "You're a reporter, aren't you? From channel four?"

She flashes a too-white grin. "I remind Kaleb every day how lucky he is to have someone on the inside."

There's a small *thud* from above us—something hitting the ground on one of the upper levels. Xander starts speaking and I tune him out as I listen for another sound, but the garage stays silent. Still, unease flickers in my chest.

"Are you *sure* that all this San Francisco Vampire nonsense is Konstantin?" Farrah asks. There's a spark of fear in her eyes, mingling with something like guilt. "You haven't actually seen him, have you?"

Kaleb clenches and unclenches his jaw. "I have. Unfortunately. Alexander and Charlotte can attest."

"Why is he even here?" Rhett asks sardonically. "I hardly think you're a threat to him."

Kaleb inclines his head, his lips curling into a threatening sneer that brings shadows to his eyes. The room recoils.

"Do explain," he says through gritted teeth.

"Explain what?" the scout leader asks, cringing a bit as though regretting his comment.

"Why you think I am so inferior to Konstantin."

Rhett pales, his mouth flapping a few times as he searches for an answer. "I didn't—I wasn't—"

"I'm sure Rhett didn't mean you any disrespect," Enzo interjects, his eyes glinting. "It's just that Konstantin is infamous. And you're, well . . . you're *you*."

Anger surges through me and I take a step toward him, ready to throw hands. "Disrespectful piece of—"

Xander grabs me by the arm. "Lottie, don't."

Enzo grins, his attention locked on Kaleb. "We both know there was only one person Konstantin truly cared about, and Miss Vesely has been dead for ages." He pauses to examine his nails before adding, "Hasn't she?"

The others exchange curious glances while Kaleb looks on with an air of disinterest.

"So you *do* know Rayna," I say, glaring at Enzo.

"Of course I do, *bellezza*. I know everyone."

Farrah frowns. "Who is Rayna?"

"Does it matter?" Rhett scoffs. "She was probably just one of the bastard's whores."

Kaleb bristles at the same time a laugh echoes through the darkness, deep and sultry and horrifyingly familiar. My heart slams against my ribs, my nerves sizzling with anticipation, with fear, with bone-chilling dread. Tension spikes in the room as cold seems to permeate the air, bringing with it a damp breeze and a sharp whiff of ozone.

There's a shuffling footstep. Another. A pale form takes shape in the shadows, materializing in front of us like a nightmare come to life. He locks eyes with me, his mouth splitting into a fanged, manic smile, and my blood runs cold.

Konstantin.

CHAPTER 59

IN 1945, I READ *DRACULA* for the first time. As a vampire myself, I had long been a fan of the story after seeing it on stage, then again in the campy movie starring Bela Lugosi. I thought it was funny to see our kind portrayed in such a melodramatic way. Most of it was completely ridiculous. Comical, even.

It wasn't until I read the book that I realized just how much I had been missing. First, and most notable, was the fact that the Dracula on page had bone-white hair and a mustache. A damn *mustache*.

Not only that, but the versions I had seen left out the unsettling nature of Count Dracula—the way he seemed so effortlessly charming, but also inherently dangerous. The way he acted and dressed like a normal man, but still managed to instill fear in everyone who crossed his path. The way there was always something *off* about him that sent chills up Mina Harker's spine. Up *my* spine. It's a feeling I've never quite been able to describe—disturbing, yes, but somehow wildly fascinating.

For weeks after I finished reading, I could see the man's face when I closed my eyes. I could feel his stare on the back of my neck, bringing goosebumps to my skin. I mentally poured over Jonathan Harker's journal entries, intrigued and unsettled and downright unnerved by one particular sentence: *The last I saw of Count Dracula was his kissing his hand to me, with a red light of triumph in his eyes, and with a smile that Judas in hell might be proud of.*

Now, as I watch Konstantin stagger from the shadows, I'm overcome by his similarities to the monster in the storybook. The same light in his eyes. The same dangerous smile, nothing short of predatory.

Only this time, my gnawing dread is far worse than anything Bram Stoker's masterpiece instilled in me. Because this monster isn't one from the stories. This monster is *real.*

The parking garage has gone ominously still as Konstantin jolts to a halt, scrutinizing us with narrowed, devious eyes. He's dressed simply tonight in dark jeans and a gray collared shirt, his ashy hair tousled and his signature gold watch gleaming at his wrist. There's a strange asymmetry in the way he holds himself, like he's a marionette with missing strings. His left shoulder is too high, scrunched toward his ear, while the same arm hangs limp, his hand twitching ever so slightly. I've seen him favor his left side before, but never like this—never so *obvious.* It makes me wonder if he has some kind of chronic injury, and just how much worse it is after Rayna slammed her fist into his back.

Xander steps forward to flank Kaleb, and I take up a place on the Alpha's other side. I expect one of them to protest—to shove me aside like they usually do—but Kaleb simply takes my hand while a growl grates in Xander's chest.

"Don't stop on my account," Konstantin says darkly, glaring daggers at Rhett. "I would love to hear more about your opinion of my 'whore.'"

It takes me a few seconds to remember what we were talking about, then I snort. "So you admit that you're a bastard?"

The words are out before I can stop them, and Kaleb's hand spasms, gripping mine too tightly. Xander abandons his usual condescending glare for a look of dull horror. Before anyone has a chance to speak, Konstantin makes a low sound of amusement, his eyes glinting.

"You would know."

I suppress a growl of my own. Visions of the cliffside flash through my mind: his wicked grin, his unyielding commands, the pure terror on

Tristan's face as he was thrown over the edge.

Kaleb glances at me sidelong, his grip easing slightly, but not completely. *Do not antagonize him, Charlotte.*

"Why are you here, Kostya?" he asks, his tone all jagged ice. "I've never known you to attend a meeting to which you weren't invited."

Konstantin laughs sharply. "Of *course* I was invited," he says in a mockery of Kaleb's British accent. "How else would I have known about it in the first place?"

"That's true," Enzo chimes in, grimacing. "How *did* you know?"

Kaleb shoots him a scathing look and the Lesser Alpha snaps his mouth shut.

"Is it so hard to believe that I have *friends*?" Konstantin asks Enzo with an exaggerated pout. He motions behind him, hand twitching, and his brow quirks as he gives Kaleb a once-over. "Not everyone favors your pathetic Alpha. Or should I say, *past* Alpha?"

Yara appears to Konstantin's left, followed by Mira on his right. Behind them, at least a dozen other vampires emerge from the shadows. One of them is Mateo—the asshole who Turned Noah—but the others are unfamiliar, ranging in age and appearance. They stand in loose pairings, making my stomach flip. I glance at Xander, who has gone bone white.

"Are those—"

"The remaining scout leaders and their seconds?" he finishes, his voice low and tight. "Yes."

Kaleb eyes them all carefully, his gaze pointedly skipping over Konstantin. He glares in accusation at a man with bronze skin and ornate tattoos covering his arms. The man stares back rigidly for a few long seconds before his face drops in shame.

"It doesn't matter *how* we found out about the meeting," Yara says through a sneer. Her *femme fatale* aura is stronger than ever tonight, her fitted black dress accentuating what were already quite a few gifts from the demonic powers-that-be. Red flashes from her Louboutin heels. "What does matter is the fact that I should have been told about it. I am your Alpha now, and you will all—"

Her next words are cut off as Konstantin backhands her across the face. I bite back a gasp as she stumbles sideways. No one bothers to help her as she catches herself against the wall, a manicured hand pressed to her cheek and blood leaking from the corner of her mouth. Her cheeks redden with embarrassment and she hastily wipes the blood away.

"I apologize for the woman's outburst," Konstantin says, almost smiling at Kaleb. "As I'm sure you know, she can be quite the self-righteous bitch."

No one moves—no one *breathes* except Yara, who looks like she's trying to decide whether to fight back or run. Ultimately, she does neither, just swipes another drop of blood from her lip and smooths her hands down the front of her dress. She straightens to attention but doesn't move to reclaim her place at Konstantin's side.

Kaleb grinds his teeth together. "Get to the point, Konstantin. What do you want?"

Konstantin's left hand spasms. "Your head on a spike."

Mira's bell-like laugh echoes hauntingly through the garage and I drop Kaleb's hand, reaching behind him to take Xander's instead. My brother clings to me, fingernails digging into my skin. Konstantin doesn't seem bothered at all by Mira's interruption. Instead, his gaze clashes with Kaleb's and he sighs dramatically.

"You never were any fun," he practically whines, but it's too pointed to be anything but menacing. "If you must know"—he takes a few jolting steps to move around us, his attention shifting to the group of vampires still loyal to Kaleb—"I am here to let all of you know that my offer still stands."

"What on earth are you talking about?" Kaleb asks slowly.

Konstantin shrugs in attempted nonchalance, but the movement is stiff. Pained. "I approached them all a few years ago with a promise: denounce their precious Alpha, or die."

Enzo snorts and it's echoed by Diego. "I think you're barking up the wrong tree, my friend."

"Yeah," Farrah adds, eyeing the scouts behind Konstantin with disgust. A few of them have the decency to look ashamed, but the rest only glare back. "If we were going to betray Kaleb, we would have done it a long time ago."

Mei nods in silent agreement, followed by Jia and Robbie. Only Rhett and Abigail remain motionless, gazes lingering on Kaleb for a too-long moment. Konstantin jumps on the hesitation.

"You two have never liked him," he hisses through a twisted grin. "I've heard the things you whisper to your little friend, Sayid." The tattooed man behind him winces and Mateo snickers. "Surely you wouldn't risk your lives to support Kaleb and his cowardly, insipid rules."

Kaleb watches the pair with an expression of careful ambivalence, even as one of his hands is yanking hard on his buttons, the other wrapped tightly around the gold hilt of a dagger at his hip. It's clear that we're already outnumbered—that Konstantin has stolen more allies from Kaleb than he had expected—but he needs to hold onto as many as he can. If Rhett and Abigail defect, that will be two fewer vampires on his side—and two more on Konstantin's.

Rhett cocks an eyebrow, making a show of crossing his arms. "Whether we like Kaleb or not is irrelevant."

"We don't have to like him," Abigail adds, "to know that he's the best damn Alpha we've had in a century. And he's a hell of a lot better than *you*."

A slow exhale is Kaleb's only indication of relief.

Konstantin's lip curls back to reveal his fangs and he shifts his weight slightly, making Mira bristle and sending a ripple of agitation through the garage. In response, Xander takes a defensive stance in front of Kaleb while Enzo and Mei join him, the others moving to form a loose semi-circle between Kaleb and Konstantin. Snarls build in their throats as they brace themselves, ready to lay down their lives for their Alpha.

In contrast, the vampires behind Konstantin remain still as statues. They only watch him in anticipation, waiting for the signal to attack. If they do, we're all dead.

I shove forward until I'm standing between Xander and Enzo, releasing my own snarl of defiance, of fear, of fury. Konstantin smiles languidly and blows me a mocking kiss, and I mime catching it and crumpling it in my fist. Kaleb hisses my name and my brother grabs at my wrist but I yank it away, walking forward until I'm standing in the middle of neutral territory, halfway between Kaleb and Konstantin. Two Alphas. Two brothers.

Konstantin has the audacity to laugh at me. "Hello, love. How is that little human of yours?"

Fury roils in my gut but I plaster on what I hope is a sincere smile.

"It doesn't have to be this way," I urge, looking straight into his eyes. They're at once wild and focused, confident and panicked. "What happened between you and Kaleb is ancient history, and you already know Rayna is never coming back to you. There is nothing left for you here."

With a slight twitch of his shoulder, Konstantin takes a few predatory steps forward, not stopping until we're breathing the same air. His pupils are blown wide as he takes me in and his tongue makes a slow pass over his upper teeth. My heart stutters involuntarily.

"Ancient history, hmm?" he murmurs, sliding his arm around me. It takes all I have to stay still as his icy fingers slip beneath the hem of my jacket. Xander and Kaleb growl behind me. "Tell me: how much do you truly know about what happened between me and Kaleb?"

I swallow, not daring to breathe too loudly. Not wanting to do something that might set him off. The touch of his fingers against my skin brings back the memory of dancing with him in our ballroom, when Ty took full advantage of my backless dress. I found him handsome, then—charming, even. But it was all a lie. *Ty* was a lie.

The only truth that exists now is Konstantin: wild and dangerous and beautiful.

"Whatever it was," I say quietly, "it's been over two hundred years. It's about damn time you got over yourself."

Konstantin jerks away as though I slapped him, his nails gouging lines into my side. There are a few gasps, a few hushed words, a few spiking heartbeats. It takes a moment for Konstantin to find his voice, and when he does, every whisper ceases.

"Charlotte, my girl," he says, the words resounding with what seems like genuine hurt. "I thought you, of all people, would understand that Kaleb Sutton is a conniving, selfish, backstabbing *coward*. But it seems he has fooled even you."

Unease prickles over my skin as I sense Kaleb's eyes boring into me.

Konstantin's head tilts to the side and he smiles again. "If this is how it's going to be, then you leave me no choice."

Mira lifts one hand in the air, palm up, and realization slams into me like a freight train.

"Ty, *don't*—"

"Kill them all."

Mira snaps her fingers once and the traitors surge forward, their snarls deafening as they leap into action.

A brunette woman barrels into me and I cry out as we crash to the floor, tumbling over one another in a writhing heap. She pins me on my back with a firm knee to my chest, clamping a strong hand around my throat. Panic takes over and I thrash against her hold, kicking and clawing at anything I can reach. I've grown too used to fighting inexperienced, wild fledglings, but this woman was one of Kaleb's most trusted—she is *far* from inexperienced. Her grip tightens, her fingers digging into my throat, and I brace myself for the moment she'll tear my throat out. For the mortal injury I won't be able to heal from. Nails pierce my skin and I see white.

"Helena!" Konstantin barks over the mayhem. "Not her."

The pressure on my neck releases and I cough reflexively, curling onto my side. The woman—Helena—sneers down at me before darting away, disappearing into the throng of fighting vampires.

Groaning, I push myself into a sitting position and touch a hand to my throat, wincing at a sharp, throbbing pain on either side of my windpipe. Battle rages around me and I barely avoid being trampled as I drag myself into a corner, waiting for the pain to subside.

Even though we have Kaleb, Xander, Enzo, and Mei on our side, we're outnumbered nearly two to one. In addition, I can see that the four of them have no desire to kill any of the defectors. They are their friends, after all. Unfortunately, Konstantin seems to have trained loyalty out of them. I watch as a woman yanks Robbie's arms behind his back while another claps her hands on either side of his head and wrenches it sideways. Blood explodes into the air and the women grin as Robbie's severed head cracks against the ground, his body slumping in the opposite direction.

For a few seconds, Farrah's furious scream is all I can hear.

"Kostya, stop this!" Kaleb cries from somewhere in the darkness. "*Please!*"

The only response is a wicked laugh.

"There you are."

I startle, looking up to see Yara staggering toward me. Her hair is a tangled mess and one of her heels has been snapped off. There's a manic smile on her face that seems strangely uncharacteristic, and it sends a shiver through me. I scramble to my feet but have quite literally backed myself into a corner. There's nowhere to run.

"What do you want?" I ask hoarsely, my throat raw and sore. "Here to chastise me for loitering?"

Yara sneers. "You're Kaleb's favorite. I can't wait to see the look on his face when he finds out I'm the one who killed you."

"Bold of you to assume I won't kill you first."

Yara lunges, fangs out, but something pale streaks across my vision, throwing her sideways. The ghost-like figure tackles her to the ground and buries its face in her neck, quickly joined by a second, then a third. Yara thrashes wildly under the creatures and the sound of her guttural screams brings all the fighting to a screeching halt.

Then suddenly, her screams cut off.

Into the silence, a chorus of rasping voices breathes two blood-curdling words: *"New blood."*

Shit.

Dozens of *immortui* pour into the garage and there's a muffled string of curses from Enzo. I can barely see our people through the mass of brawling bodies, but all thoughts of *us versus them* are lost as we focus our attention on a common enemy.

"Charlotte!" Xander's frantic voice cuts through the din as an *immortui* tears one of Konstantin's people apart. "Lottie, where are you?"

Immortui press in around me. *Breathe,* I tell myself, urging my heart to slow, my lungs to fill. The memory of the Fort Point *immortui* overtaking me—*feeding* on me—is too fresh in my mind. I can still feel the icy chill of their fingers, feel their teeth sinking into me again, again, *again.*

"Here!" I reply, shoving my way through a throng of bodies to follow my brother's voice. There are too many vampires and it's too dark for me to distinguish who is friend and who is foe, so I shove them all aside with equal force. A few sets of claws dig into my arms and I fight back another surge of panic. "I'm right here!"

In my haste, I don't see the scrawny *immortui* boy in my path until I'm two feet from him. He grins with bloodied fangs, his eyes wide and black.

"*New blood,*" he says in a voice like nails on a chalkboard, then lunges.

I throw my hands up to block him, but Xander appears from out of nowhere, slamming into the boy with a snarl.

Something hard connects with my cheek and my head snaps sideways, pain radiating through my jaw. I whirl around to see an *immortui* girl smiling at me, and my instincts take over. Wincing through the beginnings of a pounding headache, I drive my fist straight into her temple and she crumples to the ground.

The garage has descended into full-blown chaos, the air thick with the fetid stench of *immortui* blood mingling with existing grime and the strong, stale scent of vampire blood. My throat is thick with it, and I fight the urge to be sick. It's impossible to know how many *immortui* are here, but I would guess there are at least a few dozen, maybe more. I catch a glimpse of Kaleb in full Alpha mode, his fangs bright and his eyes dark. An *immortui* sinks its teeth into his forearm and he snarls in rage, flinging the creature away like a rag doll.

"Lorenzo!" he barks at the Lesser, shaking blood from his arm. "Call them off!"

Enzo appears at his side, holding an *immortui* at bay with one hand to its throat. "They're not *mine*! I've never seen these bastards in my life!"

All the blood drains from Kaleb's face.

A white-haired girl throws herself at me, teeth snapping, and I shove her away. She's wearing a San Francisco State hoodie, acrylic nails gleaming, and my heart skips a beat as I dodge her fangs. *Tristan's school.* The *immortui* at Fort Point were mostly in old-fashioned clothes, likely indicative of the time period they were originally from. This girl has a smart watch gleaming at her wrist, as do many of the others around her.

A new *immortui?* A vampire has to be truly desperate to feed on their own kind enough to change their biology. There are millions of people in San Francisco; how could there be so many new creatures in a city with so many humans to feed from? Farrah did say people were leaving the city in droves, but surely the blood supply isn't so low that vampires are already resorting to cannibalism.

The *immortui* girl lunges again and there's a dark gleam in her eye: hunger, uncontrolled. Hunger for *me*. I fend her off with a heel to the gut that sends her reeling backward. She careens into Enzo, who has his revolver pointed at another *immortui*. His arms flies sideways, the gun with it.

Bang!

A roar tears from Kaleb's throat that makes the entire garage go still, stunning even the *immortui* into silence. He clutches his shoulder, eyes burning with fury as blood spills between his fingers and soaks the front of his blazer.

I breathe through the tense silence, and it's only seconds before the *immortui* resume their attack.

"Kaleb—" Xander starts, rushing to Kaleb's side, but the Alpha interrupts him with a few unintelligible words.

I join them, tuning out the chaos around us as I put my hand over Kaleb's, blood pulsing under my palm. "What did you say?"

Kaleb has started shaking. The hollows beneath his eyes are a dangerous shade of deep plum, his fangs on full display and his hand in a claw under mine.

"Run," Kaleb hisses, grabbing me by the wrist. *"Now."*

Xander immediately starts shoving *immortui* and vampires aside, clearing a path for Kaleb and me. I don't dare look back, not wanting to know just how many the *immortui* have killed. My foot snags on something and I look down to see a creature's severed head, blackish blood leaking from its neck, its mouth open in a bloody, soundless wail. Nausea surges in my gut and I swallow hard, forcing back the bile that burns my throat.

"Come on!" Xander shouts, dragging me back into action.

We break through a knot of bodies and emerge into empty space, the garage's emergency exit only a few yards away. I sprint after Kaleb and my brother as they fly through the door, but a single word has me stalling at the threshold.

"Wait."

I freeze, turning slowly to see Konstantin locked in a battle with an *immortui*. The man is bigger than he is, but his experience more than makes up for it. On any other night, I imagine Konstantin would be able to dispatch him with a few quick strikes. Tonight, however, he's distracted. Unsteady. His left arm is curled tightly against his ribs, his chest heaving with effort. He manages to knock the *immortui* down with a sharp kick to his ribs, but the man leaps to his feet, refusing to yield.

Konstantin roars before punching a hole straight through the creature's chest.

I clap a hand to my mouth, biting back a cry of surprise. Konstantin breathes heavily for a few seconds, then his gaze snaps up to meet mine, his gray shirt torn and stained with red. At first glance, I see only anger in his eyes, but looking closer, I see he isn't angry at all.

He's *terrified*.

"Charlotte!"

Xander's panicked voice sounds from outside, but I can't tear my attention away from Konstantin. Like we're in a trance, both ready to run. Both refusing to move. It isn't until Mira appears at his side, her face decorated with blood spatters, that I'm finally able to pull away. To *run*.

"There you are," Kaleb says when I fly through the mouth of the stairwell to the street above. His breath is labored and he staggers slightly, drops of red splattering the concrete below him. His entire right side is soaked through with blood.

I catch at his wrist and he winces as Xander hurries over, wrapping his arm around Kaleb's torso. The stairwell behind me remains empty—no *immortui* in sight—and my heart slows a bit, but we're still a few blocks from Kaleb's car and the Alpha is fading quickly.

Something rustles in the shadows behind us, but Xander and Kaleb don't seem to notice. I gently nudge them forward. *Away.*

"Come on," I say, trying to ignore the phantom glow of silver eyes in the back of my mind. "Let's get out of here."

We sprint in the direction of the car, Xander and I supporting our Alpha between us. I can't help but remember the look of terror on Konstantin's face. If I hadn't seen it myself, I might have believed that he orchestrated the *immortui* attack, but there's no mistaking it: he was just as surprised to see them as we were.

And if Konstantin was surprised, then our problems just got a whole lot worse.

CHAPTER 60

Kill or be killed.

A knee to his ribs. Claws at his throat. Konstantin roars as an *immortui's* jaws snap shut on his wrist, her mouth already red with his blood. The pain barely fazes him as he flings her away, her teeth slicing up his arm before she finally releases her hold. She flies across the garage and slams against the wall with a loud *crack*.

There's a ringing in Konstantin's ears. A hitch to his gait. His vision swims as his arm seizes at his side, and he shakes his head to clear the fog, the fear, the creeping threat of madness.

No, he tells himself. *I won't survive it. Not again.*

His shoulder jerks, his head snapping sideways.

He's slipping.

Two *immortui* lunge for him and he spins out of the way, but not fast enough. One of them throws a punch that clips the corner of his jaw, sending a jolt of electricity down his neck. He curses and throws a punch of his own, straight into the *immortui's* nose. The creature howls in pain and stumbles backward, but it is quickly replaced by another.

Panic sizzles through Konstantin's nerves and he clutches at his chest, wincing at the ache that pounds through him with each stiff heartbeat. This was not part of his plan. A full *immortui* invasion is incredibly rare; he hasn't seen one since the sixteenth century, and even then, it was quickly remedied. An outbreak in a city like San Francisco is practically unheard of, and most vampires have never encountered the cannibals before.

He wanted to burn Kaleb's world to the ground, but he never expected it to happen like *this*. It should excite him to see San Francisco falling so quickly, but Konstantin is starting to worry that he might fall with it.

"Come on!"

Konstantin's head whips toward Xander's voice in time to see him drag Charlotte away from the grappling mass, heading for the garage's exit.

"*Wait.*" Konstantin's voice is raw. Disembodied. He isn't even sure he spoke aloud until Charlotte pauses at the threshold, turning to lock eyes with him.

One of the *immortui* near him reaches for his neck but he knocks him back with a sharp kick to the stomach. When the man rights himself, Konstantin wastes no time before tearing a hole through his rib cage.

The *immortui's* blood coats his forearm. His own blood leaks from splits in his knuckles. He forces a few agonizing breaths then dares to look at Charlotte, and the horror in her expression makes his chest constrict.

No. *No.* She is not supposed to be afraid of him. Charlotte *belongs* to him.

"*Charlotte!*" Xander calls after her.

She lingers for a few seconds, as though rooted to the spot. Konstantin regards her carefully, fighting his growing panic. Ignoring the numbness that has already spread down his left arm. He should tell her to stay. He *wants* to. But if he takes her now, she will only resent him. And he can't have that.

Her eyes flicker to something over Konstantin's shoulder and she breaks out of her trance, disappearing in a heartbeat. Konstantin can sense Mira as she presses close to him and he nearly gags at the too-sweet scent of her fear.

"Kostya—"

He puts a hand against her sternum and shoves. With a small cry, she staggers backward a few steps, hurt clouding her expression.

"Leave," Konstantin growls, eyes fixed on the door where Charlotte disappeared.

"But—"

"I said, *leave!*"

The fighting around him ceases for only a moment, but it's enough. Every vampire he took from Kaleb immediately turns and runs, *immortui* chasing after them in a chorus of snarls and twisted laughs.

Mira hesitates before following, flitting away like a fragile little bird.

Kill or be killed.

Konstantin staggers toward the exit. His left leg is tingling now. His ears are ringing. The scent of decay is all around him, making his stomach turn. His hands are sticky with blood. Every step he takes is agony, but he doesn't care. He *can't.*

Because Konstantin will do whatever it takes to keep Kaleb from winning this game. Even if it means putting an end to them both.

CHAPTER 61

Xander floors it through the San Francisco streets, Kaleb's Mercedes gliding smoothly through the shadows. We're surrounded by the reek of vampire blood, made worse by the accompanying scent of *immortui* rot. It will be a miracle if Kaleb can clean the blood from his seats, and even more impressive if he manages to get rid of the smell.

No one speaks. I don't think any of us want to. I can still see the sharp bite of fear in Konstantin's eyes when he told me to wait, and I half-expected him to demand I stay. But he only watched me, head and shoulder twitching, as I ran from the *immortui*. From *him*. I'm not sure what to make of it.

The supports of the Golden Gate Bridge pass by in a blur, distorted by raindrops racing along the windows. I try not to think too hard about the lack of other cars in the city, or the fact that I haven't seen another pair of headlights on the bridge.

It's too quiet. Too empty. Evidence that humans are abandoning San Francisco.

I sit in the backseat with Kaleb, whose labored breathing only grows worse the longer we're in the car. Enzo's gun was apparently loaded with silver bullets, and the shot in Kaleb's shoulder is festering.

"This is . . . ridiculous," Kaleb says between pained breaths, straightening in his seat. "I can . . . barely breathe."

"Ten minutes," Xander says, but Kaleb shakes his head.

"I can't wait that long." The Alpha looks at me, pale eyes bright. "Get it . . . out. Now. I don't care . . . how."

"No, Kaleb," I say. "We'll be back to the house soon. It will be much easier once we're there—"

"We won't have time. The moment . . . we get back . . . we're leaving."

Xander lets off the gas slightly then hits it again, making the car jolt.

"What do you mean?" he asks.

"The *immortui* . . . will soon . . . take over the city." Kaleb winces sharply, then curses under his breath as he shakily shrugs out of his blood-soaked blazer and unbuttons his shirt. It was once white, but has now been stained a striking shade of crimson. "Charlotte . . . get this *damn bullet* . . . out of me . . . and I can explain."

I frown at Xander through the rear-view mirror, then slip a knife from my boot.

"Okay, but it's going to hurt like hell."

Ignoring my shiver of apprehension, I yank Kaleb's shirt to the side, revealing the red-rimmed hole in his already-scarred shoulder. The bloodied skin is puckered and inflamed, and I can practically hear the silver sizzling.

"Charlotte," he barks. *"Now."*

With a deep breath to steady myself, I slide the knife into the wound. A snarl grinds in Kaleb's throat but he swallows it, jaw clenching. I don't see many bullet wounds, and certainly never ones made by silver bullets. Vampires are usually content to let the bullet stay rather than let someone try to dig it out. Hell, I have one lodged somewhere in my hip. I wasn't about to let Pippa come at me with a blade.

My knife scrapes against something, but I can't tell if it's bone or metal. I jab two fingers into the wound to get a better feel, and Kaleb's hand spasms before he fists it on his thigh. His eyes are shut, his teeth grinding, and a deep crease mars his brow.

"Sorry," I murmur through clenched teeth, frowning at the blood streaming between my fingers. It slinks down Kaleb's carefully-scarred torso and soaks into the waistline of his slacks. "But look at it this way: if I weren't here, Nik would probably be doing this. Or, Hell forbid, *Pippa.*"

He smirks, though it looks more like a grimace. "Ah, yes. Because you . . . have so much experience."

My finger brushes something smooth. *Aha.* Kaleb gasps as I adjust the angle of my knife, grinding the tip between the bullet and the rib where it's lodged. I pop it out then catch it between my fingers, yanking them out with a flourish and a new pulse of blood. My knife follows and Kaleb exhales slowly, letting his head fall back.

"Good *Lord,*" he groans, clapping a bloodied hand over his eyes as he sucks in a shuddering breath. "You would think I'd be used to that feeling after four hundred years. As it turns out, it still hurts like a bitch."

I snort, and Xander chuckles in the front seat.

"Wow," I say, wiping the blade clean with Kaleb's discarded blazer before slipping it back into my boot. "I don't think I've ever heard you speak so plainly."

"Yes, well." He drops his hand, glancing at me sidelong. "Perhaps I have been spending too much time with you."

"Never."

"Under the seat," he says, pointing feebly, "is a small cooler. Hand me a blood bag, will you?"

I retrieve one for him and we drive in silence for a few minutes, letting Kaleb drink and catch his breath.

"What did Enzo mean, 'they're not mine'?" I ask into the silence as we make our way through the tree-lined streets north of the bridge.

Kaleb's eyes snap open and he sits up, grimacing slightly, but some of the color has returned to his face.

"I told you about the blood bond," he says, posing it like a question. I nod. "Since Lorenzo arrived here, every *immortui* in the city has been Bound to him and no new creatures have emerged."

"Until now," I say, ice trickling through my veins. "If Enzo doesn't know these *immortui* and they're not Bound to him, where did they come from? I thought a vampire had to be beyond desperate to become a full-blown cannibal."

"That is how it started, yes." Xander catches my eye in the rear-view mirror. "But *immortui* are just another breed of vampire. They can Turn humans the same way we can."

Kaleb nods. "With the number of fledglings Konstantin is creating, they have become increasingly vicious. Less well-trained. They are Turning more and more vampires, driving up the vampire population, scaring the humans away, and lessening the food supply. All it takes is one desperate fledgling to feed on its own kind. Once it becomes an *immortui*—"

"It can Turn new ones," I finish. "And then the cycle continues, just like normal vampirism."

"Thus, the fresh horde that just attacked us," Xander says, hitting the gas hard. "All brand new. All out of control."

Good hell. That's why downtown seemed so empty. Why there were multiple police cars racing through the streets. The humans are terrified because San Francisco really is facing its own version of a zombie apocalypse. I guess Farrah's colleagues aren't far off.

"What now?" I ask as we turn into the safe house driveway. The rain is falling in sheets now, and I hear the first rumblings of distant thunder. "How do we stop the *immortui?*"

Xander puts the car into park and twists in his seat, meeting Kaleb's gaze. The Alpha communicates to him in some unspoken language and Xander purses his lips before nodding.

"We don't," they say together, then Xander hurries out of the car, sprinting for the house's front door.

"What do you mean?" I ask, my adrenaline spiking. "Are we supposed to just let them take over the city? What's to stop them from going further? What does this mean for us?"

Kaleb touches my shoulder softly, concern creasing his brow. "I have no intention of letting this get out of control. But I also under-stand that *immortui* are very dangerous. Not only will they drink your blood, but they will tear you to pieces. I will not let you or anyone else stay here when the threat of an *immortui* takeover is imminent."

I swallow a pulse of dread as I imagine the *immortui*'s teeth piercing my skin, the skeletal strength in their bone-white fingers.

"We're going to leave the city," I say. It isn't a question.

"We're going to leave the city." He opens the car door and steps into the downpour, the rain turning the dried blood on him into red rivulets. "And we must hurry. I no longer trust that we are safe here. Come help gather the others."

Following, I slide out of the backseat and shiver when the rain drenches me immediately. "What about Konstantin?"

I regret the words as soon as they leave my mouth, and I internally kick myself for asking something so stupid. For a moment I wonder if Kaleb might ignore the question, but his eyes narrow slightly, suspicion clouding his expression.

"What about him?"

I press my lips together. "Nothing. Never mind."

"Charlotte." Kaleb takes my hand, pausing for a few seconds to think, like he's choosing his next words carefully. "I have known Konstantin for a long time, and not many people have spoken so freely with him and lived to tell about it." He traps me in his icy gaze, and I swear he can see deep down into my traitorous soul. "I need you to be honest with me: have the two of you been in contact?"

Shame cuts a deep groove through my chest, and my heart spasms under the force of it. *Yes*, I want to say. *Yes, I've been talking to him. I told him everything. Henry's death was my fault. You can't trust me!* But I don't say any of it.

All that comes out is a simple, "No."

Kaleb exhales slowly before raking a hand through his rain-soaked hair, disappointment flashing in his eyes before they cool into calm ambivalence. He nods and, without another word, he turns and hurries to the house, one hand clasped to his healing shoulder. I stare after him as he disappears through the front door, wondering if I just made a huge mistake.

CHAPTER 62

THE HOUSE HAS DESCENDED INTO a flurry of chaos.

When Kaleb asked if anyone knew where we could go, Nik was quick to respond. He told us that he knew of a place that had definitely escaped Konstantin's notice, but wouldn't give any further details.

Which is probably a good thing, because I have been on pins and needles since we made the plan to leave. I want to tell Konstantin, but my phone is dead in the water. Literally. Why I still feel the compulsion to tell him everything, I don't know. It's like I physically can't help myself. Like I'm a puppet on a string, except the strings are claws and dark smiles and flashing eyes.

As of now, Kaleb has made about twenty different phone calls, Rayna is gathering every ounce of alcohol she can find, and Rose was able to coax Victoria into the Maserati. Pippa, after a few minutes of arguing, managed to convince Kaleb to bring Henry's body with us. I've been divvying up blood bags from the cellar and throwing them in various cars—Xander's Maserati, Kaleb's Mercedes, Tristan's Mazda— and I can only hope that it will be enough.

"Are we ready?" Kaleb asks as we all gather in the foyer.

It's a solemn circle—eight vampires, haggard and exhausted, ready to leave yet another "safe" place in blood-stained cars with nothing but a few under-stuffed backpacks. Rayna catches my eye and offers a forced smile, but I don't have it in me to return it.

"Ready," Xander replies, and the others murmur in assent.

A bright flash of lightning illuminates the sky, sending tendrils of electricity through the clouds over the ocean. I watch it fade as the house trembles with the inevitable crash of thunder, and I'm struck with the unmistakable feeling that we're on the cusp of something huge. And I want nothing to do with it.

"Wait," Noah says, frowning. "Where's Tristan?"

My head whips around as I search for the familiar mess of golden waves, but they're nowhere to be seen.

"He must be upstairs," I say, though it feels like a hunk of lead just dropped into my stomach. "I'll go get him. You guys go ahead. We'll catch up."

Xander gives me an uncertain look, but I motion hurriedly to the door.

"Go! I'll be right behind you, I promise."

Kaleb ushers everyone out, glancing over his shoulder to give me a look that says, *Be careful. Move quickly.*

I nod, watching as they disappear into the rain-drenched night. Everyone except Rayna.

"What are you doing?" I ask, not bothering to hide my annoyance.

"I'm not just going to leave you behind."

That startles a laugh from me. "Since *when?*"

Rayna only rolls her eyes, then calls Tristan's name. When there's no answer, she calls again. I join. She heads downstairs while I go up, dread prickling along my skin. I tell myself that Tristan is fine—that he might already be outside—but something feels off to me. Like I'm being watched, yet again.

But Konstantin doesn't know about the safe house . . . right?

I shove my way through a closed bedroom door to find Tristan asleep, buried in a huge pile of blankets. Relief cools the fire in my veins, but it rekindles quickly when I remember what we're doing.

"Tristan," I say, shoving his shoulder. "Get up."

There's a low grumble, followed by the rustle of bedding as he throws a blanket over his head. "Go away."

In response, I grab the corner of the blanket and yank, bringing the entire pile onto the floor. Tristan sits up, bleary-eyed and glaring, his hair a disheveled mess.

"*God*, Char."

"We're leaving." I raise an eyebrow in an attempt at levity, but hostility is coming off him in waves. "Didn't anyone tell you?"

Tristan stares at me bitterly.

"Don't tell me," he drawls. "Konstantin has made yet another move against Kaleb, and this place is compromised. Where are we going this time, hmm? A swanky penthouse? An elusive vineyard? An underwater hotel? I'm getting really tired of these constant threats of death—"

"Tristan," I snap, grabbing a backpack and throwing it at him. He catches it against his chest. "Shut up and *move*."

Something in my tone must spook him, because his eyes widen a fraction before he scrambles out of bed and starts shoving clothes into the backpack. I motion to the hallway as he zips it and throws it over his shoulder.

"I've got Nik and Noah in my car," he says as he squeezes past me, making it a point not to let even our clothes touch. I try not to be offended.

I did kill his sister, after all.

"Uh, no you don't," I say. He stops in the middle of the hallway and glowers over his shoulder. I shrug. "They're with Xander. Everyone else has already left."

Tristan sighs loudly and hurries down the stairs ahead of me, only to find Rayna waiting for us with her arms crossed.

"Took you long enough."

Tristan screeches to a halt. "You're telling me I have to share a car with the two of *you*? Absolutely not. I decline."

"Sorry, pretty boy," Rayna says, grabbing Tristan by the arm. "You can either come willingly or I'll Compel you. It's your choice."

She all but drags Tristan out the front door and he stumbles slightly, looking at me expectantly. I once told him that I would never Compel him, and again when he asked to forget about my confession. But right now, I don't have time to fight him. If it takes Compulsion to get him out the door, I won't stop Rayna from doing it.

When I don't jump to Tristan's defense, his expression sharpens, rain dripping from his hair. Betrayal sparks in his eyes, and they harden to fiery topaz.

Rayna throws Tristan into the backseat of his Mazda then slides into the driver's seat as I climb into the passenger's side.

"Hey," Tristan snaps, "this is *my car.*"

"Not tonight it isn't." Rayna revs the engine to life, flicking on the windshield wipers as thunder rattles the air. "No offense, kid, but I trust my driving skills over yours. Especially if things get dicey."

"Do you think they will?" I murmur, knowing that until we're far from San Francisco, we're not out of the woods.

Rayna peels out, much to Tristan's chagrin, and I watch the safe house shrink in the rear-view mirror. Rain pounds on the roof as we race up the wooded road, trees flashing by in streaks of black.

"You know, Rayna," Tristan muses, "you could end this right now if you gave yourself over to Konstantin. God knows we all wish you would."

My breath catches and Rayna scoffs, affronted, but doesn't let off the gas pedal. I whirl around to face him.

"Are you really going to do this right now?"

Tristan's eyes narrow. "Yes, Charlotte. I am."

"What the hell is wrong with you?"

"Oh, I don't know," he retorts, his tone all venom. "I'm sure if you used your brain for two seconds, you could figure it out."

I laugh once, sardonically. "If *you* used your brain for two seconds, you would know that Rayna would never go with Konstantin, and we would never let her. She may be a pain in the ass, but she's *our* pain in the ass."

"Both of you shut up," Rayna snaps as we fly around a bend in the road. "I swear, it's like I'm watching a soap opera. Charlotte, I don't need you to defend my honor. And Tristan, if you speak to me like that one more time—"

A cry escapes her and she slams on the brakes, throwing me back against the dashboard. I yelp in pain as my ribs creak and I silently curse myself for not wearing a seatbelt. Tristan's expression is indiscernible as his gaze shifts to something over my shoulder.

I glare at Rayna. "What on earth—"

But I stop short when I see the haunted look in Rayna's eyes—the all-encompassing horror that makes the amber burn. Slowly, I turn in my seat just as lightning flashes in the sky above us.

The trunk of a massive redwood is felled ahead, completely blocking the road. Standing in front of it, lightning carving his silhouette in electric white, is Konstantin. His stance is wide and his entire left side is contorted—no doubt from our fight with the *immortui*—and he grins through the storm with the confidence of an apex predator.

Rayna lifts the cross at her neck and holds it like a rosary.

"Get down," I murmur to Tristan without turning, dropping my voice as low as I can. "Get on the floor and do not move. Assume he doesn't know you're here."

Tristan hesitates for a few seconds but does as he's told, quietly unbuckling his seatbelt and doing his best to squeeze onto the limited floor space.

"What do we do?" I whisper to Rayna, but it's Konstantin who answers.

"Get out of the car, love."

His voice is deep and dark, piercing my chest like a freshly-hewn blade. Rayna is still in the driver's seat, the knuckles of her free hand turning white on the steering wheel. And while I know Konstantin is talking to *her*, I feel the urge to listen. To obey.

I open the door.

"What are you doing?" Rayna hisses as I step into the rain.

Konstantin flashes a deadly grin. "Good girl."

I take a slow step forward and the predator does the same. Something wild glints in his eye. His body still carries evidence of the *immortui* attack, but most of the blood has been washed away by the rain; there's a bruise at the corner of his jaw and his arms are decorated with various bites and claw marks. It seems he isn't as invulnerable as he wants us to think.

"I'll admit," Konstantin says through his fangs, "that my plan is going more beautifully than I had hoped. Though I didn't expect the *immortui*. That was a lovely surprise. It makes this whole ordeal all the more sinister, don't you think?"

Lightning flashes again and his left hand stiffens momentarily, fingers contorting into a claw as his shoulder ticks upward. For the first time, I notice something familiar in the movement—something that tugs at my memory, but I'm unable to grasp it.

"What's wrong with your arm?"

Konstantin freezes, head tilting to the side. "That is none of your concern."

"Yes, it is." I frown, my mind working. I feel like I'm touching on something important, I'm just not sure what it is. "I've seen your shoulder twitch like that before. Until last night, I never paid much attention, but then Rayna hit you . . ." I pause when his lips curl into a warning snarl. "What happened to you?"

"Oh, little bird." Konstantin chuckles, his grin turning feral, and his teeth flash in another bright burst of lighting. The smile tugs at my memory again. A scream. A knife. A staggered step and the stench of blood. The glint of fangs in a dark room. "You still haven't figured it out, have you?"

Little bird.

Little bird.

Stars swim in my vision as my feet carry me a step back, then another. I *have* seen that twitch before. I've heard those words. And not just in the past few weeks. Decades—*centuries* ago.

It was the morning of my nineteenth birthday in Belarus—the day that I lost my mother, my brother, my *humanity*. I can still smell Mama's blood. I can see the shadow looming over me, the kitchen knife protruding from his chest, the sharp twist of his smile, the tick of his left shoulder . . .

The taste of blood on his hand.

And his voice: deep and accented, like thunder rolling through a black sky.

You are a pretty little bird. I am sorry I have no place for you.

Another memory, only days ago: *Charlotte is mine. She always has been.*

Nausea roils through me and I barely make it to the side of the road before retching violently into the bushes. Bile scorches my throat. Hot tears sting my eyes.

"It was *you*," I choke out, fighting to regain my composure. I scrub my mouth with the back of my wrist then straighten shakily, staring at my creator. My destroyer.

Konstantin's smile goes crooked.

"There we are," he purrs. His usual swagger is gone, replaced with a sort of manic energy, but his intent gaze doesn't waver. "There's my girl."

The knowledge sinks in slowly, sending heat through my veins, part horror, part humiliation. Konstantin watches me carefully, waiting for me to speak. He has the same silver eyes, the same sharp line to his jaw, the same scar on his lip that I first saw at Pier 39. At the time, they were traits I found alluring, but now I see them for what they really are: marks of the Devil himself.

"You—you killed my mother." My voice cracks with horror. With fury. "You Turned me and Xander."

"A small world, isn't it?" He almost laughs. "Imagine my surprise when I arrived in San Francisco and realized that Kaleb had adopted two of my little protégés."

My anger flashes anew. "You're such a bastard."

"Have I ever claimed otherwise?" Konstantin is suddenly inches from me, his eyes dark. He slides his good hand behind my neck and when he speaks, I can see the deadly tips of his fangs. "Now you see why you are so valuable to me."

"But why *me?* You Turned Xander, too." I swallow, still fighting the urge to bolt. A shiver ripples through me as his thumb strokes my pulse point. "He has more influence than I do, and he's certainly stronger. And, you know, better at everything."

Konstantin chuckles and leans in, his lips grazing my ear. "Xander is not bound to me. Not like you are."

"Bound?" I balk, searching his expression for any sign of deception. But his grin is confident as ever—*earnest,* even—and all the breath rushes from my lungs. A whirlwind of Konstantin's words howls through my mind.

Do it. Kiss me.

Shut up, Charlotte. The adults are talking.

You will tell me all your plans.

Come here, my girl.

On that fateful Belarusian morning, the shadow Compelled me to be still and I obeyed. He fed me his own blood. And then he killed me.

Kaleb has warned me countless times about making such a mistake. He told me to be careful—to avoid Turning a human while they are under my Compulsion. If I do, they will be bound to me. Drawn to me. Compelled to obey my every command.

I saw a tiny glimpse of that bond with Tristan when I screwed up my Compulsion on Halloween.

With a bolt of devastating clarity, I finally understand why Konstantin has kept me close. Why he has been following me—and me *specifically*—for months. For *years.* Why I did everything he told me to do. *Everything.* Even when I knew it was wrong. Even when I was betraying my family. And some little part of me wanted to do it.

Charlotte is mine. She always has been.

Blinking at him, I whimper, "You *Sired* me?"

Konstantin smirks, his hand sliding from my neck to cup my cheek. The gesture should be comforting, but there is no tenderness in his touch. Instead, it feels possessive. Threatening.

"Yes, dear Charlotte," he murmurs, fingertips brushing my cheekbone. "As I told your beloved little human boy, you are *mine*."

My stomach turns over again, but I swallow another urge to be sick. I'm stuck by a chilling realization: my family is not safe with me. Not if I'm Sired to Konstantin. I need to distract him—to give Rayna and Tristan a chance to get away from him. Away from *me*.

"You know," I say, feigning confidence, "you're an idiot."

Konstantin's hand stiffens against my cheek. "I beg your pardon?"

A laugh bubbles out of me. "I'm *Sired* to you! This whole time, you could have asked me about Rayna. You could have demanded I tell you what I know about her. But you were so focused on getting *Kaleb* to talk that you didn't even use me properly."

Konstantin's jaw works in a few slow circles and he drops his hand, letting it rest dangerously at the base of my throat.

"You know, Charlotte," he says, menace coloring his words, "I think I've had enough of your constant insults."

"What are you going to do, *command* me to stop?"

"Believe it or not, I'm not here to strip you of your free will." He sighs through his nose, an attempt at calm. It doesn't seem to work. "I'm simply getting tired of your attitude."

"*You're* tired?" I scoff, hyper-aware of the way Konstantin's hand shifts along my throat. The ways his nails scrape against my skin. "You have *got* to be kidding me. In the past few days, we've been ambushed, overthrown, pushed off cliffs, tortured. We've been doing everything we can to stay vigilant and safe, all while trying to rescue those you deemed worthy of kidnapping. Can you blame me for being a bit obstinate?"

Konstantin shifts forward until our bodies are almost touching, and my nose fills with the metallic, electric scent of him. His eyes drop to my mouth and he smiles mischievously.

"Bring her to me."

My chest constricts, a tug that has now grown all too familiar. I once thought it was my weakness that made me obedient to Konstantin. But I now know it for what it really is: the Sire bond, strong and steady.

And completely irresistible.

"Who?" I ask, dreading the answer.

"Who do you think, love?"

Konstantin backs away, and I follow his gaze over my shoulder. Rayna is standing by the Mazda's open door, a look of disgust and horror on her rain-slicked face. Something tells me that she has been standing there the whole time, watching. Listening. Not trying to help, but rather waiting to see what information she might glean from our conversation.

And now she knows everything.

"Bring me Rayna," Konstantin murmurs, his voice a rasp, "and maybe I'll consider letting the rest of you live."

The hold on my chest tightens, tugging me backward.

"No," I blurt out, forcing my feet to stay rooted. "I won't do that."

"Actually, you will." Konstantin's tone is dark. Triumphant. "I'm sure you've realized that you cannot disobey me, even if you want to. So when I tell you to fetch Rayna for me, I mean go get her. *Right now.*"

It's like a kick to the sternum. I stagger backward, drawn by the invisible cord, and barely catch myself as I whirl around and break into a sprint. Away from Konstantin. Toward Rayna.

She startles, her eyes widening in fear before she bolts into the storm-dark trees.

CHAPTER 63

No. No. No.

The word echoes in my head in time with my heartbeat as I charge after Rayna, feet pounding the pavement like I'm running for my life. And while I know exactly what Konstantin is doing—that he's finally using me to finish this game, once and for all—there's a tiny part of me that *wants* to do what he says.

I shove through underbrush, dodging tree trunks, ignoring the sound of my inner voice screaming to *stop*. My eyes are fixed on the shock of orange hair that darts through the darkness, flashing like a beacon in the storm.

"Rayna!" I yell, shoving off a tree trunk with a burst of satisfaction. I'm gaining on her. "Rayna, stop!"

She doesn't. Instead, she vanishes between one blink and the next. Part of me loves the thrill, familiar after decades of racing with Rayna through the cobbled London streets, using my superior speed to my advantage. It was a competitive streak that pushed me then. Now I am desperate to win, and the hook buried in my chest yanks me forward. Faster. *Faster.*

Chasing the girl Rayna used to be. Hunting the girl she is now.

"Where are you going, Magdaléna?" Konstantin's voice bleeds through the trees, coming from everywhere and nowhere. Terror licks up my spine but I don't stop. I *can't.* "I only want to talk."

Lightning strikes. Thunder crashes. My feet slip and slide through the mucky earth as I gain on Rayna, and I can practically hear the hammering of her heart, smell the fear radiating from her skin. The ache in my chest becomes a sharp pain. A frenzied, physical need.

Bring her to me.

Unfortunately, while I have always been faster than Rayna, she has always been stealthier. She slips in and out of the shadows like she knows them intimately, and I have to concentrate to keep from losing her. I have no idea where she's going but I have to get her back to the road. Back to Konstantin.

Just then, the bastard appears in front of Rayna. She shrieks, skidding to a halt, then retreats back the direction we came. She side-swipes me as she passes and I'm shoved off balance, my forehead slamming into a rough tree trunk. The sharp tang of my own blood fills the air as it drips from the scrapes and into my eyes. Cursing, I scrub it away.

"What are you waiting for?" I look up to see Konstantin standing over me, forcing me back into the tree. The tilt of his smile makes my breath catch. "Go after her. And be quick about it, would you? We can't have her escaping with that little pet of yours."

I clench my teeth as I attempt to fight the command, if only for a second. "Go after her yourself."

Konstantin's eyes narrow. "I could," he says, leaning close. *Too* close. His breath chills the air between us. "But this is *much* more fun."

He doesn't wait for a response before vanishing into the mist.

I run faster, pushing harder with every step, giving myself completely to the bond, letting Konstantin's words command me. Control me.

Bring her to me.

Rayna's feet hit the road just as I fly into the air, landing on her back. She snarls as we crash to the ground, fangs flashing, claws out.

"Lottie, *stop!*" she cries, flipping me onto my back.

"I can't!" Adrenaline courses through me and I throw her sideways, leaping to my feet with a snarl. "I have to bring you to him!"

Rayna scrambles away, wiping blood from a streak of road rash on her chin. I grab at her wrist and she recoils, yanking against my hold, her whole body trembling.

"Don't do this," she whispers, genuine fear in her words.

Konstantin's deep laugh sounds behind me, and we whirl to see him standing with one hand against the fallen redwood tree.

"Rayna, darling," he says, grinning darkly, "you know she has no choice."

My feet move toward him, dragging Rayna with me. She struggles to free herself but I hold fast, even as she wraps her hands around my wrists. Our grips interlock and she swings me around until we've switched places, then she starts shoving me toward the car.

"No!" I shove back, refusing to let go. She has to come with me. *I have to bring her to him.* The desire burns in my chest, becoming more painful by the second, like my skeleton is trying to crawl out of my skin. *"Please.* I don't want to—I have to—"

"Come on, Charlotte!" Rayna fixes a fiery gaze on me, her breath coming in short gasps as I dig my heels into the asphalt. "I should have known you would be too weak to fight this."

I yank hard on Rayna's hands and she yelps, stumbling sideways as she loses her grip on my wrists. The momentum is enough to send her sprawling. Groaning, she props herself up on her elbows and stares up at me, eyes wide.

"What did you just say to me?" I growl.

Rayna's lips press into a thin line and she shoves up from the ground, swiping her hands down her sopping jeans in a fruitless attempt to clean them off. "I said you're weak, and you always have been. I only spent so much time with you because I knew you needed a babysitter." I flinch and she hastily backtracks. "I didn't mean it like *that.*"

"Then how *did* you mean it, Rayna? Were we ever actually friends, or were you having too much fun playing G—" I fight against the knot in my throat, forcing the word out through a guttural, scorching growl. *"God?"*

Surprise flashes in Rayna's eyes. "Of course we were friends, you idiot. But I did spend the majority of our time together trying to save your sorry ass."

I scoff and take a small step toward her. She takes a wary step back.

Trying to *save me*, she says. Like that somehow makes everything okay. In all the years before her "death," Rayna never left me alone. Literally. Everywhere I went, she followed me like a shadow, waiting for me to make a mess. Taking control when I did. Decades passed with me believing she was doing me a favor—that she was being the protective older sister, keeping me safe while I navigated my new life of vampirism.

Why, then, did she leave Xander to his own devices? When Kaleb found us, my brother was caught in a downward spiral, his humanity teetering on the brink of extinction. It took him years to fully recover, but Rayna never felt the need to keep him in check. Somehow, she trusted him. Why didn't she trust me?

Then again, maybe it was never about trust at all.

"You never cared about me," I snarl as I take another step. "You have spent your entire life feeding on *control*. Cowing Kaleb, humiliating Xander, making Nik believe that he was nothing without you. Everything you have ever done is to protect your own interests—to maintain control over the little world you built for yourself."

Rayna crosses her arms. "That's not true—"

"You're selfish and manipulative and controlling, just like Konstantin. We're all better off without you." The anger burning through my veins goes cold. "Maybe you should have stayed dead."

Rayna's lip curls back, revealing her fangs. "You're better without me, are you? Tell me, Lottie, how many people did you murder because I wasn't there to watch your back?" She takes a few bold steps forward in a move that is either incredibly confident or painfully stupid. Our noses brush and I bristle, even as Konstantin's command echoes in my ears. "You should be *grateful* I kept an eye on you like I did. Have you ever stopped to consider the fact that if I were here, you wouldn't have killed Tristan's sister?"

A snarl tears from me and my hand flies to Rayna's throat. She releases a choked whine and digs her nails into my wrist, but she doesn't try to pull away.

"That's just it!" I cry, hot tears pooling in my eyes. Rayna's pulse hammers erratically under my palm. I squeeze harder. "You *weren't* here! You made us believe we couldn't live without you, and then you *left*. You destroyed me with grief and ruined my life in the process. And for what?" The laugh that escapes me is black. Empty. "The pathetic woman you've become isn't even worth my tears."

With my free hand, I slip a silver knife from my waistband.

Bring her to me.

I drive the blade toward Rayna's chest . . .

But she's faster than I anticipate. Her hand flies up and catches my wrist, twisting hard. Changing my trajectory. With a slicing, searing pain, I plunge the knife straight into my own heart.

Heat lances through my chest and I open my mouth to scream, but the sound dies in my throat. My grip goes slack and Rayna catches me against her, her eyes wide and stunned, her throat a mess of mottled purple. In her expression I see a frightened young girl, a vengeful spirit, a ruthless traitor. Numbness sweeps over me as she gently lowers me to the ground, and I can do nothing as my back meets the chilly pavement.

My heart taps out a few agonizing beats, pumping fire into my veins before it goes still. The *world* goes still.

The sound of the storm fades into nothing as I stare, unblinking, into the pouring rain. Huge droplets bite into my skin, water filling my eyes and streaming down my face like tears. Warmish blood leaks from the wound on my chest.

I can't breathe.

I can't *think*.

And Rayna is looking down at me, something like resolve in her expression. Her gaze lingers on me for a few long seconds before she glances up.

"You Sired her," she says matter-of-factly, though a thread of fear winds its way through her words. "That's how you've been tracking us. Charlotte has been telling you everything, hasn't she?"

Hello? I want to yell. *I'm right here, you know!* But the silver is doing its job: pinning me down, burning me up from the inside.

I hear Konstantin's uneven footsteps splashing toward us until he, too, is standing over me. Seeing the two of them together brings a sense of foreboding, like I'm looking at a pair of ancient gods. Each one is powerful in their own right, and each was betrayed by the other. Rayna, centuries old, who left Konstantin for Kaleb, a man who was practically a brother to him. And Konstantin, who lured Rayna into his life with false promises of love and grandeur, only to use her. Abuse her. Chew her up and spit her out.

Carbon copies. Two sides of the same vengeful coin.

"A lovely little secret, don't you think?" Konstantin says, stepping closer to Rayna. She flinches as he slides two knuckles down her jaw. "Although, I suspect you already knew."

Rayna stares resolutely at Konstantin, as though trying not to drop her gaze. "I had my suspicions."

If my heart didn't already have a silver blade through it, it would have stopped.

It's Konstantin who glances down, silver eyes flashing. "You see, love? I am not the enemy here."

I can only stare up at him, a wildfire stirring in my chest, disbelief melting into fury.

Rayna *knew.*

"Still manipulating people, I see," Rayna snaps, drawing his attention. "A pity you can't earn love any other way."

Konstantin's mouth twists into what I assume is a wry smile; it's hard to see his full expression from this angle. He moves even closer, until their bodies are touching. Rayna takes a shuddering breath.

Konstantin's voice is low and earnest when he says, "I earned yours."

Rayna shivers. A beat passes. Another. There is nothing but the wind and the rain and the two ancient lovers. And me, burning alive at their feet.

"No," Rayna finally says, her confidence returning. She puts a palm to Konstantin's chest and shoves him away. He staggers backward, barely a shadow in my peripheral vision. "I never loved you. I was in love with the *idea* of you: the power, the luxury, the attention." Her voice cracks, just a little. "But it was all an illusion, because you never loved me either. If you did, I wouldn't have left you for Kaleb."

"You didn't leave me," Konstantin snarls. "Kaleb poisoned you against me. He *stole* you from me!"

"Is that really what you think, Kostya?" Rayna's laugh is sharp enough to cut glass. "We've already established that Kaleb didn't Sire me. He has no more control over my mind than you do. I always thought it was a mistake when he stabbed you with this"—she pulls a dagger from her jacket, the same one she pulled out of Nik's back—"instead of killing you outright. But I'm glad you're still alive so I can finally tell you the truth." Now it's Rayna's turn to smile. "Kaleb is the love of my life. And I would have left you for a pocketful of loose change."

Konstantin lunges forward and strikes Rayna hard across the face. She crumples to the ground—almost on top of me—and looks up at him dejectedly with a hand pressed to her cheek. Blood leaks between her fingers.

"You *bitch*," Konstantin hisses, lifting her by her jacket collar. She makes a choking sound as her feet leave the ground. "It seems you still underestimate me. Do I need to remind you of the little agreement we made all those centuries ago?"

"Please," Rayna begs, all semblance of strength gone. A little girl in a monster's clutches. "Please don't hurt him, Kostya."

Lightning cracks overhead and Konstantin's laugh follows like thunder.

"Come with me," he says, a crooked smile splitting his face, "or I kill your spineless brother. The choice is yours."

My feet have gone numb. Silver sears through every vein, every muscle, every nerve. It blurs my vision and shoots needles of pain into the base of my skull. But when Rayna's grip on her dagger loosens, something registers deep in my psyche—a subconscious realization despite the pain and the storm and the defiant expression on her face.

Impending doom.

"Take her," Rayna says, so quietly that I barely hear it.

Konstantin stills, eyes narrowing with intrigue. "What?"

"Take Charlotte." Rayna relaxes a bit as Konstantin lowers her to her feet, but he doesn't release her collar. She scrubs blood from a cut on her lip. Ice prickles through my fingertips. "If I go with you, I'll never stop fighting. But Charlotte is Sired to you." There's a pause, but her voice is firm when she says, "You can make sure she'll never *start.*"

Konstantin regards her for a moment before his eyes drop to mine, and it takes me a few seconds to decipher the emotion swirling in them: *pity.* I desperately want to look away, to run, to do *anything,* but I'm frozen in place, staring up at the man who could be my ruin.

Rayna takes a slow step away as Konstantin looses his grip on her collar, his mouth twisting into a vicious smile.

"You know," he muses in her direction, "that family of yours . . . they don't seem to like you much, do they?" I can no longer see Rayna, but her footsteps slow. "Charlotte, however, is the family darling. And I *own her.*"

Charlotte is mine. She always has been.

How right he was.

"Take her," Rayna says quietly. "And in exchange, you won't hurt Nik. Do we have a deal?"

Konstantin kneels over me, smoothing hair from my forehead in a gesture that would be comforting coming from anyone else.

"Charlotte, love," he murmurs, gripping my hand where it's still wrapped around the knife's handle. His closeness sends a shiver through me and I want to drive a fist into his nose, to kick and scream and sink my claws into his skin. Instead, I can only look at him—at the sporadic twitch of his shoulder and the awkward stiffness to his movements. His gaze darkens as it shifts to the blade. "Imagine how it would feel if the minutes were years."

Before I can figure out what he means, his free hand braces my shoulder and my stomach turns viscerally as he yanks hard on the knife. The blade slides out with a lance of pain, and it's a few torturous seconds, my eyes locked with a bemused Konstantin's, before my heart starts up a sluggish rhythm.

I gasp as the air returns to my lungs, and a fresh pulse of blood soaks into the front of my shirt. Konstantin wastes no time in sliding one arm under my back, the other under my knees, and he cradles me against his chest as he stands, his left side folding a bit under my weight. Wincing at the static in my limbs, I let my head roll sideways, just in time to see Rayna turn and sprint back to the car.

"*Rayna!*" I scream, struggling against Konstantin's hold. But my body is useless. Burning. Broken. "Rayna, *please!* Don't leave me again!"

She doesn't stop. She doesn't even slow.

Rayna is running away from Konstantin. Away from *me*. The girl I once called my best friend—my *sister,* even—is leaving me with the man who has haunted her for three hundred years. The man who destroyed her life.

The man who now controls mine.

I glance up at Konstantin, whose rigid arms hold me close as he stares at Rayna's retreating form.

"I make no promises," he murmurs after her, though I doubt she hears him.

Every ounce of fight I have left is washed away by the rain, and I fist my hand in Konstantin's shirt. It's soaked with water and grime, my blood seeping into the pale fabric, but he doesn't seem to notice or care. My nails slice through it. Spots of his blood bloom under my fingertips. In response, he holds me tighter.

Betrayal, dark and ragged, tears a hole through my chest, exposing me to agony like I've never known. Not when Konstantin killed me. Not when I drank my own mother's blood. Not when Kaleb told me he killed my best friend. Not when Xander revealed all the secrets he had been keeping.

It all seems rather silly, now.

Pain, fear, and disbelief crackle through me, swirling into a maelstrom that finds its way out in a tortured, anguished scream. My throat burns. My eyes blur. I bury my face in the crook of Konstantin's neck, accepting the fate that has been nipping at my heels since the moment I met a grinning Ty.

My life is not my own, and it never will be again.

Konstantin says nothing for a few long moments before he turns and hurtles into the trees, heading back toward the city. A distant part of my mind is screaming in terror, but another part—the one that has me wrapping desperate arms around his neck—knows that it's better this way. My family isn't safe if I'm with them—not as long as I'm Sired to Konstantin.

A fact that won't be changing anytime soon.

My Sire carries me through the darkness and he doesn't protest when my nails score parallel lines down his chest. When I scream against his skin. When I collapse into broken sobs. We leave the forested hills and emerge onto the deserted Golden Gate Bridge, a dangerous new truth swirling in my mind.

There has always been a second villain in this story. For centuries, she has watched us, manipulated us, made us believe she was on our side. She has played the part of the doting lover, the loyal friend, the victim, the messiah, but now I see her for what she truly is: a ruthless, bloody traitor. A terrified girl who will do whatever it takes to save her own skin. A powerful, arrogant vampire who learned at the feet of the master.

A villain we never saw coming.

Her name is Rayna Magdaléna Vesely, and Konstantin taught her everything he knows.

CHAPTER 64

RAYNA'S FEET POUND ON THE pavement, conviction lengthening her stride.

It was the right thing, she tells herself. *I did the right thing.*

She skids to a halt in front of the Mazda and dares a glance back over her shoulder. Konstantin and Charlotte have gone; all that remains is Charlotte's blood on the ground, barely more than a red swirl.

The right thing.

Clothing rustles in the car as Tristan moves about, likely emerging from his hiding place on the floor. Rayna doubts he saw or heard anything from that vantage point but she should Compel him, just in case. He'll never know the difference.

Though Charlotte would kill her if she knew Rayna Compelled her little boyfriend. Maybe she shouldn't—

No. She can't think about what Charlotte wants right now. All that matters is what needs to be done, and Rayna *needs* to make sure no one knows what really happened here tonight.

Compulsion it is.

There's movement in the distance—a tiny, dark shape making its way toward her. She staggers backward, legs colliding with the car's bumper. It can't be Konstantin. He wouldn't come back—not after a victory like that.

Unless Rayna missed something. She wracks her brain for any sign, any suggestion that he played her for a fool. But as the shape draws closer, she realizes it isn't Konstantin coming back to condemn her. It's someone far, far worse.

Xander flies down the road, leaping the fallen tree in one smooth bound and sliding to a graceful halt. *What the hell is he doing here?* Rayna opens her mouth to ask, but Xander beats her to it.

"Where is Charlotte?"

Rayna stills, taking a slow breath as she decides exactly how to navigate this. He can't know the truth. *No one* can know the truth. Not even Nik.

Especially not Nik.

"Konstantin," she starts, letting her voice tremble. It isn't hard— the confrontation with Kostya left her knees shaking and her heart hammering. Not to mention the fact that she just betrayed her best friend. Guilt claws its way into her chest but she shoves it away. "He felled the tree. We had no choice but to stop, and he—" She swallows hard, forcing herself not to flinch at the sharp concern in Xander's eyes. "He took her."

Panic leaks into his expression. "What do you mean, he *took her?*"

"Exactly that, Xander," Rayna says, nervously picking at her fingernails.

"No." He takes a step back, then another, fisting both hands in his sodden curls. "NO!"

Rayna almost feels bad for him. Almost.

"I'm so sorry—"

"What does he want?" he asks, too loudly. "Where did he take her?"

"I don't know." Rayna wills her voice to shake harder, like she's holding back tears. Maybe she is. "I tried to follow them, but we got separated. He chased us through the woods and I—I don't know what happened."

"Oh, so that's how you're going to play it?"

Rayna's blood turns to ice as a fierce voice sears through their conversation. Following Xander's gaze, she slowly turns to see Tristan standing next to his car, fresh rain spots on his t-shirt and fury in his eyes.

"Tristan, it's not what it looks like—" Rayna says in an attempt at Compulsion, but he cuts her off with a snarl.

"I think it's *exactly* what it looks like."

Xander looks between them wildly, waiting for an explanation. Something in Tristan's expression must tip him off, because he turns a cold glare on Rayna and his fangs slide from his gums, a crack of lighting making his emerald eyes flash.

"What did you do?" he growls.

Fear claws its way up Rayna's throat, choking her words, stealing her breath. Her vision tunnels. Regret twists in her gut, writhing like an angry viper. She clutches her chest as Tristan moves to stand next to Xander, mirroring his authoritative stance, and thunder crashes through the storm-laden sky.

"Well," the human boy says through gritted teeth, fury lacing his words, lighting turning his hair and eyes to molten gold. Charlotte's avenging angel. "Do you want to tell him what really happened here, Rayna? Or should I?"

EPILOGUE

Charlotte's tears are warm against Konstantin's neck. The storm is beginning to ease as he slows to a walk on Broadway Street and catches a glimpse of the Noviks' house, its windows dark and lifeless—a sleeping giant overlooking the Bay. For a moment, he considers taking Charlotte back to her own bedroom. But her brother lied to her, her human pet loathes her, and her best friend betrayed her. There is nothing for her there.

Perhaps it's better that Konstantin took her away. Maybe she'll be happier here. With *him*.

Besides, he couldn't just leave her there, bleeding out on the road. The moment Rayna redirected Charlotte's blade—the moment it plunged into her heart—it took everything he had not to collapse himself. After two centuries, he can still feel the bite of silver as it sliced through his back, see the look of mingled triumph and remorse in Rayna's wildfire gaze.

The scar on his back lit up like electricity when that dagger pierced Charlotte's flesh, and he felt the shift deep inside him—twisting his priorities, reshaping his worldview.

Changing his game.

All these years, he has believed that Kaleb was his undoing. That the man he called *brother* had taken his love from him, his *life* from him. But now he knows Kaleb is too soft for that. Too *weak*.

Rayna, however . . . it seems he taught her too well.

And Charlotte? Though he is loath to admit it, he has actually started to care for the girl. How unfortunate.

She shifts in his arms now only to bury herself deeper in his embrace, and he cringes at the involuntary uptick of his left shoulder. Blood soaks the front of Charlotte's shirt and seeps into his, adding fresh streaks of watery red.

"Where are you taking me?" Her words have none of their usual bite, and they're muffled where her mouth is pressed against his shirt collar.

"Damn, love," he muses, ducking into a dark alcove to avoid the passing lights of a police cruiser. "Is that the best you can do? No demands? No name-calling?" He pauses, mouth quirking. "No biting?"

Her sharp exhale could almost be mistaken for a laugh.

"What's the point?" she asks, still muffled. "If I fight, you'll just force me to stop."

Konstantin checks the street for the patrol car, but it has vanished. What he does see, however, is a pair of white-haired creatures slipping through the city's shadows, their mouths open and tasting the air. Konstantin tenses. Pain lances up his neck. He presses his back against a building, willing his heartbeat to slow, and waits until the *immortui* turn and disappear down a side street. With a slow breath of relief, he continues on his way, a renewed stiffness in his gait.

"Do you really think so little of me?" he bites out, doing his best to keep the pain from his voice.

"Yes, absolutely."

It's Konstantin's turn to laugh. "You truly don't understand how lenient I've been with you."

Charlotte's head pops up at that, and she leans away just enough to look up at him. Her wide green eyes are red-rimmed, making the scowl on her face more pathetic than menacing.

"What do you mean?"

Konstantin takes a moment to choose his words, wishing he had a free hand to wipe the smudged mascara from Charlotte's cheeks.

"I am your Sire and you are bound to me," he says matter-of-factly, tamping down a prick of emotion. "That connection is unbreakable. All-consuming. There is nothing you won't do if I command it. Why, then, have I only asked you for information?"

She frowns. "I've been wondering the same thing. Wouldn't it have been easier for you to just ask me to find Rayna? Or better yet, kill Kaleb?"

"All part of the game, I suppose," he says with a wistful sigh. His ribs creak and shudder. His head ticks. "Foolishly, I believed Rayna wouldn't be able to surprise me. I was, dare I say, too proud to use you so unabashedly. It would have been too easy."

"And let me guess: you love a challenge."

Konstantin shrugs with one shoulder, flashing her a sideways grin. "Don't you?"

He stops in the middle of the sidewalk just as dawn takes its first breath. The storm has all but passed, the spattering of raindrops few and far between, and he turns to face the familiar building with a fond smile. The scalloped facade and overgrown front lawn have become beacons of solace for him over the past eleven years. Maybe Charlotte will come to love it as he has.

"We're here, *dragoste*," Konstantin says, his blood humming with newfound anticipation. He takes a deep, agonized breath, surrounding himself with the scent of lavender and nighttime, and presses a kiss to Charlotte's forehead. "Welcome home."

APPENDIX

BELARUSIAN

Darahi
Dear

Majo kachannie
My love

Maly stín
Little shadow

Mnie choladna
I'm cold

Moj siabar
My friend

Niama
No

Repa
Turnip

Siastra
Sister

Tabie choladna?
Are you cold?

FRENCH

Amies
Friends

Mon coeur
My heart

CZECH

Co děláš?
What are you doing?

Láska
Love

Liska
Fox

Mé srdce
My heart

Moje sestra
My sister

Ne
No

Straka
Magpie

MANDARIN

Nǐ hǎo
Hello

ROMANIAN

Copilul diavolului
The Devil's child

Dragoste
Love

ITALIAN

Abbastanza
Enough

Bellezze/bellezza
Beauty/beauties

Ciao
Hello

Famme vedette
Let me see

Fermare
Stop

Porca miseria
For God's sake
(figurative slang)

SPANISH

Mi corazón
My heart

WELSH

Cariad
Love

ACKNOWLEDGMENTS

It took me a long time to write these acknowledgments because I wasn't sure how to put my mountain of feelings into words. A Ruthless Bloody Betrayal has been a labor of love in every way, and I never expected my sophomore novel to go through so much before it was released into the world, but the book is better for it. *I* am better for it.

First and foremost, a huge thank you to my husband, Garrett, for supporting and encouraging me to keep writing during the hardest moments. I wouldn't have the strength to reach for my dreams if I didn't see you doing the same thing every single day. Truly. You work so incredibly hard to provide for our family and you continue to be my biggest blessing day after month after year.

Thank you to my incredible, amazing best friend and editor, Rachel, for literally everything. Despite living hundreds or thousands of miles apart for the last five years, you have been my calm in the storm, my sounding board, my voice of reason. Without you, this book wouldn't exist. And if it did, it would suck.

Thanks to my amazing mom, who shares my love for books. I am so grateful for your love and support in my writing journey, and for the hours-long phone calls we have to fawn over any and all book characters, including my own.

To my fabulous friends, old and new: Marlee, Emily, Reba, Anna,

Delany, and many others. Thank you for reading my books and sending me the most unhinged text messages, then yelling at me again in person. It brings me true joy to know that my words have such an effect on people, and that my hardcore book-loving friends are willing to take a chance on little old me.

To my alpha and beta readers, Tia, Jess, Erin, and Karina. Thanks for sticking around for so long and helping my book get to where it needs to be. Your input and support have been invaluable and I am so grateful for your messages, Snapchats, and online friendships.

To my amazing cover artist, Fran, for putting up with me while I made changes to this cover for literal years.

To my character artist, Dezaray, for bringing my characters to life in the most insanely beautiful way.

To the members of my hype team, who have stuck with me for over three years while I announced and canceled at least three ARBB release dates. I'm sure it was a bit maddening but I'm forever grateful you didn't give up on me. You're the real heroes.

To my ARC readers, my Instagram followers, my DM friends, and everyone who continues to talk about, read, and share An Absolute Bloody Disaster. From the bottom of my heart, thank you.

And lastly, to myself. The last three years have been the best and worst of your life, but you did it. You're here. You never gave up, despite the world knocking you down again and again. This book is a testament to your passion and the love you have for your craft. When you inevitably get discouraged again in the future, always remember that you've done it before. You can do it again.

ABOUT THE AUTHOR

Lindsay Clement is a huge nerd who loves writing books almost as much as she loves talking about them. She writes paranormal and fantasy stories with memorable characters, witty banter, plot twists, and a healthy dose of romance. She currently lives in Michigan with her husband, her daughter, her golden doodle, and an obscene number of books and craft supplies.

Follow Lindsay on social media:
@novelitica
www.novelitica.com

www.ingramcontent.com/pod-product-compliance
Lightning Source LLC
Chambersburg PA
CBHW051306190726
48290CB00001B/33